BEAU GAVE JULIET
A SLOW, LAZY SMILE.

"This is the Big Easy, dawlin'—you gotta learn to leave those pantyhose in the drawer."

Enough was enough! Holding his gaze, Juliet toed off her shoes. She located the elasticized lace band at the top of one stocking through her silk dress, and raised her leg off the car seat to work the band down to her knee. Then she reached beneath her hem and, displacing her long skirt as little as possible, rolled the nylon below her calf. As it collapsed in a silken tangle around her ankle, she pointed her toes and peeled the fragile nylon free.

Beau stared at the filmy length of off-white hosiery dangling from her fingertips and croaked, "What the hell d'you think you're doin', Juliet?"

"Why, just following your excellent advice." Emboldened, she repeated the routine with her other stocking and then pointed out gently, "The light is green, Beauregard."

Swearing beneath his breath at the cars honking behind him, Beau rammed the gear shift into first and left a patch of rubber as he took off. Juliet folded her hosiery into a neat little pile and then settled back in her seat, feeling *much* more tranquil.

SUSAN ANDERSEN

Be My Baby

AVON BOOKS

An Imprint of HarperCollinsPublishers

This is a work of fiction. Names, characters, places, and incidents are products of the author's imagination or are used fictitiously and are not to be construed as real. Any resemblance to actual events, locales, organizations, or persons, living or dead, is entirely coincidental.

AVON BOOKS
An Imprint of HarperCollins*Publishers*
10 East 53rd Street
New York, New York 10022-5299

Copyright © 1999 by Susan Andersen
Inside cover author photo by Teresa Salgado Photography
Library of Congress Catalog Card Number: 98-93542
ISBN: 0-380-79512-4
www.avonromance.com

First Avon Books printing: March 1999

Avon Trademark Reg. U.S. Pat. Off. and in Other Countries, Marca Registrada, Hecho en U.S.A.
HarperCollins® is a trademark of HarperCollins Publishers Inc.

Printed in the U.S.A.

10 9

This is dedicated to the women of the industry
with much gratitude and affection

To my very good friend
and brainstorming partner,
Caroline Cross,
for hauling me out of the pits I dig myself into

To my agent, Meg Ruley,
for guidance through the mine fields

To my editor, Micki Nuding,
for making me look better

To the Avon Ladies of the Internet,
for sharing, teaching, and making me laugh

And to romance readers everywhere
Fools may attempt to pigeonhole us,
but we know exactly who we are

1

*J*uliet Rose Astor Lowell paused in the shade of the marble columns outside the Eighth District Police Station and discreetly blotted her forehead with the back of her wrist. Drawing in a deep breath, she softly expelled it. Lord, it was hot. And so humid. Just the short walk from the air-conditioned limo left her feeling limp. She peeled a clinging yard of voile away from her thighs and gave her dress a delicate shake to promote air circulation. She'd been in New Orleans less than an hour, and already things were entirely different than she'd envisioned when she left Boston.

But that was mostly due to this unscheduled stop. She had thought to have the tiniest bit more freedom down here; it seemed a small enough thing to wish for. After all, she was away from Grandmother's rigid constraints, in a city whose name was synonymous with enjoyment, and whose inhabitants certainly had no preconceived expectations of her as an Astor Lowell. And it wasn't as if she'd planned a wild spree of dancing naked across tabletops, for heaven's sake—she'd simply wanted to loosen the ever-present restraints a bit. Just enough to take a really deep breath.

But even that was to be denied her. Once again Father had arranged matters without bothering to consult her, dropping this little bombshell as a fait accompli over the limo phone. Crown Hotels had received a letter protesting the opening of the New Orleans Garden Crown. He'd read it to her over the phone, and if it had struck her as more an ardent treatise against the bastardization of a historic landmark than a threat, that simply didn't signify. Father wanted police protection for her, so here she was, all choice removed from her control. She pulled open the door and entered the building.

Her ears were still attuned to the crisp accents of New England, so the slow, soft drawls of the officers manning the counter sounded almost foreign. As she turned away from the desk and followed their directions to the captain's office, she inconspicuously—but avidly—observed everything around her. She'd never been in a police station before, and it felt both exotic and full of energy.

The man who rose from behind his desk when she tapped on his door was neither. He had the prosperous, well-fed look of a politician—Father's kind of person; exactly the sort she was accustomed to dealing with. The man's brown hair was expensively barbered, his ruddy cheeks shone from a close shave, and his suit was cleverly cut to minimize the appearance of a middle that had begun to spread. Police work must pay better than she'd thought.

"Captain Pfeffer? I'm—"

"Ms. Juliet Lowell," he overrode her enthusiastically. His voice, at least, was exotic, dripping elongated, honeyed vowels. He rounded the desk and extended a smooth, manicured hand.

Astor Lowell. She swallowed the impulse to correct him, though the desire to do so was automatic after years of conditioning at Grandmother's knee. Smiling politely, she shook his hand.

"Please," he said, patting her hand avuncularly as he led her into the office. "Do c'mon in and have a seat. Your fawtha and I had a long talk, and I've been expectin' you."

"Yes, I know." Juliet sat. Though it was most likely futile, she insisted quietly, "Father was a bit precipitous, I fear. There's truly no need for me to monopolize the services of an officer whose time could be better employed elsewhere."

"Nonsense. Sergeant Dupree is happy to be of assistance. Don't you worry your pretty little . . . well." He cleared his throat, undoubtedly seeing something in her expression that warned him he was heading down an unpopular avenue. "The New Awleens Police Department is always happy to assist a pretty lady," he substituted heartily, which was not a great improvement in Juliet's opinion. "We believe in assigning the best to the best. I was personally handpicked by the commissionah himself to be acting captain when Captain Taylor left on an extended vacation. And I in turn have handpicked the detective best suited to be your escort."

Juliet's polite smile froze, and her brows drew together. "Detective? Oh, but . . . I thought you said he was a sergeant." This just kept getting worse and worse. Bad enough to usurp the services of an officer; now she had visions of taking a detective away from a murder investigation.

"There is no official rank of detective in the NOPD. Most of 'em hold the rank of Police Officer III or Sergeant." He waved the distinction aside. "I must say we're all verra excited that Crown Hotels has decided to grace our fair city with one of their fine establishments. Why, society has hardly talked of anythin' else."

Somehow she doubted that, but she *was* proud of the Garden Crown. She'd waited years to be in charge of one from conception to start-up, and the New Orleans hotel was her baby. "Yes, we're also quite excited," she agreed.

"As well you should be. And you needn't be concerned for your safety while you go about your business, because we're heah to see to it that you aren't left alone and unprotected for a single moment."

That's exactly what Juliet was afraid of.

"I understand y'all have quite a roster of excitin' pre-opening events planned," the captain continued.

"Yes, we do." Juliet briefly summarized the upcoming social schedule. When she finished, Pfeffer looked at her so expectantly that she said with automatic courtesy, "You and your wife must join us for one."

"Why thank you, Ms. Lowell, I know she'd like that. She's a Collier, you know. From the Savannah Colliers."

"Is she." Juliet had no idea who the Savannah Colliers were, but she supposed it explained his apparent wealth. Long-standing instincts decreed it unlikely he was the descendant of old Southern wealth, for he had the too-eager-to-impress unctuousness she associated with Father's sycophants. Manners instilled from the cradle, however, dictated the only acceptable reply. "Most likely you're already on the list, then, but I'll be sure to have my assistant send you an invitation." She stole a glance at her watch.

Pfeffer caught her at it, which would have appalled Grandmother, but at least it had the benefit of hustling him along. "I realize you're busy—let me just summon Dupree."

He reached for the phone on his desk, but Juliet rose to her feet. "We needn't pull him away from his duties." Father might have a feudal belief that the welfare of the Lowells had priority over anyone else's, but Grandmother maintained that an Astor Lowell did not inconvenience others for the sake of her own comfort. And Grandmother's rules took precedence in Juliet's social training, since she had raised her from the time of Juliet's mother's death and had therefore had time to drum them into her from birth—whereas Father had merely dropped into her life from time to time to lay down a new law before departing to reimmerse himself in his precious corporation. "Please," she insisted now. "We can just as easily go to him."

Pfeffer continued to punch out numbers. "Trust me, little lady, you need to begin as you mean to go on with Sergeant Dupree. While I can assure you he's one of New Awleens' finest, he does tend to rise above himself if you give him the least little opportunity. It's bettah to make him come to us."

Juliet didn't want to be here in the first place, and having her wishes ignored with such head-patting condescension by a man she was rapidly coming to suspect was a petty little tyrant was the push that crossed the line. Gaze level and voice icy, she said, "But I insist."

Fleeting irritation registered on Pfeffer's face, but he set down the receiver and stood. "Yes, of course," he said smoothly. "Whatevah you wish." He came around the desk and then stood aside with an obsequious smile to allow her to precede him from the office. "Right this way. We'll take the elevatah."

"Josie Lee's on the warpath," Beau Dupree informed his partner gloomily. "She says I'm over-protective and smothering, and she's moving out." He looked at Luke Gardner. "You think I'm over-protective?"

"Yes."

Beau scowled. "Bullshit. Hell, if it weren't for this case, I'd pack her bags myself—I *dream* of the time I'm no longer responsible for everyone. As things stand, though, she'll move out over my dead body." He shook his head in disgust. "Overprotective, my ass."

"Beau, for Christ's sake, listen to yourself. When are you gonna let yourself off the hook for that, man? It wasn't your fault."

"The hell it wasn't." Beau's scowl deepened. He'd allowed his baby sister to come to a strip joint late at night. It didn't matter that she'd tracked him down via his cell phone, or how insistent she'd been that she had to have the car, refusing to let him get back to work until he'd agreed out of pure frustration to let a friend bring her by the club to get the keys. He should have insisted that he needed it himself, even though he'd ridden with Luke. Sure, he'd extracted her promise that the friend would then drop her off where he'd left the car parked, back near the station, and wait until she was safely inside. But big fuckin' deal.

He and Luke had been staking out the joint because of the Panty Snatcher, a man who broke into women's homes and forced them at gunpoint to strip and hand over their lingerie, terrorizing them with the unspoken possibilities of what else he might force them to do before he melted back into the night with his booty. Beau had known damn well the club was the only common denominator of the pervert's last two victims. He'd had no business letting Josie Lee anywhere near the place.

"It's not like I couldn't use the peace, Gardner. I'd love to have the house all to myself. And I live for the day that I get my old sex life back." Now, there was an understatement. He'd been fantasizing about the day for ten solid years.

Luke grinned. "Balls developin' a bluish tinge?"

Beau gave him a look. "Hey, you try raising three opinionated sisters and see what it does to your nuts. It hasn't exactly been the wild bachelor lifestyle it was before my folks died." Then he, too, grinned. "The minute Josie Lee's out the door, though, I'm picking it up right where I left off. First thing I'm gonna do is find me a little blonde with big tits."

"Uh, Beau?"

"Or maybe two blondes—or a blonde and a red-head; I'm not fussy. Then I'm climbing into bed with her or them, and I'm not comin' up for air for a week." The thought carved a smile on his face, which disintegrated when his friend kicked his foot off the lower desk drawer where it had been propped. Beau straightened in irritation. "What the hell's the matter with you?"

"Sergeant Dupree," Acting Captain Peter Pfeffer said with rigid disapproval from behind him. "You will kindly watch your language, sir. There's a lady present."

Beau turned in his seat. Oh, great—his favorite bureaucrat. And if that wasn't enough to make his day, Pissant Pfeffer was accompanied by a long-legged woman who regarded him with huge gray eyes, as if he were some unique species in the zoo. He gave her a slow once-over in return.

"I'd like to introduce you to Ms. Juliet Lowell," Pfeffer said with that snake-oil-salesman's smile that always set Beau's teeth on edge. "Your new assignment," he added with vicious triumph. "Ms. Lowell, meet Sergeant Beauregard Dupree."

Juliet felt the sudden tension of every person in the squad room, and realized she had made a mistake when she hadn't allowed Captain Pfeffer to send for his detective. This smelled suspiciously of a power play, and due to her insistence it was being played out in a public forum.

When the man whose conversation they'd interrupted had turned lazily in his seat and appraised her with black eyes so heavily lashed they drooped at the outside corners, Juliet had prayed it was the handsome bald guy with the engaging grin just beyond him who would be her new bodyguard.

No such luck, of course. Her heart began to bang against the wall of her chest as the black-haired detective climbed to his feet and gave her a comprehensive once-over. *He* wasn't particularly handsome. Which was just as well, since gorgeous looks would have been overkill. The man was extremely . . . male. He was more male than any Y-chromosome individual she'd ever come across. A snatch of his conversation whispered through her mind. *Week-long sex with multiple partners?* Dear God, did people truly *do* that sort of thing? She stared at him, repelled and yet fascinated at the same time.

He returned her gaze, one thick dark eyebrow lifted, and a corner of his mouth quirked as if he were privy to something that secretly amused him. Then he turned to face Captain Pfeffer and his black brows lowered. Every eye in the room was on him and everyone seemed to be holding their breath, as if awaiting an explosion. But he merely exchanged a glance with the other detective and

said with a mildness that Juliet instinctively knew
was fraudulent, "I already have an assignment,
Pete."

"That's Captain Pfeffer!" The ranking officer
puffed up with indignation as he spat the correc-
tion. "And your assignment is what I say it is, Dupree. *I* say it's Ms. Lowell."

The detective was only average height, maybe
five-ten or -eleven. His shoulders were wide, however, his hips were narrow, and he had the lean
muscle mass of a swimmer. Black hair feathered his
forearms and was visible behind the unbuttoned
placket of his polo shirt. His jaw, too, was dark
with five o'clock shadow, though it was only
eleven in the morning. He looked tough and com-
petent as he stared at the captain, and his cool control made his superior appear soft and nearly
hysterical in contrast. It was therefore a surprise
when the detective suddenly rolled his shoulders
and turned to her in compliance with Pfeffer's order.

"Miz Lowell," he said silkily, thrusting a hand
out at her. He, too, had a slow, lazy drawl, but
Juliet saw the energetic fury in the depths of his
black eyes. "This is my partner—"

"You don't have a partner, Dupree," Pfeffer interrupted.

"Bite me," Beau invited, but explained to Juliet,
"Luke here was my partner before the NOPD decentralized in '96, and I'm not about to start callin'
him my ex-partner at this late date." He indicated
the man with the smooth-shaven skull. "In any
case, meet Sergeant Gardner."

"Ma'am," the detective said. But although Juliet acknowledged his greeting with a polite dip of her head, she couldn't seem to pull her gaze away from Sergeant Dupree.

He was a little sweaty; she could see it in the sheen along his throat and where his black knit shirt stuck in spots to his chest and stomach muscles. But the hand he wrapped around hers to shake was dry and brown-skinned, long-fingered and hard. And it was warm, very warm.

Juliet dropped it as soon as was decently possible, feeling flustered and edgy. Curling her fingers, which retained the sensation of his touch within the shielding folds in her skirt, she felt heat climb up her cheeks. The men in her world had hands that were smooth and pale and somehow cool. A frisson of uneasiness crept down her spine.

"Beauregard will be at your service as long as you're in New Awleans," Captain Pfeffer said pompously and gave the detective a glare. "Right, Dupree?"

Keeping his eyes on her, Beau took a step that brought him much too close and cocked his head quizzically. "Is there a particular reason you need babysittin', dawlin'?"

Unaccustomed to physical contact, she stepped back. Though she was too mannerly to protest the endearment, her chin came up and she'd opened her mouth to offer a cool reply when Pfeffer jumped into the breech.

"Ms. Lowell is down heah to open the Garden Crown, a fine new jewel in the glitterin' tiara that comprises the Crown Hotels," he said expansively.

"And she's—what?—had the heap burgled already and needs a cop?" Beau's eyes were insolent as he looked down at her. "In that case, sugar, you've come to the best."

"Watch your tongue, Dupree. Ms. Lowell has received a threatening letter and I'm assigning you to keep her safe."

Breaths were sucked in throughout the room and everyone drew back as if Beau were a ticking bomb primed to go off. Juliet wished she understood what the hell was going on. Clearly there were underlying subtexts here she didn't understand. Sergeant Dupree's black eyes glittered with pure fury as his gaze wrenched from her face to the captain's.

"Guard dog duty?" he said through clenched teeth.

"Her fawtha was quite insistent, and he *is* Thomas Lowell, after all. Here's a copy of the letter." Pfeffer thrust it into Beau's hands. "I'm sure you'll want to study it. And of course you'll be gratified to know you'll also be Ms. Lowell's escort for all the hotel's pre-opening functions," he added with gusto.

"Oh, shit," someone murmured.

Beau scanned the letter. When his dark-eyed gaze raised, it locked on her face. "Daddy must have some connections," he said with soft-voiced contempt. " 'Cause this"—the white paper in one hand smacked against the long, brown fingers of his other—"is pure bullshit, but it looks as if he just bought his baby girl a brand-new boy anyway."

If his initial charm had made her heart pound,

having all that fury transferred to her added an almost frantic throb to its erratic rhythm. Somehow this man managed to wreak havoc with her usually unshakable composure, leaving her feeling entirely unstrung.

Always remember who you are. Her grandmother's arrogant exhortation offered unexpected comfort, and she needed every ounce of ammunition at her disposal.

She gave him a cool smile.

He narrowed his eyes at her and said insolently, "You don't talk much, do you, angel-face? I like that in a woman."

Gardner rolled his eyes and Captain Pfeffer snapped, "That's quite enough, Sergeant. You will mind your mannahs and address her as Ms. Lowell."

Beau's hard gaze left her face and zeroed in on the captain's. His voice lost its honeyed drawl as he lashed out, "Or you'll do what, *Acting* Captain Pfeffer? Remove me from her case and put me on somethin' a little less . . . important—like the Panty Snatcher case?"

"*Forget* that piddly-ass case!" Captain Pfeffer's polished facade cracked as he thrust his jaw pugnaciously near Beau's. "I've given you your assignment, and you'll do what you're damn well told, or I'll strip you of your gold shield." It was an idea he clearly relished.

"Oh, please—" Juliet protested in distress, but Beau cut her off.

"Come on, *Miz* Lowell." His hand wrapped

around her wrist and he headed for the door, pulling her in his wake.

"Dupree!" Pfeffer's voice behind them was a peremptory warning to halt, but Beau never slackened his pace.

Stumbling along behind him, Juliet cast a brief look over her shoulder at the captain and Sergeant Gardner and gave them a helpless shrug. Then they were lost to sight as the warm hand that held her captive yanked her out the door.

2

*G*oddam, *sonofabitchin' bureaucrat!* Beau punched the accelerator to the floor as his car sped toward the Garden District. This never would have happened if Captain Taylor were around. But then Taylor was a real cop, not a half-baked, arrogant, self-important politician like the Pissant. The thought made Beau snort. *Forget that piddly ass case, my butt.*

Okay, so he, like everyone else at the station, had considered the Panty Snatcher a bit of a joke at first. Cops dealt with some pretty grisly crimes and at least this pervert hadn't physically hurt anyone. That didn't make him harmless, of course, since his actions had terrorized more than half a dozen women who didn't *know* they weren't going to be hurt, until the Mardi Gras–masked burglar slipped away as soundlessly as he'd arrived. But so far he hadn't injured any of his victims, so with the irreverence common in squad rooms, they'd tagged him with a number of rude handles, the least offensive of which was Panty Snatcher.

Beau's insouciant attitude had dissolved like mist under the relentless noonday sun when the guy victimized Josie Lee. *That* turned it personal. Now Beau was determined to put him behind bars where he belonged.

And that was going to be a lot more difficult to accomplish with this bogus new assignment hanging around his neck. Playing guard dog to Ms. Lowell was going to eat up most of his time, and it was all due to his arresting the commissioner's teenage granddaughter.

This was his payback.

The maddening thing was he hadn't even been on duty that night, a little over a month ago—and he sure as hell wasn't a traffic cop. But as he'd roared down the Huey P. Long, he hadn't been able to ignore the way the car in front of him was weaving all over the bridge. It had come down to either pulling the vehicle over or living with himself if the obviously loaded driver ended up killing someone, when he could have prevented it. Throw in the fact that a damn drunk driver had been responsible for his parents' deaths, and he'd had no choice.

He'd pulled her over, taken her in, and landed at the top of the commissioner's shit list.

The union protected him from outright reprisal, and Beau knew his fellow detectives had just been waiting for him to invoke its name today. Playing escort to some uptight Northern socialite sure as hell wasn't a division detective's job. Ordinarily that would fall to someone way down the food chain.

But the commissioner had connections that reached deep, and this wasn't a grievance a detective could point to as severe abuse of power. He could just hear the response now. *You say you have to escort a good-lookin' woman wherever she wants to go? And the city or her hotel will pick up the tab? Oh, yeah, Dupree, we can see where you're being misused.*

There was no way around it; Beau was stuck with Ms. Lowell.

He snuck a look at his passenger as he roared down St. Charles Avenue. God, she was a priss, with those cool rainwater eyes and that honey-brown hair all slicked back in a repressed little French twist. Not to mention the oh-so-restrained gauzy dress she wore, which exposed the delicate wings of her collarbones and her slender arms and ankles and not much else. Every time he looked at her he had this crazy impulse to muss her up. . . .

No. Hell, no, what was he thinking? He yanked his attention back onto the road where it belonged. She wasn't the type of woman a guy mussed up—and that was the only kind he'd ever been drawn to.

His gaze drifted her way again and got stuck on her mouth. Even innocent of lipstick, it was surprisingly lush, like something you'd expect to see on a porn queen. The unlikely analogy tugged one side of Beau's lips into a derisive curl.

Talk about a case of false advertising—especially where he was concerned. It was hard to envision her cutting loose with any man, but he'd watched her take one look at him in particular and had seen those eyes go frosty and that aristocratic little nose go up in the air as if she'd caught a whiff of something past its prime.

Beau's shoulder hitched impatiently. Well, you won some, you lost some. It was clear, though, that she viewed him as a redneck peckerwood Louisiana cracker. And an oversexed one at that, since she'd caught the tail end of his conversation with Luke.

For just an instant everything within him stilled. Oh, shit, that was it. Why hadn't he thought of it before?

There was no way in hell the Pissant was going to let him off the hook with this assignment. It was to be Beau's personal punishment not only for the C's granddaughter, but for hacking off Pfeffer in the past as well.

Pfeffer was a confirmed ass-kisser, however, and if the prim Ms. *Lowell* were to petition for his transfer, he'd have no choice but to comply with her wishes.

Beau turned his head and gave her a big, feral grin. "What's the address, sugar?"

She blinked those gray eyes at him. "Excuse me?"

"The Garden Crown, Jules. What's the address?"

"Oh." She colored, which he'd noticed she seemed to do easily, and supplied the information.

He cornered Fourth Street and then Coliseum Street with screaming wheels and raced up the final block, roaring through the filigreed gates and coming to a screeching halt beneath the porte cochere of the former mansion that was now the Garden Crown Hotel.

Oh, God, this was brilliant. He grinned again.

It hadn't escaped his notice that little Miss Juliet didn't seem to like him invading her personal space. He licked his lips, contemplating all the possibilities such a repressed personality provided. He'd just get a little up-close-and-personal with the woman. Hell, he could kill two li'l ole birds with one stone by dragging her to some of the Big Easy's more tawdry establishments while he pursued his own case. Introduce her to a few select folk outside her rarefied social strata, and it shouldn't take any time at all before she was demanding his replacement.

He hopped out of the car and rounded the hood to open her door. "Here you are, angel face: all signed, sealed, and delivered, safe and sound as ordered." He felt almost tender toward her as he watched her unbuckle her seatbelt. Reaching out a hand, he offered his assistance out of the low car. "Why don't we go on in and take a look at your schedule."

She ignored the extended hand and sat there as if his muscle car were a throne: erect spine not quite touching the back of the leather seat, ankles together, hands folded in her lap. Those charcoal-rimmed, rainwater eyes leveled on him. "My name is Juliet," she informed him coolly. "I'd appreciate it if you'd call me Juliet, or Juliet Rose if you must, or Ms. Astor Lowell. But kindly don't shorten my name. Nicknames are vulgar."

He hadn't thought she could possibly poker up any more than she already had, but damned if she didn't actually manage it. He swallowed a smile.

"Whatever you say, Rosebud." Reaching down, he wrapped a hand around her wrist and hauled her out.

Ah, man. This was gonna be like taking candy from a baby.

Juliet's assistant, Roxanne Davies, slapped closed the appointment book that she, Juliet, and Beau had just finished perusing at the hotel's front desk, and watched the detective saunter out the front entrance and disappear into a blinding wash of light. "Ho-ly catfish, mama." Using the book to vigorously fan herself, she turned back to Juliet. "And you thought having a police escort was going to be a *bad* thing."

A hysterical bubble of laughter nearly erupted from Juliet's throat, but she managed to suppress it. "I'm still not convinced it isn't," she said with creditable coolness.

"Are you kidding? That is one whole helluva lot of man, Juliet. I can think of worse fates then to have a guy like that at your beck and call."

That's probably because you'd actually know how to handle "one whole helluva lot of man." Juliet still burned to remember the way she'd said, *Nicknames are vulgar.* Dear God, Grandmother had nothing on her—could she possibly have sounded more priggish? Aloud, she merely said, "Have you met with the Hayneses yet?"

"Don't want to talk about the studmuffin, huh?"

Juliet winced. She had hired Roxanne over her father's strenuous objections, digging in her heels with unaccustomed stubbornness when he'd objected that the young woman "isn't our kind." Perhaps she wasn't, and there were times like now when her blithe tactlessness could make Juliet cringe. But Roxanne had needed the job more than any of the Seven Sisters graduates who'd applied, she'd been fully qualified, and Juliet had rather admired her fearless frankness. It must be liberating not to weigh every blessed word before it left one's mouth.

"Come on," Roxanne coaxed her. "You do at least admit he's studly, don't you? I mean, the way he kept edging up so close to you, you must have felt the chemistry. He's definitely different than the white-bread boys you usually call escorts."

"Roxanne, I really don't care to discuss this."

"Well, all right—but I think this is shaping up to be a *most* interesting trip."

Juliet strode across the empty lobby and entered her office with Roxanne on her heels. Taking her seat behind the desk, she looked across it at her assistant. "The Hayneses?"

"Edward's a sweetie. That wonderful collection of Mardi Gras masks in the Blue Room is his, and I think it's largely due to him that the gardens are as lovely as they are."

"And Celeste?"

"Would like an appointment to discuss the list of functions she's arranged so far, as well as Crown Corporation's expectations of her duties as she understands them. She was . . . gracious, but I get the feeling dealing with a lowly assistant is a bit beneath her." Roxanne shrugged philosophically. "I set up an appointment for tomorrow afternoon at three, if that works for you."

"Thanks, Roxanne. That will be fine." Juliet had come to value her assistant's instincts about people in the year Roxanne had been working for her. She'd already known the Hayneses were impoverished Southern aristocrats who'd been charged with the care and maintenance of the lovely old Greek Revival mansion before its purchase by Crown Hotels. Now Juliet had also gained a glimpse into the personalities of the couple the corporation had retained to help open doors into New Orleans' society.

She rose to her feet. "I assume from your remark about the Blue Room that you've had a chance to look around a little. I haven't seen anything yet except this office and the lobby, and I'm dying to get a look at the renovations. Want to go exploring with me?"

It was odd how she felt so lethargic yet so restless at the same time, but she desperately sought the opportunity to move around. Her disturbing sense of anxiety was most likely a combination of the oppressive heat, which she swore she felt even within these air-conditioned walls, and knowing that she was fully responsible for the start-up of a hotel for the first time. Possibly part of it could be attributed to the necessity for police protection, too, which was a definite disruption of her routine.

It certainly had nothing to do with the escort himself, however. Why, she'd nearly forgotten he even existed.

*   *   *

It was jambalaya night in Beau's little Creole cottage in the Bywater District, and the walls of the minuscule kitchen were bursting at the seams from all the people crowded within.

Fragrant steam rose from the rice in the pot as Beau stirred in tomatoes and every seasoning his youngest sister Josie Lee could find in the cupboard. She gave him a nudge with her elbow as she located one they hadn't yet added to the pot, and without bothering to look up he reached out with one hand as he test-tasted the concoction-in-progress with the other. She slapped the container into his open palm. His middle sister Anabel stood hip to hip with him as she chopped shrimp and ham on the cutting board, Luke sautéed celery and onions on the burner next to him, and the oldest of Beau's sisters, Camilla, and her husband, Ned Fortenay, threw together a salad at the narrow table in the corner of the room. "*Heeey, good-lookin'*," Buckwheat Zydeco wailed from the CD player in the living room.

"*Whaaat* cha got cookin'?" Anabel sang along with the song, then interrupted herself to command, "Dump those veggies in the pot, Luke. I need the pan."

"Yes, ma'am." They traded places and she scraped the meat and shellfish mixture into the sauté pan. Filching a cube of ham, she popped it in her mouth and looked up at her brother. "Will you balance my checkbook after dinner? I've got all the stuff in my bag."

"Damn, Anabel," Beau groused, "you're twenty-four years old. When you gonna learn to do this for yourself?"

"You know how bad I am with numbers, Beauregard."

He made a dismissive sound and said, "Which is exactly why they invented calculators, sweet thing," but everyone present knew damn well he'd balance her checkbook after dinner. He'd accepted responsibility for his sisters a decade ago in order to keep the family together, and it was a hard habit to break.

But it sure was one he was itching to be shed of. And he would be—the minute he got Josie Lee's situation straightened out, he was bustin' free. No more constant worry and responsibility; it'd just be him and New Orleans' loosest women. He was filling his little black book against the day.

A short while later, everyone crowded around the small table at the end of the living room to eat. The ceiling fan slowly whirled, moving the humid air in thick, slow eddies as they traded friendly insults and worked their way through the jambalaya.

"I've got news," Josie Lee said into a momentary break in the conversation. "Pass that salad over here, Camilla." She dished the greens onto her plate, then resumed eating without saying what her news was.

Beau looked at her across the table. Like everyone on the Dupree side of the family, she had dark eyes. Of all his sisters, though, she looked the most like Mama, with her black curly hair, long, narrow hands and feet, and killer smile. Anabel and Camilla had inherited Daddy's sun-streaked brunette coloring, but where Josie Lee and Camilla were fairly tall and busty, Anabel had a slight build. All three were alike in that they were opinionated and outspoken, however.

"Well?" Anabel demanded now.

Camilla made a mock stab at Josie Lee with her fork.

Josie Lee grinned. "I got the job at the Eighth District," she said. "Assistant to the administrative assistant."

"Way to go, little sister," Camilla said, at the same time that Ned exclaimed, "Congratulations!"

"I don't know, Josie Lee," Anabel said with mock skepticism. "You sure you wanna be workin' cheek to hairy jowl with Beauregard and Luke?"

"Best place for her," Beau said. "I can keep a closer eye on her that way."

"How many times do I have to tell you I don't *need* looking after?" Josie Lee demanded in exasperation. "Besides, from all the talk goin' around the station while I was there this afternoon, you can't even look out for yourself. Heard you and your favorite acting captain got into it this morning." She gave her brother a look of wide-eyed innocence. "Is it true you've been assigned to escort some rich Yankee woman around town?"

Forks were suspended midbite as everyone regarded Beau with sudden interest, and he gave his sister a smile that displayed all his teeth. "Not for long, honey chile."

Luke stiffened with sudden tension and set his fork down. "Oh, shit, Beau, what're you plannin'?"

"Nothing much. Just a little friendly persuasion

to convince our Yankee rich girl to request herself a new escort."

"*What* friendly persuasion? Don't you think we oughtta discuss this?"

"What's to talk about? Hell, you met little Miz Juliet Rose—it's gonna be a cakewalk."

"Wait a minute." Luke's brows drew together. "I'm not sure I understand why you would think so. It's my understanding Ms. Lowell is down here to singlehandedly get a new hotel up and running. I wouldn't just blow her off if I were you."

Beau merely cocked one eyebrow.

Luke swore and leveled a look at his partner. "I mean it, Beau; don't go underestimatin' her. It could prove to be your downfall."

"Oh, yeah, she should be a real challenge, all right." A rude sound of derision escaped Beau's throat. "She wears floaty dresses, f'crissake."

Camilla's hand froze in the act of dishing up more jambalaya. "Excuse me?"

"I said the woman wears floaty dresses. You know the kind I'm talking about, those real girly numbers with yards of material that's sorta see-through but *still* manages to cover up every damn inch of the good stuff—" Oh, shit. His sister's dress was made of a soft, filmy material, and he suddenly recalled that it, too, was long. He promptly changed gears. "Forget what she wears. She's an uptight, prissy little Yank—"

"And how did you come by that assessment, Beauregard?" Anabel demanded. "Because she doesn't dress in skin-tight, low-cut spandex and shove her big ol' tits in your face?"

"What big ol' tits? If she's got a handful I'd be mighty surprised."

"Which is undoubtedly yet another strike against her," Josie Lee said in disgust.

Beau appealed to his partner. "Help me out here, Luke."

"I don't think so, buddy; you're on your own." Luke grinned at him across the table. Leaning back in his chair, he crossed his arms over his chest.

"Great. Thank you. Always good to know you can depend on your friends." He glanced over at his brother-in-law. "Ned?"

"Don't look at me," Ned advised. "I learned a long time ago not to try taking on all three of 'em at once." He rubbed a hand up and down Camilla's back. "Divide and conquer, that's my strategy."

"Damn." Beau's chair groaned in protest as he threw himself back in it. Gazing around the table at his sisters, all of whom wore identical you're-pond-scum expressions, he said in disgust, "Well, the hell with it. Y'all don't understand, and I'm damned if I'm gonna twist myself into a pretzel tryin' to explain it to you."

"Yes, you wouldn't want to tax our fragile little female brains," Anabel agreed.

"I didn't say that! Jez-us Joe, I really need this, on top of everything else. Why did the captain have to choose now to go to Alaska?"

"There's fish to be caught, Beauregard. Summer heat and the hurricane season to be avoided." Luke's finely shaped, smoothly shaven head gleamed beneath the overhead lights as he tilted his chair back on two legs.

Beau glared at him. As far as he was concerned, it was Luke's fault he was in this mess in the first place. If he'd just kept his two cents' worth to himself . . . "You break the legs off that chair, Gardner, you're gonna buy me a new one."

"Temper, temper," Josie Lee murmured as she rose to her feet. "I'll just fetch the coffee and Anabel's pralines—maybe that'll put you in a sweeter frame of mind." Passing behind his chair, she gave his head a patronizing little pat.

Beau snarled. *Gawd,* females could be a pain in the butt. And he really should have known better than to expect a smidgen of sympathy from these three at hearing he'd been saddled with the care and feeding of yet another of their species. Damn women always stuck together, and this time even Luke seemed to think they had a point.

Beau's shoulders twitched, throwing off their combined condemnation. Well, big deal—he'd had differences of opinions with this group before, and he'd no doubt have them again.

He still contended it wouldn't take any time at all before he was shed of the oh-so-prim Miz Lowell.

Juliet closed the suite door behind her and promptly fumbled at the back of her head to locate the long-toothed comb that anchored her French twist in place. Working it free as she walked into the sitting room, she fished out an additional handful of hairpins and, with barely a pause on her way to the bedroom, tossed everything in a hand-painted tray she'd placed atop the credenza earlier for that express purpose. Immediately her hair began to swell and grow like a sponge absorbing water, deep waves burgeoning as the thick mass sprang free of its tight confinement. Thrusting her fingers through it, she massaged her scalp vigorously with both hands. "Oh, God, that feels better."

She walked into the bedroom, where she sank onto the slipper chair to remove her flats. Peeling her thigh-high nylons down her legs, she tossed them aside, and then, with a long, contented sigh of release, slithered down the chintz-covered seat to slump on her tailbone, extending her toes as far as they'd reach in front of her and stretching her arms overhead and behind her in a reach for the far wall. She let her head fall back against the chair, her released hair an added cushion that bolstered the base of her skull.

Lessons in comportment were far too ingrained to allow such sloppy posture for long, however, and with a final stretch, she straightened in her chair. Then she rose to her feet and reached for the hidden side zipper on her dress.

It was so good to have a minute to herself. She felt as if she'd been on one emotional juggernaut after another from the instant the plane had touched down.   .

It wasn't simply the unforeseen business with the police, although that had certainly contributed. She rather thought it had more to do with the foreignness of the city, and most of all with the excitement and stress of being responsible for the success of the Garden Crown's opening.

She and Roxanne had been running flat-out practically since the moment Sergeant Dupree had elicited her agreement to stay put and departed. She'd made it a point to meet with the skeleton crew and check with each department to make sure everyone knew what they were supposed to be doing and that it was being done. She simply needed to unwind for a while, in a spot where it was possible to escape feeling her every reaction was being scrutinized, and she'd be fine.

Pulling the dress off over her head, she hung it on its padded satin hanger in the closet, then swept up her discarded nylons and put them in a net lingerie bag to be laundered later. Wearing only her skimpy bikini panties and a demi-bra of ice-blue satin and lace, she stretched luxuriously again, enjoying the cool air that washed across her freshly exposed skin. Letting her arms drop to her sides, she rotated her head.

Tight muscles began to relax and stretched nerves to unwind. Padding over to the high-mattressed bed, she tossed back the duvet.

And felt a scream rip from her throat when a huge black *thing* flew from the comforter, dropped at her feet on the floor, and scuttled for the darkness beneath her bed.

3

Seconds or hours later—she couldn't tell which—she heard a fist bang on the suite door. "Juliet!" Roxanne's voice held both urgency and anxiety. "Are you okay? Let me in."

Juliet scrambled to comply. She ran through the rooms, whipped the door open, and nearly got rapped in the face by Roxanne's upraised fist.

Her assistant's arm dropped to her side as if she'd been shot and she stared at Juliet. "My God," she breathed, "your hair is *gorgeous*. How come you never wear it down like that?"

Juliet just stood in the tiny foyer shaking and shivering, and her expression must have been as blank as her mind because Roxanne made an impatient erasing gesture with one hand and pushed her way into the suite. "Are you okay? Holy catfish, girl, you're practically naked. Nice undies, though." She wrapped an arm around Juliet's bare shoulders, and it was a measure of Juliet's state that she didn't stiffen in discomfort at the unaccustomed touch. Roxanne guided her back through the foyer to the living room.

When they reached the bedroom door, however, Juliet balked. There was no way in hell she was going back into that room.

Roxanne studied her horrified face. "What on earth happened here? Okay, never mind, hold on a second." She took a deep breath, blew it out in a loud gust, and then dashed into the room. An instant later she emerged carrying a brown and gold silk kimono and gently bundled Juliet into it. "Okay, now," she ordered firmly as she overlapped the robe's front panels and tied the garment at Juliet's waist, "tell me what's frightened you so."

"Pardon me," interrupted a cultured Southern voice from the doorway. "I heard a scream. Might I be of some assistance?"

"Oh, Mr. Haynes." Roxanne's voice held relief as she turned toward the foyer.

"Edward, dear," his voice corrected her gently. "Remember? Please, do address me as Edward—I insist."

"Yes, of course. Please, come in." When a man in his early sixties entered the living area, Roxanne reached out to lightly grip Juliet's forearm. "This is Edward Haynes, Juliet. Edward, Juliet Astor Lowell. It was she who screamed, but I haven't been able to find out why yet."

The arrival of the dapper white-haired gentleman forced Juliet to pull herself together. "In there," she said raggedly, pointing a shaking finger at the bedroom door. "It was in my bed—big, black—God, it was so ugly. And it dropped practically on top of my *foot* when I threw back the covers. I've never seen anything like it in my life. It"—she shuddered and made scurrying motions with her fingers—"ran under the bed."

"Was it an animal, dear? A rat, maybe?"

"No. A *bug*. But not little like a beetle. Big. Monstrous!"

"Wait here," Edward ordered. "Let me see what I can find." He disappeared into the room.

The women could hear him rustling around and Juliet turned to her assistant while they waited. The shock was beginning to wear off, and with relief she felt herself regain a bit of her normal composure.

For the first time since the insect had flown from the sheets, she really attended to her surroundings and noticed that Roxanne, too, had discarded her business attire in favor of a loud pair of mustard-yellow satin lounging pajamas. She'd also released her curly, ginger-colored hair from its smooth workaday topknot and pulled it into a ponytail, securing the wild cascade that exploded from the side of her head with a black seamed fishnet stocking tied in a large floppy bow. It was a flamboyant look reminiscent of the day she'd come to interview, and it occurred to Juliet that both Roxanne's work apparel and her public manner had undergone a major metamorphosis since she'd started working for Crown Corporation.

It wasn't as if Juliet had failed to notice the change before, of course—the agreement to adopt a certain look and deportment had been a proviso to Roxanne's employment. Until just this moment, however, she hadn't quite realized how very big the transformation in her assistant had been. It also suddenly occurred to her that Roxanne only indulged the more laid-back portion of her personality when they were alone together.

Juliet felt a surge of affection. "Thank you, Roxanne," she said with quiet fervency. "If you hadn't shown up so promptly and taken over, I probably would have wound up running down the corridor in my underwear, screaming my head off."

A grin flashed across Roxanne's face, and the struggle to subdue it was patent. Her sincere attempt to do so, however, gave Juliet a glimpse of how her assistant must be envisioning her at this moment—fleeing down the hallway like some underclad Gothic heroine of yore—and an inelegant snort escaped her. She immediately got herself under control, but then her gaze collided with Roxanne's and they both lost it entirely, bursting into peals of near-hysterical laughter.

"Truly," she gasped when she finally caught her breath. "Thank you."

"It was my pleasure." Roxanne wiped her eyes. "That must have been some bug, though. I've never seen you so shook."

Juliet couldn't believe how deeply she desired to just talk to Roxanne as a friend, to unload the way the insect flying out at her had accessed an almost primal fear that had knocked every rational thought from her mind. Grandmother had raised her to believe that an Astor Lowell held herself aloof from one's employees, but at the moment her assistant felt a great deal less like a subordinate than she did a warm, sympathetic woman Juliet would like to know better. She opened her mouth . . .

And then closed it again when Edward emerged from the bedroom, a pristine white handkerchief folded around an object in his hand. She didn't even know what it was she might have said, but she was left with the odd feeling that she'd just let an opportunity pass her by.

"Is this what you saw?" Edward flipped back a corner of the monogrammed handkerchief and both women drew back as one, making what Juliet suspected were identical faces of horror at the sight of the large, dead insect within its immaculately laundered folds.

"My God," Roxanne said in disgust. "What the hell is that? I've never *seen* anything so repulsive— it must be three and a half inches long."

"It's a cockroach."

"Oeeuh!" Then, with a reluctant, closer look, she said skeptically, "Get out of here. Cockroaches aren't that big."

"Oh, they come in all sizes down here, from quite small to sometimes even larger than this. Unfortunately, roaches tend to be a real problem in New Orleans, even in some of the finest establishments."

"Oh, my God," Juliet said faintly.

"We've never had them here, however. And if it's any consolation," Edward said with a sympathetic smile for the women's obvious horror, "I could only find the one, so I'm certain this is simply a random incident. I would, however, recommend calling the exterminator in the morning and having the building inspected to be on the safe side. I'd also strip the bed."

"I am not sleeping in that bed," Juliet stated categorically. She'd never get a wink of sleep in this suite now.

"I'd still be sure to have the linens properly laundered to ensure there's no spread of eggs." He reached out and gave her hand a gentle pat. "I'm so sorry, my dear. This is not how I would have chosen to introduce you to New Orleans."

"Thank you, Edward. And I apologize, also. I'm usually a little more composed than this evening's behavior might lead you to believe."

"Nonsense, dear—of course you were upset. Don't give it another thought."

"Come on, Juliet," Roxanne said gently. "I'll help you move to another room."

It didn't take long, since Juliet hadn't yet unpacked. They moved her luggage to the suite across the hall and Roxanne stayed with her while she carefully checked every inch for uninvited wildlife. When she finally climbed into bed a short while later, she was relatively certain that the cockroach had indeed simply been an unfortunate fluke.

It was nevertheless several hours before she relaxed enough to finally fall asleep.

Juliet searched for Edward the next morning and finally located him in the Blue Room, where he was ensconced in a deep chair, absorbed by a gardening magazine. An empty cup on a plate dusted with crumbs sat on the table at his elbow.

She tapped on the doorframe and leaned into the room. "Good morning. May I come in?"

"Of course, my dear!" He removed a pair of dark-rimmed reading glasses and set them aside with the magazine, rising to his feet. "I do hope you don't mind my making myself at home. This has been my special room for ... well, many a year."

"No, of course not." She realized how truly the room reflected the man. It was dapper, warm, and well-appointed, with leather chairs worn to a soft patina, bookshelves full of tomes and magazines, and that spectacularly exotic wall of Mardi Gras masks. "It must be quite difficult having strangers suddenly in charge of your home."

"Actually, having people around and seeing all the hustle and bustle around the old place is rather nice. Although I will miss this room and the garden when we leave." He gave her a gentle smile. "But I'm sure we'll find something perfectly suitable," he said graciously. "And I do hope you don't mind, my dear, but I still have one or two of my treasures locked up in here."

Guilt struck straight to Juliet's core. "Of course not. I see no reason for you to change your habits before you absolutely have to. Actually, I wouldn't intrude on your time now, but I wanted to thank you again for your assistance last night."

He proffered effusive assurances that she wasn't intruding in the least, and apologies that his home would ever afford *anyone* such a traumatic shock, let alone a woman as gracious as herself. By the time Juliet bowed out the door she didn't know whether to laugh or cry. He was such an old sweetie.

And it hadn't once occurred to her, when she'd mentally crowed over the coup of discovering the potential of the Garden Crown, that her actions would displace a wonderful old gent from his lifelong home.

"Afternoon, Miz Roxanne. Boss lady ready to roll?"

Roxanne looked up from her paperwork to observe Sergeant Dupree's loose-limbed saunter to her desk, and she couldn't prevent the slight acceleration of her heartbeat. Lord, the man was a honey. She narrowed her eyes at him, however, for she had a strong hunch he had an agenda all his own when it came to Juliet. That wasn't necessarily a bad thing, but she reserved the right to withhold judgment until she had more information.

"Have a seat, Sergeant," she said in her best, hard-earned professional manner. "I'll let Ms. Astor Lowell know you're here." Pressing down the intercom button, she passed on the information.

Roxanne adored Juliet. She was fully cognizant of the disapproval Juliet endured from her father for hiring her instead of one of those lockjawed debs who'd applied for the position. Thomas Lowell made no bones about considering Roxanne an inferior product—and nobody appreciated more than she did just how much Juliet desired to please her father. Yet Juliet had defied him, and continued to put herself between Roxanne and his disdain whenever the three of them were thrown together.

Roxanne considered Juliet to be a lady in the truest sense of the word, and she strove to emulate her in many ways, if only to prevent her boss from ever regretting climbing out on a limb to provide her with an opportunity. She wouldn't, however, object to seeing Juliet treated like a woman for once in her life.

Nobody ever *touched* her that Roxanne could see—not Juliet's tight-assed father, not her painfully proper granny, nor any of the ultra-WASPs who squired her about to various functions. Maybe some of the escorts were a little less gentlemanly in private, but Roxanne had her doubts. She covertly watched Beau impatiently flip through a magazine. Now, *there* was a man, and one who didn't look as if he'd hesitate to get down-and-dirty physical. It had tickled her to see the way he'd kept crowding Juliet yesterday.

He'd damned well better have good intentions toward her, though.

On the other side of the office door, Juliet took a deep, steadying breath and eased it out. She brushed a nonexistent speck of lint from the skirt of her dress and smoothed her palm over a French twist that required no smoothing. Arranging her features into an expression of cool politeness, she reached to open the door.

Like yesterday, her heartbeat adopted an erratic cadence the minute she walked into the small outer office and saw Beau Dupree sprawled out on one of the fragile antique reception chairs. He looked up as she approached and her mouth immediately lost all moisture. Giving her lips a surreptitious lick, she watched him toss aside his magazine and climb to his feet.

His black eyes took a lazy inventory of her person and he tipped his dark-stubbled chin in an abbreviated nod. "Miz Juliet."

"Sergeant Dupree."

One corner of his mouth crooked up. "Might as well call me Beau, dawlin'. We're going to be spendin' a lot of time together."

"Beau, then." She decided against protesting the endearment. What she should object to was being dragged away when she had a million and one things to do to get ready for the Grand Opening.

But she didn't. Sergeant Dupree had been taken from his work to provide a service they both knew was unnecessary. She owed it to him to accommodate him in return. She'd simply work extra late to make up the lost time.

"You ready to roll?" The question was clearly rhetorical, since he didn't wait for an answer but reached out to grip her arm just above the elbow and set out for the door. "See ya later, Miz Roxanne."

"I expect you to have Juliet back here by three, Sergeant. She has an appointment."

"Yes, ma'am."

The midday heat hit Juliet full force the moment they stepped out the door, overshadowing even the rough-skinned warmth of Beau's hand wrapped around her arm. The air was redolent with the ever-present swampy smell she was beginning to associate with New Orleans and overlaid by the fragrance of flowers whose varied, sultry scents she couldn't begin to identify. Her silk dress immediately stuck to her body, and pressing two fingers to her sternum, she attempted to draw in a truly deep, satisfying breath. It felt as if she were breathing through wet wool.

"Kind of overwhelmin' at first, isn't it?"

Juliet looked up at Beau as he stopped at his car and opened the passenger-side door for her. "How long does it take to become accustomed to it?"

"I'm not sure you ever do. I was born here, and I'm still not entirely used to the summer heat. Watch y'head, now."

Juliet lowered herself onto the buttery leather of the wide bucket seat and tucked in her skirt as Beau closed the door. She ran an appreciative hand along the glossy forest-green paint job outside the rolled-down window. She'd always wanted a kick-ass car like this. Instead, she drove a sedate Mercedes sedan her father had picked out for her. Yesterday she'd been too upset by the myriad unfolding events to notice details, but now, as Beau rounded the long expanse of the hood, she looked around with interest, taking in the meticulously kept interior, the small wooden steering wheel, the plush carpeting beneath her sandals. Too bad it wasn't a drop-top.

The wistful little thought made her sit up straighter. Good grief, was she actually sitting here like some starry-eyed high school girl, relishing the notion of catching a ride in a fast car? She was thirty-two years old and she'd ridden in limousines, taken the Concorde to Paris. This was hardly the Batmobile, for God's sake—it was just a low-slung, well-kept old car. Big deal.

She felt its power vibrating up her spine the minute Beau started the engine. "Nice car," she said but offered the compliment in cool tones to disguise—to him, to herself—how very much she liked feeling all that energy surging beneath her.

"This is not a *car*, sugar, it's a '69 Royal Bobcat GTO." Beau stroked the dashboard fondly. "This baby's a classic, a testimony to the genius of Detroit."

"Ah, well, forgive my ignorance," Juliet said and then murmured unthinkingly, "Lordy. Boys and their toys."

He turned his head to look at her, and she found herself pinned to her seat by the look in those heavy-lidded dark eyes. "I've got other toys I could show you, dawlin'. I'll even let you play with some of 'em, if you ask me real nice."

She was embarrassed to realize she'd actually spoken her thoughts aloud, and was eaten alive with curiosity as to whether he meant what she thought he meant. But . . . surely not. Just in case he did, however, she elevated her chin and gave him a cool, discouraging glare down the length of her nose.

He merely grinned at her, his teeth very white against the swarthiness of his skin. Then he was suddenly leaning over her, his face only inches away, his chest brushing hers as his left hand slid down her right arm and fumbled around her hip. Juliet shrank back into the seat, her heart pounding. "What do you think you're doing!"

"Gettin' your seatbelt." He seemed to be addressing her mouth, but when she licked her lips in nervous reaction, he gave his head a slight shake. Black brows snapping together, he raised his gaze to meet hers. Then he clicked the seatbelt around her and settled back behind the wheel to regard her with a quizzical little half-smile. "Why, Miz Juliet, whatever did you think I was doin'?"

"I'm sure I couldn't say." Oh, for heaven's sake, if she were any stiffer they could surf her to Havana. The damn guy seemed to have an effortless and unnerving ability to reduce her to truly idiotic utterings.

"I'm a sworn officer of the law, Rosebud—you wouldn't want me to willfully break an important statute by drivin' off with my passenger unbuckled, now, would you?"

"Oh, no, Beauregard, we certainly wouldn't want that." She couldn't believe that sarcastic tone was coming from her mouth, but he pushed buttons she'd never even known she *possessed*, and she couldn't bottle it up to save her soul.

"Didn't think so. Relax that spine a little, sweet thing, and enjoy the ride." He eased the stick shift into first gear and roared out from beneath the porte cochere, barely slowing as he approached the street.

Hot, humid wind blew through the windows as they raced out of the neighborhood, and cool jazz wailed from the speakers the instant Beau punched on the stereo. The car's engine throbbed with leashed power at every traffic light that forced it into idle, and Juliet found herself doing exactly what he'd ordered: enjoying the ride.

She held back strands of hair that were being worked loose by the wind and took in the Southern live oaks that passed in a mossy blur as the car sped down the boulevard. She turned to look at Beau. "Are the trees on the median strip as ancient as they look?"

"This is N'Awlins, dawlin'," he said with a quick grin that slashed creases next to his mouth. "We don't have medians here, we have neutral grounds. But, to answer your question: yeah, probably, dependin' on your definition of ancient. Those aren't the oldest oaks in town, but they're still over a hundred years old."

The wide boulevards soon gave way to the narrower streets of the Quarter. Juliet gazed out the window with interest as Beau cruised up and down the streets looking for a place to park.

There was litter everywhere and the air was alive with music. It was an old area of low, mostly brick buildings, narrow alleyways, and filigreed ironwork. It had a definite European look, and with the lack of skyscrapers one could almost imagine they were in the 1800s . . . except for all the strip joints, fortune telling stores, and sex shops that lined the narrow sidewalks.

Beau found a parking spot and pulled in. He helped her out of the car a moment later and, wrapping his long fingers around her wrist, immediately set off down the street. Juliet had always considered herself sophisticated, but she saw neckties in one window that were shaped like penises, a voodoo parlor with an exhibit case that seemed to be filled with dried animal parts, a porn shop that displayed objects whose use she couldn't even begin to determine, and she wanted desperately to slow down and give everything a closer inspection. It was all she could do not to gawk.

But there weren't all that many people on the street during the height of the afternoon heat to observe her. And Beauregard seemed preoccupied with reaching some undetermined destination. Given both of those factors, she cautiously indulged herself. The establishments' doors all stood wide open, and smoke and music poured out. Up ahead on the sidewalk a chalkboard advertised in quite graphic terms the live sex show going on inside. She'd never even dreamed such things *existed*, and as they passed by she lagged in Beau's grip just a bit to see if she could catch a peek.

She was still gazing back over her shoulder when he pulled her through the entrance of the establishment next door. Her pupils dilated in the sudden dimness, and the smoky haze that swirled down from the ceiling made her sneeze. "Excuse me," she murmured, rooting in her clutch for a handkerchief as she sneezed again. She was vaguely aware of a bluesy instrumental with a strong downbeat that was heavy on the horns playing over the speakers. Beau led her to a stool at the bar and seated her. Gradually her eyes adjusted to the change in lighting.

She discovered a woman with impossibly large, bare breasts, squatting on a pair of spike-heeled shoes right in front of her. Juliet's head reared back as the woman's knees suddenly spread wide, exposing her crotch, which was clothed only in a gold sequined G-string that seemed to provide less coverage than the three limp, folded dollar bills that sprouted from it. The woman braced her hands on her knees and her bottom raised slightly as she swiveled her hips in a small bump and grind that was compellingly lewd. Dear God, this was a strip joint.

How utterly fascinating.

4

Josie Lee checked her lipstick, then tilted her tiny compact this way and that as she fluffed her dark curls. The elevator eased to a stop on the second floor and she snapped the compact closed, tossing it in her shoulder bag as the doors slid open. Tugging down her top, she took a deep breath. This was it.

For as long as she could remember she'd been in love with Luke Gardner, but he'd never regarded her as anything other than his partner's kid sister. Well, that was about to change. She had a window of opportunity here while Beau's new assignment kept him out of the office, and she was about to take full advantage of it. She was making her move.

God, please don't let me throw up.

No. She could do this. She sucked in air through her nostrils and blew it out through her mouth, then patted the dampness from her palms against the linen skirt covering her thighs. *It's do or die, girlfriend; put up or shut up. You can do it.*

The moment she saw Luke, with a phone pressed to his ear and hunched so far over his desk that his shirt stretched taut over his shoulders, her nerves disappeared. She still got that whole-body hot and flushed feeling she always felt around him, but the fear dissolved like a discarded Sno-bal on a sizzling July banquette, as old-timers called the sidewalks. This was the man she'd spent what felt like forever praying to St. Frances of Rome over—figuring as she had with teenage fervor that if ever there was a saint who knew a little something about waiting, it was F of R. Josie Lee had been scared to death Luke would find someone else before she had a chance to grow up. He hadn't, thank God; at least not anyone with any staying power.

Well, she was all grown up now, and through with patiently sitting back, waiting for him to take notice. If he failed to do so this time, it wouldn't be because she'd lacked the courage to launch a campaign. Taking yet another bracing breath, she set out for his desk.

Only to ease it out again anticlimactically when she was intercepted by another of her brother's fellow officers.

Luke cradled the phone receiver to his ear with one hand and bent over his desk, rummaging through its clutter. Where the hell was his notebook? Finally locating it in a place he could have sworn he'd already checked, he rapidly thumbed through pages of cramped writing until he reached the right entry. He read the pertinent information to the cop on the other end of the line and leaned

back in his chair . . . where he found himself at eye
level with a woman's round backside.

Whoa. Very nice. He grinned, enjoying the sight.
The desks were crammed together and the woman
leaned on her palms on McDoskey's desk right in
front of him. She was bent forward in earnest conversation, an action that stretched her beige linen
skirt snugly across shapely hips and caused its already short hem to raise a fraction higher. A movement from the corner of his eye caught his attention
and Luke looked over to see Bettencourt pushing
back in his chair to also get a better look at the
woman. Their eyes met for a moment and they
both grinned. Luke blew out a breath and thumped
his hand rapidly over his heart, miming his appreciation. Then his attention returned to the woman,
where it remained riveted while he answered the
questions put to him at the other end of the line.
Man. That was one sweet butt, but it was the legs
that truly caught his attention: they were world
class. He wondered who she was.

He felt as if someone had taken a baseball bat to
his solar plexus when she turned her head and he
saw it was Beau's baby sister.

Christ. Josie Lee was just a kid. Well, maybe not
a kid, he supposed, since she'd just graduated from
Tulane and must be—what?—twenty-two now?
But still. Beau had taken him aside last night and
asked him to keep an eye on her while he was out
on assignment. Luke was pretty damn sure ogling
her ass and legs wasn't what his partner'd had in
mind.

The detective at the other end of the line asked

a question, and from his impatient tone Luke deduced this wasn't the first time the inquiry had been put to him. "What?" he said blankly. Then he shook off his unusual lapse in professionalism. "I'm sorry, something came up here that diverted my attention for a moment. Give that to me again."

He watched Josie Lee straighten. She said something to McDoskey that made the detective laugh, then she turned and strolled around Luke's desk as he concluded his conversation. He recradled the receiver just as she arrived.

"Hey, Luke," she said softly and flashed him the killer grin she had in common with her brother. "Long time no see, huh?"

Luke could see that McDoskey was still watching her, his eyes faintly dazed. For some reason it irritated him and he said brusquely, "Hey, Baby Girl." Beau called her that sometimes, and Luke knew it annoyed her.

She merely gave him an inscrutable smile, however, and hitched herself up to perch on the corner of his desk. Her short skirt slid up her thighs as she crossed her legs.

He pulled his gaze away from the mesmerizing swing of her uppermost leg and raised his eyes determinedly to her face. "Uh, this your first day on the job or you just stoppin' by to fill out the paperwork?"

"No, I started this morning. I'm on my lunch break and thought I'd run up to say hi to Beau."

"He's out today."

"Yeah, I remembered that while I was talking to McDoskey." She shrugged and slowly rotated her sandal-shod foot in first one direction and then the other. He noticed that her ankles were slim and her toenails painted red. Then her enthusiastic tone pulled his attention back to her face. "I think this job's going to be so great, Luke. It turns out Camilla's best friend's sister-in-law's brother-in-law is married to my boss." She gave him a crooked smile. "Don'tcha just love this town?"

Luke felt a slight smile tug up the corner of his own mouth. There was nothing New Orleanians loved so much as their gossip and their intrafamily connections. This was probably the largest city in the world to revel so fiercely in its small-town mind-set.

"Well, listen," Josie Lee said, and sliding off the desk, she reached out a finger and trailed it down Luke's forearm. "I'm sure you're busy, so I won't keep you. I just wanted to say hi. I'm so excited about the job and was simply dyin' to share it with someone. I'm glad you were here." She wiggled her fingers at him. "See you around."

Unable to prevent himself from watching the swing of her hips as she walked away, Luke rubbed absently at the streak of heat that lay just below the skin of his forearm and wondered what the hell had just happened here.

"Why, Beauregard Butler Dupree, as I live and breathe! I couldn't believe it when Tommy said you were lookin' for little ole me. To what do I owe this honor, sir—you finally gonna break down and take me out for a night on the town?" The skimpily clad, busty blonde waitress who'd suddenly materialized out of the bar's smoky gloom glanced beyond him to Juliet. "Oops, I guess not, huh? Or you prob'ly wouldn't a dragged along your date."

"Who, this?" Beau feigned incredulity as he looked from the waitress to Juliet and back again. "This isn't my date, Dora, dawlin', this here's my . . ." *What, genius?* He could hardly claim "sister" because Dora was a friend of the older sister of one of Anabel's friends and she'd know better. ". . . Cousin Juliet from up North. Say hi to Dora Wexler, Cousin Juliet."

"Hello, Dora, it's nice to meet you."

"You *know* I'm savin' all my lovin' for you," he assured the waitress. Actually, she was just his type; he didn't know why he hadn't asked her out already.

"Oh, I'm just sure you are, sugar." Dora ran a blood-red, inch-long fingernail down his stubbled cheek a:d rubbed her breast against his arm as she leaned past him to say to Juliet, "Rumor has it that Beauregard here was the only sixth-grader in all of Orleans Parish with a five o'clock shadow, Juliet—did you know that?"

Beau felt Juliet's gaze like inquisitive fingers against his perpetually shadowed jaw; then her attention went past him to the waitress plastered to his side. "No, I hadn't heard that," she said in her well-bred voice. "But then our branches of the . . . family . . . haven't always been close."

Dora found innovative ways to press against him as she pursued the conversation. "Is this your first trip to the Crescent City, then?"

"I've been to New Orleans before, but only

briefly. It's my first visit to the French Quarter."

"No shit? The Quarter's where you'll find all the action, hon. But I guess you're findin' that out. Tommy, there"—Dora's chin hitched in the direction of the bartender laconically swabbing down the far end of the bar—"tells me y'all caught the show. What'd you think a that?"

"It was . . . interesting." A slight smile suddenly tilted the corner of Juliet's lips. "Quite truthfully, unlike anything I've ever before seen. I found Boom Boom LaTreque, in particular, quite amazing."

"Aren't those ta-tas somethin' else again? And the really amazing thing is that they're gonna be all hers in just three more payments."

Beau shifted in his seat. It was too damn hot to have a woman draped all over him, and Dora's perfume was growing cloying. Why the hell was Juliet being so gracious? He'd thought for sure that narrow little nose of hers would be high in the air. At the very least, he'd expected a bit of condescension when she spoke to Dora—whereupon he could sit back and watch the fur fly when Dora ripped her a new one. Damn. Clearly that wasn't going to happen. It was time to quit playing around and get down to business.

He peeled Dora off of him. "I've heard Clyde Lydet is a regular here. I need to talk to him."

She regarded him sulkily. "I thought you came in to see me."

"And so I did, sugar. But I'm also on the job, and it'd be remiss of me to neglect it strictly for my own pleasure."

The music started up, presaging a new act, and Dora raised her voice to be heard over it. "So why are ya draggin' your cousin around if you're so all-fired professional?"

"An excellent question," Juliet commended the waitress and turned an inquiringly raised eyebrow on him. "Why are you dragging me around?"

"Why, Cousin Juliet, you little ol' tease, you." Noticing a lock of hair that had almost worked itself loose from her tightly pulled back 'do, he leaned close to hook it with his finger, flashing her a big ole wolfish grin when her predictable recoil tugged it free. The liberated tress immediately swelled in volume and grew surprisingly wavy. "What a card y'are, pretendin' you've forgotten how insistent you were to watch me in action." He wrapped the hair around and around one finger and rubbed it absently with his thumb as he look over at Dora. "She's such a kidder. I tried telling her I had work to do, but would she listen? No, ma'am. She kept beggin' me and beggin' me to bring her along, rhapsodizing on and on about what a golden opportunity it would be to observe the best at work." He gave a modest shrug. "What could I do?"

"Actually," Juliet said coolly, "I believe it was *you* who touted yourself as the best. And I don't recall begging to go anywhere with you. Let go of my hair, Beauregard."

He unwound the strands from his fingers while Dora commented wryly, "Y'all aren't exactly kissin' cousins, are ya?" The thought seemed to please her.

Beau's gaze went unerringly to Juliet's full, unpainted lips. Why, the situation practically *demanded* he capture a little taste, and he found himself leaning toward her. "Oh, I wouldn't say that," he murmured. "I wouldn't say that at all." This was strictly in the name of the cause, of course.

"Well, I would." Juliet slid out of reach off the far side of her barstool and stood facing them, her posture erect, the errant curl dangling down over her eye. "Dora, you're an exceedingly perceptive woman. Now, excuse me a moment, won't you? I'll just go fix my hair."

"She hates to get mussed," Beau murmured, but his self-congratulatory smile faded when Juliet disappeared down a dim hallway and he realized he'd been watching her every step of the way. He turned to Dora, all business. "Here's my card. I'm going to write down my cell and my home phone number on it, too. I want to hear from you the minute Clyde Lydet shows up. It's important, Dora."

Then he gave her a grin. "Why don't you give me your home number, too, sugar, and I'll give you a call as soon as this case is over. We'll get together."

He exchanged lazy, flirtatious comments with the waitress and watched the newest stripper until Juliet reappeared. The instant she materialized out of the gloom, he rose to his feet, ready to leave. And if there was an inexplicable sense of relief in seeing her hair all skimmed tightly back into place again, he didn't address it.

* * *

Cousin Juliet, say hi to Dora. Say hi to Charleen, Cousin Juliet. Juliet gazed stonily at the scenery flashing by as Beau raced his precious GTO through the city streets. *Hey, Tammi Mae. Meet my Cousin Jules.* What she wouldn't give to tell Lil' Abner here what she thought of his aw-shucks routine.

At first it had been amusing, but it had rapidly palled. There had even been one reckless moment in the last bar he'd dragged her to when she'd nearly smacked her palm against a portion of her anatomy an Astor Lowell never even *mentioned*, and invited him to *Kiss this, Cousin Beau.*

But of course she hadn't.

Her control should make her proud: she had remained true to her breeding, to Grandmother's upbringing. So why did she feel so sour instead?

They rolled to a stop at a red light, the threatening grumble of the GTO's pipes the only sound to break the silence that had permeated the car ever since they'd left the Quarter. Beau looked over at her. "Hey, Rosebud, you're awfully quiet. 'Course, you're always quiet, but"—he studied her with bogus concern—"you're also lookin' a mite flushed." His thick lashes lowered as his gaze dropped down to study her thighs, and Juliet's flush grew deeper when she followed his gaze and saw how they were outlined by the humidity-limp material that stuck to them. Then he brought his gaze back up to her face and gave her a slow, lazy smile. "This is the Big Easy, dawlin'—you gotta learn to leave those pantyhose in the drawer."

The man was a walking, talking menace to

women's health. She'd watched him flirt everywhere they'd gone and had seen him collect phone numbers with the enthusiasm of a kid exchanging baseball cards. He'd treated her as if she were an expensive but brainless Afghan on the end of his leash, and had tried to embarrass her by pretending he was going to kiss her. She felt hot and sweaty, manipulated and misused.

Well, enough was enough.

Holding his gaze, Juliet toed off her shoes. She located the elasticized lace band at the top of her left stocking through the silk of her dress, and raised her leg slightly to work the band down to the point where it no longer hugged her thigh. Then she reached beneath her hem and, displacing her skirt as little as possible, rolled the nylon down her leg to midcalf. As it collapsed in a silken tangle around her ankle, she pointed her toes, grasped the fragile nylon over them, and peeled the stocking free.

As a striptease went, she was certain it was deathly dull, but it was something she'd never in her life performed in front of another human being, let alone in an open-windowed car in the middle of town in front of the King of Hormones. Still, it was worth every bit of her own discomfort when he stared at the filmy length of off-white hosiery dangling from her fingertips and croaked, "Christ! What the hell d'you think you're doin', Juliet?"

"Why, just following your excellent advice." Emboldened, she repeated the routine with her right stocking and then pointed out gently, "The light is green, Beauregard."

Swearing beneath his breath at the cars that began to honk behind them, he rammed the gear shift into first and left a patch of rubber behind as he roared off the line. Juliet folded her hosiery into a neat little pile and settled back in her seat, feeling *much* more tranquil. The rush of cooling air against her overheated legs didn't hurt, either.

She should have known it wouldn't last. A short while later Beau pulled beneath the hotel's porte cochere and parked. When he rounded the hood to open her door, she gave him an empty social smile and extended her hand, hoping to forestall his habit of grasping her any old which way to haul her out of vehicles. "Well, it's been most . . . educational," she murmured as he actually assisted her with a modicum of gentleness. "I'll see you tomorrow, I imagine, as there appears to be no avoiding . . ." He hadn't bothered to move back, and her voice trailed away as she straightened from the car and found him standing much too close.

Sweat plastered his shirt to his chest and heat rolled off of him in waves. Juliet's pulse began to drum as he put his hands flat on the car roof on either side of her, hemming her in. "Forget tomorrow, sugarplum; today's not over yet. I've got five more hours on the clock."

"I beg your pardon?"

"I'm sticking with you for five more hours."

"But that's preposterous!"

"Damn right it is—you know it and I know it. But you heard 'Acting' Captain Pfeffer: my job's to guard your body. And I pride myself on my work." He sniffed the air. Then he turned his head and sniffed again near her temple, like a blood-hound scenting prey. Suddenly he lowered his head, stopping just short of burying his nose in the contour of her neck. Juliet's heart tried to bang its way out of her chest as Beau inhaled deeply through his nostrils, and she held herself very still. Slowly he raised his head again, an exhalation filtering out through his parted lips. "So this is what a rich girl smells like," he murmured, and his eyelids were heavy as he studied her. "*Nice.*"

Then he stepped back, sweeping out a lean brown hand to indicate she should go first. "Shall we go in, then?"

Juliet struggled for composure as she preceded him into the Garden Crown. He was crazy, just plain crazy. That was all there was to it.

5

What are you, friggin' nuts? The plan was to freak her into demanding a new escort, not— Beau ruthlessly chopped off the end of his thought; he didn't even want to think about how his so-called plan had turned around and bitten him on the butt. Arms crossed over his chest, feet thrust out in front of him while he slumped on his tailbone on the same chair he'd occupied outside Juliet's office before their foray into the Quarter, he scowled at Roxanne.

As if she cared. He swallowed a snort. The ginger-haired secretary reminded him of his sisters in the way she was able to ignore him with such apparent ease. And it wasn't as if he were pissed at her, anyhow; she was just a convenient substitute. He was mad at himself.

Much as he might want to ignore the reasons why, he couldn't seem to prevent his thoughts from returning to them over and over again, like a tongue probing the jagged edge of a broken tooth.

He didn't know what the hell had gotten into him. Juliet Rose Astor Lowell wasn't even his type. He liked 'em small, stacked and brassy, not middlin', willowy, and repressed. So what was he doing getting turned on by the sight of her *feet*, for chrissake?

Damn, that had to have been the most pitiful excuse of a striptease he'd ever seen in his life . . . and he got half hard all over again just thinking about it. He had to get out more; that's all there was to it. His sex life was a joke, and had been for pretty much the entire decade since his folks had been killed. But hell, what other alternative had he had: to stand back and watch his family be broken apart? Not in this lifetime—and face it, he'd hardly been in a position to bring women home: his sisters had been way too young and impressionable. Nor had there been an abundance of free hours to go out searching for action. It all added up to a pretty damn sorry and sporadic love life.

That was all going to change any day now, though, and it sure as shit didn't have to be this pathetic in the meantime. Hell, Juliet Rose hadn't even intended her little stocking removal to *be* a tease; it was simply a minor rebellion against the jibes he'd been using to drive her away. But her skin was pale gold and smooth as honey, and he'd caught glimpses of it in an exposed calf here, a slender ankle there. And her feet—man, he didn't know what it was about her feet, but they were long and slender, with high arches and long, narrow toes. Her toenails had been painted a virgin pink, where he'd expected them to be as prudishly unadorned as her fingernails. And the *smell* of her . . .

He shifted uncomfortably, muttering an obscenity.

"All right, Dupree, that does it," Roxanne suddenly snapped, and he blinked at her in surprise. He'd forgotten for a minute where he was.

She pointed to the door. "Go check out the hotel, grill the staff, walk the grounds. Do whatever it is you do, but do it someplace else. Juliet's three o'clock is due at any moment and the woman considers me her social inferior. I might have to put up with her subtle snubs, but I *don't* have to sit here and listen to you swear. Go away."

"Why, Miz Roxanne, I'm crushed." Beau shoved to his feet. "But hey, I've been kicked out of better places." Catching her skeptically raised eyebrow, he rolled his shoulders and gave her a crooked smile. "Okay, maybe not better—this is a pretty cushy crib. But I've been kicked out by tougher folks than you, for sure. How many appointments does Juliet have, anyway, not counting the snob?"

"None."

"No kidding?" That perked him up. "Think she'll be done by three-thirty?"

"Maybe. By four certainly."

"All right. Tell her to be ready to move out at four-oh-five."

She raised that eyebrow again, and shoving his hands in his pockets, he regarded her impatiently. "*What?*"

"I'll tell her you've requested the pleasure of her company—"

Beau snorted.

"—but I don't guarantee you'll get it. She may have other plans."

"Then she can just cancel them."

At Roxanne's inelegant get-real snicker, he planted his hands flat on her desk and leaned his weight on them, looming over her. "Listen, sweetheart, I'm here at her request—"

"No, *sweetheart*, you're here at her father's. You clearly don't understand Juliet at all, so you'll just have to trust me when I tell you she'd never have asked for protection on her own behalf, and doesn't want anything to do with the deferential treatment she's been given."

He straightened. "She doesn't?"

"Good Lord, no."

Well, hey, that should make little Miss Juliet Rose all the more eager to get rid of him then. He fought down the smug smile he felt rising and merely said, "Huh."

"Oh, you chatty types," Roxanne said with a perfectly deadpan expression. "How *is* a girl to get a word in edgewise?"

"You're such a card, Miz Roxanne. And just cuter 'n a button, too." Beau flashed her a crooked grin as he headed for the door. "Anyone ever tell you that?"

"All the time, Sergeant Dupree. All the time."

"Five after four," he reiterated. "Tell Juliet Rose I expect her to be ready." And with a little bit of luck, maybe by this time tomorrow he'd be back to doing what he did best: real police work.

* * *

Juliet finished tracking down the missing ship-
ment of linens for the dining room, and looked at
her watch. It was nearly three-thirty and Celeste
Haynes had yet to put in an appearance. She was
reaching with her free hand for the phone's intercom button when Roxanne's voice suddenly emanated like a summoned genie from the speaker.

"Mrs. Haynes has arrived, Juliet."

Juliet's hand settled back on the desk. "Thank
you. Please send her in."

The last word had barely left her lips when the
door opened and an exquisitely turned-out woman
in her early sixties wafted in on a subtle cloud of
expensive perfume. She was quite tiny, but something about her ramrod posture and vintage tai-
lored clothing made her appear almost tall. Juliet
stood and rounded her desk. "Celeste, how nice to
finally meet you. I'm Juliet Astor Lowell."

The older woman's white bouffant hair dipped
regally as she gave a brief nod of acknowledgment.
"Of course you are, dear." She imperiously extended a soft, beringed white hand with her fingers
curved down. No excuse was offered for her tar-
diness.

Juliet wondered if the woman expected her to
kiss the presented knuckles like some courtier of
old. She awkwardly grasped the proffered fingertips and shook. Releasing them, she said, "Please,
make yourself comfortable," and walked back
around her desk. Before she could resume her seat,
however, Celeste had bypassed the visitor's chair
and crossed to the settee on the other side of the

office. She took a seat and patted the cushion next to her invitingly.

"Do come sit down, dear. I've asked Lily to bring us a nice little repast. We must talk and get to know one another."

"Uh, Juliet?" Roxanne's voice crackled to life from the intercom speaker. "There's a woman here with a tray. She says she's been instructed to— Wait a minute, ma'am!" Her voice grew fainter as if she'd turned away from the receiver. "You can't just—"

The door opened and an ancient woman wearing a white-aproned black uniform backed into the room, balancing a large tray. Turning, she shuffled straight over to Celeste. "Here's your tea, Miz Celeste."

Celeste patted a little side table. "Set it down right here, Lily."

Roxanne appeared in the doorway and rolled her eyes. "Sorry," she mouthed with a little grimace, and Juliet gave her a slight, bemused smile. Roxanne held the door for the elderly maid and they both withdrew, Juliet's assistant pulling the door softly closed behind them.

"Come, dear, have a seat. Lily brought us a nice mint iced tea. Do you take sugar?" Celeste quirked a white eyebrow, the silver tongs suspended daintily over the Sevres bowl of sugar cubes.

"No, thank you." Juliet took a seat, wondering how on earth her business meeting had transformed into a tea party. It suddenly felt as if her beautiful hotel had metamorphosed back into a private home and she was trespassing.

"Watercress sandwich or cucumber?" Celeste extended a plate.

"Watercress, please." Juliet selected one of the quarter-sized tidbits and placed it on the fragile china plate Celeste passed her, which she then set aside. "Now. About the schedule, Celeste—"

"Cookie?" A new plate was offered.

"Thank you, no. Ab—"

"Tell me about your family, dear."

Juliet swallowed a sigh. "My father is a Lowell of the Boston Lowells. My mother was an Astor. I was raised by my maternal grandmother, Rose Elizabeth Astor." Juliet took a small sip of her iced tea.

"And a true lady she must be, dear. It's apparent in your exquisite manners."

"Thank you, that's very gracious. Now, about—"

"My Edward, of course, is a Haynes, and I am the last of the Butlers. This mansion was in the Butler family for nearly two hundred years, dear. As I'm from the distaff side, I'm ineligible to inherit, but as you know, Edward and I were charged with its maintenance until your corporation made the offer to buy it from the estate."

Actually the Butler Trust people had offered the estate to Crown Hotels, but Juliet didn't correct her. "And you maintained it beautifully," she complimented her and then said firmly, "Now, about the calendar of events you've arranged. I'd like to discuss it so I'll know how my own schedule needs to be arranged before the Grand Opening." She rose to her feet and walked over to the desk. Pressing down the intercom button, she said,

"Roxanne, come in, please, and bring the appointment book."

As she regained her seat on the settee, her assistant walked through the doorway. Juliet looked up with a smile. "Pull up a chair. Celeste, you've met my assistant Roxanne, I believe? You and she will be working together quite closely to keep the agendas coordinated."

"I understood I'd be working with you."

"And so you shall be, but naturally I'm going to be in and out of the office. Roxanne is here all the time."

"But she's only—"

"My right hand."

"Yes, of course," Celeste said primly, but Juliet wasn't fooled. Celeste's impeccable manners masked a rigid sense of societal position. The society in which Juliet moved was loaded with such women. They placed more importance upon one's antecedents than on the accomplishments that made a person who she was today, and each and every like-minded matron who'd ever had reason to come into contact with Roxanne had regarded her as nothing more than a lowly secretary.

Juliet turned to her assistant. "Sandwich, Roxanne? Celeste, is there another plate?"

"No, I'm afraid Lily only supplied the two."

"Ah, well, I'm sure you'll inform her that from now on we'll be requiring three. In the meantime, Roxanne can have mine." Juliet plucked up her tiny, crustless sandwich and held it between two fingers, her pinky crooked. She passed the translucent china plate to Roxanne, popped the watercress tidbit in her mouth, and then reached for the platter of sandwiches and presented it to her assistant. "Try one of each. Cookie?"

"Why, thank you very much." Roxanne smiled demurely. "Don't mind if I do."

Juliet passed that plate also. "Now, then, let's get down to business. Celeste, did you bring the list of functions you've arranged for me to attend?"

Usually Juliet derived extreme pleasure from the sense of accomplishment her work brought her. Today, as the meeting wore on, she merely experienced an old edgy feeling of restriction, the likes of which she hadn't encountered since she was a child watching the gardener's children run barefoot through the gardens while she was confined to her chair indoors for another interminable tea with Grandmother. She found it difficult to sit still and concentrate. Instead, she wanted to fidget and squirm. She longed to get up and run and run, to spin in balletic circles until she could spin no more and finally collapsed in a dizzy heap.

Naturally, she did not. But when the door suddenly opened and Beau stuck his head in to growl, "It's four-*thirty*. You about ready?" it took every ounce of poise she possessed not to leap from her seat, exclaiming, *Yes, yes, yes—take me* out *of here*.

"Come in, Beauregard," she said calmly and, ignoring Roxanne's raised eyebrow, turned to Celeste. "Celeste, this is Beauregard Dupree. Beau, Celeste Haynes."

"Yeah, how d'you do," Beau said and unhesitantly bent over the hand Celeste presented him and planted a kiss on her knuckles. He immediately turned back to Juliet. "So, you ready to go or what?"

She felt laughter tickle the back of her throat and pressed her lips together, swallowing hard against the urge to give in to it. Really, she shouldn't encourage his appalling manners. She turned to Celeste, who regarded Beau as if he were a wild and unpredictable animal. And no wonder: with his dark jaw, his casual clothing clinging to damp portions of his lean musculature, and the raw, palpable energy he exuded, he looked dangerous and worlds removed from his natural element.

But that wasn't to say she was about to let this opportunity pass her by.

"I'm sorry, Celeste, but our appointment has run over its allotted time, and I have another commitment. I'll leave you in Roxanne's capable hands. Do feel free to contact me in my room later this evening if you have any questions." She turned to her assistant. "Roxanne, please put together an itinerary for Beau and—"

Her instructions were cut off midstream when Beau strode for the door with her firmly in tow, but she didn't protest. Light-headed and light of heart, she felt as daring as a kid playing hooky from school. With a sensual appreciation for the cool air-conditioning that wafted against her bare legs, she trotted contentedly in his wake.

In the small, elegant office she'd left behind, Celeste pursed her lips in disapproval and sourly eyed the empty doorway. Well, really! Here she was graciously giving her time in order to ease Miss Astor Lowell's way into New Orleans' society, and for what? To be treated like this? How dare the little chit?

Celeste had been involuntarily impressed with Juliet's pedigree, but this behavior just went to show that when it came to Yankees, breeding did *not* necessarily tell.

She straightened her spine, aligned her ankles, and attended with chilly civility to the upstart typist as they concluded their arrangements. Then she snapped her appointment book closed and rose with dignity to her feet. "I'll send Lily to clear," she said coolly and sailed from the room.

As if it weren't demeaning enough that her beautiful home was being turned into a hotel, that all her and Edward's personal servants except for Lily were now employees of the Crown Corporation—the high and mighty Miss Astor Lowell had to waltz out of their meeting on the arm of a thug, too, and leave her in the company of a mere secretary? Celeste fumed as she made her way up to the set of rooms to which she and Edward were now consigned.

She should have had Lilly put a *dozen* cockroaches in the ungrateful little trollop's bed.

6

Well, that sure as hell hadn't gone the way he'd expected. Beau glanced over at Juliet as he wheeled the GTO out of the hotel drive and onto the street. What was it with her? Every time he thought he had his moves solidly down and his fingers poised to punch all her buttons, she reacted in a totally unforeseen way. Jesus Joe, she was contradictory.

As if sensing his glance, she crossed her bare ankles and tilted her knees toward the console as she swiveled in his direction. "May I?" She reached for the volume dial on the radio and lowered it several decibels without awaiting his permission.

"Hey, don't mind me, angel face," he groused. "Just make yourself at home."

He felt her studying him and cheered up. Ah, *now* he was going to get the speech about manners and the behavior she expected from a professional when dealing with a highborn Yank like herself. Hell, he should have known she wouldn't dress him down in front of Roxanne and the grande

71

dame; she was much too mannerly, and a public rebuke simply wasn't her style. She'd most likely been practicing a lecture in her head all this time—being the polite and cautious, methodical type.

From the corner of his eye he saw her fingers tracing the edge of her seat. Several heartbeats went by, and then she asked, "Who's Clyde Lydet?"

"Huh?"

"I was wondering who—"

He waved that aside. "I heard what you said, Rosebud. It's just a hundred and eighty degrees from what I was expecting." He shot her a glance before returning his attention to the road. "Clyde Lydet is a receiver of stolen arms. Not just any ol' guns, though, y'understand; he's a specialist who trades in antique firearms." He shrugged. "Only in N'Awlins, dawlin'."

"Why are you looking for him?"

"Because I think he's got a connection with the Panty Snatcher case, which you must have heard me wrangling over with the Pissant yesterday."

"The *who*?"

"Pfeffer, the clueless acting captain." He could almost swear he caught a glimpse of her full lips curling up in sly amusement, but if so, she'd reined herself in by the time he was able to take his attention from the road and look at her directly, for she met his gaze with perfect solemnity. There was something that burned in the gray depths of her eyes, however, something he'd just as soon not examine too closely, and he gave himself a sharp mental shake. "Word is Lydet's known down in the Quarter, and trying to find him beats the hell out of cooling my heels outside your office."

"What has this Panty Snatcher person done?"

"Broke into a number of women's houses and forced 'em to strip at gunpoint."

"How awful." A shiver of empathy raised a light dusting of goose bumps on her arms. "Can't someone identify him?"

"He doesn't just waltz in with his face hanging out," Beau said impatiently. "He's got an assortment of Mardi Gras masks he uses to disguise himself."

"Oh, my God." She regarded him with sudden horror. "Edward Haynes has a large collection of Mardi Gras masks."

"Everyone and his brother has at least one mask tossed in a closet somewhere," he told her. "The kind I'm talking about are a dime a dozen in this town."

"Oh, of course they are; I should have realized." Then her eyebrows puckered. "But what does Lydet's receiving stolen antique guns have to do with a man who forces women to disrobe?"

"Think about it, sweet cheeks. My sister Josie Lee was his latest victim, and—"

"Oh, Beau," Juliet interrupted. "I am so sorry. That must have been horribly traumatic for her."

He stole a look at her face, saw the sincere sympathy written there, and whipped his attention back on the road. Shit. He didn't want her to be sweet about this. He rolled his shoulders impatiently to shrug off her concern. "Yeah, well, according to her, it was more traumatic for me.

Anyhow," he rushed on, not wanting to hear her observation of that comment, "the gun the Panty Snatcher used was an antique. Josie Lee's description of it was very detailed, and I'm almost positive I've come across the same description before. Something about it rings a bell from a long time ago, and I think it may stem from the time I arrested Lydet back in my rookie days."

Juliet regarded him with something that looked suspiciously close to admiration. "Your job must be terribly exciting."

"When I'm doing real police work instead of babysitting, maybe," he said caustically.

She absorbed the snub without comment and turned to face the front, where she was silent for several moments. Then she twisted around to face him again. "I'm trying to picture you with a sister, but I can't quite visualize it."

He expelled a sharp exhalation of laughter. "No? Well, picture this: I've got three of 'em." He kept his eyes on the traffic but was aware of her gaze roaming his features.

"God, how wonderful," he heard her murmur in a voice so soft she had to be talking to herself. Then she shifted slightly and said, "I was an only child."

He felt a funny little clutch in his stomach at her wistful tone and jerked himself erect. Oh, no. No, no, no, no, no. She wasn't suckin' him in that way. He was *waaay* too savvy to fall for the sympathy bid. And where the hell had this sudden chatty streak come from, anyway? He turned his head and gave her a quick, insolent once-over. "Poor little rich girl. I'm sure daddy bought you a truckload of toys to fill the void."

He refused to feel guilty when she stared at him with stunned shock, as if he'd just backhanded her upside one of those elegant cheekbones. He nevertheless expelled the breath he'd been holding when her expression turned cool and remote.

"Actually, Father wasn't around much," she said with quiet dignity and turned her back on him to look out the side window.

Ah, fuck. Well, tough, he didn't care. He—did—not—care.

Juliet stared blindly at the scenery streaking past while she repudiated the hurt, shoving it down, enclosing it within the bleak little closet that she'd built years ago, deep in the recesses of her mind, to store the slights and disappointments of a father who rarely had time for her.

It was probably no more than she deserved, anyway, for giving in to the seductive craving for a little excitement in her life. She had too much to do in too little time as it was, and she *knew* Beau Dupree was trouble—but she'd allowed him to drag her out of the middle of a meeting anyway, without a single protest and with no more excuse than an itch of recklessness and the weak justification that Celeste Haynes had been late for their meeting and therefore deserved to have it cut short. Sucking in her ill-conceived burst of friendly curiosity, she took refuge behind a more familiar wall of reserve.

The interior of the car was like an oven. The wind, moisture-laden and heavy with scents, blew through the open window, tugging at her hair, pressing against her lungs, and the sun-faded tropical colors of crazed and peeling paint flashed exotic impressions as the car roared past the ancient buildings that sported them.

She didn't *feel* reserved—that was the problem. A kernel of resentful rebelliousness had lodged itself deep inside of her and the very lushness of the environment seemed to feed it, the way it fed and encouraged ferns to grow in the unlikeliest cracks in the sidewalks and stairs of this town. That same lushness provoked a sensuality and lassitude that made merely keeping her posture erect a burden, never mind clinging to all her stiff mores and manners. They seemed to require much more effort down here, perhaps more than they were worth.

Then she and Beau were once again back in the Quarter, with its music and noise and blatantly sexual overtones. Only this time there were crowds of people thronging the sidewalks and horse-drawn carriages slowing their passage up traffic-choked streets.

Beau found a place to park and, as usual, without so much as a by-your-leave, hauled her bodily from the car and immediately set off with her trailing an arm's length behind. Like last time, there were more things to look at than one person could absorb in a single trip, but she discreetly tried to take in as much as possible.

She was so busy looking at exotic, erotic window displays and trying to catch glimpses of the activities reflected in the full-length mirrors just inside the open doorways of strip joints and sex clubs, that when Beau stopped suddenly, she bounced off his back. His free hand whipped back to steady her, and his long fingers wrapped around the back of her thigh and burned straight through the thin material of her dress to the skin beneath. Then his hand jerked away, and he turned to face her, his features expressionless.

"I'm hungry. You eaten anything today?"

She blinked, refusing to acknowledge a lingering impression of heat at the top of her thigh. "I had a watercress sandwich with Celeste."

He made a rude noise. "I'm talkin' about real food, Rosebud."

She couldn't help it; her smile was strictly spontaneous as she remembered the less-than-bite-sized serving that was all she'd consumed. "I could eat . . . if you're talking someplace air-conditioned."

"We ain't talkin' the Ritz, sugar, but I know a place with a fountain. Nice shady spot where we can get us a po' boy, dressed."

An incredulous laugh escaped her. "I would have pegged you as more the rich-woman, naked, type."

She was immediately appalled, unable to believe she had said that. She'd trained herself years ago to keep her errant thoughts to herself, and had truly believed it to be second nature by now.

So how on earth had she allowed *that* thought to leap from mind to tongue?

Before she could gather breath to extricate herself with as much grace as possible, he'd whirled her around and sandwiched her between a display window of Mardi Gras masks and his own lean body. She blinked at his shadowed jaw, so close to her lips.

"You're the only rich girl I know, Juliet Rose," he said in a low, raspy voice, and reluctantly she raised her gaze to his heavy-lidded dark eyes. "You volunteerin' to get naked with me?"

He wasn't actually touching her, just penning her in with a hand on either side of her shoulders. But his forearms were pressed flat against the window at her back, his breath was on her lips and his scent all around her, and he was deep into the space she always kept inviolate. She wedged her hands into the minuscule gap that separated them and, flattening her fingers against the hard wall of his chest, gave him a shove. He didn't budge and the damp heat beneath her palms added to her agitation.

Her only consolation was that she sounded commendably composed when she replied, "No, Beauregard, I am not." Then, knowing it was unpardonably rude but simply not caring for once, she snapped, "You really ought to try reining in those hormones of yours. It's a radical concept for you, I'm sure, but just as a change of pace."

He licked his lower lip. "Why, Miz Juliet, I do believe I'm insulted. A woman makes a sexually loaded statement, naturally a man wants to know if it's an invitation. You'd understand what I'm talkin' about if you were a guy."

"And if you had ovaries, you probably wouldn't be such an idiot." *Oh, God, Juliet, shut up, shut up, shut up.*

"If I had *any* of your pretty pink equipment, sweet thing, I wouldn't be asking if you wanted to get naked with me in the first place." Then a crooked grin tugged up the corners of his mouth and he straight-armed himself away from the case. "So, you wanna grab a sandwich, or what?"

She ducked under his arm and straightened her dress. "I suppose," she said, and winced at the sulkiness in her tone.

"I'll take that as a yes." And once again, he manacled her wrist in his lean fingers and started off down the block.

They entered a brightly lighted establishment about the size of a closet, ripe with the rich scents of cooking, and not air-conditioned. Beau's promised fountain was nowhere in sight.

"Hey, Lou," Beau greeted the elderly black man behind the counter.

"Where y'at, Sergeant Dupree. What can I get you and your lady today?"

Beau turned to Juliet. "You need a minute to study the board?"

"Please." She stared at the selections written in neon colors on the black dry-erase board mounted on the wall above the counterman's head. A second later she said, "I'll have half a muffulatta. The number four." She reached for her wallet.

"Put your money away," Beau said tersely. "I can afford a damn sandwich." He stepped up to the counter. "We'll take a half order number four and a fried oyster po' boy, Lou."

"Oh, brother, that's just what your libido needs," Juliet muttered under her breath. "Oysters."

"You want that po' boy dressed, Sergeant?"

The smile Beau turned on Juliet was all teeth. "Yeah."

They selected beverages from a tiny free-standing cooler and took their orders outside. Juliet raised her sandwich to her mouth, but the heat and the humidity made her feel queasy, and with a grimace she lowered it untasted.

Beau watched her struggle with her fading appetite for a moment and then growled, "Come on." He led the way down a narrow passageway that ran alongside the building to a small courtyard. It was shaded by a spreading pecan tree, and the back gate opened toward the river, which intermittently offered up a breeze. A birdbath-sized fountain burbled in one corner.

"Oh," Juliet breathed. Setting her meal on a small table, she crossed over to the fountain and submerged her wrists. A throaty sound that was half sigh, half groan escaped her. "I wish I could climb right in."

"Be my guest, dawlin'." Beau gave her a heavy-lidded stare. "I'll hold your clothes for you."

"My God, Dupree, you ought to be neutered." Blotting the excess water from the insides of her wrists against her temples, she came back to the table, took a seat, and picked up her sandwich. She eyed him across the table. "Aren't you a little long in the tooth to be so libidinous all the time?"

He looked horrified. "There's an age cutoff?"

"I give up," she said and shook her head. She took a bite of the muffulatta. "Oh." Her eyes fluttered closed and she was sure her expression was downright beatific. "Oh, my. This is wonderful."

She ate half before she finally set it aside and pushed her chair back from the small table. Beau, who had just swallowed his last bite, looked over at her. "Somethin' the matter?"

"Huh-uh. I'm just full."

"You eat like a bird." He reached across the table and scooped the remaining sandwich up, grinning unrepentantly at her haughtily raised eyebrows. "Hate to see good food go to waste." He took a huge bite.

As soon as the last bite went into his mouth, they hit the streets again. Beau dragged her in and out of establishment after establishment, and each one seemed more tawdry than the last.

Juliet hadn't known so many sordid places even existed, and knew she should be appalled by them. Grandmother would be, God knew, and Father . . . well, Father most likely wouldn't be, but then he was a male and hadn't been smothered with rules and regulations his entire life. He'd certainly expect *her* to be aghast by the sleaziness to which Beau kept exposing her.

But she feared she was developing a taste for the illicit.

The sun had lowered by the time Beau escorted her into a bar whose sidewalk board read: FIFTY BEAUTIFUL WOMEN AND ONE—

"—'Whose Sex is Still in Question'?" Juliet read aloud just before they passed from the lamplit street into subterranean gloom. "What on earth does that *mean*?" Music blared out of overhead speakers, so she didn't actually expect an answer.

Sundown didn't mean a lessening of the killing

heat, apparently, and air-conditioning in the bar amounted to two overhead fans. She could feel her hair swelling against its confines as she stumbled along behind Beau on his trek for the bar.

"Hey, Beau-re-gard," a sultry voice sang out from behind the counter. "Your timing is uncanny, sugar—you're just the man I need to see."

"Hey, Shell-Ellen, how's it goin'? You're lookin' good."

"So are you. Mighty good." The bartender's smile was inviting, and she sucked in a deep breath, pulling her shoulders back and thrusting her impressive freckled chest forward. "Beau, honey, I need a teensy-weensy favor. See, I got this speedin' ticket the otha day—"

"Now, Shell, I told you the last time I fixed a ticket for you that it *was* the last time. You're simply gonna have to drive more slowly, girl."

"Oh, please," Juliet murmured. "If that isn't the pot calling the kettle black."

Beau dug an elbow into her side, and the woman behind the bar turned her attention on her. "Who's your little friend, Beau?"

Juliet braced herself to hear the Cousin Juliet routine again, but Beau evidently didn't believe in repeating himself, for he raised his black eyebrows and said, "You're joshin' me, right? Don't tell me you don't recognize her—why, this here is the famous Rosebud LaTush and her Amazing Fans. She's come to see a man about a job."

"Yeah?" Shell-Ellen looked Juliet over skeptically. "You must have an astounding act, sister, because while I'll give you long enough legs—which may or may not be reasonably hot—you sure as hell got no tits."

"I *beg* your—"

"She doesn't need 'em," Beau assured the bartender and then turned to Juliet, the devil dancing in his eyes. "Show her your fans, Rosebud."

Juliet rolled her eyes. "This is Beauregard's idea of a little joke," she informed the bartender. The woman looked confused, and Juliet shrugged. "Small minds, small ideas—what can I say? One can't always pick one's babysitter."

"Actually, one could, Rosebud, if one would only get off her shapely little butt and do it. It's the babysitter whose options are limited."

Juliet had grown so accustomed to stripper music in the background of every place Beau dragged her to that she didn't consciously attend to it anymore, except for a visceral awareness of its mysterious ability to wend its way through her system and loosen her bones. But it was difficult to ignore the sudden drumroll that preceded the next act, or the man's voice that announced excitedly over a loudspeaker, "And now, ladies and gents, the moment you've all been waiting for—Ms. *Lola Benoit*!"

The woman who strode out in rhythm to the BOOM-bumpa-BOOM-bumpa-BOOM bass thumping out of the speakers was breathtaking; there was no other word to describe her. Easily over six feet tall, auburn-haired and white-skinned, with a voluptuous body sprayed into an electric blue evening gown, she circled the stage with a stride that appeared to be hinged on ball-bearing hips. Her presence immediately captured every eye in the house and Juliet drifted over to the raised dais to more closely view the act.

It wasn't until the stripper, with hips steadily pistoning, paused at the edge of the stage right in front of Juliet that she realized Beau had followed her. It soon became apparent, however, that Lola was playing directly to him.

Her thighs appeared through slits in the sides of her gown as her hips oscillated in a sensuous bump and grind. She slowly sank onto her heels while working a long white glove down her shapely, extended arm. Once off, she held it aloft between her outstretched hands, and her arms described sinuous figure eights while her hips circled, pulling her up to her full height, sinking her back down to a squat, and then raising her again. Undulating down one last time until she rested on her heels, her firm white thighs spread wide, she dangled the opera glove from her fingertips and reached forward with a teasing smile to drape it over Beau's shoulder. Then she surged effortlessly to her full height once again and bumped her way over to another man, whom she favored with her remaining glove. Back at center stage, she wrapped first one arm around herself and then the other. She gave herself a hug and then snapped her arms wide, and her dress came away in two pieces. She was left in a pair of satin tap-pants and four-inch heels. Tossing the costume aside, she shimmied her shoulders. The movement failed to jiggle her magnificent breasts, but the audience roared its approval anyway. An original chassis was clearly not the primary consideration here.

Juliet watched in utter fascination, her own hips occasionally twitching in unconscious rhythm as she admired Lola's artistry. She held her breath as the woman teased the audience with the potential of removing her last garment, only to execute a complicated bump and grind instead and leave the garment intact.

But the music was building to a crescendo, and finally, with a flourish beneath the hot blue spotlight, Lola ripped the tap pants away.

"Oh, my God," Juliet said faintly.

For the woman was left wearing only a tiny G-string, and beneath it curled the unmistakable bulge of male genitalia. Juliet gaped at it in stunned disbelief until the woman—man? What *was* she?—left the stage.

"Come on, angel face," Beau drawled in her ear. "I'll take you backstage and introduce you."

She looked at him in confusion, as if she didn't know quite who he was, and Beau didn't feel nearly as satisfied about springing this particular surprise on her as he'd imagined he would. He nevertheless took advantage of her quiescence and pulled her along to Lola's dressing room. The sooner Miz Juliet demanded his replacement, the better off everyone would be.

After he knocked for admittance, however, he turned back to find the confusion already gone as Juliet regarded him with aloof eyes and growing speculation. He watched her paste a social smile on her lips when a light alto voice bade them enter.

Lola sat at a dressing table, long legs crossed and a satin kimono loosely tied around his waist. His auburn wig now graced a wire stand on the cluttered tabletop, and his own hair was flattened beneath a black nylon stocking that had been tied off and trimmed. He paused in creaming off his heavy stage makeup, eyes lighting as their gaze settled on Beau. "Well, hello, there."

"Hey," Beau replied and pulled Juliet forward. "This is Juliet Astor Lowell. She wanted to meet you."

"Ummm," Lola responded without noticeable interest.

"Your act was magnificent," Juliet said softly. She hesitated a second and then added, "Until I saw it, I didn't realize a striptease could be so poetic."

Lola pulled his gaze away from Beau and swiveled around. "Why, thank you, girlfriend. That's probably the nicest thing anyone's ever said to me." He looked at her more closely. "Ooh, honey, have you got possibilities."

Beau shifted restlessly. "Juliet isn't interested in her possibilities."

But Juliet studied Lola's garish makeup with every evidence of interest. "From the audience, your makeup is perfect. Exquisite, actually. You must know quite a bit about cosmetics to get the balance just right between washed out and overdone."

"It's my one claim to fame." With a rueful glance at his covered lap, Lola amended, "Well, my second claim. Anyhow, I simply adore makeup." He studied Juliet. "You should always wear lipstick, girlfriend. Women pay beaucoup bucks for that bee-stung look; you gotta accentuate it. And if I had that hair, I'd never hide its light under a bushel the way you're doing." He turned away to sift through the clutter of cosmetics on the tabletop and Beau looked at Juliet's hair. It was softer, thicker, less tightly confined than it had been earlier, and a definite wave was developing, giving its honey-brown fullness an added sheen.

He was having a tough enough time already ignoring her possibilities; he didn't need some she-male to point them out to him. It didn't make a lick of sense that he'd be attracted to little Juliet Rose at all, but good sense seemed to be conspicuously absent today.

Lola turned back from his search and extended a tube of lipstick to Juliet. "Try this. It's your color."

"No!" Beau felt almost panicky. The fact that Rosebud was too prim to call attention to the very possibilities that kept grabbing him by the balls had been the only saving grace in an increasingly uncomfortable afternoon.

Luckily, Juliet took a slight step back in perfect synchronicity to his protest. "Oh, I couldn't."

Lola's eyes cooled and he dropped the lipstick back on the table. "Of course not. Because one never knows where my mouth might have been, right?"

"No," Juliet disagreed with quiet dignity, "be-cause Grandmother drummed it into my head that one does not share one's personal grooming items, and it's difficult to kick established habits."

Lola perked right back up again. "Ooh, girlfriend, I *love* that—it's so chi-chi. Where did you *find* her?" he demanded of Beau. "Wait, wait!" He scrambled through the dressing table drawer. Finding what he was searching for, he held out a lipstick brush to Juliet. "How about this? It's brand-new, and look, I'll wipe off the lipstick." He suited action to words by picking up the duel-textured silver tube again, swiveling up a cylinder of tawny rose color, and ruthlessly removing a deep layer from the top. He held it up to Juliet.

She hesitated a moment, but then leaned forward and accepted the cosmetic brush, daubing it against the top of the lipstick. Rounding her lips, she leaned farther in to the mirror and carefully stroked the color onto her mouth. She daubed up more color and applied that, too. Then, handing the brush to Lola, she rubbed her lips together and pulled her head back a fraction to survey her reflection in the mirror. She smiled, her teeth gleaming white between newly rosy lips. "I like it."

So did Beau, and it made him want to howl.

Juliet flipped the tube over and read the label on the bottom. "Ah, Clinique." She raised her gaze to Lola. "You've probably guessed I'm from out of town. Where would I go to find a counter?"

"Dillards, girlfriend. Well, Saks, too, I suppose, but they don't know me there. Go to Dillards," he said decisively. "Tell 'em Lola Benoit sent you."

"I'll do that, Lola; thank you." Juliet exchanged chitchat for a few moments longer and then graciously eased them out the door. Her smile was warm as she took leave of Lola, and Beau watched her moodily, feeling edgy and out of sorts.

It was a considerably cooler smile she turned on him when the door closed at their backs.

"Don't mistake me for a fool," she said flatly, and he narrowed his eyes, mesmerized by that sulky, rose-colored mouth. "You think I'm completely lacking in intelligence? Well, think again, Beauregard, because it hasn't escaped me that you haven't asked after Clyde Lydet in the last several places you've taken me, and I have to believe— *Will you pay attention?* What are you looking at?"

"Nothing," he said sullenly and licked his lower lip. He dragged his gaze up to her eyes, but then her hair drew his attention. Jesus, had it grown even thicker? Wavier?

"As I was saying, that leads me to believe that our sole purpose for going to these bars was to show me the seamier side of your city. Do you harbor some illusion that the air I breathe is too rarefied to tolerate the dives you favor?"

"There's no 'harbor' about it, sweet cheeks."

"Oh, and you know me so well," she said with cool sarcasm. "After one day."

Heat beat through his veins and he stepped in close, giving her nowhere to go. "I know that you're screwing up my life, and I want it to stop." He thrust his face at her. "Go to Pfeffer, Miz Lowell. Demand a replacement. Or, I'm warning you, it's no more Mr. Nice Guy."

She gave him an incredulous look. But she didn't say what was obviously on her mind as she inspected him as if he were something that had crawled up out of a sewer at her feet.

"Tell you what, Sergeant Dupree," she finally

said. "Why don't you hold your breath while I
think about that?" And, shoving him aside, she
walked away, her skirt kicking up with every long-
legged, irate stride she took.

7

Luke was more than ready to go home by the time he left the station house. He was tense, a condition that wasn't improved appreciably when he walked into the parking lot and recognized Josie Lee's shapely butt thrusting itself skyward as she bent over the fender of a car. Her upper body was invisible beneath the hood, and eyeing the long expanse of her legs beneath her skirt's short beige hem only served to wind his tension a few degrees tighter.

He considered just walking by. She was preoccupied; he could easily slip past and be in his car and off the lot before she ever straightened. He sure as hell wasn't in the mood to play mechanic.

The only problem with that scenario was that she was hardly a mechanic herself. He could hear her tinkering and swearing, and speculated the problem probably wasn't something that would be covered by the basics Beau had taught her. Fingers shoved in his pockets, shoulders hunched, he strolled up to the car. "Need a hand?"

Josie Lee yelped in surprise and jumped, nearly bumping her head against the interior of the propped open hood. "God, Luke! You scared me half to death." She extricated herself from under the hood and turned to face him. "Are you heading home?"

"Yep."

"Good, give me a ride. Anabel loaned me her car for my first day of work—which was supposed to have been a favor, except now the damn thing won't start."

Hell. He took a reluctant step forward. "I suppose I could take a look at it."

"Oh, that's sweet, but Beau should be home in a couple of hours. I'll have him bring me back to fix it then." She swiped her forearm across her brow, then reached to unbutton the top two buttons on her sleeveless blouse. She slowly flapped the uppermost placket to promote air flow between the fabric and her damp skin. "Right now I'm hot and cranky, and I just wanna go home."

Luke found himself tracking the progress of a drop of perspiration that rolled down her throat. It zigged off at an angle as it crossed her collarbone, starting a diagonal journey across the exposed V of her chest, and he abruptly turned on his heel and stalked over to his car. Wrenching open the passenger door, he cast her an impatient look over his shoulder. "Well, come on, then, get in," he said curtly. "I'd like to get home sometime tonight, myself. I'm hungry."

She slammed the hood to Anabel's car, collected

her purse, and trotted over to his car, sliding beneath his arm and onto the seat. Smiling up at him, she tucked in her legs and tugged down her skirt hem, which had ridden up close to the indecent zone. "Thanks, Luke; I appreciate this."

Moments later he pulled out of the lot and she leaned forward into the flow of cool air beginning to emerge from the vents. "Ah, bliss, air-conditioning," she sighed, holding her lapels wider to allow the air farther beneath her blouse. "It feels so good. I wish Beau would get rid of that old heap of his and get something nice like this."

"The Goat's got AC."

"Yeah," Josie Lee agreed dryly. "Except it quit working four years ago and he's never gotten around to fixing it."

Luke shot her a hard look. "Maybe that's because all his cash was tied up in your college tuition."

Her lashes went into a flurry of blinking at his harsh tone, but she merely replied stiffly, "I earned a full scholarship, Lucas."

"Which sure as hell didn't pay for all your incidentals. Leave the Goat alone, Baby Girl; it's about the only indulgence Beau allows himself."

She swiveled in her seat to face him head-on. "You have some notion I don't know and appreciate what he's done for us?" she demanded hotly. "I'm no longer an adolescent who only recognizes her own wants and desires, Gardner, and I sure as hell don't need you to tell me what Beau's sacrificed for Camilla and Anabel 'n me. You think it's somehow escaped us that we're the reason he's always broke? Or that it doesn't break our hearts that we've cramped his love life to the point where he'll do almost anything to avoid a relationship that might tie him down?"

Luke shot her an incredulous look. "No way in hell he holds y'all responsible for his diminished love life."

"Of course he doesn't, because he loves us," Josie Lee agreed. "But has he ever had a regular girlfriend? You've seen the women he dates when he does go out. If bra sizes were brains, those bimbos would rule the world, but you know damn well he only asks out the airheads who aren't likely to be seeking marriage or—God forbid—children, 'cause he missed out on what should have been the footloose years of his life."

"Well, well. Mighty concerned words from a girl—"

"Woman."

"Whatever." He dismissed the distinction with a shrug. "Someone, at any rate, who can hardly wait to move out from under his roof."

"Have I done something to offend you, Luke?"

You look like that, dress like that, and eight hours ago you were just a kid. "No, of course not."

"Then what's your problem? Why do the two have to be mutually exclusive?" Her skirt rode up as she shifted nearer in her intensity. "Beau's been both brother and father to me. I detest the thought that caring for me has somehow robbed him of something that he can't get back. But I am not a child anymore"—she poked her finger into the side of his thigh to underscore her point—"which nobody seems willing to concede. Well, guess what?

I'm not willing to be confined to my room like some troublesome schoolgirl because I had the bad fortune to put myself in the path of a pervert."

"Could you rein in the melodrama? Beau doesn't want to restrict you to your room."

"Could you rein in the patronizing bullshit? That's exactly what he'd like to do, and you know it. I love Beau, and I owe him. But he doesn't always know what's best for me, and I'm no longer the docile baby sister who will blindly follow his every instruction."

A harsh, incredulous laugh escaped Luke's throat. "Docile? When the hell was that ever a part of your personality? And if he's overprotective, it's because he blames himself for involving you in this case."

"I'm sorry about that, because it wasn't his fault. But am I supposed to put the rest of my life on hold to make him feel better?" Her hand returned to touch his leg again, only this time the brush of her fingertips was conciliatory. "Listen, I'm not trying to be unreasonable. I'm not going to pack my bags and go storming out of the house . . . well, not until after the Panty Snatcher case is solved, at any rate. But I'm giving everyone fair notice. I'm sorry as can be if my growing up has caught y'all flat-footed. But get used to the idea, 'cause it's a fact. I'm no longer a child, and I won't tolerate being treated like one."

Part of him understood and applauded what she was saying. But the prudent part, the wary, trust-only-a-few cop part, said that this was Beau's baby sister. That to Beau, she'd always *be* a baby sister, and the smart thing for Luke to do would be to throw up the tallest damn wall he could construct against the thoughts he'd been thinking all day.

At least if he wanted to keep drawing breath. Beau's tolerance level tended to be real limited when it came to his sisters.

Luke kept his attention on the road the rest of the way to Beau's little Bywater house.

If Josie Lee noticed his silence, she didn't let on. She chatted easily during the drive, entertaining him with humorous anecdotes on the doings in her sisters' lives and those of mutual acquaintances. Rummaging through her purse, she retrieved her keys just as they pulled up in front of the house. She turned in her seat and flashed him her killer smile.

"Thanks, Luke, you're the best." She leaned over and gave him a quick peck on the mouth, then smiled as she settled back in her seat and reached out to whisk a dab of lipstick from his lower lip with her thumb. "You wanna come in? I'm going to throw together some dinner and there's plenty if you'd care to join me. I'd love to give you a proper thank-you for the ride."

His lip burned where she'd kissed him, and into his mind flashed a vision of the empty house and several ways in which she could thank him, none of which were particularly proper. He jerked back in his seat. "No . . . uh, thanks anyway, but that's not necessary. I was glad to help." Christ Almighty. This was *Josie Lee* he was thinking about— what the hell was the matter with him? If she knew the thoughts he entertained, even if only for a mo-

ment, she'd run screaming for her brother so fast
it'd make his head spin.

"Y'sure?"

"Yeah."

"Okay, then. I'll see you around." She opened
the door and climbed out, turning to lean back inside to give him a final smile. A black curl tumbled
over one eye and she flipped it back with a long,
narrow finger. "Thanks again, Luke."

He watched until she disappeared inside the
door, then heaved a sigh of relief and peeled away
from the curb.

Inside the house, Josie Lee dropped her purse,
turned on the overhead fans, and headed for her
bedroom. She smiled to herself as she kicked off
her shoes and changed out of her work clothes.

That went pretty well, she thought. Better than
she'd expected, actually. As a reward, she'd pour
herself a drink of something nice and cool to ease
her parched throat, and then she'd better call a cab.

She had to replace the rotor in Anabel's car and
get it back to her sister before Beau got home.

Juliet stalked through Lola's club in front of
Beau, but she was painfully aware that he never
allowed her to get too far ahead of him, and a temper she hadn't even known she possessed burned
a little bit hotter. He seemed happy enough to trail
in her wake until they hit the street, but then he
was suddenly right behind her, his lean, hard fingers reaching around to clamp authoritatively
around her forearm.

Feeling a combativeness that was worlds re-

moved from her normal behavior, she tried to yank
free. He not only held firm, he shifted so she was
practically glued to his side, tucked under his arm.
"Settle down," he growled. She turned a cool stare
up at him and he jerked his shadowed chin at the
foot traffic congesting the narrow sidewalks. "Take
a good look around, Rosebud. This ain't the debutante ball—you don't wanna go flouncing off on
your own."

"I beg your pardon," she replied coolly. "Astor
Lowells do not flounce." She nevertheless looked
around, as he'd suggested, and subsided, for the
first time feeling out of place in the Quarter.

It had a different, more dangerous tone at night.
The streets were inundated by noise—from the
ever-present music, to the street performers playing for change on every corner, to the constantly
shifting sounds that blasted out from one doorway
to the next as she and Beau navigated the sidewalks. Men's voices hawked the pleasures to be
found inside various establishments, and all
around them Go-cups sloshed and raucous laughter rose and fell, bouncing off the brick walls in
much the same manner as the drunks that stag-
gered from bar to club.

The French Quarter seemed to provide for adults
what Spring Break in Florida provided for college
students—a wide-open party atmosphere that allowed them to temporarily discard everyday de-
cency. She watched two separate groups of men get
importunate with the unescorted women who
passed them by, catcalling and exhibiting lewd
hand gestures and body language.

Glancing up at Beau's profile, seeing the hard set of his bristly jaw and his don't-mess-with-me cop's eyes that absorbed everything around them and made steely contact with anyone who got too close, she was suddenly grateful to have him at her side. She'd bite her tongue in two before she'd admit it, but she knew it was his presence that caused the two rowdy groups to split around them as they passed, giving her and Beau a respectable berth. It was his presence that ensured not a peep was said to her. She let her breath out. "I want to go home now."

"That's where I'm taking you, angel face. And not a minute too soon to suit me."

"Yes, I'm sure you're simply dying to get back to—"

"*Holy shit!*"

His interruption came just in time, since Juliet had been on the verge of saying something about all his women that would only have embarrassed her. That she'd think it was any of her business, let alone care, made her face flame, but luckily he wasn't even looking at her; he was staring after a car that had cruised past. His grip suddenly tightened on her arm and without warning he took off at a run down the block to where the car was parked. Caught by surprise, she stumbled, and he gave her arm an impatient tug, barely slowing his tempo.

"*Move*, dammit. I just saw Clyde Lydet."

"Where?" She didn't really expect an answer, and she didn't get one. He hauled her ruthlessly along behind him and she concentrated on not running out of her strappy little sandals. They weren't made for such activity, but she feared if she didn't keep up, he'd jerk her right off her feet.

Then they were at the car, and he swore and craned his neck to see down the street as he fumbled with the lock on the passenger door. The instant the tumblers clicked into place, he yanked it open. "Get in."

She dove in, reaching across to unlock his door. He slid in, rammed the key in the ignition, and cranked it over. The GTO's engine roared to life. "Buckle up," he ordered, his gaze on his sideview mirror. She was fitting the buckle's tongue into the slot as he peeled away from the curb in a smoking patch of rubber.

He was only able to race about fifty feet up the street before Quarter traffic conditions held him up. The avenues were narrow to begin with, and Beau swore steadily under his breath as he first dodged a tipsy reveler and then one of the tourist-trade horse and carriages. He stood on the brakes when a delivery truck that should have left the area long ago suddenly pulled out of an alleyway in front of him, and Juliet shot forward in her seat. She was throwing her hands forward to ward off collision with the dashboard when the safety harness suddenly caught and slammed her back.

Beau reached for his own belt and snapped it around him. The truck had cut too wide, and it ground its gears and reversed back into the alley. "C'mon, c'mon," he muttered as it inched backward. The instant there was minimal clearance, he hit his horn and wheeled the car around the still-reversing vehicle. Hunched over the steering wheel, he kept one eye on the traffic and the other on the streets in front of them, searching. "All right, you son of a bitch, where did you go?"

Tension emanated off of him in almost palpable waves and Juliet found it contagious. Her heart drummed with excitement as she leaned as far forward as her shoulder harness would allow. "What's he driving?"

"Looked like a Porsche, a red one." His mouth twisted. "Arms trading obviously pays a helluva lot better than public servant work."

Juliet rolled down her window and stuck her head out, scanning the alleys they passed and the streets ahead. "There! Up one—no, two—blocks, I think that's him. He's turning right, do you see him?"

"No . . . yes!" Beau's hand flashed away from the gearshift knob just long enough to administer a hard, quick squeeze to her thigh. "Good work." Moments later they made the same turn and he scowled at the taillights that had picked up quite a bit of distance once away from the heaviest flow of traffic. "Hell. Looks like he's headin' for the freeway. Brace yourself, sugar. We gotta catch up before he realizes he's got company, because that Porsche's capable of leaving us in the dust if he's not in the mood to be pulled over."

The words had no more than left Beau's mouth when he thrust his foot to the floor, and Juliet was thrown back in her seat. Her heart pounded with excitement as he slammed through the gears and the night sped past in a hot roar of wind.

They were coming up fast behind the Porsche when Lydet suddenly jumped the red light and cut across oncoming traffic. Beau swore and fumbled beneath the seat with one hand. He came up with a portable magnetic flasher, thumbed the switch that started the blue light revolving, and reached out the window to slap it on his roof. He whipped his arm back inside and jabbed the heel of his hand against the horn, holding it down as he roared through the intersection in the Porsche's wake.

A pickup truck bore down on Beau's side, and Juliet's shriek jammed in her throat as he wrenched the wheel, sending the GTO into a screaming slide before regaining control and shooting through an opening in the traffic that she would have sworn was too small to accommodate his big American car.

They hit the freeway on-ramp with a bounce just as the skies opened up in a torrential downpour. Reaching the top, Beau skidded across two lanes of traffic not far behind Lydet's Porsche, but although he pushed the GTO to its limits, dodging in and out of traffic like a maniac to keep the sports car in sight, he knew it was a lost cause. The red marvel of Stuttgart precision engineering outstripped his car when it came to power, and the best driving in the world simply couldn't compensate.

The gap between the two cars had widened considerably when he saw the Porsche roar down a distant exit. By the time he reached the surface streets in its wake, it was no longer anywhere in sight.

He could spend all night cruising up and down,

he supposed, in the hopes of getting lucky and stumbling across the Porsche again, but he accepted the bitter taste of defeat that sat firmly on the back of his tongue. He pulled over to the curb and slapped the gearshift into neutral, setting the brake. He could barely see ten feet in front of the Goat's hood through the pounding curtain of rain, and his arm got soaked when he reached out to disengage the magnetic flasher and bring it inside. He cranked up the window. Turning to Juliet, he thought at least one small triumph would come of this fiasco: she'd be screaming for his replacement without any further effort on his part.

He found her straining toward him within the restraints of her seat harness, her gray eyes huge as she stared back at him. It was neither politely repressed anger nor disdain, however, that burned in those smoky depths.

A telltale pulse throbbed crazily in the hollow of her throat, hot color flushed her high, patrician cheekbones, and her lips, still sporting that damn siren lipstick, were parted to accommodate the breath that sawed in and out between white, orthodontia-perfect teeth. Loosened strands of thick, honey-brown hair sprang out of her French twist.

"Oh, shit," he said hoarsely. "You liked it."

"Oh, my God, Beauregard; oh, my God. I never knew such excitement *existed*." She gave him a blinding smile. "Do you do this sort of thing all the time? Sweet mercy, I don't know if I could bear up under the constant exhilaration. I feel as if my heart's trying to pound its way right out of my chest.''

His gaze dropped involuntarily and he really wished it hadn't. Two rigid nipples formed peaks beneath the prim silk of her dress, and even though he knew they were most likely the result of adrenaline rush, that didn't stop his hands from reaching out for her. His fingers plunged into her hair, dislodging a precariously placed comb and several pins, and he pulled her forward, slamming his mouth down on hers.

Her lips were every bit as soft and full as he'd known they would be, and their immediate obedience to the demand of his own caused a rough sound to crawl up his throat. That lush mouth clung with a sweetness that put him in a fever to lick up all her flavors and make them his own, and his hands tightened in the soft thickness of her hair as he twisted his mouth over hers.

"Oh," she breathed, and her mouth widened in accommodation, adjusting to the forceful new demand.

Then he was inside her, and she was sweet, oh, God, so sweet. But as her head was pressed back farther and farther beneath the pressure of his kiss and her fingers fisted in the material over his chest, fervently anchoring herself, he discovered it wasn't enough. Not nearly enough. He released a fistful of hair and fumbled with their seatbelts.

The moment her shoulder harness slid free, he hauled her over the console. Rain thundered against the metal roof as he settled her sideways on his lap, and the steamed-up windows provided an illusion of privacy when he lowered his head again. The world faded away at the renewed taste of her on his tongue.

He felt her arms circle his neck, her fingers slide into his hair, and he smoothed his hand up her side until it covered her breast. The hard little nipple poked at his palm and they both sucked in a breath. He closed his fingers over the tiny nubbin and tugged. A whimper purled up her throat and he felt her thighs shift apart, pressing herself against his erection. He reached as far down her leg as his hand would reach, wanting bare Juliet but getting only a handful of material instead. He worked his hand down to warm skin, and the hem of her dress began to puddle on his wrist as he eased his fingers up the long, smooth expanse of her leg.

There was a sudden, sharp rap on the driver's-side window, and they both froze. Beau ripped his mouth away from Juliet's, and she scrambled off his lap and back onto her own seat, frantically slapping her skirt back into place. Breathing hard, they stared at each other.

Her eyes were wild with disorientation and a dawning horror, yet hazed still with the lingering remnants of lust. Her mouth was swollen and ripe, kissed free of lipstick, and ringed with the abrasion of whisker burns. He wondered blankly how the hell she ever got all that hair into the repressed little French twist she normally wore, for it was an untamed, tawny-brown cloud that tangled in her eyelashes, exploded out from behind her ears where she attempted to tuck it, and wrapped itself in clinging, wavy strands around her long throat. Sweet Mother Mary, where had the prim little socialite gone? Her nipples still stood firm behind the silk of her top and she looked like a little nun who'd just been thoroughly debauched.

Another impatient rap followed the first, and gratefully Beau wrenched his gaze away from her. Never in his life had he experienced such a lapse in professionalism.

For once in his life without a firm idea of how to handle a situation, he reached for the knob and rolled down the window.

8

How could you be so foolish? Morning sun slanted through the jalousie to form bars of light against the polished wooden floors as Juliet stood in front of the mirror, furiously dragging a brush through her hair. *No. "Foolish" is putting too kind a face on the situation. You were stupid, Juliet. Stupid, stupid, stupid!*

She twisted her hair into a tight, sleek French twist, smoothing it back so ruthlessly, her eyelids stretched. She couldn't believe that she, Juliet Rose Astor Lowell, had necked—*made out*—with an indiscriminately oversexed cop she'd known exactly two days! In the front seat of a car! Dear God, with a man who had made it abundantly clear she was a distasteful duty he'd rather do without.

And if that wasn't bad enough, she'd been caught at it by an off-duty motorcycle cop who'd looked about twelve years old.

A soft moan forced its way past her clenched teeth as she remembered the knowing, way-to-go look in the policeman's eyes as he'd taken in her disheveled state while Beau showed him his ID. To Beau's credit, he'd returned the other cop's look with a cold lack of expression until the young man had stiffly ordered them on their way. But how was she ever going to face Beauregard again? When she thought of the way she'd clung to him, the sounds she had made when he'd touched her breast, how she'd opened her legs to his advancing hand . . .

Intimacy wasn't something that came naturally to her, and the men in her world had always respected that. They were . . . urbane. Undemanding. They didn't have hot hands and urgent mouths, and eyes blacker than crow feathers. Sex with them had been an infrequent, civilized undertaking that she'd secretly considered overrated, but she'd always assumed that was her fault. She hadn't dreamed that it could be unruly, out of control. That it could heat you from the inside out, make you swell and moisten and throb like a heartbeat.

She hadn't known it could turn you into someone you didn't even recognize when you looked in the mirror.

Turning away as if the sight reflected there was the same one that had greeted her last night, she stalked over to the closet. It had been an aberration, that was all. The feverish arousal that had gripped her last night was simply a crazy by-product of a high-speed car chase over rain-slick roads. A single slip that meant nothing.

Less than nothing. And it would never happen again.

She selected a pale gold linen calf-length skirt

from the closet and a gauzy, scoop-necked tunic. Slipping them on, she adjusted the sleeveless top's beautifully crafted cut-work handkerchief hem. A long rope of pearls and tiny matching studs for her ears were her only jewelry. Opening her padded satin hosiery pouch, she chose a pair of ivory stockings. When she sat down on the slipper chair to put them on, however, she found herself simply staring down at the lacy elastic tops lying limply across her palms.

She stood up again, the hosiery dangling from her hands. She didn't care how desperately she needed to regain her old self, she could not bring herself to don them. Temperatures in this town were horrendous enough without adding to her misery by wearing nylon stockings that refused to allow a breath of air to reach her skin. She picked up a pair of ivory leather flats and sprinkled some powder into them, then stood first on one foot and then the other while she slid them on.

Roxanne was already at her desk when Juliet reached the office a short while later. She stopped next to her assistant's desk.

"I'm sorry about leaving you in the lurch yesterday."

"Hey, no problem." Exuberantly kissing her bunched fingertips at Juliet, Roxanne flashed her a smile. "If a cutie pie like Dupree came growlin' around for me, I'd be off like a shot, too."

A gasp of hysterical laughter escaped Juliet. She wanted desperately to ask Roxanne some pointed questions about men, women, and sex, but of course Astor Lowells did not discuss such things.

God, what a bunch of prigs the Astor Lowells were. Why was it so darn important to conform to all these rigid rules and restrictions that seemed to apply only to them? Oh, and to *their kind*, of course. She took a deep breath and eased it out, determined for once in her life to ignore the precepts on which she'd been raised.

And discovered in the end that training received in the formative years went to the bone. "How did it go with Celeste after I left?"

"She was quiet, very stiff. But we did get the rest of the schedule coordinated."

"You're a marvel, Roxanne. Remind me to request the salary increase form from Human Resources when we get back home."

"Why wait?" Roxanne gave her a sly smile. "It just so happens I have one right here in my forms file." She efficiently riffled through the filing cabinet and extended the paper to Juliet a moment later.

Juliet laughed. "I'll fill it out immediately. Meanwhile, please get Brentano's on the line for me. The bar glasses were supposed to be delivered two days ago, and they're still not here." She started for the inner office, but then stopped, turning back. "Would you do me a favor?"

"Sure."

"Would you call Dillards department store and order me a tube of Clinique lipstick? The color is A Different Grape. Or maybe just Different Grape."

"You want a tube of purple lipstick?"

"It's not purple, it's raisin."

Roxanne considered her. "Ooh, yes. I bet that

looks super with your coloring. How did you hear of it?"

"A very . . . interesting . . . person recommended it to me yesterday. Send the driver to pick it up."

Roxanne gave her a funny look, and Juliet knew it was because she *never* exploited her position by asking employees to run personal errands for her. If Grandmother ever heard about this she'd be severely disappointed in her, but against all sense, Juliet still harbored vestiges of yesterday's rebelliousness and she shrugged the thought away. "Please," she added softly.

"I'll make the calls right now."

Juliet held the salary increase request form aloft. "And I'll go fill this out. The smartest thing I ever did was hire you."

Juliet talked to the boss of the crew installing thermostats in the guest rooms, and she and Roxanne were deep in organizational details an hour later when the limo driver delivered the package. Roxanne barely waited for him to clear the door on his way out before she leaned forward. "Try it on. Let's see how it looks." When Juliet had complied, Roxanne leaned back in her seat and whistled softly. "Holy catfish, girl. You look great."

Feeling a bit self-conscious, Juliet gave her assistant a faint smile. "Thanks. I like the color." She smoothed her hands over the gauzy fabric of the tunic covering her hips.

Celeste tapped on the open door then and strode in, immaculately coifed head held high, back ramrod straight. "The Historical Society function is across the river and there is often a line for the ferry," she said imperiously. "So if you're ready to join Edward and me, the limousine is waiting."

"Oh, Celeste, I'm sorry, I should have told you." Juliet rose from her seat behind the desk. "You and Edward go ahead. Sergeant Dupree will be taking me." If he hadn't run for the hills after last night.

"Sergeant Dupree?" Celeste could not have sounded more astounded if Juliet had admitted to attaining her escort from the *Gambit* personals.

"Yes, you remember, you met him yesterday."

"That ill-bred young man who interrupted our meeting? He's a police officer?"

"The pride of N'Awlins PD, ma'am," Beau said from the doorway, and Juliet's head snapped up. She immediately felt flushed all over.

From embarrassment, nothing more. *He* wasn't the least bit embarrassed, she noticed, and didn't know why she'd wondered if he'd show up or not. He probably hauled women over the console of his car to kiss them silly all the time. Heat throbbed in her cheeks.

His lean cheeks shone with the satin gleam of the freshly shaven, even though an underlying bluish shadow formed a line of demarcation where his beard grew. He was dressed more formally than usual in black pleated slacks, a short-sleeved cocoa-brown silk shirt, and a black and tan tie whose knot had yet to be snugged up under his Adam's apple. Only his tan, rubber-toed high-top sneakers detracted from the look . . . or at least that's what she thought until he came closer and turned to move past Celeste. Juliet stared in horrified fascination at the hint of leather from his inside holster and the ominous pistol butt snugged just to the rear of his left hip.

"Is that truly necessary?" she inquired, nodding briefly toward the gun.

"It's the reason I was assigned to you, sugar. Hey, I read that terrifyin' ole letter from whoever you ticked off by turning this old heap into a hotel." He arched a black brow at her. "Gawd only knows what could happen at an event put on by the Historical Society. Things could turn ugly in an instant." He'd worked his way over to her by then and stopped in front of her, crowding much too close as usual.

"You're really enjoying yourself, aren't you?"

"Oh, yeah, I just purely love wearin' a tie." Then his gaze narrowed on her mouth with an abruptness that tangled his black lashes together in the outside corners, and all humor disappeared from his eyes. "Where'd you get that lipstick?" he demanded curtly. "I told you not to make a move outside this hotel without me. We both might think this assignment's a farce, but that doesn't prevent me from taking my work seriously."

Stunned, Juliet merely stared at him, and it was Roxanne who replied. "She didn't leave the hotel," she said. "The lipstick was ordered from Dillards and we had it picked up."

"Oh."

"How on earth did you know it was new? But I guess that's what they pay you detectives the big bucks for, huh?"

Dull color climbed his tanned jaw, but he was saved from having to reply by Celeste.

"If we don't want to be late we'd best be leaving," she said firmly. She extended a piece of paper to Juliet. "Here's a list of the guests who matter. I've included a brief biography of each. I was going to go over it with you in the car, but you'll simply have to study it for yourself on the way there."

Beau made a rude noise and Juliet turned on him. "Be good. It'll be a new experience." She accepted the paper from Celeste. "Thank you. This will be quite helpful."

"Hell, yeah. Wouldn't want to ignore those who matter." Beau latched onto her wrist and headed for the door. "Race y'there," he challenged Celeste, and flashed a big, barbarous smile at the chilly curl of her lips he received in return.

"Call me paranoid, Rosebud," he said as he dragged Juliet through the marble-floored lobby, "but I could almost believe that lady doesn't like me. Can you imagine?"

Celeste worked the gathering at the old antebellum plantation house like a politician at a rally, going from group to group, smiling, chatting, introducing Juliet to the more important contacts whenever both women were in the same vicinity. She knew that outwardly she looked much the same as always. Inside, however, she was in a genteelly contained panic. That rude young man with the disrespectful eyes and the manners of a low-class Yat was a *policeman*.

This was a catastrophe. Sending that letter to the Crown Corporation had clearly been a mistake if this was what she'd brought down on her head.

She'd been so furious at the idea of her ancestral home being bought out from under her nose in order to be turned into a no-account Yankee *inn* that she'd given in to the need to pen a protest, knowing even as she was doing so that it was a hopeless cause. Oh, dear. How could she have made such a huge error in judgment? Just look where her impulse had gotten her.

Exchanging effusive, insincere flattery with May Ellen Beudrey, who had never forgiven her for stealing away that dashing Lieutenant Grayson at the Debutante Cotillion back in '56, Celeste surveyed the crowd until she located Sergeant Dupree. She watched as he snagged an hors d'oeuvre from a passing tray, eyed the canapé askance from several different angles, and then tossed it in his mouth.

It was simply unacceptable to have a policeman constantly underfoot, particularly a rude, pushy one who didn't seem to recognize his betters or appreciate his proper place in life. Celeste's gaze then wandered to Edward, who was standing out in the foyer with Marcus Landry, no doubt discussing the best fertilizer to use on bougainvillea. A smile curled the corners of her lips.

She'd known the moment she'd met him that he was the one for her. They had the perfect marriage, one the youth of today would do well to emulate. There had only been that one problem years ago, the "marital duties" matter. She'd found that particular obligation rather distasteful at the best of times, yet somehow Edward had gotten the outlandish idea into his head that she'd submit to it during *daylight* hours, of all things. And not only in bed where it was at least marginally appropriate, either. Well. Some of the things he'd attempted had been downright improper, but once she'd cured him of the misconception that she was *that* kind of girl, everything had settled down nicely. Their marriage had been quite exemplary ever since.

There *was* his recently acquired hobby of collecting ladies' unmentionables, of course. She didn't know what she was going to do about that. Edward had no idea she even knew of his little diversion, and she certainly saw no reason to raise the subject. One guarded against such secrets getting out; one didn't discuss them. With anyone. Truly, though, when it came right down to it, it wasn't as if he'd appropriated them from young women of *good* family, so what was the harm?

As long as word of it never circulated within the circles that mattered. Being all but destitute was difficult enough. It was nevertheless acceptable: this was the Deep South, after all, where impoverished gentility had been raised to an art form. But people were not likely to be as understanding of Edward's little eccentricity.

Her eyes located the detective once again. She didn't like his presence in their lives; she didn't like it at all. He threatened the status quo, and that simply would not do. The problem was, she didn't see what she could do about him.

Then her spine stiffened. Well. There was always the little trick she'd learned during that ill-conceived infatuation with her father's chauffeur the summer she was sixteen, she supposed.

Granted, that was some time ago, but her memory was really quite excellent, so the mechanics of the procedure should come back to her. She was, after all, a Butler; there was little she couldn't do once she'd set her mind to it.

Excusing herself to May Ellen, she went to see what she could do about removing Sergeant Dupree from their lives once and for all.

"Don't they serve any food around here that's bigger than a quarter?"

"Behave yourself, Beauregard, and I'll buy you your very own poor boy when the party's over."

Beau hooked a finger beneath his tie and tugged at the knot. He bared his teeth at an approaching matron and watched her swerve off to intercept someone else. Then he turned his attention to the trace of amusement quirking Juliet's lips. He leaned closer. "How 'bout I behave myself and you tell the Pissant you want me removed from your case, instead?"

The tiny smile disappeared. "I'll tell you what," she replied with distant courtesy. "You let me do my job, and the minute I catch my breath I'll give the idea my utmost consideration."

Everything inside him stilled. Staring at her, he slowly straightened, lowering his hand. "You will?"

"Yes." There was no amusement in her eyes now. They were so remote when they met his, in fact, that he might have been a stranger accosting her on the street. "Excuse me, won't you? I need to circulate."

He watched her walk away. Well . . . good. That
would be the best thing for both of them. Chances
were, she was tired of the hassle, too. Tired of *him*,
no doubt. Hell, by this time tomorrow he'd probably be back on the job. That was . . . good. Great.
He grabbed a handful of hors d'oeuvres from a tray
proffered by a silent, white-coated waiter and
moved into an unoccupied corner next to the Bel-
gium marble fireplace, where he could divide his
time between casing the crowd and observing Juliet
at work.

Shindigs like this made him twitch. Too much
meaningless chatter, too many people posturing.
Not that plenty of the folks in attendance weren't
sincerely committed to the preservation of historic
homes like the one that hosted this hoedown. And
a grand old place it was, too, with its warm wood,
twelve-inch-thick brick and plaster walls, and ancient leaded glasswork in the sugarcane and pal-
metto motif. He just couldn't see getting all rabid
about it.

Listening to Juliet's polite handling of a man who
went on and on about staying true to the integrity
of the period, however, he had to admit she had
class. None of the dives he'd dragged her to had
managed to diminish it. She unfailingly treated
everyone with the same grave respect he watched
her giving to the Historical Society man.

It suddenly struck him that she didn't smile
much. Maybe life at the top wasn't all it was
cracked up to be, because last night was probably
the happiest he'd ever seen her, and it had taken a

damn high-speed chase to put that huge, uninhibited smile on her face.

He shifted uncomfortably. Thinking about last night was neither smart nor productive.

An hour later, the function began to wind down. As the crowd around Juliet thinned, Beau began closing the distance he'd been keeping from her. He watched Celeste approach and moved in even closer. Appearances seemed more important to the old dame than any safety considerations, and he didn't trust her not to propose some harebrained scheme.

His instincts were sound, for he heard her murmur, "Edward and I will be saying our good-byes in a moment. Why don't you ride home with us and save the detective"—her voice had lowered to a near-whisper, as if loath to divulge his identity to the few oblivious guests who had somehow overlooked his gun—"from making the drive."

"Yes, fine. Let me just—"

Beau stepped forward, unaccountably irritated. "You'll ride with me," he said flatly.

Celeste turned to him, five feet two inches of titanium-edged willpower in a perfumed and powdered package. "Surely, Mr. Dupree, that's unnecessary. We're going straight back to the Garden Crown. No harm will come to her."

"Necessary or not, she rides with me. And it's Sergeant Dupree." He turned to Juliet. "I do my job. And until I hear otherwise, Rosebud, that means keeping you out of trouble."

"Well, really." Celeste eyed him with chill disapproval. "She's an Astor Lowell, for gracious sake. What kind of trouble could she possibly—"

"It's all right, Celeste," Juliet interrupted. "Beau-regard will see me home."

"But—"

"Thank you for your offer, though," she said gently. "It was very kind. I'll see you at the hotel."

"Are you sure, dear?"

"Yes."

"Very well." Celeste gave Beau a searching look. She opened her mouth as if to say something further. Then, without another word, she turned and walked away.

"Let me just say my good-byes," Juliet said quietly.

Beau was still feeling inexplicably angry as he held the GTO's passenger door for her several moments later. She slid in without a word, never once looked at him, and clearly had nothing to say.

And none of it should have mattered.

It *didn't* matter. But to take his mind off an urgent desire to pound something, he centered his concentration firmly on the road, practicing a driving exercise he'd developed years ago.

His aim was to negate the need to come to a full stop. So, he didn't roar down the road with his usual breakneck speed. Perhaps he still drove too fast by most people's standards, but it took attention and a regard to detail to seamlessly avoid the use of his brakes, instead gearing down for smoother, more controlled slowdowns. On this side of the river, however, with less traffic congestion than the city and fewer lights to time, it was less of a challenge. More skill was needed by far in town.

Maybe that was why, when he finally had to use his brakes as the cut-off car in the ferry line, his temper wasn't noticeably improved. He smacked the steering wheel with his palm. "Son of a bitch!" Knowing they'd be the first car on the next boat didn't make it easier to watch this one pull away from the levy.

Juliet gave him a cool glance, then silently climbed from the car. Swearing under his breath, he got out, too.

Neither of them spoke. They stood and watched the boat traffic on the Mississippi until a new ferry jockeyed up to the slip. Then, without a word of discussion, they turned and climbed back into the car.

When the last vehicle had debarked from the boat, Beau fired up the engine and started down the ramp from the levy. It wasn't until he tapped his brakes in preparation to the sharp turn onto the side-loaded ferry that he realized they had trouble.

The peddle went to the floor.

"Shit!" He pumped the brakes, but they were gone. He yanked up on the emergency lever.

Nothing.

The metal-heavy GTO rolled onto the ferry moving much too fast.

"Beau?" Juliet's voice rose questioningly and she made a frantic grab for the dashboard.

A ferryman leaped out of the way as Beau cranked hard on the wheel, and the car swerved to the right around the wheelhouse, skidding along the deck. He double-clutched into first gear and the engine roared like a wounded lion as it wound down—but they were still approaching the front of the boat much too rapidly.

"Oh, my god, oh, my god," Juliet moaned. Then she shrieked. "Beau, we're going to go right off the end!"

"Get read to unbuckle your seat belt and swim," Beau said tensely.

A second later the car crashed through the metal end-poles and a double rope of chain, and bottomed out as its front wheels dropped clean off the end of the craft. The automobile's underside screamed as it screeched along the edge of the boat. Then the vehicle shuddered to a stop. It creaked and tipped forward. It rocked back slightly, then tipped toward the water again, rear wheels lifting off the deck.

There it settled, precarious as a compromised teeter-totter. Beau shot a sidelong glance at Juliet, who sat, white as a ghost, frozen in her seat next to him. "Stay very, very still, sugar," he warned her quietly.

One wrong breath, and they were going to slide headlong into the murky depths of the Mississippi River.

9

*P*aralyzed, Juliet stared down at the water in horror. Grungy green foam roiled and lapped at the boat's hull, churned up by the ferry's engine. She couldn't wrench her gaze away from the sight, and she felt the riled torrent was utterly capable of sucking them, car and all, right into the abyss, where it would roll them over and over as it dragged them to the bottom, the way she'd once heard crocodiles did with their prey.

Then someone cut the boat's engine, and the water slowly settled.

Hypnotized by the river that appeared a mere hairbreadth away, she was only peripherally aware of shouts and footsteps pounding toward them across the metal deck. She watched the water smooth out, saw where the sun penetrated its uppermost stratum to infuse it with a luminous, brownish green light for a short depth, before it once again turned impenetrable. She listened to the sounds of her own blood rushing through her eardrums, felt her heartbeat throbbing in her finger-tips, and was distantly aware that Beau was talking to her. She couldn't make sense of his words, although she did receive some comfort from the low, soothing tone of his voice.

"Dawlin'? Do you hear me, Juliet? Answer me, dammit."

The words bounced and rebounded in her mind like a hard rubber ball shot into an empty closet. They were just beginning to sort themselves into coherency when his hand inched across the console and touched her knee.

She jerked in surprise, and the hood of the car tipped farther toward the water. Beau swore, Juliet screamed, and the car's back wheels began to raise higher and higher off the deck. She grabbed for the dash as if stiff-arming herself away from it could counteract the dangerous new angle, and felt her eyes stretch in their sockets as the river seemed to rush up to meet them.

Then something slammed hard against the trunk of the car, and the dizzying tilt toward the water halted. The hood slowly righted itself, and she gingerly let go of the dashboard and turned her head.

The biggest man she'd ever seen sprawled across the back of the trunk. He had long greasy hair, twining snakes and naked women tattooed on his brawny arms, and a grimy white tank top that showcased an enormous beer belly and hairy shoulders. She'd never seen such a beautiful sight in her life.

He doffed his Bayou Tours baseball cap at her. "T-Ray Breaux, ma'am, at yer service. Don' you worry, you—we gon' get you outta dere faster 'n you kin say crawfish boil." Then he twisted around and yelled over his shoulder, "Gi'dat hook on down here, L'Roy!"

Juliet turned back around and unfastened her seatbelt. Beau reached over and touched her hand.

"You okay?"

Swallowing, she nodded. "What on earth happened, Beauregard?"

"Brakes were gone. There must be a leak somewhere in the line."

A tow truck backed up to them and a wiry redhead jumped out of the cab. He guided a cable-fed hook over to the GTO and squatted down to attach it to the axle. "Whoo. Glad to see yer big ole butt's good for sumpin, T-Ray. Dis here's a fine car."

"Dese babies're classic, dem," T-Ray agreed. "Hate to see one end up in da drink."

A moment later, the car lurched and bumped back onto the safety of the deck, and Beau and Juliet climbed out. The minute her feet touched the solid deck, she started to shake. Hugging herself, she turned her back on the men, mortified to be falling apart now when everything was finally all right.

Beau gently turned her back around and murmured, "Heyyy, Juliet, don't be embarrassed about a few jitters. That was a little too close for comfort."

She trembled harder.

Hooking the crook of his elbow around her neck, he pulled her into his chest. "Shhh," he breathed even though she hadn't made a sound. As she stood stiff as a post against him, he rubbed his free hand up and down her back, hugging and patting her as if she were one of his sisters. "You're okay now, Juliet Rose," he crooned, rocking her from side to side. "You're okay."

The slight stubble that had already grown from his jaw snagged at her hair as he turned his head to look at the two men. Turning her cheek against his hot, damp throat, she also looked at them as Beau said, "Thank you. I don't know where y'all came from, but you sure as hell saved our butts. Not to mention my baby, here." One of his hands left Juliet's back long enough to pat the GTO's fender.

"We was waitin' in line t'board," T-Ray said.

Leroy grinned and agreed. Then he headed for the cab of the truck. "You want me to take dis here car to a shop ova da river, I better be toinin' my rig around."

Between the mundane arrangements being made and the soothing matter-of-fact stroke of Beau's hands on her back, Juliet slowly regained her composure. She awkwardly disengaged herself and smoothed her clothes back into place.

Beau looked down at her. "You okay now?"

"Yes. I'm sorry."

"Don't you be sorry, dawlin'. I'd start to worry if you weren't shook." Then the ferry employees converged on them, and he turned away to handle the explanations.

A short while later they all climbed into the tow truck's cab, which was blessedly air-conditioned. T-Ray was so wide Juliet found herself squished between Beau and the door, but she politely declined the offer to avail herself of his lap.

T-Ray and Leroy seemed to find that hilarious, and Juliet leaned forward to peer at them. "Are you gentlemen from New York?" Their accent was a curious blend of Brooklynese and something else she couldn't quite put her finger on.

"No, ma'am. We was born 'n raised right here in Lou'siana. T-Ray 'n me, we grew up on da same banquette in da Irish Channel. Y'hoid of it?"

"I have, yes. I don't believe I know where it is, though."

"It's just across Magazine from the Garden District," Beau supplied. "Which is where Boston here is stayin' while she's in town," he explained for the men's benefit. He shifted slightly, as if trying to find a comfortable spot. Then he twisted around, plucked Juliet up, and plopped her on his lap. "There," he muttered before she could protest. "Now we've all got room to breathe."

Ignoring Leroy's and T-Ray's laughter, she faced forward, perched as primly upright as it was possible to get in the cab's limited confines. It was going to be a long ride home.

Beau stopped off at the Eighth District station early the next day on his way to the Garden Crown. Forgoing the elevator, he took the stairs two at a time up to the second floor. He shoved the door open and strode into the detective's division.

The first thing he saw was Josie Lee leaning over Luke's desk talking with great animation, and walking up behind her, he drilled a finger into her side where he knew she was ticklish.

She yelped and reached back to grab his finger and yank it away. "Don't do that! I'm trying to be professional here, and having my brother tickle me in public does not add to the image."

"You'd look a lot more professional downstairs behind your own desk."

"Oooh, aren't we a happy camper this mornin'! I'll have you know I've got five whole minutes before clock-in time, and I was just bringing Luke up to speed on your little adventure yesterday."

"She said you lost your brakes?" Luke said incredulously.

"Yeah. Damn near went off the end of the ferry. The front wheels *did* go over the end and we would've dropped clean off into the river if this big guy hadn't intervened." He explained about T-Ray and Leroy, their unlikely Samaritans. "I tell ya, Luke, I thought the Goat—not to mention Juliet and me—was gonna be swimmin' with the fishes for sure at the bottom of the Mississip."

"What the hell happened?"

"You got me." Beau plowed his fingers through his hair in frustration. "I had them haul it into the police garage, though. The guys down there said they'd give me a call as soon as someone locates the problem, but I don't know how busy they are, so it could be a while."

The phone on Luke's desk rang, and holding up a finger to indicate Beau should hang on a minute, he picked up the receiver. "Gardner here. What? Yeah, he's right here—hang on a minute." He extended the receiver to Beau. "It's for you," he said. "Pfeffer."

Beau took it and hitched a thigh over the corner of Luke's desk. "Dupree," he said. "What can I do for you, Pfeffer?"

"Actin' Captain Pfeffer," corrected the temporary division head. "Come down to my office."

"Right now?"

"Yes." The line went dead.

Beau looked at the silent receiver in his hand and shrugged. Handing it back to Luke, he straightened. "See y'all later," he said. "The Pissant requests the pleasure of my company."

"I'll walk down with you." Josie Lee straightened away from the desk also. "See you later, Lucas."

"Yeah. See you around, Baby Girl." He looked at Beau. "Don't leave without letting me know what's going on."

"Wonder what Pfeffer wants," Josie Lee murmured as they loped down the stairs a moment later.

"Who the hell knows? Probably heard I was in the buildin' and wants to rake my butt over the coals for being here instead of babysitting Juliet."

"But your shift doesn't start for another fifteen minutes, does it?"

"Honey chile, I never claimed the man was rational where I'm concerned."

She patted his cheek when they reached her office. "Try not to give him heart palpitations, okay?"

"Sure thing, sugar." He left her with a grin and strolled a few doors down to Captain Taylor's office. Grimacing to see Pfeffer had already put his nameplate on the open door, he nevertheless knocked on the doorjamb and leaned inside. "You wanted to see me?"

"C'mon in, Dupree. Shut the door."

Beau did as requested and collapsed into the visitor's chair, slumping back and crossing one ankle over the opposite knee. He looked across the desk at Pfeffer.

"I'm relievin' you of guawd duty on the Lowell case," the acting captain said without preamble.

Beau dropped his foot to the floor and sat forward. "You're what?"

"You heard me. I'm not happy about this, Dupree, but Miss Lowell insisted."

"When the hell did she do that?"

" 'Bout half an hour ago. Said she refused to waste the taxpayers' money any furtha because of one inconsequential letter that nevah should have been taken so seriously in the first place."

"Well . . . fine. Good. She's right." Beau shoved to his feet, ignoring the consternation that inexplicably knotted his stomach. He shoved his hands in his pockets and regarded Pfeffer through narrowed eyes. "I want the Panty Snatcher case back."

"Whatevah." Pfeffer shrugged. "Thomas Lowell's sure not gonna be happy when he hears about this," he murmured to himself. "But Miss Juliet's an adult and I s'pose I can't force her to accept protection." He scowled at Beau. "Are you still here? Get the hell outta here and get to work."

"Aye, aye, Cap'n Bligh." Beau snapped him an insolent salute and turned on his heel.

Luke looked up the minute he walked back into the Detective's Division. "Well?"

"Juliet had me removed from her case." He repeated what Pfeffer had told him.

"No shit? Well, congratulations, you got what you wanted." Luke studied him closely. "So why is it you don't look a little happier about it?"

"I am happy. I'm fuckin' thrilled."

Luke held his hands up. "Hey, buddy, whatever. It was just an observation."

"Yeah, well, it was a lousy one. This is exactly what I've been angling for."

"Sorry—didn't mean to tread on your toes."

Beau gave him the old Clint Eastwood expressionless stare until Luke shrugged and turned away. Then Beau stalked over to a nearby desk to use one of the computers. "Tread on my toes, my ass," he muttered. He threw himself into a chair in front of the screen. About time he got a friggin' minute to chase down this lead.

It took him a long time to focus, but he was hard at it an hour and a half later when the phone on his desk rang. He snatched it up and identified himself, but most of his attention was still on the computer screen on the other desk.

"Hey, this here's Harry, down in the garage," said the voice on the other end of the line. "I just took a look at your brake line, Sergeant, and I think you'd better come down here."

"Somebody *cut* it?" Beau craned his neck to see the spot indicated by the mechanic. He felt Luke next to him straining to do the same as they scanned the underside of the car hoisted on the overhead rack.

"Yeah. Look here." The mechanic reached for the brake line on either side of where it had been severed, and turned the ends for them to see. "Clean as a whistle. I'd say somebody doesn't like you, Dupree."

"That may be, but practically all of Lou'siana is below sea level, for chrissake—it's just blind luck that I played 'Spare the Brakes' until I reached the only hump in the entire friggin' state. What kind of candy-ass way is that to stage an accident?"

"Not so candy-ass," Luke disagreed after they thanked the mechanic and walked away. "All anybody'd have to know is how fast you always drive. Slam on the brakes in traffic, and you'd be crawlin' up the ass-end of the nearest vehicle in front of you."

"I suppose." Beau rammed his fists in his pockets and turned to scowl at his friend. "You know what this means, don't you?"

"The threat to Miz Lowell ain't the bullshit it first appeared."

"Yeah. And I've been blowin' it off."

"Yeah, you're a careless one, all right. You ever leave her unprotected on your shift?"

"Of course not, but mine *was* the only shift, and that's not acceptable—not if anyone truly believed she was in danger in the first place. Coverage is gonna have to be set up a whole lot tighter from now on."

"I thought you were off her case."

"That was before I knew someone was actually

out to hurt the woman. Now that I've been clued in, I guess I'd better go talk to the Pissant and get myself reassigned." He shrugged. "That oughtta be an easy enough sell. He'll be thrilled to be back in Daddy's good graces."

Rocking back on his heels, Luke regarded him levelly. "What about your all-important Panty Snatcher case?"

Beau grinned, surprised at how great he felt. A weight seemed to have lifted from his shoulders. "Little Miz Juliet Rose will just have to continue taggin' along while I take care of that, too, now, won't she?"

Roxanne breezed through the office door, a delicate cup and saucer balanced in one hand, a prospectus in the other. "Brought you a cup of tea," she said, setting it on the desk in front of Juliet. "Sergeant Cutie Pie's late, too. He must have got hung up in one helluva traffic snarl."

"He's not coming."

Her fanny poised over the linen slipcovered seat of her chair, Roxanne paused in the act of seating herself. She looked across the desk at her boss. "Excuse me?"

"He's not coming. I called the acting captain this morning and had him removed."

Roxanne collapsed in her seat. "Say it isn't so, Juliet." When her boss avoided her gaze by busying herself with her teacup, Roxanne demanded, "*Why?*"

"They never should have assigned anyone to me in the first place, Rox." It was a measure of Juliet's distress that she didn't even notice the familiar address. She set her cup aside. "We both know that letter didn't constitute a threat, and it certainly didn't warrant pulling a ranking officer away from serious police work in order to babysit me! It was just another instance of Father doing what he wanted to do and disregarding the opinions of anyone who disagreed."

"Ah. And Dupree disagreed?"

A caustic laugh escaped Juliet. "Let's just say that Beauregard doesn't harbor the same reverence for an Astor Lowell's position in God's great scheme of the universe as Father. And who can blame him? He could have *drowned* yesterday, Roxanne, and his car, which he loves dearly, nearly went into the river. As it is, it sustained some damage. And all because he was squiring me around per Father's decree. It was time to put my foot down."

"I see. You wouldn't dream of putting your foot down for your own benefit, but you'll do it for Dupree's."

Juliet didn't even blink. "I have no idea what you mean."

"Juliet Rose, your nose is growing. You know exactly what I mean. You like him."

Oh, God, she did. Too much. Juliet felt her face heat up. She also liked the excitement of being dragged into all those inappropriate places that would make Grandmother absolutely shudder but that made her feel so wicked and *alive,* and being thrust by him into one situation after another where he expected her to play a role, and . . .

But that wasn't who she was, or what her life was about. She sat ramrod straight and held out her hand for the prospectus. "Let's take a look at that."

Roxanne sighed, and there was disappointment in her eyes. Disappointment with *her*, Juliet knew, and she had to fight the urge to drop her gaze before her assistant's level stare. Then Roxanne put on her professional face and handed over the folder. She pointed out a potential problem, and they settled in to work.

Juliet swallowed a little kernel of belligerence. No matter what she did, she could never seem to please anybody. She constantly failed to live up to everyone's expectations of her, and God, she was tired of it, but she seemed to be stuck in a perpetual cycle. Well, she could only be who she was, and if that disappointed everybody, she was sorry.

Extremely sorry. *Eternally* sorry.

But she simply couldn't think about it right now, or she'd go crazy. She had to put it out of her mind and concentrate on the work at hand.

And she did. She did it so successfully, in fact, that her heart nearly stopped when Beau said from the doorway, "Hey, Miz Roxanne, hey, there, Rosebud. You 'bout ready to roll?"

10

*"R*oll where? I'm not going anywhere with you." Her spine snapped erect so abruptly it might have been fused to a spring-loaded rod. "What are you doing here, anyway?" Heart pounding, face hot, she was surprised she couldn't visibly track her blood's movement beneath the surface of her skin, so molten did it feel as it pumped through her veins.

"Why, reportin' for duty, dawlin', same as always. I know I'm late, but I've got a real good excuse." His smile, as he pushed away from the doorjamb and strolled into the room, was so easy and infectious, she'd bet it had gotten him out of more than one situation where women were involved.

"You're not supposed to be here at all," she said blankly, tilting her head back to look up at him as he crossed over to her desk. "I had you removed from your assignment."

"I had myself put back on." His smile brought

to mind the better-to-eat-you-with wolf from the fairy tale. He looked insufferably amused as he slapped his long hands down on her polished desktop, leaned his weight on them, and drawled, "You didn't actually think you could get rid of me that easily, did you?"

"Get *rid* of you!"

Roxanne choked in concert with Juliet's incredulous indignation, and then tried to cover it up with a fake cough. Beau turned his head to look at her. "You're excused, honey chile."

Before Juliet could protest his high-handedness, Roxanne had already melted out the door. It closed behind her with a soft click, and Juliet nearly strangled attempting to swallow the outrage that crowded up her throat. She drew in several deep breaths to regain control and pulled her gaze from the closed door to stare up at him.

"Contrary to your paranoid delusions," she stated with commendable coolness, "you were removed from my case for the simple reason that it's exactly what you've been angling for ever since the moment your captain—"

"Acting captain," he inserted smoothly, and an exasperated breath hissed through her teeth.

"—*acting* captain assigned you to my case." She studied him with genuine bafflement. "You haven't bothered to make any bones about the fact that you wanted out of this assignment, so why the sudden change of heart?"

He met her gaze squarely. "The brake line on my car was deliberately cut."

"What?" Shock deflating her pent-up choler, she

leaned into the desk in an instinctive bid to be closer to the protection he offered.

"Someone deliberately cut the Goat's brake line. Which means I was dead wrong about the serious-ness of the threat to you." It clearly didn't sit well with him, but he shrugged aside whatever twinge it might have given his ego. "I won't underestimate the danger again. You'll have 'round-the-clock pro-tection from now on."

"No," she protested faintly.

"Yes." His tone brooked no refusal. Then, brows pulling together, he rubbed a couple fingers against his sandpaper jaw, the scritchity rasp loud in her office's dignified hush. "I suppose I could always move in here—"

"*No!*"

"—but I've got my baby sister to consider." His gaze had began wandering down her, but he snapped it back up to her eyes and explained, "Since the Panty Snatcher incident, I don't like the idea of leaving her alone nights."

"And so you shouldn't," Juliet agreed fervently. "I'll be perfectly all right doing just as we've been doing. I won't venture one foot outside the door without protection."

"Damn tootin' you won't. I'm posting someone here at night, too."

"All right."

He flashed her that killer smile again. "Damn, I love an accommodatin' woman."

She surged to her feet, gritting her teeth against this newest bit of audacity. "*You,* however, will still be removed," she said in a tone that would have done Grandmother, at her most imperious, proud. She had the satisfaction of watching the smile disintegrate. "I want someone else assigned."

He circled the desk. "What you *want*, Rosebud, is the best. And that's me."

"My God. Your ego truly knows no boundaries, does it?" She held her ground when he crowded her, tilting her chin up when he thrust his belligerent face close to hers. But she blinked at the sudden ire in his dark eyes.

"Not when it comes to my work, it doesn't," he agreed tersely. "Let's get something straight right now, lady. I've been jerked around from the get-go on this assignment. The Pissant insisted on pulling me off my real cases—my sister's among 'em—to squire your highfalutin little butt around town, and there ain't no way in hell I'm going to be pulled off this one now there's actually some legitimate police work to be done on it. I'm here." He did the impossible and thrust his face nearer yet. "Get used to it."

She thrust hers right back at him. "I will *not* get used to it. I'll have you gone faster than you can whistle the redneck's anthem." Her mouth went dry from the sheer foreignness of allowing her anger to show, and she darted her tongue out to lick some moisture back into her lips.

The antagonism disappeared from his eyes as rapidly as it had appeared, and a crooked smile that made all her pulse points start to throb tipped his mouth. His sudden reversal made Juliet wary.

"Ah, I get it now," he murmured. "I'm slow, but you don't have to hit this good ol' boy over the head more'n once or twice before I finally see the light. This is about what happened in the car the other night, isn't it?"

"*What?*" The pitch of her voice went so high dogs should've started barking all over the neighborhood, but she was beyond caring about decorum. "You are certifiable, Dupree—completely certifiable. Try concentrating for a moment here. You *told* me to ask Pfeffer to replace you."

"Don't be embarrassed, Juliet Rose," he crooned in a voice that rasped every single nerve ending in her body and made her remember how it felt to be on his lap in that steamy car. Reaching out, he brushed his rough-skinned fingertips down her cheek. "You don't have to be ashamed to admit you asked for my removal because you an' me necked in my car like a couple a horny teenagers." His fingers traveled over her chin, brushed down her throat. "That's just biology, dawlin', and I can keep a rein on it if you can. Or maybe that's the problem, hey?" Spreading his legs to encompass her thighs, he insinuated himself as close as a body could get without actually being plastered to her. "Maybe you're afraid you won't be able to keep your hands off me. Is that what's botherin' you, sweet thing? Because if it is, let me assure you—"

She slapped away the fingers rasping their way down her V-shaped neckline and took a step backward, but that simply pressed her bottom up against the edge of the desk. "Don't be ridiculous," she croaked, and curled her fingers around the smooth edge to ground herself. "And don't flatter yourself. You're not that irresistible." She longed to laugh in his face, to find some truly killing words that would stomp his herculean ego into the dust once and for all. But her heart was pounding much too fast and she couldn't seem to think straight.

His face was so close she could see the way light reflected off the obsidian depths of his eyes, and his breath hitting her mouth with every rugged exhalation only added to her confusion.

"Then I guess we don't have a problem, do we?" he breathed.

Yes, they did. She just couldn't focus on exactly what it was, with him looming over her this way. She put a hand to his chest to maintain distance and leaned back, slicking a nervous tongue over her lips. "Beauregard . . ."

She felt his muscles tighten and braced herself for . . . she didn't know what. But he merely pulled his gaze away from her lips, brought it up to meet her eyes, and demanded, "*Do* we?"

Mesmerized by the look in his eyes, she shook her head.

"Good." He stepped back. "I'll leave you to get to work, then. But unless you've got a slew of appointments this afternoon, I expect you to be ready to go at one. We're gonna take a little trip down to the station."

And before she could summon even a semblance of her wits, he was gone.

As Beau had suspected, having Juliet sitting in on the meeting with Pfeffer made it impossible for him to deny Beau's request for additional person-

nel to cover her case. It wasn't simply that she was
the revered Thomas Lowell's daughter. She had a
way of looking at a person with those cool gray
eyes, and Beau enjoyed presenting his request and
then lounging back in his chair to watch the Pissant
shift uneasily beneath her patrician gaze while she
sat calmly, her spine barely skimming the back of
her seat. And if the patrolman that Pfeffer pulled
in to cover the duty rotation was a little wet behind
the ears, he was still better than leaving Juliet wide
open to attack on those evenings when Beau
wouldn't be around to see to her safety. He was
reasonably satisfied with the day's work.

More than satisfied. He swallowed a grin as they
left the captain's office. This made two times today
he'd gotten his own way, and one of them had actually involved a woman. Surprised the hell out of
him—it had to be some kind of record.

"My, my, my, aren't you lookin' mighty pleased
with yourself," drawled Josie Lee's voice as they
passed her office. "What'd you do, Beauregard,
empty a tube of Super Glue on our fearless leader's
seat?"

Shit. Beau rolled his shoulders impatiently.
"Hey, Josie Lee," he said without enthusiasm when
she appeared in the doorway. "Where y'at."

He felt Juliet come to full attention at his side.
"*You're* Josie Lee?" she demanded, and her full bottom lip dropped open as she stared at his sister.
Almost immediately, she firmed it up and extended her hand. A gurgle of laughter reverberated
up her throat as they shook. "I'm sorry. I'm Juliet
Astor Lowell. And I must sound like an idiot to be

so surprised when you obviously don't know me from Adam's aunt. It's just . . . I didn't realize you were an adult; I expected someone much younger."

"Oh, gee, where could you have possibly gotten that impression?" Josie Lee's voice was dry. She deepened it in an attempt to sound like Beau. "Did I mention my baby sister, Josie Lee? Josie Lee's the youngest, you know. Why, I was raisin' her before she needed her first trainin' bra." Her voice returned to normal. "Did he show you the picture of me he carries in his wallet? The one taken when I was in the Brownies?"

Juliet's brows puckered. "Raising you?"

Fuck. Why the hell did Jose have to get a job here, anyway? This was the one place where his competence was never called into question, and he sure as shit didn't need his role as big brother raised, not when his abilities in that arena were constantly under attack. "Well, listen," he said, trying to divert Juliet's attention, "we've gotta go on up—"

"Beau didn't tell you?" Josie Lee interrupted ruthlessly, her dark-eyed gaze on his proprietary grip on Juliet's arm. She ambled along amiably in their wake as he tugged Juliet over to the elevator, and then, when it didn't open immediately at his impatient punch of the button, to the door that led to the interior stairway. "Why, he stepped in to raise us when our folks were killed ten years ago. Me and Anabel and Camilla. Beauregard's been mama, daddy, and brother all rolled into one for us."

Beau froze with his hand on the doorknob. Son

of a bitch. He hadn't realized exactly how much he'd enjoyed Juliet's image of him as a tireless sex machine until he heard his sister's words reducing him to the boring status of what he actually was.

He felt a muscle ticking in his jaw and unclenched his teeth. Well, give him a couple of months. He'd have Josie Lee out the door and then there'd be no stopping him. He'd make up for lost time and fulfill every nonstop-orgy fantasy that'd ever gotten him through a bleak night spent worrying over his methods of raising three adolescent girls. Erasing all expression from his face, he turned to face Juliet, braced to see a difference in the way she looked at him.

Only to discover she wasn't looking at him at all. She was regarding his sister solemnly.

"You and your sisters are very fortunate," she said quietly, and the slight smile she turned on Beau held none of the reserve he'd been treated to ever since he'd coerced her into keeping him on the case. Damn, he was never going to understand women—not even if he lived to a ripe old age. They were simply a different species.

"Yeah, I know." Josie Lee grinned and gave Beau a nudge with her shoulder. "Beauregard's parenting style was unique."

Juliet choked. "I don't doubt that for a moment."

"Well, listen, Juliet's gotta get back to the preparations for her hotel's opening, and I still have to talk to Luke. We'll see you around, Jose." He opened the door and pulled Juliet through.

"Wait, I'll go up with you." She followed them up the stairs. "I'm taking a late lunch today."

Beau held his breath when she grew quiet, for he knew without looking that she was studying Juliet. His breath eked out again in relief when she merely said, "I love the color of your lipstick."

"Isn't it great? Beau introduced me to this absolute *Queen* of Cosmetics the other day, who . . ."

He grinned as he took the stairs two at a time, pulling her along behind him. He'd bet his paycheck she didn't even know she'd made a double entendre. For a woman so polished and sophisticated, she was amazingly innocent when it came to sexual things.

A sudden vision of her on his lap in his car insinuated itself into his mind. She sure as hell hadn't looked innocent then, hadn't felt innocent straining beneath his mouth and his hands. Ruthlessly he suppressed the image, as he had the countless times the image had cropped up in his mind since that night. It hadn't exactly been his finest professional hour.

He pushed open the stairwell door on the second floor and hauled Juliet through. He didn't bother holding it for Josie Lee, letting her fend for herself as he headed for his desk. Good, Luke was there; he really needed some cop-talk to counteract the effects of too damn much time spent in the company of females.

"Hey," he greeted his partner the minute Luke looked up. "Anything good goin' on?"

"Yeah," Josie Lee murmured sarcastically. "It's been—what?—a whole five hours since you were here this morning." She was clearly PO'd he'd allowed the door to bounce back on her.

Fortunately, Luke, who knew his sisters almost as well as he did, had the good sense to ignore her. "McDoskey caught a homicide at Jackson Square," he said. "And Murphy's on a burglary down on Chartres."

"And this is good?" Juliet asked with barely disguised incredulity.

Both men turned what Beau imagined were identical expressions her way—looking, no doubt, like a couple of carnivores who'd just been tossed fresh meat. God, he loved police work.

She blinked at him and then glanced questioningly at Josie Lee, who shrugged.

"Don't ask."

"Okay." She turned back to face him again. "I'll ask something else I've been wondering for a while. What type of detectives are you?"

"Good ones," Beau immediately retorted, and Luke nodded.

"The best."

"Modest individuals, aren't you," she murmured but then persisted, "No, truly, Beau, you were assigned to my case, so does that make you . . . Burglary?"

"New Orlean decentralized in the Fall of '96, Ms. Lowell," Luke explained.

"Call me Juliet," she invited. "What does that mean, 'decentralized'?"

"It means, Rosebud, that we no longer have units like the ones you're thinkin' of. This ain't like television; N'Awlins no longer has a Homicide, Narcotics, or Vice. There are—what, Luke, twenty-three?"—Luke nodded—"twenty-three detectives assigned to this district. Except for the Juvenile and Rape Investigation sections, which are highly specialized, every man and woman here covers whatever comes in, as it comes in." He turned back to Luke. "What do you know about a patrolman named Bostick?"

Luke thought about it a moment and then shrugged. "Nothing. Why?"

"Pfeffer assigned him to keep an eye on the Garden Crown in the evenings. I suspect the kid's right out of the academy, but I was kinda hopin' the Pissant selected him because he'd already managed to distinguish himself. But I guess if you haven't heard anything . . ." Shrugging his shoulders, he let the sentence trail off.

"I'll ask around."

"Thanks, I'd appreciate it. And we'll let you get back to it. Still working on that drug bust at the park?"

"Yeah. And I've got a snitch coming in at three on the Middlemyer case." He smiled wryly. "I'm not exactly holdin' my breath on that one."

"No progress, huh?" At Luke's shrug, Beau stepped back from the desk. "Well, like I said, we'll get out of your hair. See ya, Jose." He reached for Juliet's wrist and headed for the door.

"Beau, wait!" Josie Lee's voice stopped him and he pivoted back to face her, elevating an eyebrow questioningly.

"The DA's playing at Maxwell's Cabaret tonight. I was kind of hoping you'd take me."

"It's not a good night, Jose." He looked past her to his partner. "Maybe Luke could do it."

A muscle tightened in Luke's jaw and Beau immediately backpedaled. "I'm sorry, pard. You probably got a date, huh?" He had to quit expecting his friend to drop everything and babysit for him.

"No date," Luke said flatly. He hesitated a moment and then tossed his pen on the desk. "I'll take you, Baby Girl."

"Good." Beau nodded, satisfied to have the matter settled so expeditiously. His sister got a chance to go out, which would keep her from jumping all over him out of sheer boredom the moment he walked through the door tonight. And he could relax and concentrate on his own work, knowing she was in good hands. He grinned. "See y'all around." Without further ado, he opened the door to the stairway.

They were almost through it when he felt Juliet dragging against his hold. Turning his head, he saw her craning her neck around. "It was nice meeting you, Josie Lee," she called softly.

Josie Lee flashed her a smile. "Nice meetin' you, too," she said. "Hope I see you again."

Beau and Juliet didn't speak as they clattered down the stairs. Once they passed through the lobby, however, and pushed through the entrance door, Juliet paused beneath the Doric columns on the white marbled porch way, blinking in the bright sunlight. Beau watched the humidity have its predicable effect on her hair.

She looked up at him. "Your district attorney performs at a cabaret?"

"Yeah, our DA is Harry Connick, Sr."

"As in Harry Connick, *Jr.?*"

"His daddy. He plays jazz at Maxwell's sometimes. Guy's pretty damn good." A smile tugged at the corner of his mouth. "Better yet, he's a decent DA as well."

He watched her blink up at him as she absorbed the information. Then a slight smile tugged up the corners of her lips as well.

"Lordy. This is such an interesting town."

11

*"M*r. Lowell is on line two."

"Thank you, Roxanne." Juliet released the intercom button, and with a familiar, uneasy blend of pleasure and anxiety that she should have long outgrown, she punched the button for the correct line. "Hello, Father. How lovely to hear—"

His impatient voice cut her off. "What's this I hear about a brake line being cut, Juliet? You were in that car? Why the hell wasn't I apprised of the situation the moment it occurred?"

Her programmed response was to apologize, but she caught herself and drew in a deep breath instead, holding it for a moment before slowly exhaling. Mustering the composure that always, in the end, was her final defense, she said quietly, "There was nothing you could have done from up there, and I didn't see the value in worrying you." Not that she'd heard a single inquiry as to her welfare. "How have you been, Father? And how is Grandmother?"

"You might pick up a telephone and give her a call to see for yourself," he said brusquely. "She's not getting any younger, you know."

"You haven't been to see her since I left, huh?" She was immediately appalled by her uncharacteristic snideness. What on earth was the matter with her?

There was a moment of silence from the other end of the line, and she was on the verge of apologizing when her father said tightly, "I haven't seen a progress report on the Garden Crown, young lady."

She sat up straight. "Nor shall you. This is my project, Father. You wouldn't expect anyone else in the corporation to drop everything in the middle of a start-up to write a progress report; kindly grant me the same courtesy. Now, if that's all, I have quite a bit to do. Thank you for calling—give Grandmother my love when you talk to her." She replaced the receiver and dropped her head into her hands, grinding the heels into her eyes.

When would the need to please him finally go away? She was thirty-two years old and still struggling with an instinctive urge to placate, to win his approval. What was it going to take—would she have to turn thirty-five, forty-five, *fifty* before she finally learned to deal with him as one adult to another?

At least she'd stood her ground with him this time . . . and it hadn't seemed as difficult as usual. Something down here appeared to be effecting a change in her, one that could only be considered an improvement. She dropped her hands to the desktop and straightened. Reaching for the paperwork the phone call had interrupted, she caught sight of herself in the curved surface of a highly polished brass vase and leaned forward to scrutinize the reflection more closely, arrested by its eroticism. My God. Was that *her*? With those full, rose-colored lips, those sultry eyes, and the verging on out-of-control hairdo? She sat back.

Perhaps she ought to rethink this change-can-only-be-an-improvement thing. Because she didn't recognize that woman in the vase at all.

She made a conscious effort to get herself back to the woman she did know in the days that followed. A week ago that would have come naturally, but suddenly she had to work at it. Her hair wouldn't stay in its neat French twist, and she found it difficult to keep her hand from straying to the dresser top where she kept the tube of lipstick. And no matter what, she simply couldn't bring herself to don nylon stockings in this ungodly heat. She did refuse to allow Beau to drag her around town, but privately admitted in her more honest moments that she missed the excitement.

It had been almost two weeks now and nothing untoward had happened. Juliet almost wished something would, because each day that passed uneventfully added to Beau's restlessness. And a restless Beau was a definite impediment to her determination to hold onto her old self. The seductive freedom he represented was a dangerous thing.

Surely even policemen didn't court danger twenty-four hours a day. Deprive Beau of car chases, hunting down suspects in lowbrow dives, and other sundry hair-raising events, however, and he turned his attention to her. And he was growing increasingly outrageous by the day.

Yesterday he'd shown up wearing a yellow T-shirt with CALL 911 AND MAKE A COP COME emblazoned across his chest. He'd barged into the office time after time for no better reason than to drape himself over the corner of her desk and talk trash. The man could take the most innocent utterance and turn it into an innuendo, and bottling up her instinctive responses proved pointless, for he was absolutely relentless in his pursuit of one. He seemed to thrive on making her react, and didn't seem to care if that reaction was anger or sounding like a prig.

It had to be boredom.

Now, Juliet looked around the sumptuous grounds at the garden party Celeste had arranged at a River Road plantation to avoid catching Beau's eye, knowing that the sizable crowd milling throughout the gardens wouldn't hinder him at all. If someone else was within earshot, she trusted Beau to behave with absolute professionalism. Let him get her alone for a moment, though, and all bets were off. And the couple with whom she'd been conversing had just walked away.

She felt his gaze on her as she balanced her glass of iced tea in one hand and dug through her purse for her checklist and a pen with the other.

"Think you got enough stuff there, angel face?" he inquired lazily once she'd pulled everything out. "How 'bout I flag down a waiter for a couple of hors d'oeuvres?" He moved in and she felt his breath on her cheek. "Then you'll have something to occupy all your dainty little fingers."

She stepped back, straightening her spine. "Idle hands are the devil's workshop," she heard herself reply primly and could have groaned. How did he *do* that? How did he get her to utter things so prudish it would make Grandmother sound liberated by comparison?

And of course he had the last word. "Yeah, I've heard that said," he agreed in a murmur, "but busy hands'll make you go blind, dawlin'."

The checklist dropped from her fingers.

She stooped to retrieve it, glancing around for an excuse that would remove her from his immediate vicinity without giving the appearance of running away—even if she was.

He squatted down next to her. "I bet I could make you go blind," he said in a low voice and her eyes were drawn helplessly to his hands dangling over his knees. He was constantly saying things that planted images in her mind. Vivid images that never in a million years would she have thought of on her own.

She straightened her spine. "A skill learned in the devil's workshop, no doubt." If her voice sounded more like Minnie Mouse on helium than the acerbic tone she'd been shooting for, at least she'd achieved a reasonably cool delivery. She cleared her throat. "I'm afraid you'll have to practice it elsewhere, though, Beauregard. Perhaps with someone who's interested." She forced her gaze away from his long, tanned fingers. "Oh, look, there's Edward." She rose to her feet, smoothed the skirt of her dress. "Excuse me, won't you?" Her glance bounced away from the lazy amusement in his face. "I need to talk to him for a minute."

She'd nearly wondered aloud what on earth Edward was doing. Fortunately she'd caught herself, since the slightest opportunity to solve even a minuscule mystery would likely encourage Beau to tag along, and the idea was to get away from him. She was curious, however, and she watched Edward as she skirted the boxwood maze. He seemed to be cutting slips from a upright shrub in one of the Chinese pots.

"Hello," she called softly as she came up behind him.

Edward turned a singularly sweet, unrepentant smile on her. "Hello, my dear; I'm afraid you've caught me. You, too, Sergeant," he added, and Juliet suppressed a sigh when she turned to see that Beau had followed her.

"I do hope you're not going to arrest me," Edward continued without noticeable concern.

"For coppin' a few inches of branch off some bush?" Beau hitched a shoulder. "Nah. I don't think so."

"Oh, this isn't just any shrub." Edward collapsed the blade back into his penknife and slipped it into his pocket. "This is a *Hibiscus Rosa Sinensis*." He carefully folded the two slips he'd cut into a snowy handkerchief.

"Huh?"

"A Rose of China, Sergeant. It was originally presented to the Fancy Hibiscus Society by the Chinese ambassador to the United States during a hibiscus showing in Washington, D.C., in 1990. Only a few plants were distributed to very special people." He ran a reverent finger over one of the powder-puff-pink flowers that adorned the shrub. "I never thought I'd get a chance at one myself, so you can imagine my excitement."

"Uh, right . . . excitement." Beau stuffed his hands in his slacks pockets and rocked back on his heels. "The sorta stuff that gets me excited tends to be of a different variety."

"I'm sure it is." Edward regarded him solemnly. "By your very profession, you're a man of action. Flowers must seem rather tame in comparison, but we all have our passions." He turned to Juliet. "What is your passion, dear?"

Beau turned an interested gaze on her, eyebrows raised inquiringly.

The steamy interior of his GTO sprang immediately to mind, and Juliet took a hasty step backward. "My passions? I suppose that would be my work, and— Oh, I do believe Celeste is signaling me. If you'll excuse me?" Giving them her most winning social smile, she turned away, the smile immediately fading. Whew. The last subject she wanted to discuss in front of Beauregard Dupree was passion. *Excellent timing, Celeste. Thank you.*

Celeste did not like the fact that Sergeant Dupree was talking to Edward—she didn't like it one bit. She refused to give in to senseless panic, however. Chances were, it was about something entirely harmless.

She introduced Juliet to Georganne Hollister, her ostensible reason for summoning the young Northerner. Within moments, however, she'd sent Georganne on her way. The Hollisters were really quite nouveau; she hadn't the first idea how'd they managed to worm their way onto the A list that comprised today's guests. Her attention turned to Juliet. "How are you holding up, dear?"

"Fine, thank you. It's a lovely function. Father will be pleased with the number of business contacts I've made today."

"Yes, this is the crème de la crème. They're the people in a position to steer the right kind of clientele to the Garden Crown." And if strangers had to be living in *her* home, at least it would be people with close associations to members of the Boston Club, which was so exclusive not even Edward had been invited to join. Glancing across the lawn, Celeste's stomach churned. "I see your detective is talking to Edward. I can't imagine what those two could possibly have in common." But their conversation looked more intense than it had a moment ago.

"I left them discussing hobbies and passions and whether Edward's would ultimately land him in jail," Juliet said with a slight smile.

Blood roared in Celeste's ears, but she managed a credible laugh. "Oh, law, is that devil filching from the rose garden?" Patting Juliet's hand as if it were all a huge joke, she excused herself while she could still string together a few coherent words. She headed for the stand of sweet olive trees just beyond the boxwood maze, stroking the leather of

her handbag over the 1849 Pocket Model revolver
within. Heavy, awkward thing—she'd been packing it around with her for several days now, instinctively knowing the moment might come when
she'd have to use it.

It looked as if that moment had arrived. Now if
she could only remember all the steps for forcing
the balls into the front of the cylinder, and placing
the percussion caps on each of the nipples on its
backside.

Well, it would come back to her. She was a Butler
and a Hayes, after all, which by definition meant
preeminently capable. One merely needed to give
one's full attention to the task at hand. And that
she fully intended to do.

For it was time to take care of the Sergeant Dupree situation once and for all.

Storm clouds were beginning to amass to the
south, and if Beau was any judge they'd soon be
moving this way. Seeing Juliet on her own again,
he caught her eye and gave her an imperious jerk
of his chin. He grinned when her elegant little chin
racheted several notches skyward in response. She
nevertheless dutifully picked her way across the
garden toward him.

He knew he ought to muzzle himself before he
pushed her too far and she had him kicked off her
case. But she'd withdrawn behind her damn impeccable manners, and for some reason it had
plucked a chord of recklessness in him. He rolled
his shoulders to relax the tension. So, what the hell.
Giving his impulses free reign had at least nudged

her out from behind her wall. Besides, it was just so much fun to mess with her.

His amusement grew frayed around the edges, however, as he watched first one society type and then another waylay her as she wended her way through the garden. By the time she got to him, he was impatiently loosening the knot of his tie.

"You beckoned?" Her tone was ironic when she stopped in front of him and looked up into his face.

"You 'bout ready to call it a day? This hoedown looks like it's starting to wind to a close, and I don't like the look of those clouds." The sky was rapidly darkening as the roiling bank of clouds approached, but looking beyond her, he saw that while much of the crowd had begun to drift toward the parking lot on the far side of the plantation house, several diehards were still swilling tea and knocking back hors d'oeuvres. "Don't any of these folks *work* for a living?"

"Well, not all of us are cut out to be the fearless defender of law and order that you are," she informed him dryly. "Nevertheless, here's a little news flash for you. Most of the women I've met today put as much time and effort into their committee chairmanships as you do into your job."

"And that's what the world needs, all right: another charity ball."

"Why, Beauregard Dupree, you're a snob!"

He glowered at her down the length of his nose. "The hell you say."

"I do say. A reverse one, perhaps, but a snob nonetheless." And she looked downright delighted by the discovery, too. She took a step closer and reached out to give his tie a little tug. "Those charity balls that you're so contemptuous of fund a lot of very worthy causes." Tucking her little purse beneath her arm, she started to seriously mess with his neckwear, snugging the knot back up under his Adam's apple. "They raise a great deal of money for people who might otherwise go without."

He snatched the tie out of her hand. "Yeah, yeah, yeah. I suppose." He jerked the knot back down around the second button.

"Speaking of formal affairs, the pre-opening cocktail party is coming up. Do we need to rent you a tux?"

He bared his teeth at her. What was he, her charity case? "This is N'Awlins, Rosebud—Cotillion Central. Everyone owns a tux. I inherited mine from my daddy." He grabbed her encroaching hands before they could recommence fiddling with his attire, and moved her back to arm's length. "What's got you feelin' so frisky all of a sudden?"

"You think I look frisky? This isn't frisky; it simply isn't flustered, which is how you're accustomed to seeing me. It must be the lack of a blush—that's bound to confuse you."

"Yeah, well, whatever it is, you mess with my tie again, and I'm gonna be forced to get physical—"

There was a sharp crack of sound, and bark exploded on the live oak behind them. Beau swore viciously, every sense snapping to red alert. "Get down!"

Juliet looked at him with blank incomprehension, and he grabbed her and thrust her to the ground. Throwing himself over her, he heard another shot, and was reaching for the gun at the small of his back before the resulting shower of bark even drifted down on top of them. He raised his head and brought the gun around, trained in the direction from which the weapon had been discharged.

"Somebody *shot* at us?" Juliet demanded in incredulous tones beneath him.

The echoes of several women's screams died away, but there was a lot of agitated dodging about, which made it impossible to pinpoint the shooter. "Fuck," he muttered. He pushed himself into a crouch over Juliet's prone body and, without looking away from the row of sweet olives beyond the boxwood maze, wrapped his free hand around her nape. "I want you to crawl backwards 'til you get to the tree," he instructed her softly. "Then scoot behind it and stay put." She didn't respond immediately, and he demanded, "You hear me?"

"*Beau?*"

Her voice was unsteady and sounded as if she were thinking of arguing, and his fingers on her nape tightened warningly. "You hear me, Juliet Rose?"

"Yes."

"All right, then, move."

He felt her body brush his calves as she wriggled backward. Then she was gone. Sparing one quick glance to make sure she'd taken cover, he surged to his feet and ran a zigzag course past the boxwood maze.

The skies opened up just as he reached the sweet

olive trees, and he swore under his breath as he checked all the likely spots where the gunman might have stood. Great. Everyone was running for the parking lot, so not only was the physical evidence going to be severely compromised by the weather, but also half the potential witnesses would have dispersed by the time he could interview them. And leaving Juliet on her own suddenly didn't seem like such a hot idea. Somebody'd had the *cojones* to take a shot at her with sixty-five people milling about; what was to prevent him from picking her off while Beau was looking for evidence back here? The more he thought of it, the more he figured the shooter had probably melded with the crowd and slipped right past him. Pulling out his cell phone, he punched in the number for Dispatch as he loped back to the live oak tree. He summarized the situation for the dispatcher and requested Forensics and another detective, specifically Luke if he was available. Rattling off his cell phone number, he requested a call-back ASAP from whomever was coming.

Juliet was huddled with her back against the tree, hugging her knees to her chest. She'd managed to keep halfway dry, but her dress was smudged, her hair was mostly down, and there was an angry-looking scrape along her right jawline. She looked up at him with dazed eyes, and Beau squatted down, reaching out to remove a long-toothed comb that dangled from a snarl of hair. "You okay?"

Her expression clearly questioned his intelligence, and she hugged her knees tighter. "Some-body *shot* at me!"

"I know they did, dawlin.'"

"Then I guess you also know that, while it would be inappropriate for me to hike up my skirt and bend over, if I were to do so, you'd see a great big bug up my—"

"Gotcha," he interrupted. "You're not okay."

She looked like she could really use a hug, but he'd hung his badge case, badge side out, from his breast pocket, so he was now publically on duty in an official capacity. And besides, he was too pissed off. There was only one thing he did exceptionally well in this life, and that was his job. Now someone was making him look as if he were standing around twiddling his thumbs on this case. "I'm sorry, Juliet." He grasped her hands and hauled her to her feet, then gently brushed the dirt from her arms. "I know you're scared and shaken. But right now I have to concentrate on finding out who shot at you."

"And why! Why would anyone want to shoot me?"

"Right, and why. I want you to stick near me until reinforcements arrive, okay? There's too many people here, and unfortunately we don't know who can be trust—"

She dove into his arms.

Well, hell. He simply stood there for a moment, then, cautiously, he folded his arms around her. He rubbed her back. "Now, don't think I'm makin' a habit of this, 'cause I'm on the job, here." Her arms tightened around his neck, and he brought a hand up to stroke her hair. "I guess being shot at isn't exactly run-of-the-mill for you, huh?"

A bitter little laugh vibrated against his soaked shirtfront. Beau peeled her away and held her at arm's length. "I know this is hard for you, but I've got to secure as much of the crime scene as is still left to me." He peered down at her. "I need you to be strong right now. You gonna be strong?"

She took a deep breath and then blew it out, and he watched her gather her composure. That patrician spine of hers pokered right up, just the way he liked to see it. "Yes," she said.

"Good girl." Wrapping a hand around her nape, he hauled her forward and planted a kiss on her forehead, then turned her loose. "Let's go see what we can do about getting a few answers to some of our questions, then."

12

❦

*B*eau herded people away from the parking lot and into the main salon of the plantation house so swiftly that Juliet practically had to trot to remain close to his side, where he insisted she stay. He was firm as he talked to people and he was polite ... except in the few instances where someone attempted to pull social rank. Then his eyes developed a hardness and his voice a certain edge, and he became downright intimidating. In a matter of minutes everyone was gathered exactly where he wanted them.

Commandeering an antique cherrywood secretaire, he looked from it to the windows and peremptorily picked up a fragile chair and plunked it down several feet behind and to the right of the desk. He gently settled Juliet. Then he turned to a husky man. "You," he said. "Give me a hand moving this."

The man promptly moved to obey, but an outraged matron protested, "You can't simply rearrange the furniture in here! These pieces are priceless."

He and his recruit positioned the secretaire to blockade Juliet, leaving only enough room for Beau to fit in a chair for himself. Then he turned to the crowd.

"This," he told them, thumping his knuckles on the desktop, "is a very nice desk, which I will return to its proper place when I'm finished here. Essentially, however, it's an old piece of wood. This"—Juliet blinked as he indicated her—"is a woman who's just had someone take a shot at her. And I'm not leaving her sitting in line with an unprotected window. Are we all clear on this?"

No one spoke up, and he nodded. "Good. Now, we've got a situation here, and it's unfortunate y'all got caught up in it. I apologize for the inconvenience. But I need to question each of you, and if everyone cooperates things will progress smoothly. I'll try to be as brief as possible, and I'm expecting backup to arrive soon, at which time matters will proceed even faster." His cell phone rang and he excused himself.

Though a lot of folks strained with varying degrees of discretion to overhear his side of the conversation, Juliet doubted anyone actually did. His back was to her, and all she could hear was the rumble of his voice. If the unappeased curiosity on others' faces was anything to go by, no one else was any more successful than she.

Beau disconnected and stuffed the phone back in his pocket. Then he looked at the people milling about. "I'm eventually going to want to talk to everyone who was here this afternoon," he informed them. "It will expedite matters if, while you're waiting your turn, y'all put some thought into who left between the time the shot was fired and when we came in here, because I'll be asking each of you, and I want names." He pulled a notebook out of his hip pocket and tossed it on the desk. Taking a seat, he crooked his finger at the person standing nearest. "You, sir; let's begin with you," he said and got down to business.

Celeste tapped her toe impatiently as she and Edward awaited their turn to be interviewed. She ignored both the complaints and the excited speculation raging like a brush fire out of control around them.

The idiot thought she'd been aiming at *Juliet*. After she'd taken great pains and risked imminent exposure just waiting for the little chit to get out of the way. As she'd suspected from the beginning, Dupree was a fool. Unfortunately, he was a dangerous fool.

So close—she'd been so close. How was she to know the dratted Colt pulled to the left? Through sheer determination and breeding, she stood quietly at Edward's side while lava-hot frustration bubbled through her veins. It was more than a body could expect, however, to withhold a sigh of pure aggravation as well.

For she'd tied up the rest of the afternoon and soiled a perfectly good pair of summer gloves for nothing.

* * *

Somebody hated her enough to shoot at her. Juliet sat in her corner watching Beau work, and tried not to think about it. But that was a bit like telling herself not to think about pink elephants—especially with all the avid gazes watching every breath she drew. She'd never been actively *disliked* before, never mind hated, and the knowledge had a nasty tendency to keep cropping up in her mind. So much so, that she lost all track of time while she gnawed on the fact like a puppy with a T-bone.

She was grateful for the distraction when a slight commotion broke out across the room. Looking up, she saw Sergeant Gardner entering the main salon, and the crowd parted like the Red Sea before Moses as he strode toward the desk. When she saw who trailed in his wake, she surged to her feet.

Roxanne saw her at the same time. "Juliet," she screamed, and rushed across the room, squeezing behind the desk and reaching out to haul Juliet into her arms.

Her embrace was strong and comforting, and that made twice now in less than an hour that Juliet had been hugged. She still couldn't believe she'd thrown herself into Beau's arms, but all she'd been able to think about at the time was how safe she'd felt when he'd held her after the car incident on the ferry. And she'd been in desperate need of that sense of security again. It was odd, but for all his sexuality, he had a way of offering comfort that was very . . . nurturing. She imagined he must be a terrific brother to his three sisters.

Her unprecedented neediness made her uneasy, though. Grandmother had raised her to be self-sufficient, and God knows Father had hammered the precept into her often enough. She could hear both of them now, telling her an Astor Lowell stands on her own two feet. And she hadn't. She slowly stiffened in the warm circle of her assistant's hug.

Roxanne stepped back, holding her at arm's length to subject her to a thorough inspection. She reached up and gently smoothed Juliet's hair off her face. "Holy catfish, girl, I about wet my pants when Sergeant Gardner told me what happened. Thank God you're okay. But look at you! Why didn't anybody clean you up?"

Beau twisted around to shoot her a glance over his shoulder. "We've been a little busy around here, Miz Roxanne," he growled and immediately turned back to his interview.

"Well, I'm going to clean her up now."

To Juliet's surprise, Beau didn't argue. He selected two men at random and ordered them to accompany the women to the powder room, with directions to wait out in the hall and see that no one else went in while they were inside.

A small sound of dismay escaped Juliet's lips when she caught sight of herself in the antique mirror in the ladies' room a few minutes later. Her face was dirty and her hair was an explosion of snarls, tangles, and wild waves sticking out in a dozen different directions. She tilted her jaw to the right to examine the scrape. "I'm a mess."

"Yes, you are," Roxanne agreed from the sink. Craning her head around, she glanced at Juliet's reflection. "Nothing a little soap and water can't improve, though."

Juliet turned from the mirror. "Thank you for coming, Roxanne," she said with quiet fervency. "It means a lot to me—I feel much less alone with you here. What a sweetheart Sergeant Gardner is to have thought of it."

"Not Gardner, doll—it was Sergeant Cutie's idea. He instructed Gardner to pick me up."

"Beauregard did?" Juliet's heart performed a little hop.

"Yep." Roxanne turned from the sink, where she had soaked a small linen hand towel in warm water. "Sit down."

Juliet sat, but she indicated the exquisite decorative towel in her assistant's hands uncertainly. "I don't think anyone is intended to actually use that."

"Tough tomatoes. That scrape looks raw and I'm not about to use a scratchy ol' paper towel on it when there's a perfectly nice soft towel available. Besides, that's why they invented washing machines." A corner of her mouth tilted up. "I bet it was some Southern white chick who conceived the idea for the first one, too, right after the slaves were emancipated and she had to start doing her own laundry."

Juliet blinked. "Oh—you're bad."

"Nah, just a strong believer in the Necessity Is the Mother of Invention Theory." She tipped Juliet's chin up and began gently swabbing the smudges from her face. When she had cleaned everything except the scrape, she returned to the sink and thoroughly rinsed the towel. Turning off the tap, she squeezed out the excess water. Then she returned to the upholstered bench where Juliet sat and, tilting her boss's chin up, carefully dabbed at the abrasion.

Juliet sucked in a breath, and Roxanne grimaced. "I'm sorry, I know it must hurt, but I want to get all the dirt out." A few seconds later she straightened. "There. It could probably stand a dab of disinfectant, but at least it's clean." She handed Juliet the towel. "I'll let you get your arms. Oh, look at your poor hand! Come over here to the sink."

Juliet looked down at her right hand. The heel was discolored and her index and forefingers were swollen. It hadn't hurt before she saw its condition, but now it began to throb. She flexed it experimentally. "Nothing's broken. I must have jammed my fingers when I hit the ground."

She washed up at the sink, but when she tried to brush out her hair, she couldn't maintain a hold on the brush. Tears of frustration rose in her eyes, which only served to make her feel foolish on top of everything else.

"Here, let me do it." Roxanne took the brush from her hand, removed a few pins that were still caught up in the mass, and gently worked out the snarls. Then she commenced to give it a thorough brushing.

Juliet gloomily watched the volume grow thicker and wilder with each stroke. "I lost my comb and most of the pins. I'll never get it back in its French roll."

"I don't see why on earth you'd want to. How

come you never wear it down, anyway?"

"Because I look like a perfect hoyden with it loose."

The brush in her hair stilled. "Oh, wait. Let me guess. Grandmother told you that, am I right?"

All the time. Juliet didn't say so, however. She simply shrugged at Roxanne's reflection in the mirror.

"Juliet, hasn't it ever occurred to you that your granny is a tad bit . . . old-fashioned? Holy catfish, your hair is *gorgeous*—bonafide Pre-Raphaelite."

"There's way too much of it."

"Oh, poor baby." She hesitated, then said firmly, "I don't know how to break this to you, but that is not a bad thing. I know women who'd kill to have half as much body in their hair. And exactly what the hell *is* a hoyden, anyhow?"

"Someone whose hair is always in her face, who runs instead of walks, who raises her voice. Someone who has *fun*," Juliet said with sudden defiance. She studied her hair in the mirror. It really was rather pretty.

Roxanne squeezed Juliet's shoulder and handed back her brush. "Well, then, let's hear it for all the hoydens in the world."

"Yes." Rebelliously, Juliet met her assistant's gaze in the mirror as she returned the brush to her purse. "Here's to them. I've been a perfect lady my entire life, and somebody just tried to shoot me, anyway. Grandmother was wrong. Goodness is not its own reward."

The crowd had thinned considerably by the time they returned to the main salon. Snagging a chair, they transported it behind the desk next to Juliet's. There they sat, quietly talking, while Beau and Luke finished interviewing.

Finally the last person left. Beau tossed his pen on the desk and slumped back in his chair, grinding the heels of his hands into his eye sockets. Dropping his hands to the desktop a moment later, he demanded, "How the hell can forty-plus people not have seen a freakin' thing?" He looked over at Luke. "How about you—you have any better luck?"

"Nope. Let's just hope one of the people who left before you managed to stop the mass exodus will have something to share."

"Surely they would have stuck around if they'd seen anything incriminating," Juliet protested.

"We don't assume anyone saw the shooter and then simply took off," Beau told her. "But someone may have noticed a specific person down by the sweet olive trees." He rotated his head on his neck, clearly trying to stretch out the kinks. "If we could place someone in the general vicinity at the right time, it would at least give us a place to start."

Roxanne, who had walked over to the rain-streaked window, called softly across the room, "Sergeant, do you know there are men down in the lower part of the garden?"

"Yeah, it's the forensics team. They arrived while y'all were in the powder room." His gaze narrowed on Juliet with sudden intensity. "You look a little better. How're you feelin'?"

"I'll be fine." Eventually.

"Looks like one of your forensics guys is headed

this way," Roxanne said from her post overlooking the gardens.

The man entered the room a few minutes later and shook himself off like a wet dog before crossing over to Beau. "Sergeant, I thought you'd want to see this," he said and placed a baggie containing a small lead sphere on the desk. "I just dug it out of the oak."

Beau leaned over to examine it. Luke came over and perched on the corner of his desk, and without a word Beau picked up the plastic bag and passed it to him. Luke examined it also, then looked up at the forensics tech, a frown marring his handsome face. "What the hell kinda bullet is this?"

"Not the kind you can buy in your average gun shop, sir. It's a ball from an old cap-and-ball-style pistol."

Beau and Luke exchanged a look for a long, silent moment. Then, "Shit," Beau muttered in disgust. "That's just what we need. Another goddam case featuring an antique gun."

The rain finally let up, but the sun had set by the time Beau wheeled the GTO beneath the Garden Crown's porte cochere. He looked around for his evening replacement . . . and didn't see him. Anywhere. Every single muscle in his neck immediately tensed up.

What the hell was it with Pfeffer? The man stuck him with this detail when no one actually believed there was a threat to Juliet, and now that they knew there truly was, he assigned a baby cop who was nowhere around when he was needed. Only in

New fucking Orleans would someone who everyone knew was an incompetent idiot be appointed to fill in a high-ranking position while a real cop took his long-awaited vacation.

He glanced over at Juliet. Her normally golden-hued complexion looked sallow, her posture lacked its customary ramrod precision, and she frankly looked worn right down to a nub. Even her amazing hair looked slightly wilted as she leaned her head back against the headrest.

There was just one thing to do.

"Hey, Rosebud, we're here." He reached over and touched her hand lying limply in her lap, grazing a fingertip back and forth across her knuckles until she opened her eyes. Then he craned around to see in the backseat. "How 'bout you, Miz Roxanne—how you holdin' up?"

"I'm doing fine, Sergeant."

Opening the car door, he climbed out and rounded the hood to open the passenger door. He escorted the women inside, watched as they climbed the curving staircase, then pulled the cell phone from his pocket and wandered the deserted first floor as he made a couple calls. Once a few arrangements had been set in motion, he camped himself out in the lobby and tried to ignore his rumbling stomach.

Luke showed up first. Tossing him a white deli bag, from which wafted the unmistakable aroma of a fried oyster po' boy, he slid the blue nylon duffel in his other hand beneath the chair where Beau sat. "You sure you want to do this, pard?"

"I don't see where I have much choice if we want

to assure her safety." He ripped open the sack, unwrapped his sandwich, and took a large bite. "Thanks, Luke. I thought I was gonna starve to death."

"It's a damn hotel," Luke said, looking around the sumptuous lobby. "Doesn't it have a restaurant?"

"I don't think it's up and running yet. At least not for the likes of me. Not likely to be, either, once Juliet gets wind of my plan." Not even to himself did he acknowledge the tiny surge of satisfaction that plan gave him.

"I'd think she'd be tickled pink. Overflowing with gratitude, in fact." Beau gave him a look and the corner of Luke's mouth quirked up in a wry smile. "Then again, we're talkin' about the female mind here. Who the hell understands that?"

"Amen to that, brother." Beau saw his evening replacement's car cruise by the front entry and surged to his feet. "There's the little son of a bitch."

He was out the door and across the drive, yanking open the driver's-side door of the cruiser practically before the driver had a chance to put the vehicle in park. Beau reached in and hauled the rookie cop out. "Where the hell have you been?"

The patrolman blinked. "A—a Code One was called over at Sacred Heart, and I was the nearest available car," he stammered.

"The nearest *available* car?" Beau thrust his face at the young rookie's. "What was your assignment, Officer?"

"To provide surveillance—"

"At Sacred Heart?" Beau barked.

"No, sir. Here. But nothing at all was happening—"

Luke pulled Beau away and said to the rookie, "You don't even want to go there, kid."

"No, sir. You're right, sir." He straightened his shoulders and met Beau's eyes. "I apologize, Sergeant. I was derelict in my duty. It won't happen again."

"Damn right it won't," Beau snarled, muscling Luke aside and getting right back in the young man's face. "Because you're not going—"

"Beau." Luke's voice was calm, but it held a warning.

Beau pulled back. He took a deep breath and blew it out. Then he shook out his fisted hands. "Get back to your post, Officer."

"Yes, sir!" The rookie left them with alacrity.

Beau scrubbed his hands over his face as he and Luke walked back toward the hotel entrance. "Christ. Were we ever that young?"

"Yep. And committed larger screw-ups, too."

"The hell you say. We never went chasing off after bigger and better excitement when we were on the job."

"Remember the Euterpe Street debacle?"

Beau stopped dead. "Oh. Yeah." He stuffed his hands in his pockets and gave Luke a sheepish smile. "I'd forgotten all about that."

"The same way the kid over there is probably hoping to forget this." He stopped at the door. "If you don't need anything else, I think I'm gonna call it a day."

"Yeah, you go ahead. And thanks, Luke. I appreciate you bringing my stuff. Thanks for dinner, too.'' He watched his friend lope off, and then turned and contemplated the Garden Crown's imposing facade for a moment. His mood took an inexplicable upswing, and he reached for the door handle.

Time to go break the good news to Juliet Rose.

13

*J*uliet's emotions were all over the map, and she desperately wanted them under control. The knowledge that someone wanted her dead kept surfacing, though she kept shoving it away. She wished Roxanne were still here with her; yet she was glad she was alone. She was irritable and jumpy, and she paced from room to room, trying time after time to sit down and catch up on work, only to immediately toss aside whatever she attempted to read and leap to her feet, unable to sit still. When someone knocked on her room door, she hurried to open it, hoping it was Roxanne. She hastily snugged up the belt on her silk kimono as she padded barefoot to answer the summons.

The last person she expected to see was Beau, and for an instant she simply stood there staring at him. Then she gave her head a slight shake and recollected her scattered manners. "I thought you'd gone home."

"I had some stuff to clear up."

He stepped forward and Juliet found herself taking an automatic step back. The next thing she knew, he was inside and the door was closing behind him. She tilted her chin up. "Is there something I can do for you?"

"Actually, there's something I'm gonna do for you, dawlin'." His teeth were whiter than white amid the surrounding dark stubble as he gave her a charming smile. "Your luck has just taken a turn for the better. I'm movin' in."

Yes. She wanted it—God, she'd never *known* she could want something so badly. And that terrified her. "Absolutely not."

She'd have to be crazy—she'd seen this man in action. There was no way in hell she could allow herself to become dependent upon him. Sooner or later the case would be finished, and he'd turn and walk away. How was she supposed to go back and live in her world then, if she let down the guard it had taken her an entire lifetime to build?

With the killer smile she'd seen him display time after time for dazzled barmaids and strippers, he stepped forward. "Now, angel face, don't be difficult. It's not like you're gonna lose anything by admitting you need me." He reached for a tendril of hair that had fallen over her eye.

"Read my lips, Sergeant." She stepped back and blew the strand into place herself. "No. Astor Lowells pride themselves on being self-sufficient." God, she sounded like such a stuffy little prig. It made no appreciable impact on Beauregard, either, for his smile didn't diminish one iota.

"I'm sure they do. Especially Big Daddy. But

you're just gonna have to swallow that pride, sugar, because right now you're a little out of your element—and like it or not, you do need me."

"Right—like I need a galloping case of the—" She caught herself in time and cast a guilty glance his way.

The idiot had the temerity to grin wider, as if delighted by how near she'd come to saying something unacceptably crude. His dark gaze traveled slowly from her unbound hair to her bare feet, with about a half dozen stops in between before covering the same territory on the return journey. Her skin flushed, and her nipples grew tight in response. Then, right before her eyes, he turned professional on her, and she was left wondering if she'd somehow imagined that slow, knowing once-over. And if so, what did that say about her—that she was a desperate old maid?

"I know it's unexpected, Miz Lowell, and probably an inconvenience—but work with me on this. The violence is clearly beginning to escalate, and I don't like knowing that you're left unprotected in this big ol' mausoleum. The obvious solution is to have me move in. Not only will I be in a better position to see to your safety, but we stand a greatly improved chance of catching this guy if we work together on this."

That was certainly true. Her heart pounded in her chest. It was . . . logical, really. He definitely had a point.

Dismayed by how quick she was to grab at any ready excuse, she frowned at him. "I fail to see—"

"What's the matter with you?" He was clearly out of sorts when she neglected to fall for his charm or immediately succumb to his professional rationalization. "Don't you want to catch this guy?"

"Of course I do!" *I'm just scared to death that it's not my main consideration here.*

He stepped forward, looming over her. "Then use your head, woman!"

"Dammit, Beau, stop crowding me!" Slapping her hands to his chest, Juliet shoved, not taking a breath until he backed up a step. He scowled down at her and she poked her nose up in the air in rebuttal. "Fine, then, move in," she agreed coolly, as if that weren't exactly what she desired. Wondering where this ungracious, childish streak was coming from, and knowing she was overreacting, she nevertheless indicated the duffel bag in his hand and said snootily, "You obviously intend to do exactly that no matter what I say, anyway, so let's not waste any more breath arguing about it, all right? But I'm putting you in the cockroach room across the hall. And if you don't like it, that's just too bad. Take it or leave it."

Beau studied her for a moment. Then he slung the duffel over his shoulder. "I'll take it."

Luke knew he should just go straight home, but he found himself driving to Josie Lee's house instead. He'd been doing a lot of that lately.

Too damn much. It was as if his car had a homing device that locked on her, and if Beau ever discovered the way Luke was sniffing around his baby sister, there'd be hell to pay. But he couldn't seem to stay away. The problem was, the more time he spent in Josie Lee's company, the harder it was to think of her as a kid. She was funny, and articulate, and they had a lot in common. And, God, that body . . .

But it was better not to think about that. He reached down to make an adjustment for the sake of comfort, and when he pulled up in front of her house a few minutes later, he sat in the car for a while, waiting for everything to cool down. He'd been keeping it casual. It was beginning to cripple him, but he was doing it anyway. And he intended to continue on in the same vein.

Blowing out a breath, he got out of the car and walked up to the front door.

For an instant, when she opened the door to his knock, Josie Lee looked surprised. But then she gave him a smile that damn near stopped his heart. It was one of those I'm-glad-to-see-you smiles that grabbed a guy by the short hairs and made him think crazy thoughts. Oh, man. What was he doing here?

"Hey, there, Lucas," she said softly.

"Hey. I wasn't sure if you'd heard, but Beau—"

"—plans to camp out at the Garden Crown for a while," she finished his sentence for him. "I do know. I just got off the phone with him."

"You okay with that? I, um, just thought I'd stop by to make sure you don't need anything."

"C'mon in." She stepped back from the door. "This is really nice of you, Luke. Have you had anything to eat?"

"Yeah, I ate a while ago."

"Want a Dixie? No, wait"—she interrupted herself this time and flashed another soft, crooked smile. "I bet you'd rather have coffee than a beer, huh?"

She was so damn sweet. "That'd be great." Hands in his pockets, he ambled in her wake as she headed for the kitchen, trying hard to keep his gaze off the long, bare length of her legs.

"Have a seat," she invited and scraped out a chair for him as she padded past the kitchen table. "I'll get a cup." She pulled a mug from the cupboard and placed it on the table in front of him, then sank down on a chair facing him, folding one leg diagonally across the seat and perching her round butt on the sole of her foot as if she expected to be up and running at any minute. "I started a pot a few minutes ago, so it shouldn't take long."

"I'm in no hurry. It's nice not to have to do for myself for a change. So, are you really okay with being here on your own?" He tried to read her expression, but it didn't give much away. "You aren't just putting a good face on things, are you? I mean, you've never really talked about how it felt to be a victim of the Panty Snatcher." He felt heat crawl up his face. "At least that I've ever heard of. But then I guess maybe it's kind of presumptuous of me to suppose I would have. Heard something, that is." *Shut up, you idiot—you're babbling.*

She met his eyes easily. "I don't think it's presumptuous at all; I think it's sorta sweet."

"Sweet. Right. That's me." Shit.

She grinned then, that wholehearted Dupree grin she had in common with her brother. "No, truly, it *is* sweet. And refreshing. At least you're not tip-toeing around me like I was thirteen years old and the guy raped me." She planted an elbow on the tabletop and leaned her chin on her fist, gazing at him. "The fact is, it felt . . . nasty to be forced to strip in front of a stranger. But I was raised by Beauregard, Luke, and you know my upbringing was less than conventional, to say the least. Also, I'd heard y'all discussing this case before I was ever involved in it, and that alone made me different from his other victims, because I knew the way he operated. Mostly what I felt as I stood there buck naked in front of that pervert was *angry*. I wasn't afraid he'd rape me. I was just plain mad, and all I could think of was what I'd do to him if he gave me the tiniest opening."

Luke looked at her flashing eyes and flushed cheeks and found himself grinning. "I bet you woulda ripped him a new one."

"Damn right, shoog."

Shoog. Sugar. It was a common endearment used by Yat females—the blue-collar women that Up-towners called "chawmahs." It was meaningless, really; used generically for every man they came across. And chances were, Josie Lee didn't mean anything by it now.

So why did it reach down inside him and flip his guts inside out?

The coffeemaker gurgled to a halt and she popped up off her chair and circled him to go to the counter. A second later he heard her pad up behind him. Then she was leaning over his shoulder to fill his cup and her generous breasts pressed the back of his head, cushioning it for a heart-stopping moment. Rearing back in surprise, he found himself wrapped in heat from ear to ear as his smooth-shaven head snugged a place for itself between the lush fullness. He froze. "Christ, Baby Girl," he croaked.

"If there's one thing I no longer am, Luke," her voice said above him, "it's a baby." Then the heat abruptly disappeared as she stepped away.

He swiveled in his chair. She was setting the cup of coffee she'd just poured him on the counter and the pot back on the stove. An instant later, she turned to face him. Her cheeks were red, her eyes black as sin, and he didn't have to be a member of Mensa to guess her intentions.

"I don't want to play games anymore," she said in a low voice. "It's time I quit acting like a kid and started behaving like a woman. So, as a woman, I'm just gonna come out and say this flat-out. I want you, Luke."

The words had a direct and immediate effect on his dick, but he desperately tried to persevere in the course he'd set himself. Someone should be handing him a fucking *medal*, he was trying so hard. He stumbled to his feet and backed away. "You don't know what you're talkin' about. I'd better go."

"You should stay." She stepped forward. "I know exactly what I'm talking about."

"You're too young for me." Still backing up, he summoned every bit of cynicism at his disposal and gave her a derisive up-and-down. "I go for women, not kids."

If her ego was dented, it didn't show. She returned his perusal, stopping at his fly briefly before bringing her gaze back up to his. "Really? That's not what the big guy there seems to be sayin'."

His back hit the wall just this side of the doorway. "Yeah, well, the big guy's not exactly discriminating. Hell, every time I drive past Tastee Donuts he practically stands up and salutes."

Her long, narrow hands slapped softly against the wall on either side of his shoulders, and she gave him a soft, knowing smile. "Um-hmm."

"I'm serious, here." He reached up to grasp her wrists and thrust her arms away, breaking the cage of soft, scented feminine heat that pinned him to the wall.

A huge mistake, as it turned out, for without the wall to support her, she simply collapsed against his chest. Then she lifted up onto her tiptoes, nestled the full weight of her breasts comfortably against him, and leaned in to bite his lower lip.

He should have stood tough. He *intended* to stand tough. But the next thing he knew, he opened his mouth, and her tongue slipped in, and she was hot and sweet and everything he'd dreamed she would be. And then he was kissing her back, and backing her across the room to the table, which he cleared with one impatient sweep of his arm. Ignoring the crash of crockery, he laid her out on top of it, and pinning her hands to its scarred surface, he crawled up on top of her. She gave a muffled laugh and shifted her legs to make a place for him between them, bucking up challengingly against his weight.

And he was a goner.

*   *   *

Beau was restless. And hungry. He paced through the hotel, exploring the areas he hadn't already been in. At one point he came up behind a wizened little old lady, and the scents that emanated from the covered tray she carried made him follow along in her wake for a while. A guy could only shorten his stride so much, however, before he started looking like a mincing idiot. Besides, it didn't take long to figure out that her creeping shuffle had her aimed toward the private quarters that housed the Hayneses. Doubting an invitation to join them for a bite to eat would be forthcoming, he peeled off and headed for the staircase.

Dammit, he was hungry, and this was bullshit. He loped down the stairs to the second floor and then strode down the hallway, stopping in front of Juliet's room. Raising his fist, he pounded on the door.

It was quiet and he started to knock again. Then something that was not so much a sound as an intuitive sense of her on the other side of the door stayed his hand.

"What do you want, Beauregard?" She didn't open the door.

"How did you know it was me?" he demanded. The door didn't boast a peephole—something he intended to rectify.

There was a muffled sound that—coming from anyone else—he would have sworn was a snort. "I recognized your suave style of knocking."

That made him grin. "Open the door." He stroked his fingers down the rich wood.

"No, I don't think so."

"Don't make me get physical, Rosebud." Right. Like he could afford to have her calling the Pissant with a complaint that he was destroying her property. But she didn't have to know that.

It worked, too. He heard her turn the lock, and a second later she opened the door.

She was all pokered up and disapproving as she frowned up at him, but the effect was less than intimidating, given her overall condition. Her soft skin was scraped up and she was kind of wan. She still wore the brown and gold wrap thing she'd had on earlier, and although it covered her decently enough, it was a slippery material that exposed her delicate collarbone and skimmed here and clung there. And her long, sexy feet, with their high arches and those pale pink siren toenails, were bare. He wondered if she was bare all over.

Then there was her hair, which had a way of capturing his attention. Every time he saw the woman, he swore she had more hair than the time before. And he really wanted to tangle the unruly mass through his fingers, to pull her head back and expose that long throat, so he could—

He stuffed his hands in his pockets and cleared his throat. "Throw some clothes on, angel face. We're gonna go get something to eat."

He distinctly saw her eyes light up, but she poked her narrow little nose up at him. "We have a perfectly good kitchen right here in the hotel."

"I couldn't find it. You suppose it's got any grits in it?"

She made a face. "I sincerely hope not."

"Then we're going out, honey chile, 'cause I want breakfast—"

"It's eleven o'clock at night!"

"—and breakfast just ain't breakfast without grits or hush puppies. So go put on some clothes. You have ten minutes, then I'm packing you out as is. I'm starved."

"You're always hungry. What do you have, a hollow leg?"

The expression coming from her made him smile. "According to my sisters, that's exactly what I have." He glanced at his watch. "Nine minutes and thirty seconds, Rosebud."

She spun on her narrow heel and walked away. Stepping into the suite, he closed the door behind him.

She kept him waiting, of course. He occupied himself by wandering the sitting room, picking up the scattered bits of her odds and ends, examining them, and then setting them back down again when something else caught his eye. She wasn't exactly tidy, which was at odds with her neat-as-a-pin dressing style and crisp manners, but it seemed perfectly in tune with her hair the way he'd been seeing it more and more recently.

Would the real Juliet Rose please stand up?

Would the real Juliet Rose ever get her butt out here? He checked his watch impatiently. She'd dragged her feet long enough; he was starting to get a little ticked off. He strode for the bedroom, and giving the door one cursory knock, he barged right in.

She was sitting on a little girly-type chair and she

hadn't even changed out of her damn robe yet. He opened his mouth to give her hell, but with one brief look at him, she swiveled to give him her back, and he stilled.

Was she *crying*?

He saw that she wasn't when he came around the bed, but she was shaking. Shivering as if it were forty-five degrees in here instead of seventy. She sat sideways on the slipper chair, her spine perfectly erect, her neat little ankles aligned. But she hugged herself and stared straight ahead, rocking slightly.

"Heeeey." He crouched in front of her and eased his hands, then his forearms, onto the chair's cushioned seat on either side of her hips, curling his fingers over the far edge and bracketing her in. He looked up at her. "Are you okay, dawlin'? What is it?"

Her gaze left the far wall and zeroed in on his. "Somebody shot at me today, Beauregard." The trembling increased.

"Shhh, I know." He scooped her up and looked around. She'd probably fight him if he tried to go for the bed, and the little chair was a waste of perfectly good materials, if you asked him. He carried her into the sitting room and chose a good-sized armchair. Sitting down, he settled her in his lap. "Have you been chewing on it all this time?"

"I've tried really hard to *forget* . . . or at least put it aside for a while. But I can't seem to get it out of my mind." Her cheek rested against a spot between his shoulder and chest that could have been carved out just for her. Her knees were tucked up, her feet on the seat cushion between his hip and the chair's overstuffed arm, toes curled into the crevice. She tilted her head back to look up into his face. "Why would anyone want to shoot me, Beau? I've never done anything to anyone."

"I don't think it's personal, dawlin'. We're clearly dealing with a psychotic here." He reached down and wrapped his hand around one of her bare feet, curling his fingers to knead its arch with his fingertips. "It's my guess somebody's fixated on the Garden Crown as a symbol of the historical landmarks that have been lost—which frankly, in this part of the world, isn't exactly a problem of epidemic proportions." Her head rode the swell when he shrugged. "You've obviously come to symbolize the corporate destroyer in his mind."

"Terrific."

He slid his palm up her foot, kneaded her ankle. "I'm going to find whoever it is." Fingers sliding a little higher onto her shin, he squeezed. "Do you believe me?" He sat still while she searched his eyes.

She nodded. "Yes."

"Good." Thinking brotherly thoughts, he lowered his head and rewarded her excellent character-judging abilities with a soft, brief kiss.

He felt the soft ripeness of her mouth beneath his, and brotherliness was incinerated in a flash of heat. Hastily pulling back, he said hoarsely, "I don't want you to worry about a thing."

"Well, that might be asking a bit much." Looking up at him solemnly, she curled her fingers around the back of his neck and tugged. "But maybe if I could find something to distract me . . ."

Oh, shit, this was not a good idea. She was vulnerable, and he was on the job, and . . .

She shifted enough to lift her mouth up to his. With every intention of pulling away, his hands slid into her hair and molded to the shape of her head beneath the cushioning fullness.

"Please," she whispered. Then her lips, parted and warm and moist, pressed against his.

And all his good intentions went to hell.

14

❧

Juliet felt as if she'd unleashed something as elemental as lightning—an out-of-control force that had the potential to sear her to ashes. One heartbeat, Beau's hands were in her hair, resisting her sudden need for a physical connection between them. The next, they were holding her motionless against the onslaught of an appetite more voracious than anything she'd ever imagined.

His mouth twisted over hers, breaking the seal of her lips. Then he was inside her mouth, his tongue aggressive and dominant, and a feral sound rumbled in his throat. Sensations, fever-hot, sparked along her nerve endings. Her fingers inched up his nape to fist in his hair, and she clung to him helplessly, kissing him back, every stricture ever learned about self-control drowned in the river of lava that scorched its way through her veins.

Minutes, hours, days later, he lifted his head and stared down at her. "Damn, I love your mouth," he muttered. His tongue came out and moistened his lower lip. "I've seen that mouth in my dreams, made it do things I bet you've never even heard of."

Her tongue slipped over her own lips in a sympathy lick. She was disoriented, slow to respond, and just as the fog began to clear enough ask, *what things?* he wrapped a fistful of her hair around his hand, and his head descended once again. His mouth was hot and strong and demanding as it opened on hers, and she was lost.

Lord have mercy, he knew how to kiss! He was so good that her knees went weak and she heard bells ring.

He lifted his mouth away fractionally. "Ignore that," he muttered, and tilted her head to a different angle.

"Hmmm?" She sucked in a sharp breath at the feel of his lips—with the merest hint of teeth—worrying the vulnerable skin of her earlobe. Then another ring chimed softly across the room, and she realized it was the phone, not his kisses, that had caused the sound. She swallowed a bubble of hysterical laughter and struggled to sit up. Talk about a hopeless romantic.

His teeth became more than a hint on her earlobe. "Ignore it, Rosebud."

"I can't—I'll just be a minute—please."

Are you crazy, Juliet? She didn't want to talk on the phone. Deciding to forget her damn manners for once, she was startled to feel his hands slide onto her hips and ease her to the edge of his knees.

"Make it snappy, then." It wasn't a suggestion.

Juliet stumbled to her feet and crossed the room. What was it about Beau's lap, anyway? It seemed to be a dangerous place for her, for every time she landed in it, she lost all sense of decorum.

And she liked it—that was the really scary part. Losing decorum felt incredibly good.

The phone rang again, and she snatched it up. "Hello?"

"Hello, dear, this is Celeste. How are you doing after this afternoon's debacle? Are you quite recovered?"

"Oh, Celeste . . . yes. My hand is better and a nice bath took care of the stiffness." She heard a rustle behind her and glanced over her shoulder. Beau was on his feet, his gaze hot on her while he peeled out of his shirt.

The receiver dropped from her suddenly nerveless fingers.

She could hear Celeste's voice still talking and she stooped to retrieve the receiver from the floor, her gaze glued to Beau's bare torso. Shoulders, chest, and arms—he was muscular without being muscle-bound, and what she'd assumed to be a summer tan she saw now was a naturally dark complexion. Black hair feathered his forearms and spread in a fan across sculpted pectorals, and her helpless gaze followed the dwindling stripe of silky hair down his diaphragm, across a stomach that was flat and corded with muscle, to his navel, where the ribbon of hair widened. Then it narrowed again and disappeared beneath the waistband of his low-slung slacks. She saw his hands reach for his belt, saw the erection tenting his pants below, and hurriedly turned her back. She pushed dazedly to her feet and brought the receiver to her ear. "I'm sorry, Celeste, I dropped the phone. I didn't catch that."

"I said, Lily told me she saw Sergeant Dupree wandering the hallways not too long ago."

"Oh. Um, yes. He's unhappy with the way the violence seems to be escalating and has decided to move in for a while."

There was an instant of silence in which Juliet struggled to keep from turning to see what Beau was doing. Had he stripped right down to the skin? Then Celeste's voice asked, "Do you think that's wise, dear?"

Beau's chest spread heat across her back, and his warm arms wrapped around her waist. She looked down to see his long fingers unknotting her kimono's belt. "What?"

"I said, do you think that's wise?"

"I . . ."

"Is that Celeste?" Beau's chin was a sandpaper brush at her temple, his breath a warm rush of air that raised goose bumps down her entire right side.

Swallowing hard, she nodded. Had she truly thought he would be less hazardous on his feet?

The knot at her waist fell free and he spread open the kimono's sides. "Say good-bye," he ordered.

She was naked underneath except for a pair of pumpkin silk and black lace panties, and she saw as well as felt his hand as it spread possessively across her stomach. Tough-skinned and hot, it was dark and masculine against the pale gold tones of her flesh. Celeste was saying something in her ear, but she might as well have been speaking Swahili—Juliet couldn't concentrate long enough to sort out the words. "I have to go," she whispered, and fumbled the receiver onto the hook.

A sound of approval rumbled in Beau's throat and he turned her around. He kissed her hard and brushed her kimono off her shoulders. No sooner had it slithered down her body and pooled at her feet than he picked her up. A moment later, he was lowering her onto the mattress in the bedroom and following her down.

He knelt astride her hips. Reaching out a long finger, he feathered the skin next to her lips. "I should have shaved," he murmured regretfully, and, looking up at his shadowed jaw, she realized that her face probably looked as though it had been worked over by steel wool.

She didn't care.

She reached up and touched his chest with both hands. The hair covering it was springy, the muscle beneath hard and warm, and his small copper-brown nipples were smooth as worry stones. As she scratched her fingernail over one, the tiny nipple in its center grew hard as a nail head.

His gaze dropped to her own breasts, and she had a sudden desire to hide them from view. She should be wearing her Wonder-Bra—at least it gave her a hint of cleavage. Her hands left him, fluttering down to cup her modest curves.

"No." His voice sounded like gravel. "Don't cover yourself, Juliet Rose. Let me look."

"There's not much to look at. They're small." And he liked them big.

His fingers wrapped around her wrists and exerted gentle pressure until her fingers slid away. He pinned her hands to the mattress next to her shoulders. Eyes hot, he appeared totally absorbed as he studied her breasts. "They're like you—understated. And so pretty it makes me hurt."

Juliet's nipples distended and Beau sucked in his breath. "Ah, God, and so responsive." Letting loose her wrists, he trailed his fingers up her arms to the bend of her elbows, over her shoulders, then stroked them down her chest. He slid down on the mattress, making a place for himself between her legs, his hard stomach warm against the juncture of her thighs as he sprawled out, propping himself up on one forearm. The planes of his face were so taut as he gazed at her that Juliet regarded him warily. Something kept her very still.

Beau struggled to rein himself in. He couldn't remember the last time he'd felt this hot. He felt like some damn vampire who scented blood and had to hang on to his will for all it was worth to keep from falling into a feeding frenzy and scaring the bejesus out of her. He concentrated on keeping his touch gentle, cupping his hand beneath her breast and pushing the slight fullness up.

Her aureoles were luxuriant little puffs of pink that thrust her nipples forward like missiles. Her tits were so tiny and sweet, and he was utterly fascinated by them. It surprised the hell out of him, since he generally went for big and bouncy.

Suddenly, though, big and bouncy seemed sort of crass.

He smoothed his thumb up the slight swell of her breast and over the velvet arch of her aureole, until it pressed her nipple against the side of his index finger. Squeezing gently, he tugged, and her back arched, her thighs spread, and she made a low, throaty sound, as if she were a cat and he'd just set her loose in an aviary.

"Oh, shit," he whispered. "You like that. What else do you like, I wonder? This?" He bent his head to lick the straining nipple, and she shuddered. He pulled it between his lips and sucked, and her hips raised off the bed.

"Beau?" Her fingers clutched in his hair and she held his mouth to her breast. Catching the nipple lightly between his teeth and pulling, he looked up and watched as her eyes lost focus. High, mewling sounds escaped her, but she immediately stifled them, clamping her teeth over her full lower lip and biting down.

"Oh, no, you don't." He surged up and lay on her full-length. Thrusting his fingers through her warm, thick hair, he gripped her skull and tipped it back until she was looking at him. "If something makes you feel good, dammit, you don't repress it. I want to hear you." He rubbed his thumb against her captured lip and watched as its fullness slid free of her perfect upper teeth. Then he rubbed it again, savoring the fullness.

Gazing back at him with dazed eyes, she opened her mouth against the press of his thumb, and it slipped inside. She pursed her lips around it and sucked.

Seeing that porn-star mouth perform even a G-rated version of one of his more persistent fantasies made the breath explode out of his lungs. He thrust his thumb deeper, feeling the slide of her tongue and the slick walls of her inner cheeks as she drew on it. A growl rattled in his throat. He pulled his thumb free before he could give in to the impulse to instigate a suggestive rhythm. He rocked his mouth over hers, letting his tongue adopt the rhythm instead.

She tasted so sweet and pristine, and she kissed him back with untried fervor, that erotic mouth clinging to his, her breath hitching in the same crazy rhythms as his own. Her arms gripped his neck, and her long, smooth legs tangled around his thighs.

He lifted his head and stared down at her. Her gray eyes nearly matched the charcoal rings that rimmed the irises, and they gazed back at him with such a lack of focus that his stomach clenched. *Damn*, what a rush. As he felt her shift with questing restlessness beneath him, he burned to see just how out of control he could drive her.

"Beau?" She licked her luscious lips, and he kissed her hard before applying himself to the exploration of her long throat.

Juliet felt bombarded by sensations. Beau's hair brushed her jaw, his mouth was a moist, suctioning furnace at her neck, and one of his hands toyed with her left breast, massaging its meager fullness, plucking at her nipple. She couldn't think, she could barely catch a satisfying breath. She was all nerve endings, a throbbing, jagged heartbeat that seemed to be centered high up between her thighs.

"God, look at you." He pushed back to kneel astride her shins, and she stared up at him in confusion. Naked except for the gray cotton knit boxers that seemed to barely contain his massive erection, he looked dark and primal, all broad shoulders, intense eyes, and five o'clock shadow. "Look at you, Rosebud," he repeated, and his voice was a sandpaper abrasion against already overstimulated nerves.

She didn't want him looking at her. She was a galaxy removed from centerfold material, all lanky arms and legs, with no breasts or hips to speak of.

Yet he didn't seem to mind—not if his hot-eyed gaze was anything to go by. His hands reached out to trail whisper-light fingertips down her chest, up the gentle rise of her breasts and down the fuller bottom curves, before they glided onto her diaphragm.

"You've got such soft skin." His fingers spread out. Thumbs together, his hands coasted straight down her middle, fingertips curving over her sides. "Such long, gorgeous legs." He delineated the dip that defined her waist, probed the deep well of her navel with the spatulate tip of one thumb. Then his fingers curled around her slender hips and his thumbs brushed over a narrow ridge of elastic and onto pumpkin silk and black lace. Something in his face went still, and he looked into her eyes as his right thumb crested the slight rise of her pubis and firmly pressed its way down her damp, silk-covered furrow.

His touch was electric and her dew-drenched panties were the conductor that bore it straight to the heart of her. Her hips arched and he muttered, "Oh, Christ, I've got to see you," and then her panties were sliding away, and he was sprawled on his stomach between her thighs, and somehow her legs were wide open with the width of his shoulders preventing them from closing, and she could feel his *breath* there—right there, on the most intimate part of her. And she just knew she was blushing all over, for no one had ever seen her like this.

She pushed up on her elbows and said uncertainly, "Beau?"

She could have sworn he said, "God, yes, it's just like your mouth," but that didn't make a bit of sense. She certainly didn't misunderstand, however, when he looked up at her and said, "You do know I've got to taste you, don't you?"

In a flurry of pure panic mixed with a fierce anticipation that appalled her, she brought her foot up against the rounded muscle of his shoulder and tried to shove him away. But he simply wrapped his hand around her instep and brought the sole of her foot to his mouth.

He flashed his killer smile. "This first? Good idea, dawlin'. You've got the sexiest feet I've ever seen." Then the smile faded and all that was left was the intensity of his eyes looking up at her as he pressed his mouth to her arch, to the ball of her foot, to her toes. "You don't have to fight me, Juliet

Rose. I just want to make you feel good." The corner of his mouth quirked up. "Okay, and to make myself feel good, too." While his mouth paid homage to her foot, his free hand smoothed along her inner thigh, over the diminutive curve where her bottom met her leg. One long finger stole ahead of the rest, slipping between folds of slippery feminine flesh.

"*Beau*?" It came out high-pitched and breathy. Dear God, she hadn't *known* such sensations existed. Her legs spread of their own volition, and unfamiliar sounds slipped up her throat as his gentle fingers slid up and down and circled tortuously.

Beau eased her legs over his shoulders. God, she was something. So responsive, so surprisingly sexual—he should have known. She might be the poster girl of well-bred restraint, but there had been hints that he'd ignored. He'd chosen to see only the spare elegance with which she was built, the demure reserve with which she groomed herself. Her hair, her mouth, had both drawn him from the beginning, but he'd disregarded them. Now that he had her undressed, he could see other indications of a hedonistic nature—those cushy little projectile nipples, the full lips of her sex.

The latter drew him like a needle to magnetic north. It was so . . . her. Soft brown hair grew at the top of her mound in a neat little patch of curls, as if knowing an Astor Lowell would never countenance a profligate, untidy display. The lower lips, however, were smooth and plump and extravagantly slick beneath his fingers, and they virtually screamed, *Touch me, taste me, take me*. He couldn't believe hordes before him hadn't, but there was too much modesty in her movements, too much surprise at every new thing he did to her, to believe she was anything but a novice when it came to sex.

The surprising thing was how that excited him on a gut-deep, visceral level. He'd always looked for women who could teach him a thing or two—he'd never wanted someone who might turn dependent on him. But now *he* wanted to be the teacher; he wanted to be the one to drive Juliet beyond her good-girl restraint.

He leaned forward and licked the voluptuous cleft. She smelled like a million bucks, warm and clean and girly—and she tasted even better. He reveled in the incoherent little sounds that purled out of her throat, in the fingers she tangled in his hair, and the frantic little bumps of her hips. He was too damn hot to draw this out for any length of time, and he went in for the kill, moving up to focus his attentions on her clitoris.

Her hips shot up off the bed at the first touch of his tongue. "Beau? Oh! Please." Her voice was strangled, yearning. "Beauregard, *please*."

And please her he did. He drove her straight over the edge.

"Oh. My. Gaaaawwwwd." Her voice went up in pitch with each word. Her thighs clamped around his ears and she held him viced there while she rode out the sensations. The instant her grip on him relaxed, he drew back, substituted his fingers to help her through the aftershocks, and scrambled between her sprawled thighs. Aligning his erection with her opening, he pressed into her.

She was so incredibly tiny, and he managed to get no more than the head of his erection into her before she seemed to close up, leaving him nowhere to go. He smoothed a finger up and down her slippery cleft in the hopes she wouldn't notice he was forging a brand-new path into her body. "God, Rosebud," he breathed, "you have done this before, haven't you?"

"Not like this," she murmured with sleepy satisfaction, and he froze.

She was a *virgin*? Oh, God, he hadn't wanted this. It was too much responsibility; it was just asking for trouble. He felt . . . misused. "What am I, freakin' *Star Trek*?" he demanded, staring in frustration at the point where they barely joined. "I never asked to boldly go where no man's gone before."

She laughed, and he found himself raising his gaze to her face, because she didn't do that very often and she was so damn pretty when she did.

"Then you'll be happy to know you haven't," she said. He must have looked every bit as blank as he felt, for she gave him a little half-smile and said, "Rest easy, Beauregard—others have 'been' before you. Not many, but some." She wiggled her hips, and the tight ring of muscle impeding his progress suddenly relaxed and he began to sink into her. "Oh!" Her eyes lost that bright amusement and grew heavy-lidded with rekindled arousal.

His answering groan contained wholehearted agreement. Oh, in-fucking-deed. He was suddenly deep inside her, and it was furnace-hot, a muscular constriction of liquid heat that threatened to burn him alive. He pulled back slightly, then thrust forward again. "God." It hurt to force the words past his suddenly tight vocal cords, but he couldn't keep quiet. "You . . . feel . . . so . . . damn . . . good."

He leaned down to kiss her, and as always, he lost himself in the soft lips beneath his. He flattened his hands against the mattress and contracted his hips, withdrawing almost completely from her, then thrusting deeper. He did it again. Then again, setting up a steady rhythm.

"Beau?" Bracing her feet, Juliet moved her hips in time with his thrusts. He quit kissing her and she stared up at him. He returned her gaze, but she didn't think he actually saw her, for he wore a look of blind concentration on his face. His hips began to move faster, to probe a little deeper, and she began to feel that coiling tightness she'd experienced earlier. But she couldn't quite . . . It wasn't . . . quite . . . "Oh, please," she whispered and brought her inner thighs a little higher up his sides.

He rose up on his knees, and when her legs slid down over his hips and her feet skidded on the coverlet, he put a hand on the inside of her knees and spread her thighs, pressing them toward the mattress. Before she could be embarrassed by how fully it exposed her, he drove deep with a swivel of his hips, and a high, surprised squeal escaped her. It felt as if he'd touched something inside her that had never been touched before. Then he was gone. But an instant later he was back, and the rhythmic lunge and retreat of his hips grew faster and faster, and one of his hands slid up the inside of her thigh, and suddenly his thumb was keeping time in the wet curls between her legs, and he was urging her on with words no man had ever before uttered to her.

Then the iron-hard heat thrusting inside her touched something that blew her apart, and all thought fled. Feminine muscles clenched and released, clenched and released, and it felt so wonderful, and somewhere in the room a woman panted and moaned and chanted, "Ohgod ohgod ohgod ohgod," in a voice that kept getting higher and more desperate. She dug her fingernails into Beau's back to anchor herself in a world thrown into galvanic upheaval.

Beau watched Juliet's restraint vanish as she climaxed, felt her orgasm contracting around him like a thermonuclear fist, and a groan started deep in his gut and climbed up through his chest, until it tore out of his throat in a roar of triumph. Shoving himself deep, he came in hot, endless pulsations. Then, drained, gratified, he fell forward, catching himself on his palms and lowering himself gently upon her prone body. Satisfaction pulsed through him, and he buried his face in the fragrant wealth of her hair. Drifting in a spent haze, he felt like the luckiest man on earth.

Right up until the moment he realized he hadn't given one, single, sonofabitchin' thought to protection.

15

Celeste sat in her wing-backed chair, outwardly placid. She sipped her tea; she nibbled the delicate pastries Lily had brought; she exchanged desultory, even-toned chitchat with Edward. And all the while, she burned with inner fury.

Juliet had hung up on her. The little chit had invited that viper Dupree into *her* home, and then she'd hung up on her! That was simply not done . . . and she'd pay for it.

To think Celeste had felt badly that little Miss Butter-Wouldn't-Melt-in-Her-Mouth Astor Lowell had received a fright this afternoon. She'd actually gone out of her way to check up on Juliet's well-being after her mishap, and this was how she was rewarded for her thoughtfulness. Well, fine, then. Perhaps the next time she had Dupree in her sights, she *would* aim for Juliet as well.

That guttersnipe policeman was in Juliet's room right this very minute—Celeste had heard him plain as day asking if that was she on the line—

and then telling Juliet to hang up the phone. Clearly, Miss Astor Lowell was not the well-bred young woman she pretended to be . . . but then what could one expect from a Yankee?

Celeste hadn't been born yesterday—she'd recognized that tone in his voice. God knows she'd heard it often enough in Edward's before she'd broken him of the habit.

As if he'd somehow heard the echo of his name in her head, Edward suddenly rose to his feet. He gave the faultless creases in his slacks a fastidious shake. "I'm going out for a bit, dear. Don't wait up."

No! The protest screamed in her head and Celeste's heart climbed up into her throat. "At this hour?" she demanded with imperious disapproval the moment she got her breath back, and hoped against hope that it would be enough to discourage him. Sometimes using just the right tone did. "Where on earth would you need to go at this ungodly hour?" She ignored the voice in her head that whispered, *You know.* She didn't know. Not really.

Edward smiled his gentle smile. "I thought I'd stop by the club for a while, see if Yves Montague is there. He has a rare mask he's been wanting to show me. Says it might be just the thing for my collection."

"Edward, really. It's late. Wouldn't tomorrow be a more appropriate time?"

"Most likely, dear. But he mentioned he'd probably be there tonight." He leaned down and bussed her cheek. "Don't fuss. I won't be terribly late."

Celeste watched him walk out the door and held herself very still for a long while after he'd gone, fearing her inner trembling would manifest itself outwardly if she twitched so much as an eyelash. Finally, when she had herself sufficiently collected, she rose to her feet and began gathering their tea things together, placing them on a tray for Lily to collect later.

She stared blindly at the few crumbs left on the Royal Doulton plate in her hand. This was Juliet's fault. Her and her damn family-owned hotel chain. She should have left them alone to maintain this place as they were meant to do, as the Hayneses had *been* doing for decades. But no, Juliet had not only usurped their home, she'd invited that cockroach Dupree in ... and now the only thing of importance in the entire world—Celeste and Edward's rightful place in society—was imperiled because of her.

Celeste's arm moved without conscious volition, and the china plate flew across the room, where it hit the wall and exploded in a multitude of bone, blue, and golden shards. Damn that Yankee bitch. She was ruining everything.

Well, she wouldn't get away with it. Not if Celeste had anything to say about it, by God—and she was a Butler; it was her God-given *right* to have something to say about it. Taking a deep breath and blowing it out, she stalked with ramrod posture to the old-fashioned bellpull in the corner. Giving it a tug, she eyed the shards of ancient china on the floor with distaste.

Lily needed to get in here and clean up this mess.

*   *   *

Beau stared down at Juliet. He couldn't believe she'd just fallen asleep like that. She'd gotten hers and then—bam!—she'd gone out like a light. Just like a damn guy. He'd bet if he could find one of her precious etiquette books and looked up Post-coital Deportment, this wouldn't be what they advised.

Of course, she'd had a rough day. He slid down on his side, his head propped up in one hand, and reached out to finger an errant wave of hair away from her face. Damn, she looked like she'd gone ten rounds with an electric sander. He should have shaved.

He snorted, and the sound was loud in the warm, dark silence of the room. What the hell was he—the Mr. Manners poster boy? Like the worst thing either of them had to worry about was a few whisker burns. Most of the damage had been sustained when he'd thrown her to the ground this afternoon, anyway—and a bumped chin and a few bruises beat hell out of a bullet through her head.

The just-been-thoroughly-fucked look would fade. The consequences of his actions, on the other hand, could grow into something requiring a college fund. He couldn't believe he'd been so damn hot to get inside her, he hadn't even thought to put on a condom.

He'd never failed to protect a partner before—never. His father had hammered the necessity of safe, responsible sex into his head when he was a teenager, and of course later, when he was an adult with more obligations than he knew what to do with, he'd been very, very careful to be prepared. Always. Hell, the Boy Scouts of America had nothing on him. Seeing three girls through their hormone-packed, emotion-screaming teenage years, there'd been no way in hell he'd been willing to sow the seeds for another generation of Duprees.

So what had he done now? Maybe planted a mini Dupree in Juliet Astor Lowell, of all people. Jesus. He'd had no business sleeping with her at all, but he'd done it anyhow. He hadn't been able to help himself, dammit. And, God, it had been good.

Too good. He stared down at her kiss-swollen mouth, wild tangle of hair, and the soft skin of her throat and shoulders, and felt claws of panic scratching at his gut.

He had plans for the next couple of years, and they didn't include her. There was a host of women out there with his name written all over them, and *damned* if he was tying himself down to one big-eyed, long-necked Yankee princess, no matter how sweet she was in bed. If he was smart, in fact, he'd haul his sorry butt out of bed and hightail it back across the hall. Put a little professionalism back in their relationship. He pushed up against the mattress, ready to do just that, and then Juliet murmured in her sleep and rolled toward him. Her hand blindly felt across the mattress until it found his arm, then his chest, and she scooted nearer. A second later she'd curled up at his side with one of her knees drawn up perilously close to his pride and joy, and her nose pressed to his chest. Her breath fluttered warm against his nipple with each exhalation.

Well . . . shit. He eased onto his back and she immediately nestled closer, snaking an arm across his chest, her thigh across his legs, and squirming until her head found the hollow between his shoulder and chest. Then a sigh escaped her, and she went boneless and heavy, a warm, trusting weight pinning him in place.

Beau tucked his chin into his neck to look down at her. Okay, so he couldn't just dump her on her butt and go now—shaking her loose so he could slide on out the door wasn't great protocol. Besides, she'd had a hard day, and there was no sense rousting her from what looked to be the first solid sleep she'd had in days, if those shadows under her eyes were anything to go by. His fingers, which he'd kept carefully interlaced beneath his head, unlinked, and he reached down to cautiously skim his hands over her shoulders, along the arm across his chest. He finally settled with one hand on her hip and the other wrapped around her shoulder, and turned slightly to prop his chin on the top of her head. So, he'd stay tonight—he really didn't have a helluva lot of choice in the matter.

Come first thing in the morning, though, he was putting this relationship back on a professional footing where it belonged.

Juliet was surrounded by heat, and a far-off, rhythmic beat tha-thumped comfortingly beneath her ear. Yawning, she opened her eyes.

At first, all was darkness, and it wasn't until after

she'd spent several heartbeats straining to see that she realized the oppressive shadows were formed by her own hair. Sweeping it out of her face, she blinked against the bright wash of moonlight that poured through the jalousie and striped the bed with illumination.

Her new view was of a soft fan of black hair and a nickel-sized nipple leached of color in the moonlight. The memory of last night returned in a rush, and she realized she was in bed with Beau.

He was lying on his back, and she was on her side. They were intertwined, one of her legs between his and her arm thrown across his stomach, while his arms loosely encircled her, one hand lax on her hip, the other tangled in her hair.

She lay without moving, trying to sort through the multitude of sensations that coursed through her. She felt . . . good. Sort of boneless and satisfied. She also felt off balance—slightly mortified about her behavior last night, and yet powerful as a sex goddess. Before Beau had shown her otherwise, she'd never truly believed that pleasure on such a magnificent scale existed outside fiction.

There was a part of her, however, that felt just the teeniest bit inadequate about her participation in last night's events. She would love to deny it, but the truth was that Beau had done all the work. She'd mostly just hung on and moaned a lot.

Still . . .

It wasn't as if he'd appeared bothered by her lack of skill. He'd seemed, in fact, to enjoy himself immensely. But everything had moved so damn fast, and she hadn't really had a chance to explore the situation before it had slipped its bit and taken off on her like a runaway horse. She hadn't had a chance to explore him.

Most of the bedding had been kicked to the floor by their activity. Only the sheet remained, and it draped low across her waist, which put it slightly higher on Beau. Pleating its soft fabric between her fingers, she casually inched it toward her, exposing his long-boned foot, his hairy calf. Then, suddenly, the sheet was all hers, and moonlight limned him in silver.

"Oh." He was . . . *exquisite* didn't seem quite right—it wasn't a masculine enough word, and he was a study in masculinity. As curiosity stole her wits, her gaze moved lower, barely touching on the hard planes of his stomach and thighs before it zeroed in on his penis. She slithered down his side a bit to get a closer look.

She hadn't been exposed to very many of these, and had never had the freedom to actually study one up close this way. She scooted closer still, and Beau made a sleepy sound of protest as his hand slid away from her hair. She looked up at him, but he still slept soundly, and she returned her attention to his sex.

It was long and dark. Lying against his thigh in its present state, it looked a lot more harmless than it had felt last night. She slid her hand down his hard stomach. She combed her fingertips through the dense tangle of hair that surrounded his penis, ran her fingers along the inside of his thighs, rubbed the crease where they joined his torso. Her thumb inadvertently brushed the heavy sac of a testicle, and several times she came close to touching the penis itself, but shied away at the last minute. Then, beneath her fascinated gaze, it began to grow tumescent. It straightened away from his thigh in pulses, lifting until it pointed with military erectness up his abdomen. She looked up at his face again. Was he playing possum on her? No, he truly appeared to be asleep.

Her hand rubbed a circle on his stomach. Biting her lip, she reached up one questing finger. She traced the blunt, mushroom-shaped head of his penis down to the smooth ridge that delineated it from the shaft, and then ran her finger down to the thicket of hair at the base of his belly. His thighs sprawled restlessly, and she moved around to kneel between them, bending forward to look closely at this wonder.

Perhaps it was the warmth of her breath that caused it to bob upright. She wrapped her hand around its shaft with the intention of tucking it back down, but then didn't. Instead, she lightly squeezed. It felt incredibly soft-skinned on the surface, yet so rigid underneath. She moved her hand up, and then down. Beau made a sound and she raised her eyes to look up at him. He was staring down at her with sleepy eyes. The surprise of seeing him awake caused her hand to spasm involuntarily.

"Ah, God, Juliet." His voice was low and hoarse, his eyes incredibly hot. He stared at her mouth, which until that moment she hadn't realized was quite so close to his genitalia. "Kiss it," he growled.

"What?"

His hips moved a bit. "Please."

So she pursed her lips and kissed the tip, and he made a sound deep in his throat as if she were killing him. She liked that sound a lot and kissed his penis again, this time a little less primly. His hands came down and gathered all her hair to the side so he could watch her. She blushed, but opened her lips a little bit and sort of sipped the smooth-skinned head into her mouth.

His thighs went rigid, his heels dug into the bed, and he arched up off the mattress. It pushed him deeper into the heat of her mouth, and she wrapped her hand around the base of his shaft and tried synchronizing the various movements. Her technique seemed terribly inexpert to her, but he looked as if he'd died and gone to heaven, which gave her an incredible feeling of power. Oh, my. She liked this.

She wasn't the only one. Beau felt as if he'd awakened in the midst of his favorite wet dream. It was like being offered a slice of paradise right here on earth, and he loved everything about it— the sight, the feel, the look in those big gray eyes before she quickly lowered them. A corner of his mouth jerked up in amusement. He'd seen the knowledge of her dominion over him gleaming there, and that demure drop of her lashes didn't fool him one bit.

His breath grew choppy and his hips began to instigate their own fierce rhythm, and he tugged a little frantically on her hair in his hands.

She made a protesting sound in her throat, increasing the suction of everything that held him captive, and he closed his eyes for a second, so tempted. Then he pulled harder on her hair.

"You gotta stop, dawlin'," he panted. Then, "Oh, Christ, Juliet, that feels so—" He forced his hips back on the bed. "You gotta stop now, before you get a whole lot more than you bargained for. Come up here and kiss me."

She released him and sat back between his legs. Her little breasts rose and fell as she stared at him. Then, falling forward onto her hands, she began to pick her way over him on all fours like some sleek, overgrown cat. Her tongue came out and licked the corner of her mouth. "I enjoyed that, Beauregard."

"Yeah. I could tell." His laugh was a little short on breath, but he was probably lucky to be breathing at all. "Me, too." He reached for the back of her neck and hauled her forward.

If his kiss was a little out of control, well, a guy could only be so strong. He reached between them to cup her breast, and the deep sound of arousal she made caused his hips to surge up off the bed in primal search of the wet heat between her legs. He'd nearly gotten the two parts aligned when the bedside phone rang.

Juliet whimpered in distress. The phone rang again and he looked up at her. "You want to get that?"

"No." The denial sounded instinctive and definite, but then she blinked at him in indecision. "It's the middle of the night, though, and I've got a grandmother who's getting up there in years."

"Yeah. And I've got sisters."

She took a deep breath and let it out. "It might be an emergency."

"Shit." He reached out and ripped the receiver off its hook, passing it to Juliet.

"Hello?" She sounded so cool and efficient, she might have been in her office in the middle of the afternoon. Then her brows drew together. "Yes, he is. Please hold a moment." She handed the phone to him and reached for the sheet, wrapping it around herself as she climbed not only off of him, but off the bed as well.

Beau brought it to his ear. "Yeah. Dupree. This had better be good."

"Sorry, Beau," Luke said. "I tried your beeper first—the battery must be dead."

Or it could be that the beeper was still on the belt of his discarded pants, which he'd left in the other room. "What's up?"

"I just thought you'd wanna know—Bettencourt beeped me. He caught a new case, and from all indications, the Panty Snatcher's struck again. Looks like we've got us a new victim."

16

The pounding on Roxanne's door awakened her. Focusing bleary eyes on her bedside clock, she saw that the red numbers read 4:15. She pushed her hair from her eyes, stumbled out of bed, and reached for her robe. Who on earth came calling at this hour of the morning?

She recognized Beau's voice on the other side of the door before she even reached for the knob. "Yeah, well, humor me," he growled. "It's either this or leaving you to the tender mercies of Celeste Haynes. Those are your choices, Rosebud—live with 'em."

He thrust Juliet into the suite the moment Roxanne opened the door. "Hey, Miz Roxanne—gotta favor to ask."

"I'm sorry, Roxanne," Juliet murmured. "I tried to talk him out of disturbing you, but I think 'Bullheaded' is his middle name."

"Close," Beau agreed. "It's 'Prudence.' "

Snorts that were long on disbelief escaped both

women, and he treated them to a flash of his killer smile. Roxanne blinked to be on the receiving end of it. "Nice threads," he commented with a nod at her mustard satin robe and partially revealed fire-engine-red nightie. "I do admire a woman who's not afraid of a little color."

Then he wrapped his hand around the nape of Juliet's neck and hauled her up on her toes. Roxanne half expected him to kiss her, but he didn't—he just thrust his face aggressively close. "Stay put," he commanded roughly and set her free. Fingers flexing at his side, he stared at her, momentary indecision crossing his face. Then he stepped out into the hallway. He dragged his gaze from Juliet and gave Roxanne a fierce look. "Lock this door, and don't let anyone in. She stays here until I get back. We clear on that, Roxanne?"

"No problem."

"Good. There's an officer outside, and I'll be back as soon as I can, but it'll probably be a few hours." With a last glance at Juliet, he closed the door between them.

Roxanne locked it as she'd been instructed and turned to Juliet, looking at her closely for the first time. "Holy catfish," she murmured. "You've really gotta get that man to shave more often."

She half expected Juliet to politely freeze her out, but instead her boss touched careful fingertips to the skin around her mouth and said, "I'm not convinced it would help. You can practically see his beard grow." A soft smile curled her lips. "Rumor has it he had a five o'clock shadow way back in the sixth grade. Or so some woman in a bar told me.''

"Then perhaps you oughtta start keeping a supply of skim milk on hand to bathe the inflammation.''

Juliet raised an inquiring eyebrow, and Roxanne grinned at her. "Trust me, not only is it good for the waistline, it does wonders at soothing whisker rash. Unfortunately, I'm fresh out at the moment, but come into the bathroom with me—I do have some cortisone cream you can put on it. Where's the sergeant off to in such an all-fired hurry, anyway?''

As she listened to Juliet's explanation, Roxanne noticed that the whisker burn wasn't strictly confined to her boss's face, but she forbore mentioning it . . . or Juliet's wild, unbound hair or swollen mouth. And, walking a few paces behind her as she herded Juliet toward the bathroom, she noticed the languorousness of Juliet's normally faultless posture. Her lips curled up in a tiny smile of satisfaction.

Beau wasn't thrilled to hear the Panty Snatcher had racked up yet another tally on his growing list of victims . . . but he had to give the pervert credit for a superb sense of timing, at least.

Dammit, he'd gone to sleep swearing to put his relationship with Juliet back on a professional footing, but what had he done instead? Awakened with a raging hard-on and come *this close* to trying his hand at the Let's-Populate-the-World-with-Little-Duprees Lotto. Again. Shit. Why not just play

Russian roulette with his service pistol?

He was leaving Juliet Rose alone from this moment forward, and that's all there was to it. The
GTO's engine roared as Beau slammed down
through the gears in response to a red light that
loomed up ahead. He'd do his damn job, see to it
that she remained safe, and then send her the hell
on her way.

And his life could get back to normal.

The new victim lived above a gay bar in a
second-floor apartment whose only touch of elegance was one of the ubiquitous narrow,
lacy-looking, iron-trimmed galleries. It overlooked
one of the Quarter's busier streets.

Beau walked around to the courtyard and
climbed the stairs. It didn't take any detective work
to determine which apartment was hers: the door
stood wide open, light poured out onto the land-
ing, and several voices within seemed to all be talking at once.

It turned out there were fewer people inside than
the noise level indicated. There was a forensics cop
Beau assumed must be new, since he had never
met him, Bettencourt from his district, a bleached
blonde with tits out to here and a royally pissed-
off expression, and an elderly gray-haired black
woman. The latter sat next to the blonde on a
shabby couch, patting her hand consolingly. The
recipient of her tender ministrations looked as if
she could chew nails.

The forensics cop paused in his attempt to lift
prints off the doorknob and raised green eyes to
give Beau one of those suspicious who-the-hell-are-

you narrow-eyed once-overs that cops were so good at. The minute his gaze reached the badge Beau had hung around his neck, however, he went back to the business at hand. Beau approached the remaining three.

Bettencourt looked up. "Hey, Beau," he said.

"Hey. You mind if I sit in on your interview?"

"Not at all. Let me introduce you. This is Shirl Jahncke and her neighbor Ernestine Betts. Miz Jahncke, this here's Sergeant Dupree—he's worked a number of these cases."

The blonde glared up at him. "So you the one responsible for the sonzabitch what did this still bein' on the street? You better hope you catch him before I do, hawt, cuz I'm telling ya, I ever get my hands on the little asshole, I'll rip his friggin' head off and scream down his throat."

"Now, Shirl," soothed the black woman at her side. "You gotta calm down, girl."

"Calm down, my ass. I don't give a damn he made me take my clothes off—hell, I do that for a livin' anyway. But he took my brand-new Frederick's of Hollywood crotchless panties! I just got the damn things from the cat'log Monday, and they don't exactly give 'em away, I'll tell you what." She divided her displeasure impartially between Beau and Bettencourt. "From my lips to Satan's ear, I ever run into that prissy-voice sonzabitch again, you can forget playin' by the book. I won't bother callin' y'all—I'll drag that boy's sorry butt out to the bayou and let the gators have 'im."

"What do you mean by prissy-voiced?" Beau hunkered down on his heels in front of the couch.

"I mean, it was Miss this and Miss that, and would I 'kindly' hand over my panties, fer chrissake, like we was at some fuckin' tea party." She blew out an exasperated breath and glared at him. "Cap wasn't from my neighborhood, you can bet yer ass. Come to think of it, he dressed pretty damn dapper, too. Bet if he hadn't a had that fancy old gun I coulda took him easy."

"What color hair did he have?"

"Don' ax me—how the hell I know what color hair he's got? He was wearing one a those Carnival masks that covers the whole head, ya know what I'm sayin? That one with the big, hooked nose that looks like some sorta bird beak or sumpin'. And he stood in the shadows over there"—she indicated a spot to the left of the window, behind a freestanding lamp—"so I couldn't really see his eyes, neither. Freakin' pervert."

Beau spent another hour and a half interviewing the victim with his fellow detective and collecting information. Bettencourt introduced him to the new forensics cop as the man was closing up his case and preparing to go. His name was Chris Andersen, and although he had lifted several prints, his preliminary assessment was that they probably belonged to the victim or her friends. The theory would be proved or disproved back at the lab.

In the end, Beau was left with the same statistics he already knew—the Panty Snatcher's height and approximate weight and his preferred style of mask. It was damn little. The fact that the man was cultured was a new tidbit to throw into the mix, but then again, given the victim's place on the New

Orleans social scale and all things being relative, who was to say how cultured that actually made the guy? He'd have to question Josie Lee about that particular aspect.

The smell of the river wrapped around him when he stepped out into the pre-dawn air a while later. Hands in his pockets, he rocked back on his heels for a few minutes while he ran all the events of the night through his mind and tried to figure out what to do next.

Then he fished his keys from his pocket and headed for the car.

Josie Lee sauntered up behind Luke in the kitchen and wrapped her arms around his waist, flattening her breasts against the hard wall of his bare back as she snuggled up to him spoon-fashion. "Hey, Big Boy," she murmured, and then yawned lustily.

He craned his head around to grin at her over his shoulder. "You sound like a woman who didn't get enough sleep last night."

"I know." She dug her chin into his shoulder and smiled at him, feeling wonderful. "Don't you just hate it when things get in the way of your beauty rest?"

"Oh, absolutely," he agreed. "Beauty rest is right up there, toppin' my priorities." He boogied his muscular butt into her stomach, and then turned back around to peer into the pan on the stove. He turned off the burner. "Hush puppies are done. Grab yourself a plate."

"I'll just have some coffee."

"The hell you say." He turned to face her. "What bogus kinda way is that to start the day?" But the indignation faded and his eyes went heavy-lidded when he got his first full look at her. "God Almighty, you look good," he said hoarsely and reached for her.

He'd lifted her onto the countertop and had his face buried in the skimpy ribbed-cotton tank top that covered her breasts when Beau walked in.

It was a toss-up who was most surprised. All three of them froze for an instant, Josie Lee on the counter, Luke hunched over her with his chin turned to look over his shoulder, and Beau in the doorway. Then Josie Lee's heartbeat began to pound. With a wordless roar, Beau charged across the room, and Luke straightened, turning to face him.

"I know what this looks like," he said, hands spread wide of his body, "but—"

Beau's fist smashed into his mouth.

Josie Lee screamed and scrambled down from the counter as her lover lurched back several steps. Luke touched the back of his hand to his mouth, and saw a smear of blood on it when he lifted it away. "Well, fuck," he murmured. Then he took a step toward Beau with the express purpose of returning the favor.

Luke drew up short as he saw Josie Lee grab the frying pan off the burner and dump the contents on the counter in one motion, then swing its bottom at her brother's butt. It connected soundly.

"Sonovabitch, Jose!" Grabbing at his buttock, Beau pivoted to face his sister, and Josie Lee reversed her swing and brought the flat of the pan crashing into his gut with enough force to knock the wind out of him.

"*You hit him!*" she snarled. "You keep your filthy hands off him, Beauregard Butler Dupree, or I'll make you rue the day you were born!" Clearly beside herself with fury, her arm came up over her head, and Luke, fearing for Beau's head, waded in and plucked her up, swinging her out of striking range. Her lush breasts lifted and fell against his constraining arm as she panted for breath, and she knuckled a black curl out of her eyes, glowering at her brother.

"Jesus, Josie Lee, the freakin' pan was *hot*." Beau lifted his shirt and stared down at the large, slightly reddened blotch on his stomach.

"Good! How *dare* you punch Luke and treat me like I'm twelve years old! When are you going to get a *clue*, Beauregard?" She thrust out an arm, pointing an imperious finger at the door. "You're not welcome here. I want you to leave."

Beau opened his mouth, but then shut it again. He narrowed his eyes at Luke and said, "Don't even think this is the end of it, Bud. You and I'll talk again when she's not armed."

Then he turned and stalked out of the room, and Luke set Josie Lee back on her feet. He gently pried the frying pan from her fingers and set it on the stove next to their discarded breakfast. "That was some defense, Baby Girl," he said and reached out to touch her hot cheek. "Remind me never to piss you off in the kitchen."

* * *

Beau felt like kicking down Roxanne's door, but he contented himself with one brisk knock before he stuffed his hands in his pockets and stepped back out of temptation's range.

It had taken him a while to drive from the By-water to the Garden District; then he'd spent a good fifteen minutes grilling the rookie who'd kept an eye on the front entrance while he was gone, to determine that no one had tried to get in and that the other two entrances were still securely locked with no signs of tampering. Finally, he'd stopped by his hotel room long enough to shower, shave, and change into clean clothes.

And yet none of that had provided nearly enough time to quell the frustration that filled him, the livid anger and sense of betrayal he was forced to swallow whole. He didn't have time to worry about his personal problems now, though; he still had a job to do. Taking a deep breath, he hunched his shoulders, stretched out the tense muscles in his neck, and vowed that he would, by God, do one thing right today. He'd behave professionally with Juliet if it was the last thing he did . . . and think about Josie Lee later.

But in the back of his head, an enraged voice kept repeating, *I can't believe my partner, my good and true friend, is screwing my baby sister!* And he wanted to hit something.

He gave the door another rap instead. A moment later, Roxanne's voice asked who was there.

"It's Dupree. Open up."

She opened the door and blinked up at him. "Sergeant, hello. I'm sorry . . . have you been out here long? I fell asleep and only now heard your knock."

"I just got here, Miz Roxanne. Y'wanna get Juliet for me?"

"Yes, sure. Come in." Leaving the door open, she turned and padded back into the salon. By the time Beau sauntered into the room in her wake, she was in the bedroom. He heard her enter the bathroom, then she dashed back out again, her face several shades paler, the freckles across the bridge of her nose standing out like a sprinkling of ginger on skim milk. "She's gone."

Beau snarled an obscenity and ran from the room. He skidded to a halt in front of Juliet's suite a moment later and pounded on the door. Glancing over his shoulder at Roxanne, who had followed him, he demanded, "Do you have a key to this room?"

"No."

"Shit." Drawing his gun, he took a step back, prepared to kick the door in.

Then it opened and Juliet stood there, her silk robe plastered damply to her body in several spots, water glistening on her throat and bare feet, a towel wrapped turban-style around her hair. She looked from the gun in his hand to his face. "Beau? Is something wrong?"

"Oh, boy," he heard Roxanne murmur, and he felt rather than saw her leave, presumably to return to her room.

"Wrong?" he said softly and, holstering his weapon, advanced on Juliet. Something must have shown in his face, for she took a step back for every one he took forward until they were in the salon. "What could possibly be wrong?"

She stopped in the middle of the room. "You're angry."

"You rich girls are an astute lot, aren't you?"

That put a poker up her backside. Lifting her chin, she gave him one of those you're-the-shit-on-the-bottom-of-my-shoe looks she was so good at. But she didn't say a thing—which for some reason was like throwing gasoline on the fire.

Beau reined himself in, holding his temper on a very short leash. "Did I or did I not tell you to stay put?" he demanded through gritted teeth.

She raised a supercilious eyebrow.

She might as well have said, *Bite me, peon*, and Beau saw red. But he was in control here—he was cool. "You think I issue orders just to hear myself speak, Rosebud? We've had too many incidents involving your safety already, and when I tell you to stay somewhere, I do it for a damn good reason."

"I needed a shower."

"And Roxanne's was out of order?"

"I wanted my own shower."

"So you risked your safety because—let me take a wild stab here—Grandma taught you never to use somebody else's bar of soap, am I right?"

He could tell from her expression he'd hit the nail squarely on the head. She thrust out her elegantly chiseled chin. "For heaven's sake, Beau, I was careful. I made sure no one was around when I left Roxanne's room and I locked my door securely behind me."

His ire cranked another degree higher and he

took a step toward her. "And if someone had gotten in here anyway, you planned to do what, exactly—freeze him with your good manners?"

She stepped back, chin still high. "I'm perfectly capable of handling myself."

He stepped forward. "Oh, yeah, I can see you're all kinds of courageous, all right. A regular little tough guy." Disregarding the voice in his head that whispered his fury was disproportionate to her crime, he stalked her as she backed across the room. The nervousness that sprang into her eyes gave him a grim satisfaction. "Forget the fact that whoever wants you hurt is most likely armed. For argument's sake we'll say that this time he isn't."

Her back hit a wall, and he slapped his hands on either side of her shoulders, pinning her in place. He leaned in close. "Let's just suppose for a minute that I'm him. The Boogeyman. It wasn't exactly strenuous backing you into a corner, sugar." His finger trailed down the side of her neck, over her collarbone, and along the edge of the robe's neckline to the place where it overlapped between her breasts. He crooked his finger beneath the fabric and tugged the opening wider. "And once he's got you in a corner, in a room all alone, he can do any damn thing he wants to you, without a soul to stop him."

Her breasts rose and fell more quickly beneath the silky material, but she met his eyes squarely. "But no one did do any of that. Only you. And I'm not afraid of you."

"You should be, angel face," he insisted softly. He pulled on the robe to completely expose one breast. "You should be very, very afraid of me." And his hand slid onto her breast as he lowered his mouth against the erotic fullness of hers.

It wasn't a gentle wooing—he used his teeth, the strength of his mouth—but she didn't fight him. She kissed him back hard, and just that fast he was out of control. He was aware of those gorgeous lips cushioning his, and her taste, hot and sweet, on his tongue. Then it was all flashing impressions—of him sucking her breast into his mouth, and her back arching to give him more; of her hands first gripping his hair, then moving down to his fly to fight with the zipper while one of her thighs rubbed up his leg to hook over his hip. Next thing he knew, his pants were pushed down far enough to free him and he'd lifted her against the wall and was starting to push into her.

"Wait, wait," she whispered and stiff-armed him away with her hands on his shoulders. "We've got to be smart this time, Beau. We need to use a condom."

He froze, his chest rising and falling as he struggled for breath. "Oh, God, Juliet. I don't have one. Please, dawlin'. I'll pull out. . . ."

"I've got one. Roxanne gave me a handful. She said I was probably going to need them more than she."

"Where?" When she told him, he lifted her off him and set her on her feet. He kicked off his pants. "Don't budge."

It was probably the fastest he'd ever moved in his life, and he was back in a moment, appropriately attired for the occasion, to find her still leaning against the wall, her hair towel on the floor at her feet, her silky robe hanging open. He picked her up and sheathed himself in one smooth movement, pinning her to the wall. Then, eyes closed to fully appreciate the feel of her surrounding him, he held himself very still. "Ah, Gawd—*there*," he breathed reverently. "It's been such a shitty night and you feel so good."

She made a restless, yearning movement. "Beau?"

He began to move slowly, languorously, wanting to draw this out and make it last. For all the stimulation, there was something almost . . . spiritual . . . about being inside her. That was crazy—he knew it was crazy—and most likely just the mood he was in. Yet being with her like this washed away the frustration of the preceding hours, if only for a little while. So he slid into her inch by inch, pulled back until he was nearly out, then slowly plunged deep again.

His reward was the yearning little noises she made. She framed his cheeks in her hands and kissed him deeply. Moments later she pulled back, panting. "Oh, Lord, Beau. Please." Her thumbs rubbed restlessly back and forth along his cheeks, and her gaze suddenly focused on his face. "Oh. It's *smooth*. I didn't know it was possible for your jaw to feel this way." Then she arched her back, thrusting her breasts against his chest. Her hands lowered to grip his shoulders and she attempted to move against him, but being sandwiched against the wall severely constrained her range of movement. "Please, Beau, a little harder?"

"Tell me what you want, Juliet Rose. Talk dirty to me."

She blinked. Her gray eyes were heavy-lidded and seemed to have difficulty focusing on him. "What?"

"Talk dirty to me and I'll give you this"—he thrust deep—"a little harder."

She looked scandalized. "I can't do that!"

"As you wish." His hips ceased to thrust and withdraw. Instead, like stirring molasses, they instigated the slowest, faintest of oscillations. He bent his head to her breast.

Juliet withstood it for several moments. Then she breathed a command in his ear with a blunt Anglo-Saxon term she'd probably never used in her life. His hips picked up a little speed, and she said it again . . . and then again, and again, and again, as he gave her what she wanted and began to thrust into her. His hips picked up speed and force, and he drove her right off the edge of the world, reveling in her little screech of satisfaction. Beau jerked convulsively as he followed her into oblivion.

They were both limp and covered in sweat, and Beau sank to his knees with her draped astride him. He felt boneless and utterly free of tension.

Juliet raised her head up off his shoulder and stared down at him. Her hair was a wild tangle of half dried, out-of-control waves, and she thrust a hank of it out of her face. "We seem to keep doing this, Beauregard." Blushing, she searched his face as if looking for something. "I can't believe you made me say that."

He couldn't, either, now that he thought about

it, but he said somewhat defensively, "You liked it."

She gave a delicate shrug of one silk-covered shoulder. "Maybe. Maybe not. But it certainly points up the differences in our experience. And in regards to that—particularly your propensity for unprotected sex—I really need to know about your health record."

17

Juliet was already feeling mortified by how quickly she'd succumbed to Beau's demand for sex talk. The last thing she needed was to have him stare at her openmouthed and then throw back his head and roar with laughter. She got her feet under her and slapped her hands to his shoulders to shove herself upright, face flaming anew as she felt him slide out of her.

He hooked an arm around her waist and pulled her back down. One of her heels skidded out from under her and she landed in a sprawl astride his thighs.

"I'm sorry," he said. He made an obvious attempt to control his mirth. "It's just—given my history—it really is pretty funny. Listen—"

"I'm so glad you're amused," she said icily. "I'm sure—given your history—I'll laugh all the way to the clinic. That is, if you don't have something truly nasty to share."

"No, dawlin', that's just it." He thrust his long

fingers through his hair. "I'm clean as a whistle—I swear it. God, I really hate to admit this, because your view of me as some red-hot sex pistol is the greatest stroke my ego's ever gotten. Truth is, though, honey chile, I've been so busy raisin' my sisters the past ten years that my sex life has been all but nonexistent. And the little I have gotten, it's been Rubbers 'R' Us all the way." He stroked his free hand up and down her thigh. "You're the only one who's ever gotten me so hot I've forgotten to suit up."

"Do I have 'Gullible' stamped on my forehead, Beauregard?" She felt betrayed that he valued her intelligence so little he'd try to fob her off with such a patent cock-and-bull story. She made her voice particularly smarmy when she lowered it to approximate his and said, "*Trust me, baby, you're the one.*" Her voice returned to normal. "You're forgetting I've seen you in action. Don't mistake relative inexperience with idiocy."

"I'm not messin' with you, Rosebud. It's the honest-to-God truth. Call my sisters; call Luke." His face suddenly went expressionless and Juliet looked at him suspiciously.

"What?"

"Maybe Luke's not the one to call. He's a little busy right now, screwing my baby sister."

"Excuse me?" The bitterness in his voice caused Juliet to look more closely into his face. Something there made her decide that perhaps he wasn't jerking her around after all.

"I stopped home on my way back here this morning to talk to Josie Lee about something that came up on that case I went out on." An expression Juliet couldn't interpret flitted across his face and then was gone. "I found her and Luke in a . . . compromising position, shall we say?"

Juliet felt the tension in his body. "And this is not a good thing, I take it."

"She's my baby sister!"

"But she's not a baby. I took her to be in her early twenties. Was I mistaken?"

He shrugged sullenly. "She's twenty-two." Underlying the surface cool and the flickering glimpses of anger was something that looked suspiciously like . . . hurt.

Juliet knew she was in big trouble when that fleeting sign of vulnerability got to her. Oh, God, she had a bad, bad feeling she was falling in love with him. "Do you suspect Luke is coercing your sister in some way?"

The muscles in Beau's thighs sprang into prominent relief beneath her legs and he surged to his feet, a forearm scooped under her bottom to hold her in place. Juliet emitted an undignified sound, like a young girl startled by a mouse. She grabbed at his shoulders and clasped his hips with her legs. He walked a few steps over to the chair and collapsed in it, rearranging her legs to tuck them alongside his. Then he shook his head. "No. I'd give a month's pay to be able to say otherwise, but when I popped him, Jose attacked me with a hot frying pan."

"You *hit* him?"

He looked at her as if she'd said something inexpressibly stupid. "Hell, yes, I hit him—haven't you been paying attention? I walked in to find him putting the moves to my little sister, and I did what a brother's supposed to do: I tried to rearrange his face. And no good deed ever goes unpunished, let me tell you." He yanked up his shirt. "Look what she did to me: *this* is what a guy gets for his efforts."

There was a dull red patch on his hard stomach, but that wasn't what Juliet found herself staring at. Except for the condom, Beau was naked from the waist down, and she straddled his lap wearing only her robe, which hung open. Face hot, she tugged it together and tied the belt.

He followed her gaze and removed the condom. Tying it off, he tossed it into a nearby wastebasket, then grasped one corner of her robe's hem and draped it over his loins. "Better?" He cocked an eyebrow at her. "Never let it be said Beau Dupree is too uncivilized to follow Miss Manners's rules of postcoital etiquette."

"Good lord, she wrote a book about that, too? That's one Grandmother never added to my must-read list."

He gave her a crooked grin, but it faded almost immediately. "What am I going to do about Josie Lee, Juliet? It's making me crazy."

"I can see that, but I'm not certain I understand why, precisely," she admitted cautiously. "I mean, don't you think it's something of a double standard to say it's all right for you and me to make love, but your adult sister and her partner of choice ought to remain chaste?" Knowing now that Beau wasn't entirely rational where his youngest sister's love life was concerned, she braced herself for his anger.

But he surprised her. "I don't know—maybe. Hell, on an intellectual level, I'm sure you're right. But on a gut level, I wanna stomp Luke right into the ground and lock Josie Lee in her room until she's thirty." He ground the heels of his hands against the ridge of his brow as if to contain a headache trying to pound its way free. Then, blowing out a deep breath, he dropped his hands to Juliet's thighs and looked up at her.

"Maybe it's because Jose was only twelve when Mom and Dad died. Of the four of us, it hit her the hardest—I mean, that's an age when a girl really needs her mama the most, don't you think? But all she had for was me, and I was twenty-four when I inherited the job, so who the hell knows how effective I was? I always felt the most inadequate with her, and some things never change. Hell, five, six weeks ago I couldn't even keep her safe from the damn Panty Snatcher. She refuses to admit that her encounter with that pervert was the least bit traumatic, but I know damn well it had to have been." His black brows gathered above his nose, making him look thunderous. "And now here's good ol' Luke stickin' it to her."

"Oh, there's a lovely way of putting it."

"Yeah, well, I'm sorry, but that's the way it feels, okay?" He glared at her, his hands tense on her legs. "Christ, Juliet, she tossed me out of my own house, just because I got a little physical with her precious Luke—that Judas bastard."

Ah, now she got it. "It sounds as if you've got a case of separation anxiety."

"Say what?"

"Separation anxiety. Your baby's growing up, leaving the nest and depending on another man instead of you, and it hurts." She smiled at him and reached out to run her fingertips over his smoothly shaven jaw. "It's rather sweet, actually." Dangerously sweet: it caused a serious meltdown of all the guards she'd erected to hold his cataclysmic effect on her at bay.

"It's *bullshit,* is what it is." He looked at her as if she'd somehow insulted his masculinity. "I don't have any damn separation anxiety—hell, I've been counting the days till she moves out." Giving her a deliberately sexual look, he undid the knot belting her robe closed. He pulled the two overlapping sides wide, exposing her and himself in one swift movement. "Sweet, my ass. Where the hell are those condoms—I'll show you sweet."

Beau pushed the bathroom door closed with his foot, shutting out the sight of Juliet's bed with Juliet in it. He looked at his face in the mirror. Just when a guy thought he was standing on firm ground . . .

What the hell had happened to his life? One minute everything was running smoothly, and in the next breath he was ass-deep in alligators again.

He'd thought woman trouble was finally a thing of the past, that the only problem he was going to have on the female front from now on was deciding who to call up for a hot date each night. But here he was with un uptight Yankee he couldn't keep his hands off of, and a little sister who'd just as soon smack him upside the head with a frying pan as look at him.

Shit.

He slapped on the cold water faucet. He knew from experience there was only one thing to do when too many women and all their attendant problems started taking over a guy's every waking moment. Lose himself in work.

He splashed water against his face, turned off the tap, and reached for a towel. After a brief examination of his teeth in the mirror, he found Juliet's toothpaste, squeezed out a dab on his finger, and did what he could with it.

The truth was, he hadn't been taking care of business for the past week or so—not in any manner he recognized, anyhow. But that was about to change. He was through being a babysitter, no matter how sweet the babe. He was a cop, dammit. It was time to start acting like one again.

He strode into the bedroom. Juliet sat on the far side of the bed with her back to him. She had a long, narrow back, and the delicate knobs of her vertebrae pushed against tawny skin as she bent forward, sweeping the floor with her hand as if in search of something. The bumps retracted into the smooth groove of her spine as she straightened up and twisted around to look at him over her shoulder. Then she rose to her feet, pulling the sheet off the bed and wrapping it around herself as she turned to face him. Gentle color bloomed in her cheeks.

"You hiding something I haven't already seen, angel face?"

Her chin angled up regally. "Not all of us have the great good fortune to be as comfortable in our nudity as you are, Beauregard."

He glanced down and saw that things were, indeed, dangling out there at half mast for all the world to admire, and he looked back at her and grinned. "My clothes are out in the other room. You want me to put them on?"

"Only if you have an urge to accomplish anything today."

She had a point there, and he strolled into the other room and scouted around until he found his slacks. Sliding them on, he gingerly zipped up and looked over to see that Juliet had trailed him as far as the doorway. "What were you looking for on the floor just now?"

"My panties."

He smiled reminiscently. "You weren't wearing any when I showed up, sugar."

"Yes, so I recalled."

Oh, man, she was at her primmest best, and he wanted like crazy to snag that sheet out of her hands and muss her up until all the starch left her backbone.

But he was going to have to backburner the impulse. He straightened. "Get dressed, Juliet Rose. I've got a proposition to put to you."

She arched one well-groomed brow at him as if she could just imagine what sort of lurid offer would come out of his mouth. But she didn't argue.

Turning on her heel, she disappeared back into the bedroom.

She was back out in under ten minutes, looking once again like the very proper Ms. Astor Lowell, with her hair ruthlessly controlled in a sophisticated French twist, and those voluptuous touches on her spare body once more hidden behind a floaty, floral dress. Only her long, bare feet with their siren polish on the toenails, the come-on-and-kiss-me lipstick on her generous lips, and the still-healing scrape on her chin belied the prim image. Beau directed her to a chair before he could give in to his baser instincts to go mining for the sensuous woman he knew lurked beneath all that spit and polish. He squatted down in front of her.

"Okay, listen. It's occurred to me that I've been reactive rather than proactive when it comes to your case. And it's time for that to change."

"Beau, you've dragged me all over the French Quarter from day one. That's hardly what I'd call reactive."

"That was in regards to the Panty Snatcher case, not yours," he disagreed. "Although, now that an antique gun has surfaced in yours, too, I suppose a case could be made for your theory." He shook his head. "But that's neither here nor there, dawlin'. The fact is, it's time for me to do what I do best."

She glanced toward the bedroom and he laughed. "No, not that. Detective work."

"Oh." Her color deepened. Then she laughed— a laugh so surprisingly bawdy it left him blinking. "Then you must be very good indeed."

He gripped the arms of her chair. "You make it damn hard not to take you back in there and give you another taste of my second best talent." He pushed himself to his feet. "But I'm a man on a mission. How would you like to play cop for a while?"

"Me?"

"Well, not actually do cop work, but hang with me while I do the job I was trained for."

"Beau, I've got a hotel that's only days away from the pre-opening cocktail party—"

"I know you do, Rosebud. That's where my proposition comes in. I don't like the way things have been shaking down around you lately, and the idea of leaving you unprotected while I track down the source of these attacks strikes me as counterproductive. So how about we compromise? How 'bout we give the mornings over to your work, the afternoons to running down computer files or paperwork on old cases that involve antique guns, and the evenings to tracking down Lydet, who can conceivably help us kill two birds with one stone?"

"Sounds busy."

"But productive. You game?"

"Yes."

"Good girl." He leaned forward and gave her a brief, hard kiss. He was disinclined to pull back, which gave him a flicker of unease. But hell, Juliet's time in New Orleans was finite—there was no reason he couldn't enjoy this relationship as long as she was around. There'd be time enough to fall back on his long-anticipated Plan A once she returned to the cold North. And if the thought of her back up in Boston with her stuffy family gave him a pang, well, it was probably just hunger pains.

It was way past breakfast time, after all.

"You been avoiding me, Baby Girl?"

Josie Lee looked up from her computer to see Luke standing in the doorway. She glanced over at the administrative assistant whom she assisted and then back at Luke. "Sergeant Gardner, this really isn't an appropriate—"

He reached over her desk and wrapped his hand around her upper arm. Turning his head, he looked at the AA. "Excuse us a moment, won't you, Constance?" It was clearly less a request than a demand.

Constance Warner gave him a half-smile. "Certainly. In fact, why don't you take your break now, Josie Lee. You've been working straight since lunch."

Josie Lee grimaced wryly. "Thank you. I won't be long." She allowed Luke to drag her out of the office, but extricated her arm once they had pushed through the front door and out onto the square marble porch way. She faced him coolly. "Was it really necessary to do that in front of my boss, Luke?"

"Probably not." He slicked his hand over his smooth-shaven head and stared at her in frustration. "But I get the impression you're avoiding me, Jose, and it's scarin' the shit out of me."

She looked at him standing there, hand wrapped around the base of his skull, his elbow jutting toward the sky, and her heart contracted. Her priorities also reestablished themselves. "I'm sorry," she said. "I have been avoiding you, and it's so stupid that I don't even know if I can explain the reason why, exactly." She brushed her fingers down his triceps, and he dropped his arm to his side. "This is going to sound crazy," she said, "because I know Beau was dead wrong this morning. But somehow, once I cooled down, I couldn't stop thinking about the look on his face when I kicked him out of the house, and I feel . . ." She blew an exasperated breath. "Oh, God, this is so absurd."

"You feel guilty," Luke said.

"Yes! Do you feel it, too?"

"Oh, yeah." His gaze pinned her in place. "But not enough to give you up."

"You'd *better* not—that's the last thing I want." She laughed then, but the sound wasn't filled with humor. "What I want, I suppose, is to have it all, and I want it to be *easy*. But I don't think I can have it both ways." She stepped closer. "If it comes down to a choice, though, Luke, I choose you. I do. I just got sidetracked for a while this afternoon."

"You're not going to have to choose between us, baby. It will never come to that. Beau'll come around—I promise." He stepped back into the shadow of one of the Doric columns and pulled her into his arms. "But you gotta promise me something: Don't go hiding from me if you've got a problem. It makes me kinda crazy." His arms tightened and he ground his chin into the top of her head. "Jesus, Jose, how'd you get to be so important to me so fast?"

"Does it seem fast to you? That's funny—I feel like I've been waiting for you all my life." She squeezed him hard. "And you're officially mine now, you know. You all but made a declaration of intent in front of Constance." Tipping back her head, she grinned up at him. "It'll be all over the building by quittin' time."

18

Juliet was sleeping soundly when the beeping started. It was an intermittent but persistent noise that was fortunately soft enough to ignore. Exhaustion sucked at the edges of her consciousness like an undertow in a black sea, and she was on the verge of being dragged back into the depths of oblivion when Beau stirred. With a quiet oath, he eased her off his chest and rolled toward the edge of the bed, and when the beeps abruptly ceased, Juliet deduced in a far corner of her mind that the sound must have originated in his beeper.

She was already drifting toward unconsciousness again when he began punching out numbers on the telephone. The first word out of his mouth, however, startled her awake.

"Anabel? This had better be good, sugar—it's one o'clock in the morning." He listened a moment and then said with low-pitched incredulousness, "There's a *what* in the bedroom? For Gawd's sake, dawlin' I'm working here—get a broom! What?

251

No, Ana, take care of it yourself. Yes, you can. Then close the damn door and sleep on the couch . . . All right . . . all *right*! Take a deep breath and settle down. Just keep the door closed until I get there—I'm on my way."

By the time he'd rolled to sit on the edge of the bed, Juliet had pushed the hair out of her eyes and propped herself up on one elbow. His tone had been laced with the familiarity of a long-term relationship, and an awful thought suddenly occurred to her.

"Are you married, Beauregard?" Her voice emerged all froggy-sounding, and she cleared her throat, moving to sit against the headboard, the sheet pulled up and tucked beneath her armpits.

He made a rude noise as he twisted around to face her. "No, I'm not married—and don't go thinking that's gonna change in the near future, either. I've been up to my armpits in female problems since I was twenty-four years old, and it's way past time it stopped." He climbed to his feet and pulled on a pair of pants.

"It wouldn't occur to you, I suppose, that it's a bit insulting to assume I have designs on your bachelorhood simply because we've slept together a couple of times." She kept her tone mild—and in truth, at the moment she was simply too tired to take offense.

"Hey, what can I say—I lost my head. I know a rich girl like you has no long-term need of a guy like me." And for some reason that didn't seem to set well with him, either. He scowled down at her.

"Get dressed. We gotta go rout a baby 'gator from a bedroom."

She looked at him blankly and he added ironically, "Welcome to my world."

Ten minutes later they were climbing into his car. Beau fired up the engine, and Juliet buckled her seatbelt and leaned back in her seat, politely covering her yawn.

They'd been working flat-out from daybreak to nearly midnight the past few days, and although she had questions she would love to have answered—such as exactly where they were headed—she couldn't quite wake up enough to form the words. The familiar rumble of the GTO's engine lulled her, the soft worn leather of the wide bucket seat embraced her, and the next thing she knew, Beau had parked the car on a quiet side street somewhere and was squatting outside the opened passenger door, reaching in to massage her shoulder where it curved to meet her neck.

"Wake up, Juliet Rose," he murmured. "Come on, sugar, we're here."

"Where's here?" She unlatched her seatbelt and swung one leg out of the car. A big yawn caught her unaware and she gave vent to it, not bothering to cover her mouth as she stretched luxuriously. Climbing to her feet, she leaned sleepily against Beau. "Who calls you at one in the morning to come clear her bedroom of alligators?"

"My sister Anabel." He slammed the car door behind her and escorted her into a courtyard. "She thinks I was put on earth expressly to take care of any little inconvenience life puts in her path."

"I would think an alligator in the bedroom is a rather large inconvenience."

Beau shrugged. "Whatever." He stopped in front of a royal blue door and rapped on it.

It was immediately opened by a tiny brunette. "Thank God you're here, Beau." She blinked in surprise at Juliet. "Oh! Hello."

"Hi."

"Juliet, this is my sister Anabel. Anabel, Juliet Astor Lowell."

"Oh?" Anabel's dark brow lifted as if wondering where this unexpected companion fit in her brother's life. Then her eyes rounded in comprehension. "Oh! The lady you've been assigned to protect!"

Beau pushed Juliet over the threshold and stepped in behind her, closing the door. "I told you I was on the job, Ana. When you rousted me, you rousted her. You better at least have some of your pralines to offer us."

He sounded grumpy, but Juliet was charmed by the whole situation. She tried to imagine Father climbing out of bed and driving halfway across town to come to her rescue . . . but simply couldn't. He'd probably hire someone to address the problem.

"I'll need a pillowcase," Beau said, and when Anabel had fetched it for him, he commanded, "Y'all go in the kitchen while I deal with this." Then he bent his head to his sister's. "You okay, Anabel? How the hell did a 'gator get in your room, anyhow?"

"All I can think of is that it must've come up

through the plumbing in the bathroom. Either that or it got in earlier when I had the front door open." She shuddered, and touched her brother's stubble-roughened cheek. "Thanks for coming, Beau. I'm sorry I got you out of bed, but I sorta freaked when I saw that thing in the dark, movin' across my floor."

"Yeah, yeah, yeah," he groused, but hauled her in for a brief, commiserating hug. Setting her free, he opened the bedroom door a crack, slid into the room, and pulled the door closed behind him.

Anabel turned to Juliet. "I'm so sorry to drag you out of bed before the crack of dawn. You must think I'm crazy."

"Actually, I was thinking you're rather lucky to have somebody who'll come running when things go bump in the night."

"Yeah, Beau's our Galahad—bad temper, rusty armor, and all." Anabel's grin was full of affection. "C'mon into the kitchen—let me fix you a cup of tea."

They drank tea and ate Anabel's homemade pralines, and exchanged desultory conversation in counterpoint to the occasional thumps and curses coming from the bedroom. Beau emerged a short while later, the pillowcase in his fist swinging gently, weighted now at the bottom. The expediency and prowess with which he'd accomplished his mission made Juliet think of other things he did with the same exceptional skill. He looked so intensely cocky as he walked up the short hallway, so dark and masculine and full of himself, that Ju-

liet felt her cheeks heat and her bare toes curl in
her sandals.

He grinned as he entered the kitchen and victo-
riously thrust the pillowcase aloft, then he
thumped his other fist against his chest. Anabel
laughed and jumped up to congratulate him. Juliet
sat nailed to her seat, immobilized by a shocking
lust for ownership.

She'd never yearned to possess a man in her life,
but she wanted to possess Beau Dupree. Worse, she
wanted to *belong* to him, to be one of the chosen
few for whom he'd get out of bed in the middle of
the night to go rescue. Watching him, she would
have liked nothing better than to believe it was
only his audacity, merely a case of an exceptionally
charismatic sex appeal, that drew her in.

But it was more than that, and she knew it. Way
more. It was the endearing way he looked out for
his sisters, the way he concentrated all his attention
when he made love to *her*, his obvious love for his
job, his humor—oh, God, she had to quit dancing
around it the way she'd been doing the past couple
of days and just come right out and admit it. She
was in love with him.

Beau pulled out a chair and swung it around,
straddling it backward. He dropped the pillowcase
at his feet and it rustled furiously. Anabel jumped
back with a screech, and he gave her a crooked
smile.

"It's okay—I tied it off at the top. He's not gonna
get out." He slapped his palms down on the tabletop. "Where's my reward?"

Anabel pushed the plate of pralines across to

him. "You want coffee to go with that or milk?"

"Milk." He looked across at Juliet. "So how 'bout you, Rosebud—aren't you gonna tell me what a hero I am?" He crooked his fingers at her in a gimme gesture. "C'mon, I can take it."

Feeling uncharacteristically flustered, she smoothed back her flyaway hair and unthinkingly twisted it into a French roll. Then, scraping together every bit of composure at her disposal, she batted her eyes at him. "Oh, Beauregard. You're so big and strong."

"Damn straight, sugar. Just wrestled me an alligator." But the cocky grin fell off his face and something dark and intense replaced it as he stared at her neck.

"What?" She straightened self-consciously in her seat, her hands dropping away from her hair. It slid down her neck to cover whatever had captured his attention.

But not quite soon enough, apparently. Anabel suddenly sat forward and reached out a finger to sweep Juliet's hair away from her neck. She looked at the exposed skin for a moment, then turned incredulous eyes on her brother. Letting Juliet's hair drop, she pointed the finger accusingly at Beau.

Juliet's hand went to her throat, but she didn't feel anything different. "What?" she demanded. "What are you two looking at?"

Beau crossed his arms over his chest and directed cool defiance at his sister. She shook her finger at him like an incensed mother. Juliet reached for her purse, determined to find her small pocket mirror and see exactly what it was that was drawing so much attention.

"Beauregard Butler Dupree!" Anabel exclaimed. "When you said that rousting you meant rousting her, I thought you meant from another room." She shook her finger beneath his nose and demanded, "But you're the one responsible for all these love bites on her neck, aren't you?"

Juliet quit looking for her mirror and slapped a hand to the side of her throat. She stared at the siblings in horror. "For the *what*?"

Celeste poked her head into Juliet's office. "Hello, dear," she said, ignoring the sergeant sprawled out in a chair in the corner. She was perfectly aware that after one brief, penetrating look at her, he went back to reading his computer printout, but she chose to concentrate on Juliet.

She was a bit taken aback to see Juliet's hair down. She'd never before seen it thus, and it was quite . . . unruly. Rather common-looking, actually, the way the thick waves bobbed and swayed with every motion of the young woman's head. Juliet looked up, and Celeste tore her eyes away from the uncivilized coiffure to focus instead on Juliet's eyes, which at least were appropriately neutral in color— even if they did have that flamboyant charcoal rim around the iris. "I stopped by to discuss the cocktail party Friday night," she said primly. "I thought it would be helpful if I knew the agenda."

Juliet smiled warmly. "Please, come in. I know Roxanne put one here somewhere." She riffled through a stack of papers on her desk.

Celeste crossed the room. "I'm quite pleased to report I've had several RSVPs from people I hadn't *dared* to dream would attend. People who belong to the Boston Club. I want to be sure we don't duplicate our efforts by scheduling your introductions to them during a time already allotted elsewhere."

"I believe the only time set in stone is when I give the thank-you speech, but let me just find that . . ." Juliet pulled forth a sheet of paper. "Here we go. Beau?" When he looked up she gestured at the chair in front of her desk. "Would you bring that around for Celeste so she and I can go over this together?"

He got up and sauntered over to the desk. Picking up the chair in one hand, he thumped it down to the side of the desk and made an after-you gesture to Celeste before he turned away and returned to his own chair.

It appalled Celeste that such a rude young man had the potential to be the instrument of her and Edward's downfall. But she buried her feelings and took her seat.

They were concluding their meeting when Celeste noticed the marks on Juliet's throat. The young woman's hair swayed away from her neck for a moment, and exposed blood-dark splotches that caused Celeste to stiffen in outrage. She knew what those were. Those were love bites—hickeys, the vulgar young called them. Oh! And to think the little slut was in charge of *her* home. Well, Miss Astor Lowell's antecedents might be impeccable, but she had clearly been swayed off the righteous path by that low-class Yat in the corner.

It was all Celeste could do to excuse herself civilly. Unlike some she could name, however, she knew her duty and icily attended to the courtesies. Then she fumed all the way back to her and Edward's rooms. The moment she entered their apartments, she crossed to the bellpull in the corner and gave it an emphatic yank.

She knew what she had to do now, and she knew exactly when it needed to be done. It was simply poetic justice that Juliet herself had handed her the timetable. All Celeste needed to do was supply the means.

Speaking of which, where was that Lily? She was so abominably *slow* these days. Time was limited and Celeste had an errand for her, but she could hardly send the woman to do it if she kept taking her own sweet time about answering the summons, now, could she? Well, the minute Lily got here, she could just turn right around and trot down to the garden shed. Celeste needed the saw.

Two days later, Beau still found himself gnawing on the way he'd felt upon seeing those love bites on Juliet's neck. There'd been an uneasy sort of shame in realizing that marking her gave him so much juvenile satisfaction. And it bugged him that he had such perfect recall of how it had felt to be sprawled out on top of her, their fingers linked while he stretched her arms high above her head and latched his mouth to her arched throat. Then there was the fact that, for the first time he could remember, one of his sisters' opinions didn't matter. In fact, when Anabel had dared chastise him like some randy teenager, his visceral reaction had been to snarl at her to back off. He'd barely managed to confine himself to a look guaranteed to discourage her from butting into his business.

A quiet snort escaped him. Yeah, right. Like one fish-eyed stare was likely to stop her. Half of New Orleans probably knew about the hickeys on Juliet's neck by now.

But who had time to worry about that? He'd been spending what little free time they'd had cajoling Juliet out of her coolly contained snit. She didn't scream or slam doors like his sisters would have done, but it was amazing how much displeasure she could display without ever raising her voice.

He glanced at her sitting at a desk over by the water cooler. Since there was no safer place than a cop shop, he'd taken to bringing her to the station the past few days. She had dragged Roxanne along with her today, so the two of them could go over hotel stuff while he searched the computer's data banks for cases involving antique guns. He noticed, however, that Roxanne appeared less than her usual efficient self today. She seemed to spend more time flirting with Bettencourt than working with Juliet, but Juliet apparently didn't mind. She'd been scribbling notes and talking on her cell phone almost nonstop since they'd arrived.

The marks on her neck had faded to the point where she could once again sweep her hair up in that regal, French coil thing. She'd worn it down until this morning, and returning his attention to the computer, he scowled down at the screen in front of him. He did *not* feel a need to brand her all over again.

"You plannin' on avoiding your sister and me forever, Dupree?"

Beau looked up to see Luke standing to the side of his desk, looking aggressive and restless. Beau tipped back in his seat and looked his erstwhile friend in the eye. "I'm not avoiding either one of you."

"The hell you say. You haven't been back to your house in—what—four days? And you've been in and out of here a couple of times, but you sure as hell haven't talked to me or stopped by to see Josie Lee." Luke narrowed his eyes. "I can live with your anger, Beau. But she misses you."

"I doubt that." Beau knew his own eyes had probably gone flat in that don't-fuck-with-me cop mode, but it couldn't be helped. The truth was he missed Josie Lee, too, but he couldn't get the image of her and his ex–best friend out of his mind. "I'm sure you've managed to keep her real busy."

"What's that supposed to mean? You talkin' about in bed? Dammit, Beau, she's not thirteen anymore!"

Suddenly Beau was on his feet and the two of them were facing off, the belligerent thrusts of their jaws only inches apart. But he kept his voice low. "I know she's not thirteen," he said through gritted teeth. "But she's certainly young enough to be taken advantage of by someone old enough to know better, isn't she?"

"You don't know your sister for shit if you think anyone could take advantage of her." Luke thrust his face a little closer. "But the same can't be said about you, can it, Dupree?" He jerked his head in Juliet's direction. "She have any idea yet about your big dream to screw half the eligible women in New Orleans? Why don't you whisper *that* in her ear the next time you're suckin' the blood up to the surface of her neck? Or maybe you just plan on fucking her right up to the moment her job's done and you can hustle her onto a plane back to Boston, huh?"

He took a large step back, slicking a hand over his shaven skull. "Shit. I swore I wouldn't get into this. I don't know why I bother, anyhow—you're so goddam blind once you've made up your mind to something." He turned and stalked away.

Beau resumed his seat, but when he looked at the computer screen, all the words blurred together. He was breathing much too fast and made a conscious effort to inhale deeper, holding the breath in his lungs for several counts before exhaling. It was hard to hold on to rational thought when his heart was trying to beat its way out of his chest in anger.

Clearly Anabel had been shooting off her mouth. Well, big deal, what the hell. His sex life had been so barren that linking him with any woman, let alone one whose connection to him was supposed to be strictly professional, was probably really hot news on the Dupree grapevine. And trust Luke to take the knowledge and run with it to make his own duplicity palatable.

Well, Beau didn't buy it. There was no way in hell he was taking advantage of Juliet the way Luke was of Josie Lee. Juliet knew the score: she was a thirty-two-year-old woman, not a kid fresh out of college. Maybe he hadn't exactly sat her down to spell out the terms of their relationship, but it wasn't as if she was looking for love everlasting from a debt-ridden, middle-class Southern cop anyway. She'd be going back to her own kind when her job here was finished, and would probably be thrilled to do so, too. And he would finally get around to pursuing his long-held fantasy.

No way in hell did that make him the hypocrite Luke tried to paint him to be. It only made him a realist.

19

*T*he Garden Crown was ablaze with lights and packed with people, and Juliet finally found herself with a spare moment to catch her breath. Celeste had been dragging her from one person to another all evening long, and while Juliet didn't doubt that the Boston Club members were all very nice people, they differed very little from the society in which she'd moved her entire life—which perhaps explained her failure to share in Celeste's excitement. She was much more interested in seeing how the pre-opening cocktail party fared overall, and this was the first opportunity she'd had to assess the result of their efforts.

They were lucky to have pulled it off as well as they had, she decided, looking at the beautifully attired crowd milling throughout the first floor and the discreet servers who wove between them, bearing trays of champagne and hors d'oeuvres. The tilers had worked right up to the last minute on the ladies' room floor, and the workers laying the temporary dance floor had been in and out all day, competing with caterers, florists, and the wine steward for her attention. Thank God for Roxanne. While Juliet was stuck with the Boston Club people, she'd seen her assistant directing servers and trouble-shooting a myriad of last-minute details.

"Wonderful affair, Miz Lowell."

Juliet turned. "Acting Captain Pfeffer." She had forgotten all about sending him an invitation, but extended her hand with automatic courtesy. "How nice that you could attend. And this must be Mrs. Pfeffer."

"Yes, ma'am, mah bettah half." He performed the introductions.

Juliet felt a presence at her elbow and knew before turning that it was Beau. She drew him forward. "You know the acting captain, of course. Have you met Mrs. Pfeffer?"

God, he looked devastating. You'd never know he'd inherited his tux from his father; it fit him like a glove, and the pristine white of his shirtfront set off his swarthy coloring. He'd even shaved again just before the event began and his lean cheeks gleamed with a sleek, satin sheen.

The charm he turned on Mrs. Pfeffer left the woman nearly stammering, but his eyes turned cool when they settled on her husband. "You've got one helluva nerve showing up here after ignoring my requests for more personnel," he growled, but kept his voice low enough that Juliet doubted even Mrs. Pfeffer overheard. "It's been a logistical nightmare trying to keep track of the people comin' in and out of this joint the past few days."

Ignoring the criticism, Captain Pfeffer turned to Juliet. "May we expect to meet your fawtha this evenin'?"

She made herself relax against the stiffness his question induced in her posture. "No, Father is tied up on another project at the moment."

Beau's hand spread warmth across her back. "Care to dance, dawlin'?"

"Yes, please, I'd like that." She smiled at Pfeffer and his wife. "I haven't had the opportunity to try out the band yet. Please excuse us, won't you?"

"Stupid son of a bitch," Beau muttered as he led her onto the dance floor and turned her into his arms. "It's idiots like the Pissant that keep everybody jawin' on about corruption in the New Orleans Police Department."

Juliet's head came up. "You said New Orleans."

"Well, of course I said New Orleans. What was I suppose to say, St. Louis?"

"N'Awlins."

He looked at her down his nose. "Only tourists call it N'Awlins, dawlin'."

"But I've never heard you call it anything *but*—" She didn't need to watch that one black brow lift to cut herself short. "Ah, of course. It was all part of your hey-shucks-howdy, let's-pull-the-wool-over-the-ignorant-Yankee's-eyes routine."

"No, it was part of the persona I put on back when I was still dumb enough to think I could actually make you ask for a replacement." He skimmed his hand down her side. "And for what it's worth, that was before I realized there was any actual danger that you needed to be defended from." His shoulder shifted beneath her hand. "Or pretty soon afterwards, anyhow." He looked down at her and blatantly changed the subject. "So, Big Daddy's tied up on another project, huh?"

"Oh, yes."

"Otherwise he'd be here for your big night?"

A cynical laugh escaped before Juliet could prevent it.

Beau moved in a little closer, wrapped the arm around her waist a little tighter, as they swayed to the sounds of the six-piece band. "He wouldn't be?"

"He wasn't there for my first piano recital. Or when I graduated high school or college." She made certain her expression was bland as she met his gaze. "No, I think it's safe to say he wouldn't be here."

"Well, that sorry-ass son of a bitch." He seemed far more incensed about it than she, and for some reason his rigid jaw made Juliet's heart lighten. Then the frown between his eyebrows smoothed out. He brought her right hand, which he'd been holding in approved waltz position, up to his shoulder and then wrapped his arms around her and tugged her close. "Did I mention you look really, really pretty tonight?"

"Thank you, Beau."

"I like that dress a lot. It actually shows a little skin."

She rolled her eyes.

"Hey, you gotta admit, this is a whole lot sexier than the good-girl dresses you usually wear. Now the world knows you've actually got legs." He craned his head around to look down at them and then flashed her a white grin. "Great legs."

"What's wrong with the dresses I usually wear?"

"Nothin', I suppose. They just make you look like a good little girl."

Feeling faintly insulted, she raised a haughty brow. "Perhaps I simply wear what I am."

"Can't argue with that, honey chile. Gawd knows, you are very, *very* . . . good." His tone was low and insinuating. "No doubt about it."

Heat flashed through her veins. Lord, he made her feel sexy. Impulsively, she dipped her head and pressed a kiss on the side of his neck. When she pulled back she noticed the lipstick imprint she'd left behind, and unhooked an arm from around his neck to wipe it away.

She stopped with her thumb poised over the kiss-shaped smudge. Then, smiling slightly to herself, she wrapped her arms around his neck again.

He pulled his head back to study her with sudden wariness. "What?"

"Hmmm?" Her lips curled up a bit more at the corners.

"Oh, man. It scares the bejesus outta me when a female smiles like that, because it always means I'm just about to get mine, big-time."

Juliet laughed. "What an imagination you have, Beauregard."

"Imagination, hell. You're up to something, sugar."

"I haven't the faintest idea what you're talking about." Okay, so maybe she understood a little better about that urge to brand thing now. Maybe it wasn't only trailer park people who felt the compulsion to leave their mark behind. She sighed and rested her forehead against his throat.

"You nervous, Rosebud?"

"About what?"

"The speech you have to give?"

"Oh, no. It's what I've been groomed for."

His step seemed to hesitate a fraction of an instant, but perhaps that was merely her imagination, for he swirled her around in the next breath. "Yeah? Groomed in what way?"

"Oh, Lord, in every way. For as long as I can remember, until the day I left for college, I attended a daily two-hour tea with my grandmother, where she would test me on my elocution, my manners, my grasp of etiquette—you name it."

"And you were how old?"

"I don't know—a toddler. When I said for as long as I remember, I meant it literally."

Beau frowned. "And you spent two hours every friggin' day playing little Lady Astor Lowell?"

He sounded so incredulous that she impulsively confessed, "Sometimes I just wanted to jump up and run around and around in circles until I collapsed in a dizzy heap. I really envied the gardener's kids, because they got to play games outside that looked wonderfully fun."

He muttered something under his breath that she didn't quite catch, but when she asked him to repeat it, he gave her a dazzling smile and said it wasn't important.

The next hour was magical. She felt pretty and sexy and much wittier than she knew she actually was, and she was in love. God, so deeply, desperately, ecstatically in love. She really ought to tell Beau, but the right moment just never seemed to present itself. And that was okay. For the time being it was fun simply to drag him from group to group, introduce him around, and laugh and flirt and dance with him.

At eleven o'clock, with Beau right behind her, she climbed the grand, open staircase to the gallery that overlooked the lobby. She picked up the little handbell they'd placed on a small table earlier and rang it to get everyone's attention.

As the lobby quieted down, she set down the bell and picked up a handheld microphone. "I promise not to interrupt the festivities for more than a few moments," she said with a smile as she looked down at the faces raised up to her. "But it would be terribly remiss of me if I didn't take this opportunity to thank you all for coming. The Crown Corporation is proud that we'll soon be opening this new hotel in your beautiful city, and as you might imagine, it takes the cooperation of many people to bring a project of this size from conception to fruition. The Garden Crown is my particular baby, and it's been my great good fortune to have the help of some amazing people while I've been here. Your own Edward and Celeste Haynes have gone out of their way to introduce me to most of you gathered here this evening." She went on to thank a few of the individuals and societies that had hosted the events introducing her to the cream of New Orleans' aristocracy. Then she arrived at the acknowledgment she most wanted to make. "Matters have occasionally gotten a bit crazy around here," she said, in what she considered a fine understatement for having been publicly shot at. "And I would especially like to introduce you to the woman who's been my right hand throughout sane times and mad times alike. Roxanne, would you come up here, please?"

Juliet saw her assistant's startled face in the crowd below, and smiled in delight and gestured her forward. While Roxanne picked her way through the crowd and up the stairs, Juliet explained to the gathering, "In an undertaking like this there is always a multitude of details that require strict attention, and it's a rare individual who, without being asked, is both willing and able to step in and attend to them." As Beau stepped aside to allow Roxanne access, Juliet turned and reached out an arm to encircle her assistant's shoulders and drew her forward. "Not only did Roxanne attend to her own overburdened allotment of details with grace and efficiency, she took up the slack and attended to mine as well when I was unable. So please join me in recognizing Roxanne Davies." Guiding Roxanne to stand slightly in front of her, she dropped her arm and brought her hands together in applause. Lowering the microphone, she said for her assistant's ears only, "Thank you, Roxanne, from the bottom of my heart. You've been a godsend." She extended the mike. "You want to say a few words to the people?"

Roxanne's face was so flushed that her ginger freckles had disappeared entirely, and it belatedly occurred to Juliet she might have embarrassed her assistant beyond belief. Oh, damn, why hadn't she thought this through? If Roxanne's white-knuckled grip on the gallery railing was any indication, she was miserably self-conscious at being the center of attention.

The applause died down and Juliet raised the mike back to her lips. "Thank you all for coming. Please continue to enjoy the food and wine and the marvelous band." Setting the microphone on the little table, she turned back to her assistant, who had sagged against the railing. "Roxanne, I'm so sorry—I didn't think. I wouldn't have embarrassed you for the world."

Her color still high, Roxanne turned. "Holy catfish, don't apologize." She gave Juliet a sheepish smile. "I'm so proud that you would honor me this way, and it's just plain ridiculous the way I simply *freeze* when I have to get up in front of people. You had no way of knowing: it's not as if I'm ever at a loss for words under ordinary circumstances." Straightening, she frowned and turned again toward the railing, reaching out a hand to give it a hard, impatient shake. "What is it with this thing? It feels awfully—" It broke off in her hands, abruptly leaving a three-foot gap in what seconds ago had been a secure barrier.

It caught her off balance, and Juliet watched in

horror as her assistant teetered on the edge of the opening. Then Roxanne's right foot slipped off the edge, and Juliet dove forward to grab her. Her hands closed around Roxanne's forearm just as her assistant's left foot toppled into space, and the sudden dead weight at the end of her grip pulled Juliet into a tottering, headlong race toward the abyss as well.

"No!" Amid the screams from below, Beau's roared denial echoed in her ears, and she felt his muscular arm wrap around her waist and jerk her against his body. She bent double, and her shoulders screamed at the weight that abruptly yanked the ball joints against their sockets.

Roxanne's white face stared up at her as she dangled in space. She twisted in a half circle and then rotated back again, and it petrified Juliet that the only thing standing between her assistant and a sheer drop to the marble-floored lobby below was her own puny upper-body strength. Even as the thought scudded through her mind, Roxanne's arm slipped an inch through Juliet's grasp.

"No!" Tears of frustration and fear rose in her eyes, blurring Roxanne's terrified face. Her hands were rapidly losing strength, and Roxanne slipped another fraction of an inch.

Then Beau reached over her back and his long fingers closed around Roxanne's forearm just above her own grip. She felt the muscles of his thighs bunch as he braced himself.

"Let go of her and—"

"No!"

"Juliet, listen to me," he commanded in a voice

that brooked no insubordination. "Let go of her and slide out of the way. I've got her—I promise you I've got her. But I can't get any leverage to pull her up with you in my way."

It was the hardest thing she'd ever done, to loosen her grip on her assistant, but she peeled her fingers away one by one. When Roxanne didn't immediately crash to her death on the floor below, Juliet scrambled to one side, clearing the way for Beau. She knelt in place, panting for breath and watching as he braced himself firmly on his knees.

"Miz Roxanne, can you hear me?" he said. "Look at me, sugar—that's good, that's good, keep your eyes up here. Now I want you to reach up with your other arm. No, don't look down! Just give me your other hand and I'll have you out of this mess in nothin' flat, okay?"

Roxanne didn't reply, but finger by finger she disengaged her death grip on the loose section of railing still in her hand, and it tumbled away.

"No, don't watch it go," Beau commanded as it smashed to the floor below. "Just give me your hand, Roxanne. Come on, now—that's it sugar, that's it—I've got you!" And his shoulder, back, and upper arm muscles strained against his tux jacket as he hauled her to safety.

He handed her to Juliet the moment she cleared the gap in the railing, and the two women knelt, breast to breast, clinging to each other. Juliet was vaguely aware of Beau commanding someone to cordon off the gap as she pulled away far enough to smooth Roxanne's hair off her face with fierce tenderness.

"Are you all right? My God, I'm so sorry, Roxanne—I'm so very, very sorry."

"It's . . . not . . . your . . . fault," Roxanne gasped.

"It *is* my fault. Someone clearly meant that for me—they probably thought I'd lean on the railing during my speech."

"Then they don't know beans about your granny's training, do they?" Roxanne's mouth slanted. "As if an Astor Lowell would ever be caught dead leaning."

A hysterical giggle escaped Juliet's throat. "Caught dead. Oh, God. I'm so sorry."

"Hey." Roxanne gave her a stern look. "I know you Astor Lowells like to believe you're up there at the right hand of God, but get over yourself, girlfriend—only He could have foreseen this."

"You're right. This is not about me. I'm not only being arrogant, but self-indulgent." Juliet lightly gripped Roxanne's shoulders and held her away to inspect her. "How are you feeling? Can you get up?"

They struggled to their feet, and Juliet smoothed Roxanne's cocktail dress into place. "You know what we need?"

"Barring tranquilizers, you mean?"

"Yes, barring about ten milligrams of valium, we could both stand a great big glass of champagne. A huge glass, I daresay."

"Or maybe the entire magnum," Roxanne agreed. She gazed down at the buzzing, milling crowd below, then looked back at Juliet. "Well, one thing's for certain," she said dryly. "I bet the Garden Crown's gonna take off like a rocket. It might not be exactly what your daddy would've ordered, but we couldn't *buy* the kind of publicity this little episode is going to give us. Especially on the heels of you getting yourself shot at last week."

20

❧

*R*age burned through Beau's veins. Sure as hell, it was no fluke that the balustrade had broken apart the way it had. Even if he believed in that kind of coincidence, it would have taken only one fast glance to disabuse him of the notion. The railing had been sawn through. With premeditated intent, someone had meant Juliet Rose Astor Lowell to fall through sometime during her thank-you speech.

He couldn't for the life of him think of a logical reason why anyone would want to do that. But he would, by God, find the person responsible and slam his sorry ass in jail.

With all the people who had been in and out of here this past week, though, it wasn't going to be a walk in the park. The cocktail party's schedule hadn't exactly been posted in the lobby for everyone to see, but all the staff knew what it was, and there was nothing New Orleanians loved more than to talk. There was no end of opportunity for anyone with a strong enough desire to dig out exactly what they wanted to know.

Considering that statistically most suspects turned out to be either a family member or a significant other, though, maybe he'd just start with Big Daddy and see what sort of motives shook free. More than likely Rosebud was the recipient of a trust fund, and profit was the biggest incentive going when it came to criminal behavior. Just possibly, Thomas Lowell had a pressing need of his baby girl's money to bail him out of a bad investment—it would be interesting to see who her beneficiaries were. God knew her old man didn't sound like the world's most loving parent. And her little ol' grandma was frankly beyond his ken, too.

Minutes after hauling Roxanne to safety, he went looking for answers. His first stop was the Pissant, whom he found being his usual ineffectual self down in the lobby. Grasping him by the elbow, he whirled the man around without regard to the social-register type whose conversation he interrupted. "I want Gardner assigned to this," he demanded through his teeth, "and I want him now."

Wisely, Pfeffer didn't argue with him—probably because he knew his hide could be tacked to the wall if Beau chose, after ignoring his many requests this past week for additional personnel to prevent this exact type of security breech. Pfeffer reached into his tux jacket's inner breast pocket and pulled out a slim cell phone. Three minutes later, he flipped the phone closed and returned it to his jacket. "He'll be here in ten minutes."

Beau didn't bother to say thank you. Turning on his heel, he went to corral two of the burliest servers he could find to cover the exits until the professionals arrived. No one was leaving before he or Luke had a chance to talk to everyone, if he had anything to say about it.

As it turned out, no one appeared to have any intention of leaving. Champagne disappeared from trays, and the decibel level of excited chatter rose apace. Apparently, a near death made the cocktail party a hotter ticket than attendance at the Comus Carnival Ball, which until tonight had been the most sought-after invitation in New Orleans' society.

He was nevertheless relieved to see Luke and three uniforms walk through the hotel entrance a short while later. He sent two of the uniforms to relieve the servers he'd posted and the other to stand guard over Juliet and Roxanne. Then he turned to Luke and filled him in on the evening's events.

"This is fucking nuts," was Luke's baffled response.

"Yeah, that's pretty much my assessment," Beau agreed. "If it's the work of a fanatic preservationist who thinks he'll run the Garden Crown out of business, he's sure going about it all wrong. Hell, this sorta shit is guaranteed to bring in *more* publicity, not less. It might not land on the society or business pages where Crown Hotels would prefer to see it, but people being what they are, they'll flock here in droves anyhow just to meet Juliet and see what kind of woman inspires so much off-the-wall passion. And if it isn't some save-the-historic-building lunatic . . . well, I'll run some checks on her family tomorrow."

"You think Daddy might be in some kind of cash crunch?"

"I don't know what I think at this point, but I'm damn well going to make sure I cover all the bases. And I know that antique gun fits into the equation somewhere, Luke. My gut tells me it's the key, and I'm gonna run it down if it's the last thing I do. There's something about this whole thing that just doesn't smell right."

"I hear that," Luke agreed. "I can't pin it down myself, but something's off, for damn sure."

"Thanks, Luke. I knew you'd be the best one to work with me on this." Beau hesitated, then said reluctantly, "Listen . . . about Josie Lee. Maybe I've overreacted a bit about your relationship with her."

"Ya think?" Luke snorted. "There's an understatement—you've overreacted a ton."

Beau scowled. "I might've been a little off base."

"You've been out of the friggin' ball park, bud."

Beau thrust his face up to Luke's. "Listen, you asshole, I'm tryin' to apologize here."

"You call that an apology?" Luke thrust his chin right back at him. "All I'm hearin' is a bunch of maybes and might haves. You made your sister cry, you dipshit, and not just once, either. You think I went looking for this to happen between me and Josie Lee? Think again. But I'm so over-the-moon crazy about her that I can hardly see straight, and I don't like seein' her crying because of you."

"Crying, my ass." Beau was disgusted that his

friend would flat-out lie like that. "Don't insult my intelligence, Gardner. She came after me with a freakin' frying pan."

"Jesus, Beau, for a guy who's normally so self-aware, you're incredibly dense these days. Josie Lee idolizes the ground you walk on. She wants your approval, man, but she's *in love* with me, get it? We're not talking about puppy love or a high school crush here—we're talkin' adult, I-accept-you-warts-and-all *love*. She. Is. No. Longer. A. Kid." He spaced the words out between his teeth. *"Get it?"*

"I get it; all right, already," Beau muttered. And he truly was beginning to. But it made something inside him hurt.

"Then get this, too. It puts her between a rock and a hard place, because as much as she loves you and wants your stamp of approval, she's not about to give me up just because you refuse to realize she's a woman. And if that's too hard a concept for you to grasp, then, dammit, you know *me*. You know damn well I've never chased younger women in my life. I don't need a teenybopper to make me feel like a big man, and I'm sure as shit not searching for some sweet young thing I can dominate."

That elicited a snort of amusement out of Beau. "As if anyone could ever control Jose. I'd pay big bucks to see that happen."

Luke grinned. "Yeah. Me, too."

Beau rolled his shoulders uncomfortably. "So maybe I'll stop by the house tomorrow and talk to her." It was painful, but the truth was he did know

Luke, and deep down he knew his sister, too, so he took a deep breath and just said it. "Give her my, uh, stamp of approval."

"Good plan."

Beau looked at his partner for a moment. "You hurt her, though, Gardner, and I'll come gunnin' for you."

"Wouldn't expect it any other way, Dupree."

"Okay, then." Edgy, Beau looked around the crowded lobby. Everything seemed to be slipping beyond his control these days. "Let's get to work. I gotta wrap this thing up and get my life back to normal."

The look Luke gave him struck him as suspiciously pitying, as if his partner knew something that he ought to. Beau straightened and said defensively, "I *will* get it back to normal."

"Hey, sure, whatever. If it makes you happy to think so, bud."

Celeste was not happy. Sourly, she eyed Juliet, who still hovered over her upstart secretary. Good Lord, she'd seen flea-bitten alley cats with fewer lives than the Yankee trollop seemed to have. And didn't it just *figure* her mongrel typist would be the one to lean on the railing during the thank-you ceremony, and screw everything up? It wasn't easy being surrounded by incompetents.

Between that sorry exhibition the two of them and Dupree had put on like so many cut-rate circus performers, and the way the Yat cop had then cut through group after group of the people who mattered like a demented bull in a crystal shop, at the very least she should have had the satisfaction of watching everyone flee in disgust, never to darken the Garden Crown's doorstep again. After all, the crème de la crème that she'd lured here tonight were people with delicate sensibilities and rigid rules. But for some odd reason, everyone seemed to be treating tonight's incident as some sort of lark, as if it had been staged purely for their delectation. She'd expected better of the Boston Club people; she really had.

The only highlight in the whole dreary evening was that rather than finding her position tarnished by this fiasco—which she'd risked and had rather feared—she'd had several people seek her out, thank her for thinking of them when she'd issued the invitations, and hint they'd love to attend the Grand Opening as well. There'd even been indications that a reciprocal invitation would be forthcoming for next year's Comus Ball. She should be thrilled, for it was an unforeseen reward and something toward which she'd strived her entire adult life. Goodness, she and Edward had just moved one rung higher up the ladder. And that was as it should be—it was wonderful. The only thing was . . .

She now had that much farther to fall.

Juliet had begun to think the night would never end, when suddenly it did. She watched the door close behind the last guest and immediately sank down upon an armchair. "At last," she murmured. The starch melted out of her spine, leaving her wilted.

"Well, if you didn't have such a Puritan work ethic," Roxanne chided as she took an adjoining chair, "you could have gone upstairs hours ago and let the party wind down on its own."

"Look who's talking." She looked at her assistant. Exhaustion and stress had given her skin a grayish tinge. "I am so sorry you got caught up in this mess, Roxanne. I wouldn't blame you a bit if you caught the first flight back to Boston."

"What, and miss all the excitement?" Roxanne reached over and squeezed Juliet's hand. "I'm afraid you're stuck with me for the duration. Lord, girl, this is like being an improv actor in a Southern Gothic play. It's terrifying, but titillating, too, in a thrills and chills sorta way. Besides"—her smile was game, if bone-weary—"I've got a hot date with that cute Officer Bettencourt tomorrow night, and it's the first chance I've had to rub up against a little testosterone-fed beefcake since we've come down here. No way I'm passing that opportunity by."

Juliet squeezed Roxanne's hand in return. "You are the best, you know that? And not only as an asset to the Crown. You're so funny and smart and insightful, and I would really, truly be honored if you'd consider me your friend. You've certainly been a good friend to me."

Roxanne looked at her without speaking for a moment. Then she burst into tears.

Horrified, Juliet scooted forward and wrapped her arms around her assistant, offering a stiff but genuine hug. "Oh, my God, I'm so sorry. It wasn't my intention to put you on the spot." She patted

Roxanne's shoulder. "That was very gauche—
friendship is certainly not requisite to your job or
anything."

A strangled laugh erupted out of Roxanne as she
emerged from Juliet's embrace. "That's not it, Juliet!"

"It's not?" *Thank you, God.*

"Of course not. Oh, shit, I feel like such an idiot."
Roxanne knuckled away the tears pooling beneath
her eyes. "I can be tough as nails when things get
rough, you know. Hey, drop me off a balcony—
I'm cool. Nerves of steel. But say something nice,
and I fall to pieces." She looked at Juliet, who sat,
her spine very erect, on the edge of her chair, and
added gently, "And that *was* very nice. I honestly
can't think of anything I'd like more than to be
your friend." The corner of her mouth tipped up
in an irreverent smile. "Well, except maybe to get
laid sometime before the end of the millennium."

Juliet smiled with such radiance it made Roxanne blink. "Wow," she said. "And me without my
shades. If this is the sorta reaction I get, you must
not have many friends."

"I don't," Juliet confessed. "I've got a ton of acquaintances handpicked for me by Grandmother.
And they're perfectly nice women, you know? But
I always felt somehow—I don't know—*different*
from them." She tapped her breast with a gentle
fist.

"Probably because you've spent your entire life
trying to repress a shipload of passion, the likes of
which most of those white-bread chicks wouldn't

recognize if it came up and bit 'em on their blue-blooded butts."

"Oh, no, I don't think that's the reas . . . well, yes, I suppose I do have more, um, passion than one might have previously suspected—" Breaking off, she flashed a delighted smile. "White-bread chicks?"

"Oh, definitely."

"As opposed to myself, who is . . . ?"

"A babe. Refined, but nevertheless red-hot." And looking at her friend in her sleek evening gown, with most of her hair slipped free of its confines and her cheeks flushed, she was entirely serious.

"Oh, my." Juliet's sudden laugh sounded self-conscious but pleased. "Oh, my." Then, abruptly, she sobered. "I shouldn't be so tickled, Rox," she said guiltily. "Someone's trying to kill me." Her fist clenched in her lap as she stared at Roxanne. "Lord. I can't quite get a grasp on that."

"I'm not surprised. I can only imagine how it must make you feel."

"Embarrassed," Juliet promptly supplied. "As if I've committed some major social faux pas."

"Good God, Juliet." Roxanne felt her eyes roll up. "We have got to work on your attitude. Is that really what you'd like to see inscribed on your tombstone: 'Here lies Juliet. She apologizes for being murdered'?"

"I would rather avoid being murdered entirely, if it's all the same to you."

"That's exactly the kind of attitude adjustment I like to see. It's much better to be a little pissed than apologetic. None of this is your fault," Roxanne stated firmly. "You've just got to keep that thought solidly in mind." Looking up, she saw Beau bearing down on them, looking grim and determined. "And here comes the guy who will ultimately unravel this mess. If anyone can get to the bottom of things, Juliet, I'd put my money on Sergeant Cutie."

It was late when Beau finally called it a night and went up to Juliet's room. Sending the man standing guard between the two women's rooms down to Roxanne's door, he let himself in.

He half expected Juliet to be asleep, but although she was in bed, she sat up the moment he entered the room. He shed his tux jacket, kicked off his shoes, and made his way over to the bed, sliding his bow tie from beneath his collar. Juliet had scrambled to her knees by the time he reached it, and she reached out to undo his shirt studs. Between them, they had him stripped in seconds flat, and she immediately pressed herself against his chest, wrapping her slender arms around his neck. "Hold me, Beau. Please."

He did, but it was soon clear she didn't simply crave the comfort of his arms. She moved against him, pressed restless kisses to his throat and chest, and within moments he was wrestling her down onto the mattress, looking for the same sweet oblivion that she sought.

Foreplay was minimal, and soon he was deep inside her, and it was rough and hot and fast, and the tension that had kept his neck and shoulder muscles knotted all night was finally—finally!—beginning to abate when he heard Juliet's voice, muffled against his throat, begin a soft little chant. Dragging his attention back from its hot, mindless free-fall through space, he tuned in to what she was saying.

"I love you, Beauregard," she murmured into his skin. "I love you, love you, love you."

And just like that, the tension was back.

21

❧

*B*eau leaned in the office door. "Afternoon, ladies."

Juliet and Roxanne, working with their heads together at Juliet's desk, looked up and returned his greeting. Her pulse rate picking up, Juliet gave him a swift and discreet once-over, wishing she had the ability to read minds. Last night he'd made love to her with a fierce intensity that had left her boneless and able to drift immediately into sleep. But this morning she'd sensed an uncharacteristic reserve, the origin of which she couldn't begin to pin down. She'd wanted to ask him if anything was the matter, but it was an asinine question that he'd undoubtedly answer with a snort and a where-do-I-start? response. Her life was a Keystone Kops comedy these days—of course there was something the matter.

His professional mask seemed firmly in place this afternoon, too. But no—she had to put a lid on the paranoia. He simply had a lot on his mind.

"You about ready to go?" He stepped farther into the room. "I've exhausted the computer files in my search for the antique gun, so we're going to Cop Central today to check out the records room."

That startled a laugh out of her. "Cop Central?"

"Police headquarters. You comin' along, Miz Roxanne?"

"No, I've got work here I have to get done."

"Sure." Hands in his pockets, he shrugged. "Just in case you're nervous about being left here alone, though, I want you to know I've got a man posted outside your office. I don't anticipate a problem, but I'm establishing a few precautionary measures now that I finally have some decent manpower to work with."

"Thanks, Sergeant. You're a pip."

Juliet hesitated, then forced herself to say, "As long as you have somebody to stand guard, Beau, perhaps I ought to stay, as well." It was actually the very last thing she wanted, and yet . . . "We're up to our eyebrows in preparation for the Grand Opening, and there's a hundred details that still need my attention."

Beau's gut instinct said to tell her flatly and un-equivocally to forget it. Then he thought of the way his long-held fantasy seemed to be getting all screwed up, and that sinking feeling he'd gotten in the pit of his gut last night—as if a steel-barred door were clanging shut behind him—and he took a step back, rubbing his hands down his thighs. "Yeah, okay, whatever. As long as you don't make a move outside your office without my man dog-

gin' your footsteps." Hell, the freedom to get some
uninterrupted police work done would be welcome—just what the doctor ordered, in fact. "Y'all
come on out here with me for a minute, and I'll
introduce you to the guard."

A few moments later the introductions were
complete, and Roxanne disappeared back into the
office. Juliet trailed Beau to the front door.

"Well, hey," he said and edged toward the main
entrance. "I guess I'll, uh, see you la—"

"Would you do something for me?"

He was so surprised to hear Juliet Rose Astor
Lowell interrupt anyone that he dropped his hand
from the door handle and looked down at her.

"Sure. Shoot."

"I'd like to invite your sisters to the Grand Opening—"

"Oh, hey, really, dawlin', that's not at all necessary." Panic gnawed his vitals with sharp little rat
teeth at the very thought.

"Please. It's something I'd very much like to do,
only it's quite late to be sending out formal invitations. I apologize for not thinking of it sooner,
but . . . will you invite them for me? Or give me
their numbers so I can call them myself?"

"Yeah, sure, okay." She looked up at him with
her serious gray eyes, and his shoulders twitched.
"I'll pass the invitation along, okay? Listen, I gotta
go."

"I know."

"Then move it, sugar. I'm not budging an inch
until you're in range of the guard dog."

"He has a name, Beauregard."

"I know he has a name. Benton, okay? Get over
to where he has you firmly in his sights, angel face,
so I can go do my job."

She leaned forward to kiss him good-bye, but
with some vague notion that it would be easier to
put distance between them if he avoided it, he
shifted out of range. "I'll see you this evening."

Her chin elevated slightly, and the dignity in her
level gaze made him feel like a worm. Then, without a word, she turned and walked away. He
watched until she strode like a queen past Benton
and the office door closed behind her ramrod-
straight back. Then he headed for the car.

She'd be just fine, he assured himself as he
steered the GTO through midcity traffic, her and
Roxanne both. He'd chosen Benton himself, and besides, he needed breathing room.

Still, he was edgy and out of sorts when he arrived at the records room on the second floor of
the HQ building, and the hours spent searching
through spool after spool of hard-to-read film
failed to improve his mood. He nevertheless kept
at it, doggedly threading new reels onto the microfiche and skimming the information that scrolled
up the screen until his eyes burned.

And found nothing.

At a quarter to six, he pushed back from the machine and ground the heels of his hands into his
eyes. Then he made a note of the most recent date
checked, gathered up the latest stack of reels, and
returned them to the clerk on duty.

On his way back to the Garden District he decided to stop at home. He'd told Luke he'd make

up with his sister, and he felt a sudden need to touch base with his real life.

The house was closed up and hotter than hell's anteroom when he arrived. Josie Lee wasn't home yet, so he grabbed the lone bottle of beer out of the fridge door, turned on the overhead fans, and put T-Bone Walker on the compact disc player. Then he sprawled on the couch with his feet propped on the coffee table as he flipped through his stack of mail.

When the whining guitar licks, tenor sax, and bump-and-grind drumbeat of "Blues Rock" drifted out of the speakers, he looked up from his bills. The instrumental always reminded him of music to take it off by, which made him think of strip joints, which led inevitably to thoughts of Juliet. He looked around the living room and wondered idly what she'd think of his place. It was hardly the palatial digs she was accustomed to.

His feet hit the floor with a thud as he sat up. Shit. Where had that come from? It was stupid, useless speculation—she was never going to see it. And it wasn't as if he wanted her to, anyway. Plenty of other women would, and he imagined *they'd* like it just dandy. He tipped the beer bottle up to drain the last sip from it.

The screen door creaked as it opened and then slapped shut behind his sister and Luke. Beau winced at the wariness that appeared in her dark eyes the instant she spotted him.

In inimitable Josie Lee fashion, however, she recovered quickly. "Well, well. Would you look what the cat dragged in. How goes it, Beauregard—stopping by to check the lock on my chastity belt?"

"Jose," Luke remonstrated, but Beau shook his head at his partner and climbed to his feet.

He watched his sister assume a combative stance and approached her cautiously. "Nope. You're too close to the kitchen for that; a guy could get hurt." Thrusting his hands in his pockets, he stepped up to her and tilted his head to one side. "The truth is, sugar, if I had my way you would die a virgin at the ripe old age of ninety-five. I can't help it— it's the way I feel. But Luke said I had to play nice or risk driving you away, so I'm here to apologize."

The look she gave him was bemused and distrustful, and he nudged her arm with his elbow. "Come on, Jose, let's kiss and make up, whataya say?"

Her black lashes went into a flurry of motion. "Let me see if I've got this straight. You're apologizing."

"Yep."

"To me."

He bristled. "You act as if I've never said I was wrong before."

Her mouth dropped open. "You're saying you were *wrong*?"

He was starting to get seriously insulted here. He opened his mouth to blast her, but then she laughed like a loon and threw herself at his chest. Staggering back, he pulled his hands from his pockets and hugged her. He gave the top of her head a noogie with his chin and murmured, "I overreacted, Jose—I'm sorry."

"Yeah, you were a jerk."

"So Luke tells me."

She pulled back to look into his face, her own suddenly serious. "I've loved him for as long as I can remember, Beau."

"Have you? Well, you could do worse, I guess. He's okay."

"*Okay!*" She punched him. "He's the *best*."

"Yeah. He's a good man."

"Aw, shucks, all this effusive praise has me shufflin' my feet in modesty," Luke inserted dryly. "I'm such a swell guy, I think I deserve a beer. Excuse me while I go fetch one."

"That might be kinda difficult, since I drank it," Beau said.

"You drank my last beer?"

Beau narrowed his eyes. "Last time I looked, my name was on the mortgage. And since Jose is an iced tea freak, you'll just have to excuse the hell outta me if I assumed it was one I'd bought before I got bumped up to the high life at the Garden Crown."

"Speaking of which," said Josie Lee, "how is *your* love life?"

I love you, Beauregard. Beau shut out the voice and set his sister loose. "None of your business."

"C'mon, Beau! You didn't hesitate to critique my love life; turnabout's fair play."

"Yeah, well, I gotta head back to the Garden Crown now. Otherwise, I'd just love to spill my guts for your amusement. Tell you what, though." He gathered up his bills and stuffed them in his hip pocket, then stopped to look at his sister. "Juliet wants y'all to come to the hotel's grand opening next week. You're welcome to try your hand at pickin' her brains." *And good luck, little sister.* He'd trust in Juliet's impeccable manners and level gaze to stop rude questions in their tracks any day.

And as he'd hoped, Josie Lee was sidetracked. "We're invited to the opening? Ooh. Is it formal? I bet it's formal."

"Yeah, it's a golden opportunity for y'all to wow 'em in the aisles, so pass the word along to Camilla and Anabel, huh?"

"I'll go call them right now." She stood on her toes to give him a peck and then dashed for the phone.

The wry quirk of Luke's lips was admiring. "Nice work. How'd you do that?"

"A guy can't live in a house full of women for as long as I have without learning a trick or two." He pushed the screen door open. "Tell Jose 'bye for me. I've gotta go do something I should have taken care of a while ago. I'll catch you later."

The minute Juliet saw Beau's face, she knew he was going to say something she didn't want to hear. Her stomach sank, but in her heart she had known there was a problem from the moment he'd avoided her good-bye peck. Beau Dupree—who had probably never passed up an opportunity for some intimate physicality in his life—sidestepping a kiss? Oh, yes, she'd known.

"We've got to talk," he said.

Juliet leaned out the door to peer up and down the hall. "Where's Benton?" The man had insisted on following her up to her room to stand guard when she and Roxanne had finally called it a day a short while ago.

"I sent him down to get dinner."

"Oh." She stepped back. "Come in."

He followed her into the sitting room, but when she turned to face him he thrust his hands in his pockets and shifted restlessly.

"Has something happened?" Her instincts insisted this was personal, but she could hope she was mistaken. All she knew for certain was that his mood was beginning to affect her. Heart drumming, she asked, "Did you find the information you were searching for at headquarters?"

"No. No, this's got nothing to do with the case. It's just . . . you and I have never discussed what we expect out of this relationship, Juliet, and I . . . uh, realized today it's something we need to talk about."

"And you look like your dog's just been run over because . . . ?"

He regarded her with unfathomable eyes. "Look, I just think it's important that you don't get the wrong idea."

For the first time since she'd set foot in Louisiana, she felt cold—cold to the bone. Resisting the urge to hug herself, she inquired coolly, "And what might that wrong idea be, Beauregard? That you care?"

"No, dammit! I do care. It's just—"

"Will you quit saying that!"

"What?"

" 'Just.' It's 'just' that we never discussed where

we saw this relationship heading. You 'just' think it's important I don't get the wrong idea. You care, but it's 'just' . . ."

"Hey, excuse the hell outta me, lady. I didn't have the benefit of your posh upbringing. Is that one of the things Grandmother taught you during your daily tea parties—never to repeat yourself?"

God, how soon he'd managed to use that against her. Well, she would not let him see her bleed—she wouldn't. She tilted her chin up. "Tell you what, Beau. Why don't you *just* spit out whatever it is you want to say?"

He shoveled a hand through his hair and then let it drop to his side. "Look . . ." He drew in a deep breath and looked around the room, lending his attention to everything but her. Then, suddenly, he exhaled and faced her squarely. "I inherited the care of my sisters when I was twenty-four years old, Juliet. I wanted to do right by them, so except for rare occasions, I pretty much gave up the idea of a love life. You can't exactly bring lovers home to where your little sisters are living."

"And it's very commendable of you," she said. "Although I'm not certain I comprehend how this is pertinent to our relationship." But deep inside, she was afraid that perhaps she did.

"It's pertinent because while I lacked a sex life, what I did have was a plan for the day I'd have my freedom again—and I gotta tell you honestly, it got me through many a night when I didn't have a clue what the hell I was doing."

"And that plan involves the little book you're always collecting phone numbers in, I take it."

"Yeah. I always planned to go ape-shit as soon as Josie Lee moved out, to date a different woman every night of the week to make up for lost time."

The awful thing was, she could see the justice of his dream. He deserved to see it fulfilled. But that didn't help the grinding hurt eating through her heart. "Why are you telling me this now? It seems to me you have a pretty good thing going for yourself here. Regular sex, no pressure. Or—oh, God." She regarded him with sudden horror. "It's grown distasteful? *Boring?*"

"No!" He took a huge step toward her, then checked himself. "You know better than that—you know it's been the best."

"Then why didn't you simply wait until I went back to Boston? You could have spared both of us this."

"Dammit, Rosebud, you said you loved me last night!"

That stopped her dead. "What?" She'd been biting back the words for several days now—she certainly didn't remember uttering them last night. "I didn't."

"Yes. You did—when we were making love. You said you loved me."

"Ah. Well." She faced him coolly. "Sex talk."

He took another step toward her. "Bullshit."

"It was a stressful night."

"Yeah, it was. But you meant it."

"Did I? Well, you'd be the expert, wouldn't you? But you might want to consider that it was you who introduced me to the kind of sex that has me saying just about *anything*—and certainly things I'd never say under ordinary circumstances."

God, she was tired. It seemed that all her life she'd been seeking someone's approval: Father's, Grandmother's . . . hell, all of society's. Well, she was through. She hadn't asked for anything this time—not a blessed thing—but even that wasn't good enough.

"I tell you what, Beau. I don't want to be a rock around anyone's neck, so why don't you consider yourself free as a bird." She grasped his arm and guided him toward the door. "Really. It's been fun, and I thank you for the experience." She opened the door and shoved him over the threshold. "Have a good life." She closed the door in his face. And then she was alone again, just as she'd been most of her life.

She turned until her back pressed against the solid panels of the door. Sliding slowly down its surface, she sank to the floor and buried her face in her knees. And tears like acid rolled silently down her cheeks.

22

For the third day in a row, Beau sat planted in front of a microfiche in the HQ records room, examining films of old police reports. It was painstaking, frustrating, and thus far unrewarding work, and his mind had a tendency to drift from the business at hand. Unfortunately, where it drifted, more often than not, was to Juliet.

He should be pleased—hell, relieved, even—that she'd made it so easy for him to walk away. She'd done him a favor. Well, maybe *walk away* wasn't precisely the way it had happened—not with the door hitting him in the butt as she shoved him over the threshold. And hadn't she given up on their relationship mighty damn fast? For someone who professed to love him?

Christ. He scrubbed his hands over his face before reaching for a new spool and threading it onto the machine. He had to quit thinking about her. It was making him nuts. She'd cut him loose, and that was exactly what he'd wanted. *Exactly*. End of story.

He nevertheless continued to chew on it endlessly, and had nearly scrolled through an entire report before it sank in that he'd skimmed past a reference to two antique guns. Going back to the beginning, he saw it was a stolen property report from several years ago. Among the items taken was a matched set of Colt 1849 Pocket Model revolvers—two .31-caliber, cap-and-ball percussion, five-shot pistols, which matched the forensics report on the lead ball removed from the tree at the garden party. He checked further for the name of the officer who had taken the report.

It wasn't one he recognized, but the report had been filed in the Garden District. If he was lucky, the patrolman was still around and would remember something about the case. Odds were against that, but it was a place to start, at least.

Hell, an even better source would be the victim. An experience that was routine for the cop was much more likely to stand out in the victim's mind. He quickly scrolled the report up the screen, searching for a name.

And cursed beneath his breath when he found it. For the theft had been reported by one Edward Haynes—at an address Beau recognized only too well.

The intercom on Juliet's desk buzzed. Without looking up from her work, she reached for the button to open the line. "Yes?"

"Your father's on line two, Juliet," Roxanne said.

"Oh, perfect," she whispered. Taking a deep breath to calm herself, she blew it out again and carefully placed her pen in perfect alignment with the invoices she'd been studying.

Roxanne's voice was professional but sympathetic when she said, "Do you want me to put him off?"

"Thanks, Rox; I appreciate the offer. But . . . no. Go ahead and put him through."

"Are you sure?"

"Yeah." The concern in her assistant's voice warmed her and she punched down the button that opened line two. "Hello, Father. To what I do owe this honor?"

"Is that flippancy I hear in your voice, Juliet Rose?" His voice was coldly displeased.

It never failed to amaze her how effortlessly he could reduce her to a little girl eager to please, and she caught herself correcting her posture as if he were right there in the room to notice that it had degenerated into something less than perfect. "No, Father." Swallowing a sigh, she said levelly, "But I am up to my eyebrows in details for the opening, so perhaps we should get to the point."

"I have a newspaper clipping here in front of me, Juliet. Would you like to know what it features?"

She bit back her impatience. "I haven't had time to keep up with the *Boston Globe*, I'm afraid."

"This isn't the *Globe*, Juliet Rose, it's the *New Orleans Times-Picayune*. With a very nice write-up of the Garden Crown's pre-opener the other night."

"Well . . . good."

"Yes, it is, for the most part. But there's a picture in the spread that disturbs me greatly."

"Oh, Lord, don't tell me they got a shot of Roxanne dangling from the gallery." She sighed. "Well, it's not the sort of publicity I would have hoped for, Father, but it was hardly her fault."

"This has nothing to do with your ill-bred little assistant, Juliet. This is a photograph—a rather prominent photograph—of you looking entirely too chummy with the man purported to be your bodyguard."

"Sergeant Dupree?" It was like having a barely healed-over scab ripped free. She'd been trying to think of Beau as little as possible for the past two days. For all she was worth, she had been attempting that.

"Yes, Dupree. Captured on film, making a vulgar display of you for all the world to see. I don't think I need tell you I don't approve of this, Juliet. Captain Pfeffer has told me something of this man, and Dupree is clearly not our kind."

"You've discussed Sergeant Dupree with *Pfeffer*? That ineffectual toady? Have the two of you also discussed me?" Resentment stirred, but she did her best not to let it color her voice. "Did Pfeffer send the article to you, Father, or do you have other spies checking up on me?"

"Who sent it isn't important. And I don't like your tone, young lady."

"*I* don't like having my life reported back to you. I'm not a child to be yanked back in line when she does something of which her parent disapproves."

"Perhaps not. But you're a fool if you believe anything will ever come of a relationship with a blue-collar, debt-ridden policeman. He's probably after your money."

She could have set his mind at ease and told him the relationship with Beau was yesterday's news.

"Thank you, Father; that's a very flattering assessment of my desirability. Considering you've never even met the man and are taking Pfeffer's word as gospel, however, you'll have to excuse me if I'm not overwhelmed by your acumen. But here's a bit of information for you, straight from the source: I'm thirty-two years old, and my love life is none of your affair. Stay out of it." Leaning forward, she reseated the receiver in its cradle and then depressed the intercom button. "If Father should call back," she said crisply the moment Roxanne answered, "I'm not in."

"Gotcha. He gave you a hard time over something, I take it."

"Let me put it this way: I'll probably get my period next—and then I'll just have it all."

"I can't believe I never once checked the obvious," Beau said as he slapped a copy of the stolen property report down on Luke's desk.

Looking up from his own report, Luke growled, "I realize this is bound to come as a surprise, buddy, but I happen to be hip-deep in work of my own—and *I've* got more than one case." When Beau just looked at him, he picked up the copy and read it. "Want to give me a clue as to what I'm lookin' for?"

"Edward-friggin'-Haynes."

"Who is . . . ?"

"Yeah, that would be the sixty-thousand-dollar question, all right." Beau's laugh was short and sharp. "I did some digging and found out that Haynes and his wife the grande dame have called the Garden Crown their home for the past thirty years or so. Seems it was part of Miz Haynes's heritage, only the women in her family aren't allowed to inherit. So the Hayneses were appointed caretakers and lived there rent-free instead—until Crown Corporation bought the estate out from under them to turn it into a hotel." He planted his knuckles on Luke's desk and leaned his weight on them. "You beginnin' to see glimmers of a motive here, pal?"

"Yeah. The original letter finally begins to make sense, doesn't it?"

"Not to mention that Haynes has been present every single time one of those horseshit 'accidents' happened or an attempt on Juliet's life was made."

"And the antique guns?"

Beau threw himself into a chair and propped his ankle on his knee. He bounced his leg. "What do you wanna bet they were never stolen at all? It's my guess Haynes padded the report for insurance purposes."

"I'm sure you're right, but supposition's not enough for a warrant."

"I know, but it will be, after I do more digging. It only took me a couple of hours to unearth this inheritance info."

Luke gave him a curious look. "Why didn't you just ask Juliet? She must have known."

Beau lost a little of the juice that had him jazzed. He shifted in his seat. "She's, uh, not exactly talkin' to me at the moment."

"No shit?" Luke straightened. "What did you do?"

"Why the hell would you assume it was something I did? I didn't do anything," Beau said flatly. When his ex-partner simply looked at him, he gave his shoulders an uneasy hitch. "I don't wanna talk about it, okay?"

"Well, sonuvabitch, Dupree, that hardly seems fair. You know everything there is to know about my love life."

Beau looked at him from beneath lowered brows. "Don't remind me," he said glumly. "I'm still struggling to come to terms with that one."

"And gettin' closer to it every minute. Just look at how good you were with Josie Lee yesterday. I was proud of ya, bud."

"I guess I can sleep easy now." Beau eyed his ex-partner sourly. "It would never occur to you, I suppose, that I was lying through my teeth so Jose wouldn't be mad at me anymore."

"Nah, the idea of me and her is growing on you. Admit it."

"I admit I'm not gagging quite as often."

"See? You're coming right along. Why, before you know it, you'll probably be walking her down the aisle, and I'll be callin' you Dad."

"Do that, Gardner, and I'll make her a widow."

Luke's teeth flashed white against his dark goatee. "You're such a card."

"A freakin' barrel of laughs—that's me." He tapped his finger against the report on Luke's desk. "You going to sit around all day crackin' wise, or are you gonna give me a hand?"

Luke threaded his fingers together at the back of his head and leaned back in his chair. "Just tell me what you need, oh impatient one. I'm your boy."

For the past two days, Juliet had done everything in her power to avoid Beau. So she was less than thrilled to find him waiting for her after her discussion with the restaurant manager and the chef about Saturday night's Grand Opening menu.

He pushed away from the marble pillar he'd been leaning against. "We need to consult."

She would have loved to find an excuse to avoid talking to him, but she stifled the longing in true Astor-Lowell fashion. In any event, he'd said consult, not talk, so chances were he wasn't looking for an intimate tête-à-tête any more than she was. She could handle this. She could handle anything as long as it wasn't personal.

"I was on my way to check the preparations in the Blue Room. We can talk there if you'd like."

"Sure." Hands in his pockets, he ambled along at her side.

He was wearing his noncommittal cop face. Otherwise, he seemed so perfectly at ease that he could have been out for a stroll with one of his sisters. And it hurt. He looked the same, moved the same, and it brought to mind everything they had ever done together. Things they'd never do together again. Which apparently didn't matter to him a whit.

Well, fine. She would lick a cockroach before she'd let him see it was tearing her into a trillion little pieces.

It might have helped her if she knew that Beau wasn't nearly as insouciant as he appeared. Juliet was close enough that hints of her elusive scent made his palms itch. He knew full well the information he needed would be in her office, yet he didn't insist they go there. God only knew why.

He stole a sidelong glance at her face as they made their way to the Blue Room. She was so damn cool, with her ramrod-erect spine, and it irritated the hell out of him—even though he had no legitimate right to feel that way. But she wore her breeding like some high-class impenetrable body suit, and it made him want to shake her up, to elicit the sort of reaction her grandma wouldn't sanction in a million years. He stuffed his hands in his pockets and compressed his lips to prevent himself from doing or saying something irrevocably stupid.

But his nerves stretched thinner with every silent stride they took.

He peeled away from her the minute they entered the Blue Room, relieved to put some distance between him and her scent. Stopping in front of the wall of Mardi Gras masks, he rocked back on his heels to study them.

The collection could be a good lead-in to Haynes, since he couldn't compromise the case by warning Juliet about him. If her manner around Haynes were to suddenly change, it might alert the man that his anonymity had been blown. Beau looked over at her. "This is one hell of a collection."

"Yes," she agreed distantly as she moved around the room making notes on the clipboard she carried. "Right now we're renting the use of it, and we're looking into replacing it when the Hayneses leave. Obviously whatever we come up with at first won't include pieces as rare as many of these, but the overall effect is so evocative of New Orleans that I hate to give up the display entirely."

"Why would the Hayneses leave? I thought they worked for you."

"Only temporarily." With aloof politeness, but not so much as a glance in his direction, she briefly explained the Hayneses' connection to the Crown Corporation—information that might have saved them all some heartache had he known about it earlier. "They'll be moving out on the first," she concluded, and when she finally deigned to glance up, it was to look right through him. "Was this the matter you wanted to discuss, Sergeant?"

Sergeant? Her frozen good manners ate at something he didn't care to examine too closely, and he took a giant step in her direction. "No. I need to know who the photographer was at the cocktail party."

"That information is in my office. If you'd care to check with Roxanne . . . ?" She continued to make notes.

"Dammit, Rosebud!"

"*Don't*"—visibly reining in her composure, she modulated her sharp tone of voice and finished mildly—"call me that." She stooped to examine the soil in a potted plant.

He took another step nearer, blood racing hot through his veins. "What *do* I call you, then, dawlin'? Miz Astor Lowell?"

"Yes. That will do nicely."

"The hell you say!" He took the step that brought him towering over her. "Don't you think that's just the tiniest bit formal for someone who's seen you naked as often as I have?"

She faced him with cool composure. "I might be inclined to agree with you, Sergeant, if we were talking about someone who had a prayer of ever seeing me naked again." Her rainwater eyes met his levelly. "But we're talking about you."

Denial reared up on its hind legs and roared like an enraged bear. He reached out and jerked her close, thrusting his face next hers. "God, such pretty, pretty composure," he said in a hoarse voice. "Not for Ms. Astor Lowell the pesky, disorderly emotions that rule the rest of us. How does it feel to live in your world, I wonder?" He knew he was being unfair, but he didn't care. *Never, never, never* chanted in his mind and he wanted to erase it, eradicate it from the English language. "Doesn't it ever get lonely, Juliet Rose? Don't you get tired of being Daddy's good little girl all the time, of being too damn pristine to go after what you want?"

How dare he—oh, God, how *dare* he? Laser-white rage exploded in Juliet's brain. Slapping her hands to his chest, she shoved as hard as she could and felt bitter satisfaction when his hold on her upper arms broke and he stumbled back a couple of paces.

"*Pristine?*" she demanded through her teeth. "It's not enough that you dump me so you can have sex with every large-breasted woman in New Orleans—now you're saying I didn't get *down and dirty* enough for you?" She thumped her fist hard on his chest.

"No . . . Juliet . . . dawlin' . . . that's not what I—" He backed up step by step, his arms spread wide in entreaty.

"What's the matter, Beauregard, too *emotional* for you?" She stalked forward with every step he took. "You hypocrite. You don't want my emotions. It was my saying I loved you that sent you running in the first place." She laughed bitterly. "God, the thought of getting trapped in a monogamous relationship must have struck terror to your very soul."

His back hit the wall and she stabbed her finger in his sternum. "But it wasn't sufficient that I gave you an out, was it? Oh, no, not for Loverboy Dupree." She thrust her face up to his in a most unmannerly way. "Why? Didn't it satisfy your lust for drama? Just out of curiosity, Beau, what exactly did you expect me to do—dog your footsteps? Cry? *Beg* for affection? Well, screw you, Dupree."

He knocked her finger aside and cupped his long hands around her jaw, tilting it up and holding her in place while he rocked his mouth over hers.

And, oh. God. It felt so good. Juliet kissed him back, but desperately held a part of herself aloof. When he raised his head, she tamped down her screaming hormones and simply stared at him.

He rubbed his thumb over her bottom lip. "I'm sorry, Rosebud, I was wrong. I—"

"No. I was." She reached up and disengaged his hands, stepping back. "I've said it before, but clearly you weren't listening. I—don't—want—to be—a rock—around—anyone's—neck," she said slowly and concisely. "And I refuse to spend my life trying to make amends for *loving* someone. So you go do whatever it is you've been dying to do. Run barefoot through a field of bare breasts, if that's what makes you happy. Just stay the hell away from me."

"Juliet, wait—"

"No." She took one step back and then another, holding up a hand when he opened his mouth. "I have always come in a poor third with the people whose affection I most craved. Well, you know what? I'll be damned if I'll settle for that from you, too. I deserve better. It's taken me a while to realize it, but I do. So do your job, and stay out of my way. And for the record, Beau, when *Daddy* insisted you weren't our kind, I told him to butt out, too." Stooping, she picked up her clipboard and swept across the room, making an exit that even Grandmother would have applauded.

And if her heart was breaking with every step she took, at least *he* would never know.

23

❧

*B*eau was riding the crest of a piss-poor attitude when he walked into the bar. Pulling out a chair at the first table he came to, he swung his leg over its seat, planted his butt, and tossed his case folder onto the minuscule tabletop.

This wasn't the choicest spot in town to get any work done, and he knew it. The light was dim, the music loud, and the crowd who watched the stripper on stage full of raucous, mostly illegal suggestions. It was also from here that the Panty Snatcher had chosen three of his victims, including Josie Lee. Offhand, Beau could think of a dozen places better suited for studying the case he was struggling to build against Haynes.

But he was hot, tired, and frustrated, and without thinking he'd found himself in the Goat driving out of his way to get here. For the past two days he'd knocked himself out trying to put together something substantive in this case, but the results were skimpy, to say the least. So, the hell with it.

This joint was an armpit, a dive—and *just* the sort of low brow establishment to suit his mood.

A coaster landed on the table next to his folder, and a dulcet voice inquired, "What can I getcha, hawt?"

Beau looked up to see a wet dream in spike heels and a sequined G-string hovering at his side. She was blond, she was built, and she had an expression that said she was no better than she oughtta be. She was, in short, exactly the kind of woman he'd fantasized about for the past decade—and it made him extremely nervous to realize he didn't feel the slightest bit stirred. To compensate, he flashed her his most killing smile. "Give me a bottle of Dixie, sugar."

When she inhaled a deep breath, her abbreviated crop top wasn't equal to the task of containing the lush bottom curves of a truly spectacular set of breasts. Thrusting them close to his face and returning a carnivorous smile of her own, she said, "Why don'tcha pick up your whatchacallit, there, shoog, and I'll clean off that sticky ol' table for you."

Obediently he lifted the folder. The waitress leaned over him to wash off the table, and her left breast swayed into teasing contact with the side of his face with every swipe of her arm. To his disgust, what popped into his head was not that old primeval male desire for a little horizontal boogaloo with a brand-new partner. Rather, it was the look on Juliet's face when she'd said, *I have always come in a poor third with the people whose affection I most craved.*

Damn her. Blinking the apparition away, he straightened in his seat. In defiance of the ghost that simply would not leave him be, he raised his hand and curved it around the indentation where the barmaid's waist flowed into bare, lush hip. "So. I bet you dance here, too, huh?"

"That I do, shoog. You wanna see my stuff, I'd be happy to give you a private table dance right now."

Beau felt a sudden weariness. "Maybe later." He slid his hand off her hip and tapped the folder in front of him. "Much as I'd love that, I've got a mess of work here that needs lookin' over."

The look she gave him cast doubts upon his sexuality, as if the heterosexual who could pass up her abundantly displayed charms for the sake of a slim manila folder had yet to be born. But she merely shrugged and said, "You think about it, shoog. I'll be back with your beer in a minute."

She ceased to exist for him the moment she walked away. Opening the folder, he spread the contents across the table. He set aside the forensics reports, having nearly memorized them. He lined up the black and white proofs he'd picked up from the photographer half an hour ago, knowing that it was highly debatable they'd have anything new to teach him at this late date.

It was nevertheless a disappointment to be proved right. He studied the garden party shots first. They were stamped with a date and time, and while he was able to locate Edward in two of them, neither photo placed the man anywhere near the sweet olive trees at the time of the shooting. Beau moved on to the cocktail party photos.

He separated out a nice clear shot of Edward and Celeste and thumbed through the rest to see if he'd missed anything. When he found himself lingering over a shot of himself and Juliet, tracing his thumb over her two-dimensional, black-and-white features, he impatiently shuffled it to the back of the stack. He studied the rest and then put them back in the folder, leaving out only the three photos in which Edward was featured.

"Here's your Dixie, hawt." The barmaid gave the pictures on the table a brief, disinterested glance as she set the bottle on the coaster next to them. "That'll be . . ." Her voice trailed off as she leaned forward to give the photographs a closer look. "Hey, that's Dapper Dan." She turned her head to look at Beau. "What are you doin' with his picture, hon? You a whatchamacallit? A photographer?"

Beau's blood started to thrum hot and heavy through his veins, and he said, "You know this guy?"

"Well, not *know* him know him, shoog. But he comes in here sometimes." She straightened. "That'll be four-fifty for the beer."

Beau fished his wallet out of his back pocket and pulled out a twenty. He handed it to her. "And his name is Dan, you say?"

"You got me, shoog. That's just what we call him—Dapper Dan. Well, look here, you can see for yourself." She reached out to tap one long, blood-red fingernail against the photograph of Edward wearing a tuxedo at the Garden Crown's pre-opening. "On account of the way he dresses, ya know? And his manners. He's got really nice manners." Pulling back, she deposited the twenty in a box on her tray and made change, which she extended to Beau.

He gave her a huge grin. He could *kiss* the woman. Damn, were his instincts hot, or what— how else to explain what had driven him to this dive at this moment? *Edward was the friggin' Panty Snatcher.* He waved away the change. "Keep it."

"Hey, thanks, hawt." She put the change in a separate envelope in the back of her money box.

"Don't mention it, sugar—you're gonna earn it. Here." He pulled out the chair next to him. "Have a seat. I've got a lot of questions for you."

Roxanne looked up and eyed him with cold disfavor when he walked through her office door a couple hours later. "What do you want, Dupree?" There wasn't so much as a token pretense of civility in her tone.

Good question. If he could think of any other way to get the information he sought, you wouldn't see him within ten miles of this joint. "I need to talk to Juliet. She in?"

"Not for you."

Defensiveness settled hot and heavy in his gut, and it made him resentful. "You'll have to excuse the hell outta me if I don't just take your word for it." He gestured peremptorily at the intercom button on her phone. "Ask her. I'm here on business."

Roxanne curled her upper lip at him, but picked up the receiver and punched the intercom button. "Juliet? Sergeant Dupree is here to see you. He says it's about business." She listened for a moment, then said in a noncommittal tone, "Will do," and reseated the receiver. She looked up at Beau, but made him sweat it out for several heartbeats before she said, "You can go in."

It surprised him to feel his heart thud heavily against the wall of his chest. Crossing the ante-room, he paused at the door to the inner office and glanced back at Roxanne. She met his gaze head-on, and if contempt were lethal, he would have dropped in his tracks. Since he was still standing, he turned the knob and opened the door.

Juliet looked up when he walked in, but she nei-ther pushed back from her desk nor rose. She folded her hands atop a stack of papers on the desk and regarded him with aloof, polite patience, as if he were a stranger who had wandered into the wrong place.

He hadn't known it would bother him this much to see her look at him so dispassionately. He licked his bottom lip. "Uh, you look good." And she did. She'd clearly tried to button herself back into her prim and proper Ms. Astor Lowell persona, but New Orleans heat had a way of softening her best efforts. She was damp and rumpled, and with the renegade lock of hair that wrapped its wavy strands around her throat, she looked altogether touchable.

"Thank you," she said coolly. "But I'm sure that's not what you're here to discuss. And since we're both busy . . . ?"

"Okay." He shoved his hands in his pockets. She wanted professional—he could be professional. "I believe I'm making progress in the investigation."

"Congratulations."

"Uh, yeah, thanks. But I could use your help."

One golden brown eyebrow rose. "What possible help could I provide?"

"Information. You can tell me if Edward Haynes has a favorite spot in the hotel where he hangs out . . . or if he spends all his time up in his apartment." In which case, Beau's case would go straight down the tubes.

For just a second her impenetrable composure cracked and she shot him a look that clearly questioned his sanity. "*Excuse* me?"

"You heard me, dawlin.' "

"Why in heaven's name would you want to know where Edward spends his spare time?"

"I'm not at liberty to say." He would have sworn it wasn't possible for her back to get any straighter, but it did.

"Fine. Then you know where the door is."

"Dammit, Juliet!"

"Don't you swear at me, Beauregard Dupree." She rose to her feet, every inch of her radiating a lifetime of good breeding. "If you want information from me, you'll explain why. If you're unwilling to do that, then you can just trot your arrogant carcass out of my office and quit wasting my time. I have work to do."

Beau wasn't accustomed to having his authority challenged. Under ordinary circumstances he wouldn't tell a civilian squat, and he'd let his fingernails be ripped from their beds before he'd allow anyone to dictate terms where a case of his was concerned.

But he was in desperate need of probable cause, or Edward Haynes was going to get off scot-free. Moreover, he realized that he trusted Juliet's judgment.

He didn't know why that should catch him by surprise. Idiot that he was, hadn't he told her about his decade-long fantasy to bed every able-bodied woman in New Orleans? He'd never entrusted that to a soul but Luke. Besides—and he had to swallow back a snort—God knew her discretion was reliable. To see her facing him down now, one would never guess that she had ever lain in his arms panting and whispering dark, raw demands in his ear. So, she sure as hell wasn't likely to give anything away to Haynes before Beau was ready to make his move.

"Okay," he said. "I've got several leads that implicate Edward not only in the attempts on your life, but in the Panty Snatcher case as well."

Juliet felt the shock clear down to her toes. Sweet, gentle Edward? She shook her head. "I don't believe it."

"He's connected to a set of antique pistols that are consistent with the one used to take a shot at you."

"*Consistent* with?"

"My sister also identified it as the type used to force her to take off her clothes."

"And this gun is one of a kind?"

"No, but how many antique guns do you think

are out there being used in the commission of *two* separate crimes?"

"He's a *collector*. It isn't necessarily the same gun."

"A barmaid in a place we've established as the common denominator in several of the Panty Snatcher incidents identified his picture, Juliet."

"For heaven's sake—he dropped by for a drink in a bar. Does that make him a criminal?"

"Dammit, do you think I'm just stringing this crap together for the fun of it?" He was suddenly standing much too close, his dark eyes glaring down at her. "I've been a cop for a long time— give me some friggin' credit for my instincts."

Resentment boiled in her veins. "I've been on the receiving end of your instincts," she snapped. "You'll have to excuse me if I'm not impressed."

His face was suddenly bent so near to hers she felt his breath hot against her mouth. "I'm talking *professional* instincts, not . . ." Backing up a step, he shoved a hand through his hair. Kneading the back of his neck, he exhaled and said quietly, "I showed his photo at three other places where a victim had either worked or been to, and he was positively identified at them, too. And these four places are dives, Juliet. Bottom-of-the-barrel strip joints. Can you honestly picture Edward patronizing such places under ordinary circumstances?"

His unemotional professionalism in the face of his frustration with her was frighteningly convincing. "It all sounds so circumstantial." She hated that her tone practically pleaded with him to say it was a mistake.

"Right now that's exactly what it is. Which is why I need to know if there's a place in the hotel besides his living quarters where he spends a great deal of time."

She knew by his sudden alertness that her face must have given her away. "Show me," he said. "And I'll need your permission to search it."

"You're wrong, Beau."

"Then prove it to me and I'll drop the whole line of inquiry. You might consider, though, that your corporation displaced Edward and his wife from a home they'd lived in for more than twenty-five years—which would have been helpful to have known before this week. And that it was shortly thereafter the threats began on your life."

"This is crazy."

"Like I said, prove me wrong."

"Fine. I will." She stalked past him and stopped by Roxanne's desk on their way through her office. "Do we have keys for the Blue Room?"

"Let me look." Sparing them a covert glance, Roxanne bent to her bottom drawer. "Celeste handed all this stuff over the day we arrived." She sorted through tangled sets of tagged keys. "Ah, here we go." Straightening, she extended a ring containing two skeleton keys.

Juliet waited until they were out of Roxanne's hearing before she turned to Beau. "Edward actually spends most of his time in two places. The gardening shed and the Blue Room."

Beau was silent for a moment. "He collects souvenirs," he finally said. "And he'd want to keep them in a fairly immaculate state. The Blue Room."

They headed off, and Juliet was aware of him beside her every step of the way. There was a tension about him, an energetic anticipation that she could only assume was part of being a cop on the hunt. *Her* stomach was tied up in knots, and only half of that had to do with being forced to be this near Beau when their relationship was such a screwed-up mess.

The Blue Room was empty when they got there and Beau paused in the doorway, looking around. "Do I have your express permission to search here?"

She swallowed hard. "Yes."

"Let's open up the locked stuff, then. There's far too many people in and out of here for him to risk leaving anything incriminating in plain sight."

She wanted to protest Edward's innocence again, but she held her tongue and handed Beau the key ring. He'd taken her seriously when she refused to divulge Edward's habits without an explanation, and even knowing she was furious with him, he had trusted her with sensitive information. It was more faith than she was accustomed to receiving, and he deserved equal respect.

One of the keys fit the set of cabinets on either side of the ornately carved built-in bookcases. Neither contained whatever it was Beau sought. He fit the remaining key into the drawer keyhole of a small antique desk, and Juliet held her breath when he pulled it open.

"Shit."

She exhaled again. "It *isn't* him."

"It is, Juliet. I feel it in my gut."

"Well, your gut is wrong."

Beau merely grunted and started removing books. Soon there were stacks surrounding their feet, but there was nothing to see except empty shelves. Swearing in frustration, Beau smacked one of the carved decorations with the flat of his hand.

A panel in the back of the wall slid silently open.

They both just stared at the dim opening for a moment. Then a crack of incredulous, exultant laughter exploded out of Beau, and he planted a hard, fast kiss on Juliet's dumbstruck mouth and flashed her a crooked, self-deprecatory smile. "You gotta admire crackerjack detective work, huh? See if that little lamp will stretch over here."

It did, and Juliet peered over Beau's shoulder into the space it illuminated. Her heart immediately sank to her heels.

For an old-fashioned-looking pistol lay within, nestled atop a sizable pile of women's underwear.

24

Celeste completed her toilette and leaned forward to regard herself in the mirror. She picked up the Butler pearls and fastened them around her neck, shutting out the muffled sounds of footsteps and voices in the hallway outside her and Edward's apartment.

It was an hour before the Grand Opening Ball was scheduled to begin, and there had been much coming and going since four o'clock this afternoon as the rooms on their floor slowly filled. She'd heard Juliet mention that the hotel was booked at eighty percent capacity for the evening, and Celeste had seen the reservations book for herself. It read like a virtual Who's Who of the very cream of Louisiana society. Even several of the Boston Club people planned to spend the night, and they had perfectly grand homes of their own right here in town.

She wasn't certain what she thought about that. Taking a sip from the minuscule glass of sherry on her dressing table, she sat back in her seat. While part of her was thrilled to have such luminaries in her home for the second time in such a short space of time, this was no longer her home. And yet. . . .

All things considered, she felt rather . . . euphoric.

Juliet was scheduled to leave soon. Celeste hadn't heard an exact date mentioned, but the young woman's job would be done once tonight's event was over. Perhaps she'd even leave as soon as tomorrow, if there was a God in His heaven. More importantly, that rude young Yat of a policeman had barely been around recently—and Lily had told her it was the talk of the staff that when he *was* here evenings, he slept in his own room. It was beginning to look as if she'd worried herself sick for nothing.

She and Edward had until the end of the month before they were required to give up their apartment here. Maybe tomorrow she'd begin looking for a new abode. Something small, yet elegant, in the right neighborhood, naturally. This evening would be a perfect time to query the people who mattered about the best places to begin her search.

With the money the Crown Corporation had contracted to pay her and Edward for being displaced from their home and for their services in introducing Juliet to the right people, a lovely little nest egg had been accumulated. If she could just convince Edward to sell them his mask collection as well, or at least a portion of it, money would never again be an issue.

She took another sip of sherry and reached for

her pearl earbobs, clipping them on and giving her reflection a nod of approval. She would simply regard the upcoming change as an adventure. For truly, although it was wrenching to lose the Butler estate, life was a trade-off. They'd always had the address but never the money that went along with it. Now, not only could they afford the amenities that made life worth living, but the one thing that was absolutely crucial to their quality of life—their standing in New Orleans' society—was firmly intact. It had actually risen. Life was certainly strange sometimes, the way it seemed to hand one a problem of gargantuan proportions, only to have the reality turn out quite differently.

All things considered, her reality looked bright.

Juliet set down her mascara, smoothed her hair one last time, and checked her lipstick. She slid her hands up the halter straps of her bronze evening gown to the narrow band that connected them at her nape, making sure the six strands of amber beads draped correctly between the band and their attachments at the gown's low-cut V back. Picking up a hand mirror, she turned to check the results.

They fell in perfect alignment, and she knew she really ought to hurry. The ball would begin in less than an hour and there were still a dozen details that needed attending. Instead, she found herself doing something she'd done far too much of recently: gazing blindly into the distance and thinking of Beau.

God, what was she going to do about him? By rights, she ought to hop the first plane out of here tomorrow morning and head back to Boston, where she understood all the rules. Yet she hadn't even called for flight schedules.

She was deranged; there was just no getting around it. Beau had flat-out told her he dreamed of a free and easy lifestyle that didn't include her, so why was she considering hanging around New Orleans like some lovesick fool? She had more pride than that—at least she always had in the past.

And yet . . .

She *was* in love, and he kept giving her so many mixed signals. If he was all through with her, why did he keep kissing her? How could she tuck tail and run if there was a chance for them? She rather *liked* operating without a full understanding of all the rules when it came to him—even if it was stressful at the moment.

Wondering what on earth Beau was up to in regards to Edward Haynes added another dimension to her edginess. Not knowing when the police might arrive with the search and arrest warrants he'd left to get yesterday was a lot like waiting for the other shoe to drop in an old Hitchcock movie— and something she could easily do without.

She hadn't seen a glimpse of Beau since he'd had her point out a pair of pruning shears that Edward routinely used, and bagged it to take with him for a fingerprint check. The two messages she'd left him at work had gone unanswered, and if he'd returned here to sleep last night, it was long past the time she'd finally given up waiting and fallen asleep. She didn't even know whether he planned to appear at tonight's ball.

Giving herself a mental shake, she straightened her spine. She could go on like this all night, and accomplish absolutely nothing. She had a Grand Opening to conduct—an event her entire career had been building toward. She'd best be smart and see to it.

She could worry about the state of her love life tomorrow.

The ball was well under way and Juliet's "to do" list had finally been whittled down to almost nothing when a woman's voice spoke her name.

"Juliet, hello. Do you remember me?"

Turning from imparting final instructions to Roxanne, Juliet saw Beau's petite sister approaching with Josie Lee and Luke and another couple. "Anabel! Of course I remember you; how have you been? You haven't had any more reptiles in your bedroom, I hope." She smiled at the man and woman she didn't know and said, "Hello, Luke, Josie Lee." For just a moment, before she caught herself, she looked beyond the small group in search of Beau.

"You've never met my sister Camilla, have you?" Anabel said. "And this is her husband, Ned Fortenay."

Camilla smiled and extended her hand. "It's so nice to finally meet you. And thank you for inviting us. It's a wonderful affair."

Warmth bloomed in Juliet's stomach, and she gave Beau's sister a smile that was entirely genuine—a rare occurrence for her this evening. "Oh, bless you for saying that. My assistant and I have been so crazed trying to keep up with the details, we haven't had a moment to stop and assess how we're actually doing. It's nice to know it's all hanging together."

"It's doing more than that," Josie Lee assured her. She snagged a glass of champagne from a roving waiter and saluted Juliet. "It's a fabulous party. The food is wonderful, the music is spectacular even by New Orleans' standards, and it's a blast to see so many gorgeous gowns in one place."

"Yours is certainly lovely." A smile tugged up the corner of Juliet's mouth as she admired Josie Lee's floor-length, tomato-red, form-fitting sheath and added with an honesty she'd been trained to suppress, "I wish *I* had the wherewithal to hold up a strapless gown."

"Me, too," Anabel agreed gloomily. "All the boobs in the family went to these two. Talk about unfair, huh? So, where is Beau?"

Juliet found herself the cynosure of three pairs of dark, curious eyes, and was grateful to Luke when he said, "Beau has an assignment tonight."

"I thought Juliet was his assignment," Camilla protested.

"Not tonight. Something else came up."

"But, Luke, what if someone attempts to harm her again—" Josie Lee grimaced at her tactlessness. "Sorry, Juliet. Sometimes my mouth works faster than my brain."

"No one's gonna get to her, anyway. Look around you, Baby Girl. Your brother made sure the place was crawlin' with cops. You probably just didn't recognize them right away because they're wearing tuxes. And I'm here," he added, striking a wryly macho pose. "Speaking of which"—he ran his hand down Josie Lee's bare arm—"you mind if I ask our hostess to dance?"

"Of course not."

Luke turned to Juliet. "Would you care to dance?"

"I'd like that very much," she said and excused herself to Beau's sisters. With relief, she allowed Luke to lead her to the dance floor.

Holding her a respectful few inches away, Luke gazed down at her as they danced. "You okay?"

She looked up at him. "Oh, God, you know, don't you?"

"Not the details. Beau just said you weren't talking to him."

She nearly strangled on her bitter laugh. "Yes, silly me. I tend to get a bit testy when I'm dumped so a man can fulfill his fantasy of sleeping with every woman in New Orleans."

Luke stopped dead on the dance floor. "He *told* you that?"

People around them gawked in a subtle, well-bred sort of way, and Luke picked up the rhythm again. He shook his head, looking utterly bemused. "I can't believe he told you that. He's never talked about that to anyone but me."

"Well, aren't I the lucky little buckaroo."

"I'm sorry," he said contritely. "I'm making everything worse."

"No, I'm sorry. You were discreet in front of

Beau's family and you're being wonderfully sweet. I'm the one behaving abominably."

"No," Luke disagreed grimly. "That would be the idiot Dupree."

She smiled. "You're a nice man, Luke Gardener. Josie Lee's extremely lucky."

Suddenly there was a subtle sense of agitation around them—less a sound than a rustle of movement. Juliet glanced around to see what had caused it, and froze when she saw Beau bearing down on them.

His eyes were bloodshot, and with his shadowed jaw, grim expression, and old, worn jeans and a collarless denim shirt with the sleeves rolled up his forearms, he looked dark, angry, and out of place. The first words out of his mouth did nothing to dispel the notion.

"What the hell are you doing dancing with Juliet Rose, Gardner? I thought you were supposed to be moon-faced in love with my sister."

Although Beau was under the gun and racing a clock, something about seeing Juliet smiling up at his best friend ripped open an unknown streak of jealousy. But he forced himself to shake it off. "I'm sorry, that's not what I meant to say at all. I'm actually glad you're here, Luke—some serious shit is about to hit the fan."

He reached out to stroke a fingertip down the smooth-skinned curve of Juliet's shoulder. She looked so great in her sexy little gown, and he regretted he couldn't take the time to appreciate it. He regretted a lot of things. "I'm sorry, dawlin'. I wouldn't see your big night ruined for anything, but the Pissant got wind of my investigation and he's determined to turn it into a freakin' side-show."

"What the hell are you talkin' about, Dupree?" Luke herded them from the dance floor into a quiet corner.

"I'm saying I'm maybe ten minutes ahead of him, Luke. Pfeffer's taken the results of my investigation and plans to use them to very publicly search the Blue Room and arrest Edward Haynes. Here. Tonight. The sonofabitch is gonna wreck Rosebud's big night just to get his face on the eleven o'clock news." He scrubbed his hands across his face, then let them fall to his sides. "I walked in on him a while ago calling up the local stations. I disconnected him from Channel Eight, but you can be damn sure he called them back the minute I left—then probably went on to talk to Four and Six as well."

"He's going to arrest Edward here, tonight?" Juliet's face was rapidly losing color. "At my Grand Opening?"

"Yes."

"*Why?*"

"Because he's a pompous bureaucrat with political aspirations."

"But . . . I thought he was so enamored of my father."

"That was yesterday, angel face. Today Daddy isn't a registered voter in the parish of Orleans." The look on her face was killing him. "I'm sorry— I'd planned to do this last night more privately, but by the time we matched up Haynes's prints to some taken from the crime scenes, I couldn't track down a judge to sign the warrants. Look, do you know where Edward is? I have the warrants now and if I move real fast, I might be able to do this before Pfeffer gets here."

"But what will that do to your career, Beau?"

"Not a damn thing." Or so he hoped. Either way, he owed her—he'd been messing up her life right and left since the moment she'd hit town. "Let's just find Haynes."

They weren't quick enough.

Beau had no sooner spotted Edward standing with Celeste over by the dining room entrance and alerted Luke and Juliet than the main door banged open and a group led by Peter Pfeffer swarmed through the entrance in a confusion of bright lights and loud voices. Pfeffer paused on the threshold to look around, got a bead on Edward Haynes, and made a beeline straight for him.

"Son of a bitch." Beau stopped dead and turned to Juliet. And was hit with a sudden revelation that made his stomach burn and his hands go cold.

Oh, man. He loved her. After doing everything possible to flush it all down the tubes, he loved her.

Despite her pale, expressionless composure, he knew she felt sick underneath—and knew he'd do anything, give anything, to make things right for her. Why had it taken him so long to realize that his carefree bachelor days were far more fun in retrospect than in reality? Now, he'd probably blown the one chance he'd had for something really special.

He wrapped his hands around the back of Juliet's neck and gently tilted her chin up with his thumbs. "I've gotta go administer whatever damage control I can. I'm really sorry about this shit exploding all over your big night, Juliet Rose."

She didn't say anything; merely blinked those big gray eyes once as she stared up at him.

He felt a sudden sense of urgency. "Listen, dawlin', don't go leavin' town, okay? Promise me you won't go back to Boston before I can talk to you."

"Edward Haynes," Pfeffer's voice intoned loudly, "you are under arrest for burglary in the first degree, with sexual motivation. You have the right to remain silent. You have the right . . ."

Beau swore viciously and kissed Juliet hard. Releasing her, he ordered, "Don't leave," and spun away.

He didn't look back as he waded into the crowd toward the scene being played out near the dining room entrance.

Juliet stood numb and unmoving for several long moments. Finally, she took a deep breath and shook out her hands. Hearing the excited chatter around her, she approached the band leader and asked him to resume the music. She corralled the nearest waiter, who stood gawking with everyone else, and reminded him to keep the champagne circling.

Roxanne approached. "What can I do?"

"Keep our servers moving. Let's try to recoup our losses as best we can."

"They say there's no such thing as bad publicity," Roxanne offered.

"That's what I keep telling myself." Juliet touched her friend's hand. "I saw Beau go into the Blue Room. I'd like to go see what's happening and perhaps get an idea of how soon we can expect the police to be out of here."

"You go ahead. I'll circle the wagons here."

"Thanks, Rox."

She passed Edward, barricaded by policemen, and Celeste, who stood white-faced just outside of the phalanx of tuxedoed cops. Every camera and minicam in the place was trained on the tableau. Pfeffer postured for the media's benefit, but before Juliet could detour over to him, Beau pushed his way past the crowd that blocked the door to the Blue Room. He carried a clear plastic parcel containing the pistol and panties they had discovered yesterday.

The media immediately turned their cameras on him, but he thwarted them by tucking the packet under his shirt. Ignoring Pfeffer, he edged through the line of cops to stop in front of Edward.

"Mr. Haynes, I'm going to take you to headquarters now."

Edward looked at him for an instant and then gave a brief nod.

"I'll leave the cuffs off until we get outside." Gently grasping the older man's elbow, he headed for the door.

Juliet watched them go, then turned to see Pfeffer holding forth with the press.

"Through hard detective work, we've arrived at this moment where once again the streets are a little bit safer," he said pedantically. "We have reason to believe Edward Haynes is the perpetrator who has plagued the city in recent months with a series of—"

Juliet inserted herself between him and the cameras, burning to tell the media that the hard detective work was not Pfeffer's doing. "You're not welcome here, sir. I'd like you to leave."

Dark color surged beneath Pfeffer's skin. "We're conductin' a police investigation here, young lady."

"Since all the evidence and your suspect have gone downtown, sir, there's nothing left for you to investigate, is there? Please leave."

"It's mah understanding that this is an establishment open to the public."

"Your understanding is correct. We do, however, reserve the right to deny service to anyone we wish. You have outstayed your welcome." She turned to the media. "Turn off those cameras. I want you all out of here now."

They had no recourse but to comply with her wishes, and she stood sentinel until the last one was out the door. Then, suppressing a sigh, she turned to do what she could to salvage her event.

25

*L*uke found Josie Lee standing with her sisters. Anabel leaned into her from one side, Camilla's arm was wrapped around her shoulders from the other, and Ned stood at her back. He stopped in front of her. "You okay, Jose?"

"Yeah." She stepped into his arms. "That really was the Panty Snatcher, then?"

He wrapped her in his arms. "Yeah."

"I thought so, but I wasn't absolutely sure." She shivered and his arms tightened around her.

"I'm sorry, Baby Girl. I had no idea that would go down tonight. Neither did Beau. It must have been some kinda tough to get caught unprepared like that, huh?"

"I always imagined that if I ever saw the guy, I'd want to rip his face from his skull with my bare hands. But he looked like a confused old man, Luke."

"I know. It's that 'best laid plans' thing, I guess."

"Speaking of which, poor Juliet! Pfeffer sure

made a mess of her grand opening. Couldn't the idiot have waited until tomorrow?"

"I'll bet Beau's livid," Anabel chimed in. "Her bein' his sweetie, and all."

Luke wasn't about to get into the convoluted relationship between Beau and Juliet. "He's less than thrilled, all right."

"And the way that acting captain talked to the press, you'd think he'd done all the detective work himself," Camilla said indignantly. "I don't *think* so." Her husband rubbed his hand up and down her bare arm.

"Why *would* he handle it this way, Luke?" Anabel demanded. "It seemed pretty unnecessary."

"Well, his position's about to disappear at the end of the month. Beau guesses it's political aspirations."

"Oh, goody," Josie Lee said glumly. "Just what New Orleans needs—another politician looking out for Number One." Then she made a visible effort to shake off the bitter mood. "What d'y'all say we don't let this ruin our evening?"

"Yeah," Anabel agreed. "How often do we get an opportunity to get all dressed up like this, anyway?"

"Exactly. Let's find Juliet and see if there's anything we can do to help her salvage her party."

The individual districts no longer possessed holding cells of their own, so Beau took Edward to police headquarters to conduct the interrogation and have the evidence processed. He closed the interview room door behind them and pulled out a

chair at the small table in the center. "Have a seat,
Mr. Haynes."

Edward sat, looking around with vague eyes at
his surroundings. Beau removed the handcuffs and
then circled the table. He pulled out a chair for
himself and straddled the seat, crossing his arms
over the top rail of its back.

"You want a cup of coffee or anything?"

Edward's gaze returned to him. "No, thank
you."

"You wanna tell me why you've been breaking
into women's houses and making them strip at
gunpoint?"

"I like looking at naked girls," Edward replied,
as if it were a perfectly reasonable explanation. "I
like it a lot—and Celeste would never let me look
at her. Girls are so pretty, don't you think? I like
their skin. And the way they smell."

Sweet Mother Mary. "Did you ever stop to consider they might not like stripping for a stranger?"

Edward blinked. "Why? All of them either
worked for or frequented burlesque clubs; I figured
they liked being looked at. I never hurt anyone,
Sergeant. I just wanted to study them somewhere
a bit more private than a bar." Then he smiled
sweetly. "I would have enjoyed doing more than
that, of course, but I knew it wouldn't be proper."

"If all you planned to do was study them in the
nude, you should have just bought yourself a girlie
magazine," Beau said flatly.

Edward shook his head. "Celeste would never
allow one of those brought into the house," he said
with wistful regret.

There was a tap on the wall, and Beau glanced at the two-way mirror, from behind which the assistant DA monitored the interview. He pushed a legal pad and a pen across the table. "I've gotta go out for a few minutes. While I'm gone, I'd like you to write down everything you can remember about all the girls you've 'asked' to undress for you. Give me details about how you let yourself into their homes and what happened once you were there." He watched Edward for a moment as they elderly man picked up the pen and began to write on the yellow ruled paper. "I'll be right back."

He joined the assistant district attorney out in the hall. The man immediately demanded, "So, what do you think?"

"He never so much as asked for an attorney," Beau admitted. "And he's in there right now, writing out his confession. He could be feeling his way toward an insanity plea, I suppose, but I don't think so. I sort of have to question his competency."

The ADA sighed. "Yeah, that was my thought, too. I'll schedule an appointment to have our psychiatrist take a look at him." He shook his head. "Sure coulda used a whole lot less publicity surrounding this arrest, Dupree."

"Tell me about it. Captain Taylor's due back at the beginning of the month, and it can't come a second too soon for me." He blew out a breath. "I still need to question Haynes about some attempts that were made on his employer's life."

The lawyer glanced down at his paperwork. "I don't see any charges to that effect here."

"No—we don't have a shred of proof at this point. But he seems to be in a forthcoming frame of mind, so I might as well see what shakes loose." Unease nagged him over the differences between Haynes's nonviolent encounters as the Panty Snatcher and the aggression that had been used against Juliet. But the antique guns linked the crimes. Anything else would be too damn coincidental for words. His instincts nevertheless urged him to move this along. "I'd better get back to it. I'll book Haynes when I'm through and stick him in holding."

"Sounds good." The ADA snapped his folder closed. "I'll see if I can set up an appointment with the shrink for first thing in the morning."

"She oughtta be thrilled to be called in on a Sunday morning," Beau said dryly, and the young man grinned.

"I know. That's the highlight of my night." He strolled away, whistling tunelessly.

Beau let himself back into the interview room. "How you doing, Mr. Haynes?"

Edward glanced up, then went back to his writing. "I'll be done in a moment."

"Take your time."

They sat in a silence broken only by the scratch of Edward's pen. A short while later, Edward set it down and straightened, opening and closing his hand upon the tabletop as if easing a writer's cramp.

Beau reached across the table for the stack of handwritten pages. "You finished?"

Edward nodded.

"Sign your name to it." As soon as Edward had complied, he pulled the stack to his side of the table and began to read. His jaw tightened once, when he read the appreciative comment Haynes had made about Josie Lee's breasts, but he swallowed his instinctive challenge. A moment later, he set the paper aside. "Let's talk about Juliet Astor Lowell for a moment."

Edward flashed a sweet smile. "A lovely young woman."

"Yes, she is. So why did you write her that threatening letter regarding the Garden Crown?"

Edward dropped his gaze. "Oh, dear, that was rather bad of us, wasn't it? But Celeste was upset about being displaced from the Butler estates. And it really wasn't a threat, you know." He looked up again, meeting Beau's eyes while he carefully straightened the sleeves of his tux. "It was simply a little dissertation to protest the loss of yet another piece of history to crass commercialism. And of course, it was before we'd actually met the dear girl."

Us. We. Beau was beginning to get a very bad feeling.

"And I suppose you didn't cut the brake line, either. Or take a shot at her at the garden party. Or saw through the banister in hopes that she'd fall while giving her welcome speech at the cocktail party."

Edward's posture grew erect, all offended dignity. "Certainly not."

"Then who did, Mr. Haynes?"

*   *   *

"Roxanne, do you know where Celeste went? I've been so busy, I failed to even notice the poor woman had slipped away."

Eyebrows raised skeptically, Roxanne made a rude noise. "Poor woman, my—"

"I know she hasn't treated you particularly well." Juliet reached out to touch her assistant's arm. "But she's so proud of her position in New Orleans' society, and Edward's arrest must have been a teriffic blow."

"And it couldn't have happened to a more deserving—" Roxanne cut herself off and grimaced ruefully. "Sorry. The person I can't help feeling sorry for, though, is Edward. Whatever he's done, I bet the dragon lady drove him to it."

Juliet swallowed a smile. One could always count on Roxanne for unrelenting honesty. Celeste *was* difficult. But no one deserved the kind of public humiliation she'd been subjected to tonight. And from the older woman's point of view, the timing probably couldn't have been more horrific. "I'll check her rooms."

She looked around at the party. Wine flowed, people danced, and the decibel level was a steady hum as folks laughed and gossiped. "I guess we worried prematurely about the guests leaving in droves, huh?" She shook her head. "I feel for the poor new general manager—for sheer scandal and sensationalism, our last two events are going to be difficult to top."

Her eyes met Roxanne's, and they both burst into slightly hysterical laughter. Juliet tried to rein her amusement in, for surely it wasn't appropriate, but the corners of her lips kept curling up despite her staunchest efforts. "God, I love this town," she confessed. "It's a world unto itself."

"So, maybe we ought to stay."

Juliet stilled, every atom of her being quivering to attention in agreement. "Start our own business and give Father a run for his money, you mean?"

"Yeah, why not? Not that I've got a helluva lot to contribute."

"I beg to differ. You've got loads to contribute."

"Juliet—"

"Perhaps not financially, Roxanne. But you've got one of the most organized minds I've ever encountered. Things don't slip through the cracks with you in charge. And I have contacts and a trust fund that's never been touched." The entire concept sparked her imagination. "I'm going to give this some real thought. That is . . ." She shot her friend an uncertain glance. "You *are* serious?"

A tiny smile curved Roxanne's mouth. "Oh, yeah. I am if you are."

"Oh, God, I truly think I am." She laughed, because the whole idea felt so right. "We'll have to talk about it in more depth later. Right now, I'd better check on Celeste and make sure she's all right."

She couldn't get the idea out of her mind as she made her way through the revelers to the open stairway. Sometime during her stay in New Orleans, she had evolved into someone she actually liked. Although much of what Grandmother had drummed into her head had merit, many of the rules she'd been taught were designed strictly for appearance's sake, and she was finally learning to do what most of her peers had undoubtedly figured out during their adolescence—to take the best of her upbringing and disregard the rest.

And if Beau didn't like her decision to stay when he heard about it? Well, as much as she loved him, she didn't need a man to be complete. This town was big enough for the two of them. And if he didn't think so, he could always move.

Ruined. Celeste stared into the mirror over her dressing table. She was ruined. There would be no recouping their position in society after this. That horrid man who'd talked to the media had made Edward's little hobby sound *deviant*, for pity's sake, and she could hear the sound of doors closing in her face all over town.

Well, she'd make them sorry. She knocked back her thimbleful of sherry and pulled open a drawer in her dressing table, reaching in to extract the pistol. Loading the ammunition into the front of the cylinder, she used the attached rammer to push the bullet to the back. Then she placed a percussion cap on one of the cylinder nipples. Each of the six bullets called for its own cap, but she only needed one for what she had in mind. Cocking the hammer, she raised the barrel to her temple.

Then she lowered it to the marble tabletop and poured herself another drop of wine from the bottle at her elbow. Opening another drawer, she pulled out a stack of stationery and a pen.

To Whom It May Concern, she wrote.

It was that bitch Juliet's fault that she had come

to such a pass. It wasn't bad enough that she'd taken over her home; she'd brought her rude policeman into their lives, too. After scribbling a note to that effect, however, Celeste balled it up and tossed it to the floor. Whiners never garnered any sympathy, and she was determined that everyone who mattered would feel compunction at her passing.

She drank her sherry and poured another shot. What she needed was something with punch that would make her most persistent enemy weep with regret. Picking up her pen again, she wrote, *I find I can no longer go on in the face of Edward's disgrace* . . .

That was better, but it still lacked emotional pathos. She needed something that would grab the reader's attention right off the bat, something . . . Oh! She knew.

Dear cruel world, she wrote at the top of the page. After adding several more phrases that brought tears to *her* eyes, she finally signed her name, folded the paper in half, and picked up the pocket revolver again. She was raising it into position when there was a tap at the door.

Now what? Heaving a sigh, she set the gun down. "Who is it?"

"It's Juliet, Celeste. May I come in?"

Just like that, Celeste's plan changed. Swiveling to face the door, she slid the revolver onto the seat of her vanity bench and spread her starched taffeta skirt over it. She aligned her ankles just so and folded her hands in her lap. "By all means," she said grimly to the closed portal. "Please do."

* * *

Juliet eased the door open and poked her head in. "I'm so sorry about Edward," she said and stepped into the room, closing the door behind her. Picking her way through the family antiques that ate up every free inch of space, she approached Celeste, who sat like a dowager queen at her dressing table.

The older woman's rigid silence made her uneasy, and she continued, "The public nature of his arrest was inexcusable, and asking if you're all right is surely asinine. But is there someone I could perhaps call to come sit with you?"

The fleeting expression that crossed Celeste's face almost gave her pause, but she moved closer, reaching out an impulsive hand.

"You should have never come," Celeste said flatly.

Juliet's hand dropped to her side. "I'm sorry," she said and berated herself for feeling rebuffed. "I won't impose if you want to be alone. I just hate the thought of you sitting up here all by yourself. What Peter Pfeffer did tonight was unconscionable. Have you contacted a lawyer?"

"Butter wouldn't melt in your mouth, would it, you phony little hussy?"

Shock jolted Juliet. "Excuse me?"

"You heard me. Don't be a hypocrite, Juliet. Don't pretend a concern you don't feel."

"I *am* concerned."

Celeste emitted a genteel snort. "Please. If you and your precious Crown Hotels had stayed in Boston where you belong, none of this would have happened."

Juliet's sympathy dissipated faster than morning fog beneath the Louisiana sun. "Neither I nor Crown Corporation had anything to do with Edward forcing young women to take their clothes off, Celeste. That started long before we arrived." Her chin raised in an unconscious imitation of Grandmother. "Obviously my presence here is unwelcome, however. I won't inflict it upon you any further." She turned to go.

"Sit down."

Drawing herself up, Juliet turned back once again. "I beg your pardon?"

Celeste's hand slipped beneath her skirt and came out with a revolver, which she pointed straight at Juliet. "I said sit."

The strength leaving her knees, Juliet sat.

"I repeat, Mr. Haynes, if you didn't do all those things in an attempt to harm Juliet, who did?"

"I have no idea."

Looking at him, Beau decided he probably didn't. "Was it your idea to send her that first letter?"

"Heaven's no, dear boy, that was Celeste. It's never sat right with her that the females of the family can't inherit—"

"Where's the other gun, Mr. Haynes?"

Edward blinked. "The other . . . ?"

"Gun. The revolver we collected from your hiding place was part of a set. What became of the other one?"

"I don't know—I'm sure it's around somewhere."

Beau surged out of his seat and went to the phone in the corner. Punching out numbers, he listened impatiently as the phone on the other end of the line rang once, twice, three times. "This is Sergeant Dupree from the Eighth," he said the moment it was picked up. "I submitted a stack of evidence a while ago to be tested, part of which is an antique handgun. Has anyone checked yet to see if it's been fired recently?" His ire grew as he listened to the bureaucratic complaints on the other end of the line. "I know it's after hours, dammit. And I know you're busy, too. But I've got a woman whose life could be in immediate danger if that gun's never been fired. Don't make me come down there. Yeah, okay. Here's my cell phone number. I expect to hear from you before the half hour is up."

Resisting the urge to slam down the receiver, he gently reseated it and turned to Edward. "We're going to book you now, Mr. Haynes."

He walked Edward through the process, and twenty-five minutes later locked him up in a holding cell. Though the guy was a pervert—one who had accosted his sister—the lost look on the elderly man's face made Beau hesitate. "I'll be back in a minute," he said.

He found a detective typing a report in one of the squad rooms. "Anyone around here read skin magazines?"

The cop looked up. "Say what?"

"Girly magazines." He felt like an idiot, and any attempt to explain his real reasons would sound too damn lame for words, so he said, "I've got a prisoner who's bound to drive you nuts all night long if I don't supply him with something to engage his interest."

"Oh, Christ, a yeller?" The detective took Beau's shrug as assent. "Yeah, try Playdel's desk—the fourth one over. Bottom drawer on the left."

Playdel had quite an assortment, and Beau helped himself to two of the tamest. "Thanks."

He was an idiot, no two ways about it. Nevertheless, when he walked away after handing the magazines through the bars a couple of minutes later, he took with him the sight of Edward's gentle smile of delight.

He was loping down the stairs when his cell phone rang. "Yeah, Dupree here."

"Sergeant, this is Maxwell from the lab. We tested that gun, as you requested, and it hasn't been fired for a very long time."

"Son of a *bitch*." Beau disconnected, and running for the door nearest the garage where he'd parked, he punched in Luke's number.

An instant later the connection went through. "Hey," Luke answered breezily, and music and laughter came through the receiver.

"Man, we've got trouble." Beau filled his friend in on the situation. "I'm on my way," he said, unlocking the GTO's door and climbing in. "Just find Juliet for me and make sure she stays the hell away from Celeste until I get there."

26

Juliet stared down the barrel of Celeste's gun, and could have sworn it had a bore the size of a cannon. All the moisture in her mouth dried up. She licked her lips several times but her tongue lacked any dampness to transfer.

Celeste, watching her, smiled unpleasantly. "I'd offer you a sip of wine, but I only have one glass."

Screw the glass. "Then just pass the bottle." She wouldn't talk her way out of this mess if she couldn't even unstick her lips from her teeth.

The older woman's lip curled in fastidious disapproval, but holding the gun steadily on Juliet, she leaned forward and extended the bottle by its neck.

Juliet grasped it and brought it to her mouth. She took a greedy gulp and felt an overwhelming appreciation for the warmth that exploded in her stomach. Lowering the bottle, she curled her hand around its neck and hugged it to her chest.

Celeste regarded her with disgust. "Spend

enough time with the lower classes and one begins to act just like them."

As opposed to the good breeding shown by holding a person at gunpoint, you mean? Since she was neither stupid nor entirely suicidal, she swallowed the thought unspoken.

Celeste's lips tightened and she said waspishly, "I didn't set out to harm you, you know. It's your own fault we've come to this."

Juliet felt as enraged as a raped woman who'd just been told she'd deserved it because she wore her skirt too short and tight. She took a tiny sip of wine and said in a carefully nonconfrontational tone, "How is it my fault?"

"Because you wouldn't go away! It wasn't enough for you to take over my house and turn it into a common boardinghouse—"

The ridiculous exaggeration aside, Juliet was truly perplexed by the woman's reasoning. "But Celeste, it was going to be sold, regardless. The Butler Trust people came to us—we didn't seek them out."

As though she hadn't spoken at all, the older woman continued, "You didn't even have the refinement to be driven away by a nasty cockroach."

Juliet snapped upright. "*You* put that thing in my bed?"

"Certainly not. Loathsome creatures." Celeste shuddered. "I had Lily do it." Catching Juliet raising the wine bottle to her lips again, she glared. "Look at you! You're a disgrace. But I gave you a chance to leave peacefully. I even sent a warning letter."

Juliet's head was beginning to swirl. Though she was certain it wasn't due to the alcohol she was putting into her empty stomach, she carefully set the bottle on the floor next to her chair.

"But did you heed it?" Celeste demanded indignantly. "Oh, no, you came anyway. And even that might have turned out all right . . . but then you had to drag that uncouth policeman into the midst of our lives."

"Actually," Juliet said mildly, "Beau was brought in because of the letter."

Celeste blinked. "What?"

"Your threatening—pardon me, *warning*—letter. It caused Father to demand police protection for me."

The sheer rage that transformed Celeste's face made Juliet's stomach do a slow slide. And it revealed a truth she should have tumbled to much, much sooner. "Oh, my God." She breathed slowly through her nostrils for a moment until she got the roiling queasiness under control. "It was you who tried to kill me. The brakes, the gunshot . . ."

"Oh, don't be any more asinine than you can help," Celeste snapped. Juliet was just inhaling a deep breath of relief and feeling foolish over her accusation when the older woman added acerbically, "It was that pesky Sergeant Dupree I wanted to be rid of—you simply happened to be there."

"You were trying to kill *Beau*?"

Celeste tipped her head in a condescendingly regal nod.

"*Why?*" Then the light bulb went on over her head. "Oh, of course—Edward."

"Yes. It was crucial that word of Edward's little hobby didn't spread to the people who matter."

And now that it had, Edward had clearly ceased to matter himself. The old bitch hadn't made so much as one inquiry into her husband's welfare.

Anger building inside her, she studied the gun that now rested in Celeste's lap but was still pointed directly at her. It looked old. Didn't those old-time guns only hold one bullet? No, it had a barrel like a revolver, which meant a bullet went into each chamber. Unfortunately, there was no way to tell whether the chambers were all loaded.

She was concentrating so hard on the pistol that the sudden sharp rap on the door made her think for an instant that the gun had gone off. A squeak escaping her throat, she slapped her hand in sheer reflex to her pounding heart.

Celeste didn't even blink. "Who is it?" she demanded testily.

"It's Sergeant Gardner, Mrs. Haynes. I need to speak to Juliet."

The calvary had arrived! Hope soared in Juliet, only to be immediately dashed when Celeste snapped with autocratic finality, "Go away."

"I'm sorry, I can't do that. Juliet, are you all right?"

"Um, not exactly."

"I'm coming in."

Celeste fired a shot at the door.

"Dear God!" Juliet surged to her feet. "Luke! Are you hurt?" She was relieved to hear a steady stream of obscenity coming from the other side of the door, since it meant he wasn't dead. He could still be seriously injured, however.

Then he said, "No. I'm okay, I'm fine." Raising his voice a bit, he added, "Lady, you shouldn't have done that, because now I'm pissed. And you don't want to piss off the NOPD."

Celeste looked so crazed that Juliet feared bullets would start to fly at any moment—and she refused to simply sit there and catch one. Picking up the wine bottle, she took several cautious steps toward Celeste, staying on the older woman's blind side, while Celeste's attention was still focused on Luke.

Celeste must have caught a movement from the corner of her eye, because she abruptly swung around, and Juliet froze as her gaze locked on the barrel pointed straight at her heart. She was vaguely aware of feet pounding up the corridor outside, but her attention was locked on Celeste as the older woman cocked back the hammer with her thumb.

"Go ahead, you trashy little chit," Celeste said frigidly. "Give me an excuse to pull the trigger."

"*Rosebud!*" The voice was a primal roar of outrage.

"*Beau?*" Juliet swung to face the door. Oh, God, he was here, he was here, he was here!

Celeste turned in that direction, too, her face a mask of fury. She raised the gun, her veined finger squeezing the trigger.

"*No!*" The empty clicks didn't register until after Juliet had swung the wine bottle at the back of Celeste's immaculate white coiffure. It connected with a horrible thunk, and the pistol dropped to the floor with a clatter. Celeste collapsed in a heap next to it an instant later.

Moaning, "Oh, God, oh, God, oh, God," Juliet stepped over her, then bent down and gingerly pinched the gun's hammer between her thumb and index finger. Holding the revolver at arm's length in front of her, she raced to the door. The horrendous noise of an unrelenting battering on the portal's wooden panels made her shudder.

"Juliet Rose!" Beau roared. "Talk to me—what the hell's goin' on in there?"

She jerked opened the door and nearly got his fist in her face. He pulled the punch just in time, his eyes wild as his gaze raced up and down her body.

"No blood," he croaked. "Thank you, God." Reaching out, he removed the revolver from her fingertips and handed it to Luke as he yanked her to him with his free arm. A second later, both arms were wrapped around her.

His grip was so tight she could barely breathe, but Juliet didn't complain. She buried her nose in the little notch at the base of Beau's throat and breathed in his scent, felt his heat penetrate everywhere they touched. The pounding of his heart reverberated through her own clothing and skin.

"It was her, Beau. It was her all along." Her words tumbling over each other, she hoarsely related the details into his collarbone.

Beau felt her trembling and stroked his hands soothingly up and down her back. The strings of beads at the back of her gown kept getting in his way, and he slid one hand beneath them, closing his eyes at the feel of her warm, silken skin. "Shhh," he crooned over and over again in a hypnotic chant. His right hand stroked her from nape to waist, the beads grazing his knuckles. "It's all right, dawlin'. It's over now, and I'm here. It's all right."

He didn't know who he was trying to comfort more—her or himself. The thought of that despotic old dame as a wild-eyed pistol waver with Juliet Rose firmly in her sights was enough to make a grown man quail. He rubbed his jaw against her temple. "I love you, angel face. You're not alone now—I'm here and I love you."

She shoved away from him so abruptly it was all he could do to avoid ripping her fragile beads from their moorings. Hands tightening on the soft skin on either side of her spine, he looked down into her face and saw her gray eyes blazing at him.

"Don't patronize me, Beau," she snapped. "It's been a rough night and I'm in no mood."

"Huh?" He didn't know what the hell she was talking about, but he petted her soothingly. "That's okay, dawlin'," he assured her. "You don't have to make perfect sense. I know how it can unhinge a person to have a gun stuck in her face."

She made a sound like steam escaping a teakettle. "Bully for you. But I'm not some puppy that needs to be tossed a bone, so keep your phony protestations of love to yourself."

A smile tugged crookedly at the corners of his mouth. "I'm afraid that's just not possible. Daddy'll probably take out a contract on me when he hears the news, and God knows I never pictured myself falling for some uppity Yankee princess, but trust me, sugar—my protestations are the real deal."

"Pfff." Pretty lips pursed, her skepticism couldn't have been plainer. He noticed, however, that she'd ceased to strain against his hold.

He lowered his head to kiss the side of her throat, encouraged when she shivered and shifted the tiniest bit closer.

But Juliet Rose Astor Lowell was nobody's pushover, and she leaned back again. "And what about the much-awaited revolving door in your bedroom, Beauregard?"

"Don't want it."

"Not tonight while your emotions are running high with everything that's happened, maybe—"

He blew out a breath. Okay, in all fairness he couldn't expect to simply waltz back into her life—not after the way he'd treated her. He'd lived with women long enough to know that a certain amount of groveling was required before she'd even consider taking him back. But come hell or high water, he was determined she'd do that—and then some. Freeing an arm, he kept her tucked beneath the other as he poked his head into the Hayneses' apartment. "Luke, you got everything under control?"

"On my worst day, pard."

"Good. I'll be down—"

"Is Mrs. Haynes all right?" Juliet craned to see into the room. "I didn't kill her, did I?"

Celeste sat on the floor with her hand to the back of her head. Feeling Juliet sag with relief, Beau called to Luke, "I'll be in Juliet's room if you need me."

"Ain't gonna need you, bud." Luke looked up and grinned at them.

Beau grinned back. "Good." He wheeled Juliet around and marched her down to her room. "Got a key?"

She fished one out of a clever little pocket sewn into the inside of her dress between her breasts.

Beau felt his temperature spike. "Maybe I oughtta pat you down for concealed weapons."

Her nose tilted up. "As if my puny weapons would interest a man with a preference for bazookas."

"Ah, dawlin', I've hurt you, and I'm sorry about that. I'd like a chance to explain."

She shrugged one delicate shoulder and let them into the sitting room, making a point to keep her distance.

He looked at her, all golden-skinned and coolly defiant in her slinky little gown, and he wanted her with an ache he felt deep in his bones. Looking her in the eye, he stated categorically, "I love you. Let's get that straight right now."

"I'm sure you believe that tonight"—her shoulder inched up once again—"while you're feeling guilty."

He didn't appreciate being told what he felt, and forgot for a minute that he'd planned to be gentle and persuasive. "Yeah? And what the hell have I got to feel guilty about?"

"Ruining my—how did you put it?—my big night."

He made a rude noise. "I didn't ruin your big night—that was the Pissant's doing. Besides"—he started stalking her and was pleased as punch to see her backing up nervously—"I'm a real selfish sonofabitch. I don't feel guilt."

Her back hit the wall, but starch infused her spine and her chin angled up at him. "If you were so almighty selfish, you never would have accepted the responsibility of raising your sisters." She touched soft fingertips to his jaw briefly then snatched her hand back and concluded coolly, "And now you finally have the opportunity to follow your dream."

"Uh-huh." Hands on the wall, he leaned over her. "And you approve of me playing sexual suicide with an unending line of bimbos, do you?"

The look she gave him seriously questioned his intelligence. "Of course not. I think it stinks."

"I don't know if *stinks* is the word I'd use, but I did realize tonight that the idea doesn't rev my engine the way I always expected it would."

"Exactly," she agreed insistently, as if he'd just made her argument for her. "You realized *tonight*."

"Dammit, Rosebud, if I'd really wanted to chase puss—um, women all over town, I've had years and years to do so."

"Your sisters—"

"Didn't have a clue what my schedule was half the time. I could have been with a thousand women, and they never would've known the difference."

"That's not what you were saying the other day."

"Yeah, well, the other day I was still clinging to an outdated goal. But it's a fact. I could've been makin' time all along if that was what I'd truly wanted."

"So you're telling me you've been celibate all these years because—"

"Not celibate, exactly. Just . . . discriminating." He kissed her temple. "And there's nothin' puny about your weapons, sugar." His hand slid down to cup her left breast. "Trust me, they're killer."

Her spine wilted against the wall a bit, but she was by no means vanquished. She pinned him in place with those big eyes of hers and demanded, "You're no longer interested in big breasts, then?"

"Dawlin', I'll be interested in breasts till the day I die." He grinned crookedly at her. "Big ones, little ones, I'll look at 'em all—it's just plain built into the guy chromosome. But I swear to God I won't lay a finger on any but these." He stroked his thumb over her nipple and breathed into her ear, "Tell me that you love me."

"No." But her voice was breathy and she shifted restlessly against the wall.

"Tell me, Juliet Rose."

She remained silent.

"God, you're stubborn. Okay, I'll tell you, then. I love you." He stared into her eyes. "It hit me like a brick upside the head, right about the time all that shit was coming down with Edward's arrest. And when I thought you might leave town before I had the chance to tell you—it was not a good moment, Juliet."

Her fists thunked against his chest. "I don't

know what you *want* from me," she wailed.

"I want you to trust me again. I want you to say you love me and that you could give up a few of the luxuries you're accustomed to and come be my woman, be my wife—maybe even have my babies."

"I don't want to be responsible for tying you down. You've raised your family. You want to have sex with two women at once."

"Oh, dawlin.' " He rested his forehead against hers. "Don't hold that idiocy against me forever. I was really scared when I took over raising my sisters. Scared that I couldn't do it, that I'd mess them up with my ineptitude. The fantasy was an escape hatch for all those nights when I thought I was going to drown beneath the weight of too much responsibility. But it's not what I really want." He finessed the long-toothed comb from her French twist and pulled out the pins, raising his head to watch in satisfaction as the mass immediately swelled away from her scalp in honey-brown waves. "It doesn't keep me warm at night, Rosebud. It doesn't make me laugh or my heart pound, and it sure as hell doesn't make me want to throttle a woman one moment and strip her down to the skin the next."

"I love you, Beau." Juliet's voice came out weak because telling him was a risk—but one she could no longer keep herself from taking. She watched his dark eyes light up and his teeth flash white against his five o'clock shadow as he grinned down at her.

"Yeah?" His chest brushed hers with the deep breath he drew.

"Oh, yeah." She wrapped her arms around his neck. "So much it scares me."

"Ah, sugar, don't you be scared. You and me, we're gonna have us the time of our lives." He threw back his head and laughed. Plunging his long fingers into her hair, he kissed her, then pulled back and demanded, "So. You gonna marry me, or what?"

She swallowed hard but answered in the only way she could. "Yes."

"All right! And I didn't even have to bring out the big persuader."

"The big what?"

"Persuader, dawlin'. The definitive weapon in my arsenal."

"Ah." She brushed her hips against his erection. "Well, don't you worry; you'll have plenty of opportunity to use it in the future."

"I'm countin' on it, angel face." His grin was skewed and an unholy light shone from his eyes. "But I was, uh, referring to all the raunchy places in the Quarter I've yet to show you."

Her mouth dropped open. "What makes you think *that* would persuade me?"

"Don't kid a kidder, dawlin'—those joints fascinate you right down to your dainty little toes."

She tilted her nose up. "I might find them moderately interesting."

"You might find them downright stimulatin'."

"Oh! You are such a hound." Heat swept up her face and she buried it in his throat—then laughed.

"Just for that, I'm going to let you break the news to Father."

"Fine with me. Just don't expect me to ask his permission. I'm *telling* him how it's gonna be."

And he wouldn't blink an eye at Father's bluster, either, Juliet knew. Suffused with happiness and a sense of security she'd never known before, she grinned up at him. "You're absolutely right, Beuregard. You and I are really going to have the time of our lives, aren't we?"

"Damn tootin', honey chile." He kissed her, hard, and then flashed his killer smile. "That we are."

Epilogue

❧

*I*t was red beans and rice night at Beau and Juliet's little Creole cottage in the Bywater District, and the house was bursting at the seams. Anabel and Roxanne jostled for space at the stove, Josie Lee argued with Camilla over what needed to go into the salad they were throwing together over at the table in the corner, and Luke was drafted to dig through the refrigerator for each new item they swore was necessary to the success of their mission. Juliet slathered garlic butter on French bread at the counter and passed it off to Beau to cut, who then passed it off to Ned to reassemble into a loaf on a sheet of aluminum foil. Aaron Neville crooned a duet with Linda Ronstadt from the CD player in the living room, and the late October wind rattled the steamed-over windows.

Juliet blotted perspiration from her brow with the back of her wrist and edged around Beau to assemble plates and silverware. "Grab the dressing while you're in there," she instructed Luke, who was rummaging for green onions in the fridge. "Jose, hand me the napkins?" She accepted a stack of them from her sister-in-law and set the table at the near end of the living room.

"Hey, Juliet," Luke called through the doorway. "I heard today that Celeste Haynes was judged fit to stand trial after all. The insanity plea didn't hold up."

Juliet walked back to the doorway, where she was met by Beau. Talk of Celeste always made him protective of her, and he pulled her in front of him and tugged her close, wrapping his arms around her waist. "Good," he growled. "Edward belongs in the Antebellum Home for the Insane, I suppose, but I always felt the old battle-ax drove him there."

"Amen," Roxanne agreed.

"And you two are so unbiased," Juliet said dryly. "You were never exactly her biggest fan to begin with, Rox, and Beau thinks being denied sexually is a legitimate defense in a competency hearing."

His arms tightened around her and the stubble on his chin tangled her hair at her temple as he rubbed it back and forth. "Damn straight, sugar. I'd go crazy, too, if you'd cut me off from practically Day One of our marriage. But Celeste knew exactly what she was doing when she tried to knock us off to preserve her place on the precious Social Register. Prison orange should be a good look for her. And if there's any justice in the world, there'll be an inmate named Big Bertha just waiting to meet her bus."

It was a crush when they were all seated around

the table a short while later. Juliet still had occasional moments of being overwhelmed by the close
quarters they lived in, but it was a small price to
pay for being included in the give and take of
Beau's noisy family.

"I've got news," Camilla said when the edge had
been taken off of everyone's hunger. She shifted
away slightly from her sister. "Josie Lee, would
you get your elbow out of my side?"

"Hey, excuse the hell outta me. Where exactly
do you want me to put it?" Then she grinned.
"Don't answer that."

"Maybe you oughtta have the next dinner at
your place," Beau suggested and reached past Juliet for the bowl of rice.

"Oh, right—it's even smaller than this. Maybe
we should have the next one at Juliet's and Rox's
new hotel."

"We don't even have the kitchen in yet—the
whole place is still pretty much gutted." Juliet
looked across the table at Camilla. "What's your
news?"

"Ned and I are gonna have a baby."

Anabel and Josie Lee screamed, Juliet laughed,
Luke slapped Ned on the shoulder, and Beau said
fervently, "Please, Jesus, I've been outnumbered all
my life—make it the kind that pees standing up."

"Oh, get a grip, Beau," Anabel said. "Nobody
feels sorry for you, and besides, the odds are beginning to even out."

Juliet grew rather quiet after that, and Beau
wanted to know why. The front door had barely

closed behind their last guest when he tackled her with it. "What's the matter, dawlin'?"

She blinked. "Nothing."

"God, I hate it when women do that—it's such a chick response. Is the house startin' to crowd you?" This place was a cracker box compared to the mansion she'd grown up in.

"No. Every couple of weeks I get a little claustrophobic, but it always passes. I like it. It's got you."

"So, you aren't gettin' tired of the marriage, then?"

"No!" She pushed him down on the couch and knelt astride his lap. "My God, Beauregard, we're practically still on our honeymoon. Where would you get such a crazy notion?"

"Well, something's bothering you. Did you talk to your grandmother today?" The old bat wasn't the coziest person Beau had ever met, and neither was Juliet's father. When Juliet shook her head, but failed to elaborate, he growled, "Don't make me break out the bright lights and rubber hose here, angel face."

"Boy, you sure can tell you're a cop—you're so suspicious." She squeezed his biceps. "Beau, there's nothing wrong. I was just thinking about babies."

Beau stilled. "What?" His gaze dropped to her flat stomach. "You're not . . . ?"

"No! Oh, no." Juliet laughed. "Camilla's announcement just made me wonder what kind of mother I would make, is all."

"A great one."

"You think so? I know you'd be good at parenting, but I don't have any experience with little kids, and I'm terrified I might be a total flop."

"Trust me, dawlin'—you allow people to be exactly who they are, and you treat 'em with respect no matter what that is. You'd be a really great mother. You want a kid? I'll give you a kid—just say the word." He'd give her the moon, if that was what she wanted.

"No, I'm not ready. I'm having too much fun to settle down quite yet. It just made me wonder for a while, is all."

"Well, then I'll tell you what." He tipped her over onto the couch cushions and rolled to prop himself over her. "Whata'ya say we practice *makin'* babies?" Hands moving with speed and skill, he began to divest her of her clothing. "That way, when you're ready, we'll know exactly what we're doin'."

"It's very important for one to know what one is doing," she agreed solemnly, as she unbuttoned his shirt and pushed it off his shoulders.

"Oh, yeah. Absolutely. My thoughts exactly."

Listen to
New York Times Bestselling Author
SUSAN ELIZABETH PHILLIPS

Breathing Room
ISBN: 0-06-009259-9
$25.95/$38.95 Can.
6 hours/4 cassettes
Performed by Kate Forbes

Also available in a LargePrint edition
ISBN: 0-06-009391-9
$24.95/$37.95 Can.

This Heart of Mine
ISBN: 0-694-52493-X
$25.00/$37.50 Can.
6 hours/4 cassettes
Performed by Jennifer Van Dyck

Also available in a LargePrint edition
ISBN: 0-06-018803-0
$24.00/$36.50 Can.

Available wherever books are sold or call 1-800-331-3761 to order.

HarperAudio
An Imprint of HarperCollins*Publishers*
www.harpercollins.com

Harper LARGE PRINT Edition

SPA 1002